MY WIFE'S

HUSBAND

A FAMILY THRILLER

ISBN: 978-1-950381-27-2

Cover design:Jonathan Morizet-Davis
Cover photo: E.H. Davis

This book is set in Sabon LT Pro
Printed in the United States

Published by
Piscataqua Press
32 Daniel St.
Portsmouth, NH 03801

MY WIFE'S HUSBAND

A FAMILY THRILLER

E.H. DAVIS

PISCATAQUA
PRESS

"But in the murderer, such a murderer as a poet will condescend to, there must be raging some great storm of passion — jealousy, ambition, vengeance, hatred — which will create a hell within him; and into this hell we are to look."
Thomas De Quincey, "On the Knocking on the Gate in *Macbeth*"

"Mortui vivos docent" — the dead teach the living

Dedication

To Jonathan, my son; my wife, Chris;
my teachers John Yount, Thomas Williams
& Donald Shojai

PART ONE

Chapter One

Armand Laurent picked a summer night when the moon, in its last quarter, shrouded his hiding place in total darkness.

Dressed in black, lying in a thicket a hundred yards from the target, he was nearly invisible. He peered through his binoculars at the farmhouse. Dark except for a fluorescent lamp over the kitchen window. An hour had passed since the other lights in the house had been put out — enough time for all to be asleep. In prison he'd learned the virtues of Zen-like patience and stillness, and could endure long hours motionless, especially if it meant the difference between life and death.

He rose silently from his makeshift blind, stretching, flexing, untensing. He was a big man, six foot four, with a weightlifter's bulked arms and chest, and a neck as wide as a fireplug. His massive head was tucked between his shoulders, like a prizefighter.

He patted his coat pockets, feeling for the rope cut in measured lengths, duct tape, and a folded commando knife. He had no need to check on his gun, a .44 magnum, tucked snugly into the small of his back.

He would have little trouble gaining entry through the sliding glass kitchen door at the back of the house. They always left it unlocked. He'd been watching for days, always arriving after dark, disappearing before dawn, careful not to leave any signs behind.

He was familiar with all their habits. They had a French

bulldog he overheard them calling "Bruzza," who usually slept indoors with the family. Sometimes they left him out, like tonight. Laurent had sedated him earlier with a tranquilizer-laced Big Mac, which he'd tossed into the doghouse.

All things were in place. This was *his* time, the night, with its comforting solitude. He was ready, come to take back what belonged to him. Because of what society, the law had done to him — years of incarceration for a crime he was innocent of — he no longer considered the consequences of his actions.

Once past the snoring dog, he slipped inside the kitchen by raising the sliding glass door a hair to reduce friction. He stood still, barely breathing, hidden from the cone of light above the sink, listening for sounds from the upstairs bedrooms.

Hugging the shadows, he made his way up the carpeted stairs to the second floor, where Corbin slept alongside Vivian in the master bedroom. Down the hall was the son, finally done with his Xbox marathon, signaled by the end of the flickering lightshow on his window shade.

Laurent led the way with his pistol. Though he'd had it in his possession only a few days, repeated handling made it feel familiar.

A step groaned under his weight and he stopped, listening for any sound before continuing.

How will Vivian react when she sees him now, transformed by the hard years served in her honor? Will she recognize him, truly see him — strip away the dross of jail to reveal the true face of the young lover he once was?

In his fantasy, she stirs from the warm bed of the usurper — her husband for almost as long as his imprisonment — and leaps with a joyful cry into his arms. They'll make a new life — in Canada or Mexico, wherever. How could it be otherwise?

Of course, the boy, her son and Corbin's — a geeky teen, Teddy she calls him — has to stay behind. She will understand that he'd be in the way. He pushed aside the thought of having his own son one day; didn't know if there'd be room in their new lives.

As for Corbin, he'd provide the wherewithal, the cash, to make it all happen. And keep his mouth shut if he wanted to go on living.

Wrapped in equal parts of hope and rage, Laurent mounted the last few steps of the stairs, intent on trampling this union of man and wife, and replacing it with his own.

Chapter Two

Jens Corbin, middle-aged novelist of some note, slumbered deeply if uncomfortably, caught in the grip of a repeated dream, one which had haunted him since adolescence.

Despite all the trappings of success — winner of the prestigious Mystery Writers Poe Award, a book on the bestseller list (but not too recently), two homes and two late model cars, a son in private school and a handsome, talented, accomplished wife snoring beside him — he was troubled.

In that state between reverie and consciousness, when fragments of ideas mix with shards of the past, he rehashed certain events, *ad nauseam*, before launching into the dream.

Two teenage boys walk silently along a wooded path banked by oak and maple, branches fluttering with rust-colored leaves. They cradle scoped rifles in their arms, pointed down, like trained hunters. Whenever Jens, five years younger, anxious, inexperienced, begins babbling, older brother Nils hushes him with a severe glance. Jens, who hates hunting, did not want to come, but Nils insisted. Jens idolizes Nils.

They spot a matted knoll where a deer herd was bedded down for the night. They go on alert, following spoor and the trail of waist-high broken branches, leading deeper into the woods. The thunder of the herd fleeing at their scent, trampling brush and snapping low tree limbs, sets them swinging their rifles up. But the deer are already gone. A ghostly silence descends in their wake, gathering, growing with menace.

He stirred restlessly in his sleep, moaned, rising up through the stages of REM as he tried to stop the familiar nightmare.

And with it, the knowledge that he killed his older brother that day.

Chapter Three

In the Corbin's bedroom, hidden in the shadows cast by an inconstant moon, Laurent observed Vivian toss an arm and a leg carelessly over Corbin, a gesture at once familiar and intimate, intended to rouse him from his nightmare.

With growing horror, Laurent watched as she began to massage the crotch of the man he'd convinced himself she only tolerated — not loved — as a means to an end. That end being *their* reunion. No fool, he'd long ago accepted the inevitability of *their* coupling, but never expected to be condemned to acknowledge, let alone witness it.

Hadn't she kept an ember of their love alive over the years, just as he, faithfully, had fanned his in the solitude of his prison cell? Hadn't she read the letters he'd mailed her in the last few weeks, announcing, after years of silence, his release from Concord State and his arrival in Portsmouth, to be with her? Wasn't she expecting him?

He was unable to look away as Corbin responded to her ministrations. Eyes clenched, Corbin embraced her in a ceremony of love that both aroused and repulsed Laurent, especially when he saw how willingly she responded, even dominated their lovemaking.

In a welter of nausea, Laurent aimed his pistol at the proverbial double-backed creature, an icon of lovers as old as original sin. He aimed first at Vivian, writhing atop her lover, then at Corbin, as they switched places.

How could she? How *could* she?

His pain carried him from the room, down the carpeted stairs, out the sliding kitchen door. He left it open, unsure if he was coming back that night to finish the job. Unsure what the job was, exactly, now that everything had turned to ashes.

Stumbling into the woods, his gun hand smacked against his thigh.

A shot rang out, *booming*, seemingly without end.

He ran into the night.

Chapter Four

Unable to stem the tide of recriminations that always accompanied his nightmare, Jens slipped silently from the bed, careful not to disturb Vivian, a light sleeper. Her back to him, she slumbered on, cheating him of the chance to see her face, see if a faint trace of their lovemaking lingered.

She'd surprised him by taking the initiative last night. And though he hadn't expected, or received in the aftermath, any indication of a truce in their ongoing cold war, let alone pillow talk expressing rekindled love, still he would have welcomed a softly spoken word from her, accompanied by a goodnight kiss on the lips. Instead, she'd turned away abruptly and begun snoring.

He stepped into the bathroom and gently closed the door. Stared at himself in the mirror, ran his hands through his hair, noting again with dismay his receding hairline and sprinkling of salt-and-pepper rising from his sideburns. There were liver-colored dark bags under his eyes. He back-handed the stubble on his cheeks and decided to shave, even though it was Saturday and he was taking Teddy up to their log cabin in Jackson. The stubble made him look old, like a wizened reprobate — not the best foot to put forward when trying to bond with your teenage son. He turned on the tap, splashed hot water on his face, lathered up.

A muffled "Pop!" sounded distantly from somewhere in the woods behind the house. Early morning poachers jacking a deer caught in their headlights? He imagined a pair of local yahoos capitalizing on the serendipitous moment, after a long night of doping and drinking.

Jens pulled aside the curtain and looked into the backyard, still dark. Nothing.

He went back to his shaving, resolved to investigate the

woods later, check his assumption about poachers. It occurred to him that the "pop" he'd heard, or thought he'd heard, lacked the resonance of a rifle crack as the bullet broke the sound barrier, followed by the lingering *thump* of the round fired. It was a "sound worm" that he knew only too well from his nightmares. Pistol, then? Could mean a wounded deer. He'd definitely have to investigate.

But he forgot all about it in the rush to have breakfast with Teddy and say goodbye to Vivian, who'd deigned to drag herself out of bed and see them off, so they could get on the Kancamagus Highway north before the tourists.

Evil had come calling. An apt complication for a fictional character, but not for a man with a stake in life.

Chapter Five

Teddy, also a light sleeper, overwrought by the electronic games he was obsessed with, especially those featuring hard men, efficient killers, like Desmond Miles from Assassin's Creed, came downstairs to investigate the noise that had awakened him.

Finding the kitchen door open, he examined it for a break-in, found none, and stepped out onto the porch, ready to vanquish any and all, weaponless except for his wiry arms and legs, which he imagined were registered weapons of destruction.

This image of himself as a fearless warrior was the alter-ego he privately cultivated. He hadn't told his dad yet, but he planned to join the Marines out of high school. Good thing, as he was failing most subjects except for physical education, but was willing to pass them for the Marines.

Satisfied that the noise he'd heard was likely a jet on maneuvers from the nearby airport breaking the sound barrier, he was about to return to the comfort of his bed when he noticed that Bruzza, a barker, was oddly quiet in the wake of the *boom*, whatever it was.

He found the dog inside his doghouse, snoring loudly, his jowly head resting on black and tan paws. Lost in thought, Teddy hit his head on the low roof, forgetting to duck.

That's when he saw it — a thin wedge of pickle in the far corner, chewed and discarded.

Really?

He backed out, the pickle gingerly held. Oddly, it was still moist. At once he recognized it as coming from a McDonald's burger.

Now, where the fuck did this come from? he wondered, peering into the bleak woods, looking for an intruder who may have — what? — shared his late-night snack with Bruzza.

Baffled, he plunged a few steps into the woods, then halted, restrained by darkness, wishing he had night goggles like a proper warrior.

"You out there, fucker," he hissed, spooking himself. More boldly: "I'll get you, you bastard." He pointed an imaginary gun into the dark. "Come out!"

No answer was forthcoming, only silence wrapped in mystery, the kind that Teddy had to come to relish.

Like about his mother's letters from a man named Laurent that he'd been intercepting for the past few months. Had she really been with a convicted murderer before marrying Dad? What else didn't he know about her?

And what did that make him?

Chapter Six

By the time Jens and Teddy had breakfasted, said their goodbyes to Vivian and Bruzza, and loaded up the Subaru with their fishing gear, clothes, and a carton of Teddy's Xbox and games, Laurent was just emerging from the woods onto Calef Highway.

He was exhausted from his fiasco at the Corbins' and his long ramble through the woods and farmlands. He'd taken the long way out to avoid the farmhouses and barns where armed citizens, alerted by watchdogs, might not take kindly to a suspicious-looking trespasser on their property in the middle of the night.

At one farm, he'd been attacked by a German Shepherd. In the scramble to get away, he'd lost his gun — adding to his failure. He doubted he would find it even now, in daylight.

Then, it had taken him hours to get to the Shell Station on 125 near Epping. Happy to find the garage open for business, the bay doors up, the ratcheting mechanics' drills humming purposefully within, he waved to the clerk at the register inside the station and mimed *restroom?*

The cashier gave him a cursory nod, indicating with his thumb that the bathroom around back was open and he was free to use to it. Though his scowl suggested he'd be happier if Laurent bought something to justify its use.

Laurent waved back, mimed drinking coffee, and went around back. Like roadside gas stations most everywhere, the dank bathroom stunk of urine and trucker perspiration. He relieved himself and washed up at the grease-smeared sink, inured to like facilities in prison.

He eyed himself in the mirror, wondering how he'd let his well-planned home invasion at Vivian's go south. He hadn't anticipated his reaction to her being in bed with Corbin. He dried his face and hands with toilet paper, finding no towels in the dispenser.

Refreshed in spite of everything, he pushed out of the bathroom and turned the corner to the station to get coffee and a sweet roll.

And pulled back suddenly when he saw Corbin gassing up his Subaru at the pump. The boy, Teddy, was entering the store. Before Corbin looked his way, Laurent withdrew to the bushes alongside the garage and made himself invisible.

He watched, boiling with rage, wrestling with his impulse to carjack Corbin and take him back to the house in Lee, force him to give up the goods, while Vivian watched.

But he knew better than to act in broad daylight with witnesses present.

Instead, he surrendered to fantasies about what he was going to do Corbin when the time came. He knew he needed a plan. A way to get at him. Through the boy?

Just then Teddy loped to the car, a bottle of water in each hand, and opened the door on the passenger's side.

"Want a water, Dad?"

Corbin, shaking his head, replaced the nozzle on the pump. He went to the hatchback and fished around in the bags, emerging with two apples.

Laurent thought of all the years this Sancho had been sleeping with *his* wife.

Before he knew it, he'd picked up a baseball-sized rock and hurled it at Corbin's head with all his might.

Corbin, lowering the hatchback, incidentally ducked.

The hatchback closed just as Laurent's projectile bounced off the window, fissuring it with a loud *pop*. The rock skittered away unseen into the bushes as Corbin flinched away from the sudden noise.

"What was that?" Teddy, lurched from the car, alarmed.

His father shook his head. "Freak thing. Slammed it too hard."

Teddy studied him. "You okay, Dad?"

"Let's go," Corbin answered. "Can't let a little thing like a cracked window spoil our trip."

He got in and they drove off.

Leaving Laurent cursing himself for not curtailing his anger. He knew better. He was trained. A thousand sleepless nights had taught him the virtue of mastering his emotions.

But would he be able to, now that he was back in the real world?

Chapter Seven

At last she lay in the claw-foot tub she so loved, up to her neck in bubbles, celebrating her solitude now that she'd shipped Jens and Teddy off to the mountains with the admonishment to be nice to each other.

With a pleasurable moan, she sank down into her sudsy heaven, submerging, surfacing — a submarine breaching the depths — the sea rolling off her breasts, belly, and thighs, her skin tingling, steaming.

What luxury, not to have to worry about anyone else. Not attend to the needs of others. No after-school pickups, doctor's appointments, shopping, liaising with teachers, guidance counselors, or parents on Teddy's behalf. Truth be known, though, Jens shared equally the burdens, if not the joys, of raising their son. True, he handled most of the family business, too: banking, insurance, utilities, home and car maintenance.

And moi? Mother, artist, dreamer, creator, lover.

She spat out a mouthful of soapy water inhaled with her laughter. She sponged her arms, torso, and legs, all the while thinking about the painting she'd been working on.

A watercolor of the Hampton Beach salt marshes captured in late August, the leafy trees and grasses shimmering, resplendent, in tones foreshadowing fall's color riot — of cranberry, chrome green, lambent yellow, pale white, lilac, vermillion and, her favorite, the scintillating ultra blue of the sky.

Hyperrealist, painting from color prints from her camera, she wasn't satisfied with her rendition of the marshes. In her painting, grass greens and stalk browns bled into the white areas — *unacceptable* — destroying the illusion of silhouetted blades of grass.

The thought of this imperfection roused her from her bath.

She rinsed off, skipped shaving her legs, which she did only occasionally to please Jens, which was less and less often.

She dried off, wrapped a towel around her wet hair, and stepped from the tub into flip flops and her terry cloth robe. She thought about her loss of desire. *Was it hormonal?* At thirty-nine, wasn't she was too young for menopause? No hot flashes yet, thank God. Still, it had been a long time since she thought about making love to her husband as other than a duty. Despite last night, which she could not account for.

The part of her past that she had disciplined herself never to glimpse or acknowledge, *not ever*, pushed itself into consciousness. The image of the man she'd once loved, her childhood sweetheart, dead to her for decades, reappeared. Teasing, tantalizing her painfully with the icon of their bittersweet love, the kind that comes only once in a lifetime, if we're lucky.

In flashes, vivid fragments from *their time* fluttered behind her eyes, tormenting, beckoning. Why now?

Oh, God! She was a teen again, uncomfortable in her woman's body, desperate to escape the unnamable shame at the core of her being. Shame generated by the monster, who'd come to live with her and her mother after her father died, isolating and tormenting her, cutting her off, making her willing to do anything to escape her sordid life.

Enter her savior, young Armand Laurent, handsome, well-spoken, educated. An aspiring artist from a family of pulp paper manufacturers, looked upon as landed aristocracy in the mill town of Berlin, New Hampshire. She'd cleaved to him with abandon, loving him with that part of her that was unspoiled, intact, despite the cuttings and the suicide attempts and the *bloody* forced abortion.

Even after she'd betrayed Laurent, long after he'd been taken away for murder, she'd been faithful to him — in her heart. But the years had passed, and he'd pushed her away to do his time. She'd gone off to university and started a career as an artist, loved another man, married, and had a son. And now?

"Armand," she whispered, choked with emotion. His luminous, teen-handsome face beamed down upon her as he wiped her tears and murmured endearments, bringing her back from the edge, from the abyss. As he always had.

"Armand," she whispered. "Forgive me."

Chapter Eight

Driving in their Subaru, father and son were approaching the crossing of the White Mountain Highway and Route 16 near the town of Ossipee when a speeding Escalade suddenly appeared behind them, bearing down as it pulled out to pass.

"What's he doing, ninety?" Teddy's head turned as the Escalade blew past, then swerved recklessly in front of them onto the exit ramp, nearly clipping them.

Jens cursed under his breath.

"Eight thousand pounds of gas-guzzling road hog."

To anyone born and bred in the conservative atmosphere of New England in the late 70s, like Jens, driving a Cadillac, let alone an Escalade, was like giving everyone else on the road the finger.

"Asshole," they said in unison, breaking into laughter. Exchanging looks with Teddy, Jens proudly noted that his son had grown a half a foot taller, seemingly overnight.

"Can we stop for drinks?" Teddy pointed to a strip mall ahead on the right.

Jens pulled off the shoulder into the parking lot of a convenience store named Foothills Pickup.

As they exited the car, he pushed from his mind his perennial concern for his son, who suffered from attention deficit and processing issues, which materialized primarily as an utter disinclination for anything academic, and accounted for his poor grades. It seemed he was only interested in working out, girls, and Xbox.

Jens had come to fathering in his 30s and couldn't help indulging his only offspring, who brought him back to a time of innocence and promise. Recalling his own preoccupations at that age, he reminded himself that sex had been on his radar, very much so. But so were books, theatre, art.

Vivian was quick to accuse him of being too hard on their son, for not accepting him as he was — with his *differences*, not limitations. She warned him that his severity with Teddy over his studies was planting deep seeds of resentment. This weekend, Jens had set himself the task of not showing his disappointment and simply enjoying the boy's company.

That's what the hurried "don't worry" he'd tossed Vivian, as they loaded up the car this morning, was meant to convey. Skeptical as always, she'd only raised an eyebrow.

She'd hugged Teddy but not Jens, which he interpreted as her way of saying, "You got yours last night." Vivian, Jens reminded himself, was not one to confuse sex with sentiment, and he tried not to take such slights personally, common as they were. But how could he not?

Inside the store, Jens drew himself a coffee from the urn of "gourmet" blend and smiled at the dowdy, gray-haired woman behind the counter. She stared back at him, a sheen of sweat on her brow, despite the droning air conditioner.

"That be all?" Her voice was a breathless rasp.

Jens nodded as he added a dab of milk to his coffee and watched it dissolve, sending his thoughts back to the scene he'd been writing the previous day, of a body face down in a tidewater pool framed by sea grass. Like all of his crime novels — this was his fourth — it began with the discovery of a body, the *corpus delicti*, revealing the details of his story with seasoned reliability.

But this time, that wasn't happening. He was blocked, and had been for too long to remember. Despite his patience, an array of corpses *in situ* had come and gone, but none had triggered the usual flow of imagery, character, and plot needed for writing a novel.

The *shucking* of the cash register as it opened brought him back to the present. The woman behind the counter was silent as she made change. Jens noticed her labored breathing. He glanced at Teddy to see if he'd noticed.

Just then the SUV that cut them off earlier careened into the lot and parked. A spry old man with a shock of white hair and a harried yet authoritative air pushed into the store, made a beeline for the drinks cooler, and grabbed several cans of Red Bull.

"Look who's here." Jens glanced at Teddy.

"The A-hole who cut us off." Teddy seemed perplexed. "Must have gone off road for a while, or he'd be here before us."

Jens nodded, discretely eyeing the older man.

"White Gold Rolex Presidential — 18k dial with diamonds and sapphire markers," he whispered.

This was a familiar game they played, guessing at a stranger's identity and background from clues, like a character in a novel.

"Distinctive, elegant, and *very* expensive," answered Teddy, enjoying the game.

Jens smiled at his word choices, which constantly surprised him with their sophistication, despite his son's aversion to academics. It reminded him of the precocious transitional words and phrases Teddy used as a first grader, like "incidentally," "in contrast," and "decidedly," which amazed his teacher, though she thought him slow in other respects, and had been the first to raise the alarm about his attention deficit.

"That watch would pay the taxes on the house in Lee for the next few years."

"Retired?" Teddy discreetly looked the stranger up and down.

Jens nodded, deciding Mr. Red Bull, for lack of a name, had fulfilled a position of authority in life, as he still projected an aura of self-importance.

The old man, his face lined with fatigue, plopped his cans on the counter in front of Jens.

"Do you mind?" Not waiting for an answer, he waved a large bill at the cashier.

Jens held up a mollifying hand.

"You go right ahead since you seem to be in a hurry."

Red Bull glared, reaching over him to pay.

Stepping aside, Jens noted his manicured hands, too delicate for a man his size. He was wearing wrinkled cotton pants and shirt, both of light ply. Jens glanced outside at his dirt-caked Escalade, looking for a plate to confirm his suspicions, but the SUV was parked nose in, with no license plate in front.

"From Florida, doctor, most likely," he told Teddy, no longer concerned about the rude stranger overhearing.

"I get Florida. Why doctor?" Teddy hissed.

"Hands — manicured, educated."

Teddy nodded, dubious.

"Want a bag?" the cashier asked the impatient older man. She seemed distant, her face pasty with sweat. "Well?" she insisted, her voice a hoarse whisper.

Suddenly, she put a hand to her throat, and her face turned red, contorted with pain. With a gasp, she clutched her chest and stumbled back, pawing the air.

"Can't ... breathe."

As she fell backward, her arms strobed the shelves of cigarettes, cigars, and candy behind her, sending everything crashing. She collapsed onto the floor, sucking for air, eyes filled with terror.

Jens bolted into action, charging around the counter to where she lay. Her face was livid, her body rigid. He turned to the older man.

"Don't be offended, friend, but I know you know what's wrong with this woman and what to do about it. You're a doctor, aren't you?"

He didn't reply. His mouth was drawn tightly, deliberating.

Meanwhile, the woman clawed her throat, unable to draw a breath. Her eyes fluttered and closed. She went limp, her skin damp, pallid.

Jens tore his eyes away from her, found Teddy.

"Call 911!"

Jens glared at the man he knew was a doctor.

"You going to help or what?"

Teddy came around the counter and scrambled for the phone in its cradle on the wall. Jens slid his knees under the cashier's head, lifting her gingerly, overcoming his reluctance at handling a stranger.

In the background, Teddy could be heard reporting the nature of the emergency and their location, his voice rising shrilly. Jens looked up at the older man, who observed the woman's condition and Jens's desperation with ambivalence.

Finally, the stranger came around the counter and stooped beside her, his movements steady and economical, as he positioned her on Jens's knees so that her head was raised higher. Then he took her hand, felt her pulse, pried open her eyelids, and noted her labored breathing. He seemed to nod to himself, certain of his diagnosis.

He groped in the woman's pockets. Not finding what he was looking for, he turned and probed under the counter, finding the woman's pocketbook and dumping the contents onto the counter. He shook his head, stood, and scanned the immediate shelves.

"What do you need?" asked Jens, voice strained.

"Aspirin," he answered. "She's having a heart attack. Apparently this is her first; otherwise she'd have digitalis handy. Have to thin her blood," he added.

Jens exchanged looks with Teddy, who dropped the phone and peeled off toward the aisles, hands fumbling along the shelves until he found the aspirin.

"Which kind?" he shouted, holding a handful of bottles aloft.

"Bring the lot," answered the older man.

Teddy spilled his cache on the counter. The old man scanned the labels on the bottles, broke the seal on one, removed the lid, and shook out two tablets.

He bent over beside the woman, forced her mouth open, and inserted the tablets between her teeth. He manipulated her jaws, forcing her to bite down on the aspirin and masticate. He massaged her throat until her swallowing reflex took over. Within a few minutes her breathing subsided and the color returned to her face. She opened her eyes.

"Where am I?" she croaked, her voice a whisper. She clutched at her heart. "It hurts something awful."

"You've had a heart attack." The older man stood. "You'll be okay until the medics arrive. In the meantime, just rest easy."

Jens looked at him in disbelief.

"You can't leave now — she needs you."

He held Jens's eyes for a long moment, started to speak, shook his head. He walked to the door without a moment's hesitation, pulled it open, and left.

Chapter Nine

The next day, at the New Hampshire Art League Gallery in Portsmouth, Laurent stood in front of one of Vivian's signature watercolors, striking an unlikely pose, chin in palm, arm supported at the elbow.

Scenes from his fiasco at Vivian's home in Lee and his recklessness at the gas station disturbed his vision, overlayed like transparencies.

Finally, back at his motel room in Kittery, he'd collapsed on his bed and slept until late morning, as though drugged. Freed from the roar of white noise that cons learn to sleep through, it had taken him a while to block out the random noises of life in the civilian world and fall asleep. Now, without the routine of prison, he slept like the dead.

In his dream, he's in the Corbins' bedroom pointing a gun at Corbin, smiling, mouthing, "Dead-Bang! Gotcha!" He pulls the trigger.

Boom!

He lurched awake, groping madly for his Glock.

Then he remembered.

He'd lost it, running from Corbin's farmhouse last night.

"My name is Belinda and I'll be your art consultant today. Do you have any questions?"

Laurent jolted back to the present.

"What can you tell me about the artist?"

Belinda Crockett, the lanky, straw-haired woman with sharp eyes who'd greeted him at the door, now surveyed him.

In his new clothes — belted trousers, open muslin dress shirt, Bostonian loafers, bought with a thick wad of cash tucked into his pants pocket — he looked better than he had when he'd gotten off the bus from Concord State Prison a week ago.

Given his rugged features, he knew he appeared intimidating.

27

But dressed decently now, he could pass. He was a tourist, up on a day bus from Boston, taking in the quaint sights, buying overpriced baubles, rubbing elbows with the locals in the trendy breweries along the wharf.

He'd shopped earlier with the money he'd earned in prison — $1.50/day for two decades working in the library, minus expenses for cigarettes, soap, stamps, razors — leaving him with a tidy sum of $3200, in the form of a registered government check, handed him upon his release. At the only check cashing place that would take it without a state-issued ID, he'd had to pay the maximum cashing fee of 12%. *Bastards!* Still, the cash bought him time and time is what he needed. His Rambo act just wasn't going to cut it with Vivian.

"I can see why you like her art," said Belinda, pushing back a strand of hair, striking her own pose. A hand on her hip, the other gesturing at the painting, she extolled its virtues. Her delivery was rote, as if she wanted to get it over with, move on to a more refined client.

"It's a fine example of hyper-realism ... keen eye for detail, precise, accurate strokes." She smiled; Laurent could see it was an effort for her.

"You from the Seacoast?" She didn't wait for an answer. "Well, if you were, you'd recognize the location — a few miles south of here, on Route 1A, between here and —"

"Uh-uh." Laurent pretended to be listening.

"— Hampton Beach ..." she droned on, her hands fluttering at the painting, birds on a string. "Golden light ... luminescent ... transcends the literal ..."

Laurent tuned her out, let his mind wander back to a day when he and Vivian were in high school, before they were married, before the "thing" happened and he'd gone to jail.

They'd been taking the bus down to Boston on Sundays, to tour the art museums, her passion. Dragging him from one museum to another, treating him to a visual smorgasbord, from the Renaissance to Cubism. They had to see it all, she'd insisted.

Her obsession: the artists' use of light — whether abstract or representational — as a commentary on the presence of good and evil. Her intensity, as she wavered between insight and perplexity, repelled and attracted him. She was on a crusade, her holy grail an answer to the question of why evil exists.

What was behind her madness? he'd wondered then, flattered to be a part of her quest, all the while knowing that he couldn't help her, only witness, mutely, whatever was driving her. He knew it was connected with her father's death, but how he couldn't say. Only later did he find out the truth.

He stared blankly at the gallery consultant, watching her lips move but not registering what she was saying.

"So, how would you like to pay for this, cash or credit card?" she repeated, presumptuously extending the watercolor toward him, urging him to take it. Her insistence brought him back to the present, to the gallery in Prescott Park, to his imposture. To his yearning to be back with the one person who mattered.

Instinctively, he reached for the wad of cash in his pants pocket to make sure she hadn't somehow dazzled him into paying with her polished sales pitch. Her smile, pretentious and insincere, was all the wakeup call he needed.

He scowled at her.

"Sir, are you all right?"

He backed up, waving his clumsy hands, feeling his face flush with embarrassment, mouthing *no, no, no,* as he stumbled from the gallery amid the stares of the patrons, their polite hum of conversation arrested by his muffled curses.

She'd tried to shame him.

"Screw you, lady!"

He went on cursing, not caring who heard; past the wharf, across State St. to Market, down Bow. Undaunted, he passed through the crowds. He hated every one of them, these ciphers, with their careful, privileged lives, as they clung to the illusion of safety and goodness in the universe.

"Screw you all!"

That's when he decided — stealing Vivan back was not enough. He had to kill Jens for usurping his place, for stealing his life. The boy would have to die, too. There would be no place for Corbin's son in his and Vivian's new life together.

Resolved, he kept on, his feet swallowing up pavement, past Portsmouth's iconic tugboats and salt piles; over the bridge; through Kittery and the Point. Not stopping until he got to his motel room, where he began to plot his resurrection.

Chapter Ten

Back at the farmhouse in Lee, Vivian, arms wrapped around Teddy's mountain of dirty clothes — stuffed in the hamper sweaty from gym if he bothered with it at all — picked her way carefully down from his bedroom to the laundry room off the kitchen and piled his load into the washing machine. She poured in extra detergent and dialed to the hottest wash possible, colors or not.

After a long day at her easel, during which she rejected her numerous attempts at getting the marsh scene right, she finally came up with a technique to preserve the highlights — adhering strips of masking tape. Success at last! The painting, in all its shimmering glory of shadow and light, was ready in her opinion to join her series on the four seasons on display at the New Hampshire Art League exhibition on the wharf.

Without her art, she would be destroyed. She tried that for a time after Teddy's birth, only to descend into a low so abysmal that it took meds and the threat of electroshock to snap her out of it. She never wanted to go there again, not ever. Though she fought depression constantly, she managed to stay afloat. Her marriage, though unsatisfying emotionally and spiritually, served a purpose — it allowed her to paint and be around her son.

Standing in the laundry room, she listened to the sound of the washing machine filling with water. A movement outside the window, the backyard shrouded in darkness, drew her attention, but she paid it no mind, assuming it was Bruzza making his rounds.

Sure, she loved Jens on some level, distantly. But wasn't he distant too, involved more with his stories than her? Granted, it was his single-mindedness that made his novels successful and paid the bills. If she were honest, she would have to admit that she resented his success.

Self-doubt dogged her constantly. She wasn't a good enough artist, a good enough mother, a good enough human being — she wasn't, was she? So, she compensated with these acts of kindness on Teddy's behalf. The laundry, a case in point.

Hey, he's old enough to take care of his own laundry.

At his age she'd been forced to wash her own clothes, her mom's, too, and Uncle ... she stopped herself.

Isn't it time for a drink?

After rewarding herself with a glass of wine for doing the laundry, good mother that she was, she'd had a few more glasses, just to mollify her ubiquitous annoyance with Jens. And a few more after that — to celebrate her solitude. And a few more to ... well ... just because Jens was not around to slow down her drinking with disapproving looks.

Asshole!

By the time she trudged upstairs to Teddy's room with the stack of folded laundry, she was pleasantly muzzy. She dumped it all onto a chair — the bed was unmade of course — and opened Teddy's closet to put it away. As usual, dress pants and shirts Teddy had worn only once — serviceable if hung up properly — were stuffed onto a shelf.

She shook her head, stopping herself from cursing.

He's just a boy, after all. And a great kid at that!

She shoved his dirty laundry onto the floor. That's when she noticed the gray metal box at the back of the shelf.

Curious, she sat on the bed with the box in her lap, debating whether or not to invade her son's privacy; telling herself she had to. It might be drugs, which wouldn't surprise her. She'd been warned at school meetings about the dangers of teens abusing drugs and alcohol, and drunk driving. Or worse, mixing "cocktails" of prescription drugs from their parents' medicine cabinets, resulting in sudden death.

What to do?

The latch was unlocked. She opened it.

A stack of letters, the envelopes torn open.

Rifling through the lot with mounting dread, she recognized *his* handwriting. His flowing script, the familiar "V" of his "Vivian" tilted forward, chasing the letters that followed.

Could there be any doubt?

There, addressed to her, was her name, not "Corbin" but her maiden name, "D'Arcy," which she hadn't thought about in years, for all the anguish it summoned. She viewed the return address, stamped in red ink: New Hampshire State Prison for Men." With trembling fingers, she reached for the topmost envelope, dated less than a month ago.

My dearest, darling, Vivian, I'm coming for you — soon. I forgive you for not writing back, not even once, even though I asked you not to. Really, darling, I know how hard it must have been, all these years, to keep up the facade of marriage with Corbin, a man you tolerate at best. Soon we'll be together — we'll figure out how. I know you have a son; we'll work that out. It will all take some getting used to, I'm sure. I've changed over the years — but I've never let jail poison my love for you. I've kept that love pure, along with the picture of you imprinted in my heart, from the last time you visited me here, in this place. I will come for you when I know it's safe.

On an impulse, she went to the window and drew the curtain aside, scanning the darkened landscape that surrounded the farmhouse. Looking for what?

Was that someone?

There — at the edge of the trees!

Or was it just her imagination?

Shivering, she dropped the curtain and backed away.

Suddenly, it all made sense. The strange phone calls lately, met by silence when she answered, abruptly disconnected. The sense, suppressed as paranoia, that someone was watching her and that her home, even the bedroom, had been violated.

In a panic, she booted up Teddy's desktop computer and looked Laurent up on the webpage for the New Hampshire

Inmate Locator — *Armand Laurent, Released August 5.*

"Armand," she whispered. "You're back."

She didn't know whether to be excited or repulsed. Or terrified.

Chapter Eleven

He stood at the edge of the vast manicured lawn that fronts the administration building of Phillips-Exeter Academy, that venerable institution.

Laurent shielded his eyes against the slanted late summer sun flashing off the white-spired cupola atop the landmark Academy Building, the center of this august universe of higher education.

It was Sunday morning and the sprawling, ivied campus was deserted but for a gaggle of students who'd remained on campus over the long weekend.

With a pang of regret, he reminded himself that this is where the children of America's aristocracy traditionally attended as a stepping stone to an Ivy-League education and a place at the trough of wealth and power.

He, too, would have attended here if he hadn't fallen in love with Vivi and his life hadn't taken a turn for the worse. He laughed bitterly at this understatement, sneering at the hand fate had dealt him.

This is where Corbin and Vivi's son attended. This is where he could fetch him, should he need him as a pawn in his plot to reclaim what was rightfully his.

As he strolled about the campus, he couldn't help feeling jealous and resentful of Teddy.

Once in Teddy's dormitory — which he'd had no difficulty tracking down — he resolved to deal Teddy the kind of blow fate had bestowed on him.

What form would the fatal stroke take?

Well, that depended entirely on Corbin. His generosity, his cooperativeness.

And Vivi, of course. How well she received him.

He had done his homework. He had learned valuable computer skills in prison — most legal, some not. Add to that a

35

few simple phone calls, using the account number and address from the Comcast bill he had stolen from Corbin's mailbox, and the profile grew and took shape. Identity theft was easy as pie if you knew what you were doing.

Tonight, knowing what he now knew from his research, about her husband's properties, their art, his literary assets, he would call her.

He tried the knob to the dorm room he'd identified as Teddy's, to see exactly how the little prince lived.

It was locked.

"Can I help you, sir? Are you lost?"

The young man in sweats, unconsciously bouncing a field hockey stick off his shoulder, smiled at him helpfully.

Laurent returned his smile.

"My son will be attending in the fall. Just wanted to see what the rooms actually look like before signing on the dotted line."

"No problem," the boy said, turning to go on his way. "There's a model room on display at the end of the hall. Good luck, sir."

"The same to you ... son."

The word stuck in his throat. It called to mind everything that he'd forfeited. Why should Corbin have the life he, Laurent, was meant to have?

Perhaps it was time that someone else suffered a loss as great as his own.

And know what it's like to curse God for abandoning you.

He left campus, walking briskly along the wooded paths to Main Street, to his bus stop back to Portsmouth.

Along the way, he memorized the cul-de-sacs where he could hide when it came time to snatch Teddy, and the escape routes affording an easy getaway to the car he'd steal for the occasion.

And, if Vivi wouldn't have him?

First the father, then the son.

Chapter Twelve

Afterwards, the old man, the doctor, tore up The Kancamagus Highway in his black Escalade SUV, cursing himself for getting manipulated into rescuing that poor woman, the cashier at the convenience store back in Conway. That obnoxious man and his son, somehow they knew he was a doctor, and had shamed him into feeding her aspirin to arrest her heart attack.

He'd only stopped to pick up more Red Bull to stay awake. Driving for over twenty-four hours, straight from Florida, he had less than an hour to go.

He'd even forgotten his Red Bull, which he didn't need any more, charged as he was on adrenalin and self-loathing. He'd sworn never to lift another finger to uphold his Hippocratic Oath, not after what had happened back in Ft. Lauderdale.

The Escalade seemed to know where it was going — back to that lookout facing Black Mountain Ridge, back to where it all began so many years ago, back to where it would all end, in a few hours.

He stomped on the gas, anxious to join his wife's ghost.

———

He maneuvered the Escalade over the last few bumps in the switchback. The paved road leading to Black Mountain Lookout was swollen in places from previous winter thaws, forcing him to drive around the moguls.

He turned into the lot at the foot of the trail, finding it much the same as he remembered it years ago. A corral of seasoned post-and-rail fence encircled the dirt lot. At the far end, the official trail forked to the right. Beyond, at the foot of the mountain, a cottage sat surrounded by shade trees and rose trellises.

Everywhere he looked, summer's end was in abundance. Conifers and firs towered over thickets of wintergreen and partridge berry. Amid the bracken and fern, a plum-colored Canadian wildflower bobbed in the mid-afternoon breeze.

He stopped the SUV, opened the driver's window, turned off the motor. In rushed the sounds of nature, dominated by trees rustling in the breeze. Warm air wafted down, riffling fields of hay toasted by the sun. How his heart ached. He was home. Back to where it had all begun. He jerked open his door and tumbled out, swept away in feeling.

If he was going to do this right, he needed to make a clean sweep — leave no trace of himself. He lurched back to the car and tore open the passenger's door. From the glove compartment, he took out the registration and insurance. Then he ransacked the car, removing anything else that might identify him, obsessed with the idea of effacing all traces of his earthly existence. Why, he couldn't say, only that it felt right: neat and final, like a doctor caring for his patients.

A nearby trash barrel loaded with tinder-dry refuse caught fire almost instantly when he dropped a match into it. He fed the remnants of his life into the flames, watching it all go up.

The ritual over, he was ready. He ducked back into the car and emerged holding his semi-automatic.

Discarding the canvas holster as he ran, he charged past the quaint cottage and mounted the trail that canted uphill.

———

The bear — a black sow of the family *Ursus americanus*, with a summer-thick pelt thinning where she'd purposely rubbed against low-lying tree limbs — caught scent of the fire burning in the trash barrel at the foot of the trail. Having pupped in the spring, she was still nursing her litter, and her dugs were full and cumbersome. They swayed heavily as she dropped nimbly from her perch in the tree, where she'd been scavenging ants, eating to store up food for the long winter.

Her primal fear of fire made her anxious for her five-month-old cubs, playing outside a den she'd fashioned of boughs dragged against a leeward outcropping of rock, on a high ridge, downwind from the trail. Standing on her hind legs and sniffing furtively, she rose to her full height, revealing herself to be, at nearly five-and-half feet, as tall as the male of her species. She easily weighed two hundred and fifty pounds.

She began running, the muscles beneath her pelt scissoring her haunches and paws in a powerful loping motion, as she picked up speed in a blur of black maternal fury.

———

A few miles east on the trail to Black Mountain Ledge, father and son trudged through the long grass edging the woods, in pleasant conversation, warmed by the slanting sun. Seen from afar, they configured silhouettes in a time-honored rite of passage.

What would the future bring for Teddy? Jens silently mused, as they passed under a canopy of pine and spruce. *What promise lay in the boy's soul? What seeds of greatness might emerge? How could he, Jens, water the seeds? Wasn't that a father's job?*

Lost in thought, he was startled when Teddy called out to him from a bend in the trail, which led to the dirt parking lot at the foot of the mountain.

"You won't believe it — it's the Escalade." Teddy shuffled backwards, arms swinging.

The enigmatic man at the convenience store, the presumed doctor they'd dubbed "Red Bull," had continued to occupy Jens and Teddy's conversation all the way to Jackson and farther, to their cabin atop Mt. Ledge Road, where they left the car and set off on foot to hike the nearby Ridge. What had bothered them most was that Red Bull had bolted from the convenience store immediately after saving the clerk.

Waiting for the ambulance, Teddy had wondered what sort of man would act so callously, doctor or not. Jens didn't have a ready answer. He'd held the stricken woman's hand and reassured her that she'd be all right.

And here was his dust-covered vehicle, parked at the turnout to the very same ridge they'd come to climb. Coincidences like this were unacceptable in fiction and suspicious in real life. Jens' hackles were up. Was Red Bull stalking them?

Teddy waited around the bend at the SUV while Jens caught up. While he may not be as spry as his son, who was thirty years younger, Jens was in good shape — working out daily in his home gym as part of his fitness program as a writer. He prided himself on being able to go the distance. Diligence and hard work had earned him his accomplishments in life and promised more — so long as he went the distance.

Suddenly the air was acrid with smoke. At the same time, Jens noticed the SUV's rear plate, from Florida, as he'd predicted.

Teddy inched closer to get a look inside. "The keys are in the ignition."

"Don't touch anything, something's not right."

Jens glanced around nervously, noticing the trash can off to the side emitting a thread of smoke. He went to the can and peered inside.

Teddy joined him at the barrel. "Look, a wallet."

Jens picked up a stick and poked inside the barrel, stirring up the ashes; he scooped up the still-smoking wallet, dropped it onto the ground to let it cool.

"What do you think happened?"

Jens shook his head. He poked the wallet with his finger, peeled it open, and removed the driver's license. The plastic coating had melted, blurring the name and address.

Teddy peered over his shoulder, trying to decipher what the fire hadn't completely eradicated.

"'D'... 'a'" he read with difficulty. He looked closer. "The last name has no first letter, but the second is an 'o'; then there's an 'm' followed by more letters, but I can't make them out."

Jens nodded, swiveled his head around, all the while expecting the peculiar man from the convenience store, *Dr. Red Bull*, to charge out of the woods and do what? Attack?

Given what they'd found, it seemed to Jens that anything was possible. He felt like one of his fictional protagonists sorting through the clues at the scene of a crime, only this was real. What kind of man destroys his identification?

"Shouldn't we call the police? You brought your cell phone, right?"

Jens shook his head. "No signal up here." He opened the wallet again, looking for another form of identification. Plastic credit cards had melded together in a wad, leaving no trace of a name.

He pulled open all the compartments. Stuck to the lining of one was a black and white passport photo of a young woman, early twenties. Pretty, her short light-colored hair worn in a style long out of fashion — perm-curls piled on top. Her blouse was high-collared, prim. Jens handed it to Teddy.

He gave it back with a smirk. "Looks like from your time."

Jens put it in his jacket pocket along with the charred license. "I'll keep that in mind the next time you ask to play Xbox."

———

The bear charged uphill through the dense woods, forepaws clawing, hind legs springing. She grunted as she ran, making a mewling sound as she called out to her cubs, warning them of danger, assuring them she was coming. Her paws landed heavily, pulverizing dead limbs in her path, snapping them with a loud *kerak*. She had to get back to her cubs.

———

Father and son mounted the same trail as the doctor had earlier, the path ascending steeply within a few yards. Teddy, wearing the prized Dunham hiking boots Vivian had bought for him, bounded ahead, seemingly liberated by the woods.

Jens trudged after, conserving his strength.

"You and Mom — you're getting along okay, aren't you?"

Jens caught up with him

"No better or worse than usual. Maybe even better than usual," he added, recalling their lovemaking. "Why do you ask?"

"Ah, no particular reason." He shrugged.

Jens glanced at him, trying to read between the lines.

"You worried we're going to split up?"

"Nah ... it's just that a lot of kids at school, their parents are divorced or getting divorced." He smiled reassuringly. "It's a trend."

Jens thought about what to say. He didn't want to say something that would deny or discredit Teddy's intuition. They trudged on, the sound of their boots blending with the encompassing hush of the woods.

Teddy picked up a sturdy fallen tree limb, splintered at one end where it had broken from a tree.

"Take it." He held it out to Jens.

Jens shook his head. Was this a peace offering? he wondered. For what?

"You're kidding, right?"

"You'll need it soon, old man." He flashed Jens his gamin grin. "For when the going gets tough —"

Jens finished their ritual with a smile: "The tough get going."

He caught the limb Teddy tossed him, swung it under his arm like a baton, and decided to keep it. They trekked on, the incline ever steeper, forcing them to lean forward, nearly perpendicular. Teddy chattered away, about the beauty of the woods and how much he liked the peace and quiet — unaware, noted his father, of the irony.

Jens climbed on silently, enjoying the workout. With each

step, the cane Teddy gave him bit into the web of his hand, soon blistering the skin. He gripped it firmly, trudging on, letting it bite: uncomplaining, unwilling to show weakness, the mystique of his identity wrapped up in stoicism, learned by default. From the father he'd loved but had not loved him back, and had decked him at the dinner table for accidentally saying the f-word. Young as he was at the time, Jens, dry-eyed, had picked himself off the floor and glared at his father until his father, exasperated, had left the table.

Kerak.

Something large — Jens couldn't say what — was crashing through the woods. Turning reflexively, he saw a dark form, low to the ground, knifing through the trees.

What the —? At first, he thought it was a man on all fours, dressed in black, scrambling up the ridge. *How absurd.* The hackles on Jens' neck stood up.

Bear! Shit.

He watched it pounce uphill, mewling ferociously. Keeping an eye on the beast's progress, he picked up a rock, ready to do battle. In the other hand was his knobby staff.

———

The old man winced with pain as he climbed the last few feet of the path to the lookout. He grabbed an overhanging tree branch to steady himself. Heaving, out of breath, he took in the view, a spectacular one-hundred-eighty-degree panorama. It was just as he remembered it. Miles to the north across the steppes lay the Black Mountains, smoky-blue in the afternoon sun, beasts at rest. South, to his dismay, the forested ridges were desecrated with a sprawl of red-roofed developments, clinging to the hillsides, sprung up in his absence. Exhausted, he drew in the crisp mountain air, fighting to clear his head.

He collapsed onto the weathered granite outcropping that capped the trail, perspiring and heaving with exhaustion. He lay still, looking up at the vast sheltering sky, thinking of his wife, Leah, whom he'd be joining shortly.

He patted the gun in his pocket, confirming that it hadn't fallen out during the climb. All his life he had played God with the lives of his patients; now it was his turn.

A noise in the thicket below the ledge caught his attention. It sounded like *growling* dogs, though higher pitched, more primitive.

He got up from the rock and peered over the edge, holding onto a sapling, careful of his footing.

He jerked back as though struck — then risked another look.

Below, three cubs cavorted behind a barrier of bracken and tree limbs, trapped against a hollow in the granite wall. He smiled as they paused in their play, sniffing the air tentatively because of him. They soon lost interest and returned to their ritual of dominance: pouncing, rearing, surrendering.

Back on the ledge, the old man made his peace with himself and the world. He had no need of last-minute declarations of love — he was ready. Leah was waiting.

With hands accustomed to healing, he put the gun to his temple without hesitation, placed his finger on the trigger, and squeezed.

———

Teddy was farther along on the trail, leaping like a mountain bock, oblivious to any danger. Jens glanced warily in his direction, told himself that black bears rarely attack humans. For all the good it did. His primitive brain had taken over; he was ready for fight or flight. He scrambled to catch up with Teddy.

"Teddy — *bear.*"

Shooshing, he pointed in the direction of where he'd seen her disappear into the woods.

"Where? Don't see him." Teddy sidled up to his father,

scanning the woods. "You seeing things, old man?" He slung his arm around Jens.

Jens gave him a gentle elbow in the ribs. "I saw what I saw."

Nothing happened outside of an impotent *click*. The old man lowered the gun and studied it. Shaking his head at his stupidity, he fumbled with the gun until he figured out how to pull back the slide and drop a round into the firing chamber.

This time, though it was a difficult angle, he raised the pistol to a point between his eyes, confident that the .44 caliber bullet would punch through his skull and cerebral cortex, destroy his autonomic nervous system, and kill him instantly.

He tightened his finger on the trigger and — squeezed.

At the exact same instant, there was a *roar*.

He barely registered a dark flurry of movement out of the corner of his eye, hurtling toward him.

Bear.

She was on him, claws extended, teeth bared.

Roaring.

Time stopped. He heard the plaintive *yips* of the cubs calling to their mother; a cloud cluster spoke to him of eternity; a glimpse of blue sky disappeared behind the bulk of the bear, as she bore down on him with all her terrifying certitude of muscle, bone, gristle, and pelt.

The shot rang out — *BOOM* — reverberating loudly in the thin mountain air.

Coveys of birds darted out from under the ledges and trees, arching in different directions, as though pointing the way to the beyond.

Back on the trail, Jens exchanged a wary glance with Teddy. *Did Red Bull have a gun*, wondered Jens? With the sound of gunshot, the mystifying evidence back in the parking lot jelled into certainty. *Red Bull shot himself.*

"Hope that's not what I think it is." Teddy lurched up the trail before Jens could react.

"Wait!" Jens scrambled after him.

"Don't shoot!" Jens turned the blind bend onto the ledge.

Teddy, first to arrive, stood frozen, speechless.

The bear had the old man's head in her jaws and was shaking him violently from side to side, his body limp as a rag doll, the whites of his eyes showing. As she clawed his flesh with her talons, her drool slathered her jaws and spilled onto her prey, mixing with blood from the gashes.

Trembling, Teddy inched forward, reaching behind him for Jen's cane. "Give!" he hissed.

Jens pushed in front of him and jabbed the stick at the bear's head as she crunched down on the old man's skull with a bone-splintering snap of her jaws.

Jens gripped the stick and let loose a terrified bellow.

"Hey, you — you son of a bitch!"

Panting furiously, the bear looked up, showing bloodied yellow fangs and feverish red eyes. She roared and jawed down on her captive.

Stepping in like a batter meeting a pitch, Jens swung the thick staff with all his might, landing it with a resounding *thwack* on the enormous head. She ignored him.

He rained down blow after blow, striking her all over, but she continued to ignore him, caught in a frenzy of destruction meant only for the old man. Jens readied to make another assault on her while Teddy groped for the pistol in the grass.

"Don't!" Jens lunged for the gun.

The bear looked up, seeing — as though for the first time — Jens then Teddy. She dropped her victim and launched herself at Teddy, scrambling on all fours. She was nearly on him.

Jens fired a shot into the air. *Boom!* She was still going for Teddy. He fired again, *Boom.* The bullet creased her furred scalp.

As though recovering a buried memory — of man and his cunning weapons — she stopped, rose up on her hinds, and *roared* and *roared.*

Terrified, Jens stepped back, his arm extended rigidly, his finger on the trigger, aiming at her head. He didn't want to kill her, but he would, cubs or not.

They glared at each other, the beast heaving with fury; the man shivering with resolve.

The barking of the cubs furled up from the ledge below. Mewling loudly, the sow dropped onto all fours with a grunt and scrambled off the ledge toward her children.

Later, when Jens sat down to write about this moment, he would wonder at the mysterious understanding that seemingly had passed between them, man and beast, parent to parent.

Awed, Teddy stumbled over to him, halted.

"Hey. You okay?"

Jens wondered why he was whispering. He shook his head, not sure what he was feeling. He gripped the gun, fist white-knuckled, his look turned inward.

Again, softly: "Dad, *Dad*, we gotta get help."

Jens stooped beside Daniel. Blood was pooling from the gashes on his head; there was a raw wound behind his ear, the edges singed with gunpowder.

He felt his neck for a pulse.

"He's alive!"

Chapter Thirteen

He'd sent Teddy tearing down to the cottage at the foot of the trail, where telephone lines confirmed the existence of a landline, to call the police and send an ambulance.

Jens stood watching the medics as they carried the injured man to the trail on a stretcher. He was strapped down, an oxygen mask over his face, a plastic bag of vital fluids attached to an arm drip. Jens' makeshift bandage had been replaced with sterile pads and gauze. The medics had loaned him a green scrub top to replace the bloodied shirt he'd used to wrap around the old man's head.

Still pumped on adrenalin from his second confrontation with death in the same day, Jens breathed deeply, trying to regain his balance. His thoughts racing ahead, he found himself silently giving thanks for the safety of his son and that of the man whose life he'd saved.

It had been his turn to save a life. The image of his deceased brother Nils, lurking always at the feathery edge of consciousness, fluttered back into the depths. Was Nils trying to tell him something? An unconscious shiver passed through him as he seemed to sense the proximity of the world of the dead with that of the living.

He was ready to go down the mountain, to resume his routine duties and responsibilities as a father and husband, and reclaim the rarer joys of his work as a writer. Nearing fifty, his own father's age at the time of his death, Jens felt a sharp twinge of mortality. Would he be here next year to welcome the golden days of Indian summer? To watch his boy grow into a man?

He gave the granite rock on the ledge a final scan, to impress it in his mind for future use as the scene of ordinary miracles, in a story. His reverie was interrupted by Teddy calling to him from around a bend in the trail below.

"You coming, Dad?"

A flash of gold in the late afternoon sun caught Jens' eye as he turned to go. Lying in the grass alongside the granite rock was the Rolex he had seen the stranger wearing earlier. Jens scooped it up, marveling it at its dense utility. He turned it over in his hand, admiring the bejeweled face and the elegant gold band. On the back cover was an inscription: "To Daniel, Always, Leah."

The stranger had a name. Daniel.

––––––

As they went down the mountain, he reassured Teddy that they would turn the Rolex over to the police. Teddy was all for keeping it, they'd saved Daniel's life after all. Jens laughed, shook his head.

Teddy gave his father a troubled look.

"Something terrible must have made that man want to take his own life."

Jens didn't answer, preoccupied with his concern for the man they now knew as Daniel. But Teddy's comment lingered. Already his writer's mind was spinning possible scenarios for the man from Florida: the sad man, the erstwhile doctor, Daniel, who was loved, or had been loved, by a woman named Leah.

––––––

At the bottom of the trail they were met by a New Hampshire State Trooper, a woman in her late 20s, early 30s, whose name tag identified her as Sgt. F. Morrison. In Jens' experience, most "staties" approached the good citizenry under their purview with liberal doses of sarcasm, faux civility, and arrogance. Sgt. Morrison was no exception, female or not.

"Taking in the sights on the way down, *gentlemen*?"

Her clipped speech reminded Jens that they were in northern New Hampshire, within a hundred miles of the Canadian border.

He held her sharp gaze, noting that even without makeup she was attractive — her eyes piercing blue, long-lashed; pert nose; lips well-formed despite being pulled back in what appeared to be a perpetual grimace. Her sandy hair was shorn military style, fringing the brim of her Smokey the Bear hat; her uniform tight over a sculpted torso.

Something blatantly masculine in the mix. A pose, predicated by the job, or natural, wondered Jens, his writer's eye instantly registering her as a character of interest. Gender preferences had become the new hot potato in culture and politics, and he was not indifferent. He watched as she pulled down on the brim of her hat, worn full tilt over the eyes to intimidate. No different from her chauvinist male counterparts.

"I've been debating whether or not to go on up and bring you down myself."

Jens gestured to the ambulance where the EMTs were loading Daniel's stretcher onboard. "Is he going to make it, officer?"

"Dad, the SUV is gone." Teddy pointed to the place in the parking lot where the Escalade had been parked.

"Maybe the police towed it." Jens turned back to Sgt. F. Morrison.

The trooper cleared her throat. "Tell you what, Mr.—?"

"Corbin, Jens Corbin. This is my son, Teddy. Mind telling me what hospital they're taking the injured man to?"

"May I see some identification, Mr. Corbin, *sir*?" she said with feigned civility, eyes taut, hands on her Sam Browne belt. She wore her holstered gun high on her right hip. Making her right-handed, noted Jens. He also noted the gun was not standard issue, it was a revolver of some kind, and he knew from his book research that most troopers carried an automatic pistol. He observed everyone as if they might be a character in his next book.

He rewarded her with the look of a tolerant parent.

Something clicked in her. She nodded to herself, inhaled,

exhaled, took her hands off the Sam Browne belt. Away from her gun.

Jens produced a thin billfold he used when hiking. He fished around inside, purposely taking his time. Finally, he handed his driver's license to F. Morrison, who glanced at it, matching the picture with the man standing before her.

"And the boy?"

"My son."

Jens pulled out a student ID card for Teddy, issued by his school in the event he went missing.

Sgt. Morrison put Teddy through the same scrutiny, though gentler.

"Mind stepping over to the cruiser, Mr. Corbin?"

They waited while she ran Jens' license through the DMV.

She handed back their IDs.

"You want to tell me what happened up there on the ledge? Got part of the story from the medics. Something about a bear."

"What's the man's condition?" asked Jens.

"Mind if I ask the questions." It wasn't a question.

"Jeez, what a —" blurted Teddy, silenced with a glare from Jens.

Arms folded over her chest, Trooper Morrison glanced from father to son, assessing while Jens recounted the story of the man they presumed to be a doctor, who had tried to take his own life but was thwarted by the bear.

Jens wondered if her suspicion was an acquired trait, requisite for her job, or one that came naturally to her.

Jens recounted the incident with Daniel at the convenience store in Ossipee, and how he knew he was a doctor because, along with other clues, he had saved the life of the cashier. Jens explained how he and Teddy deduced he was from Florida. He described how they'd found his SUV with the doors open, keys in the ignition.

All the while, Trooper F. Morrison wore a sour expression that reminded Jens of a redneck sucking on a tooth.

52

"What line of work you in?" She adjusted her belt, rolled her shoulders like a weightlifter.

Jens smiled, knowing what was coming.

"Writer. Crime novels."

"Leave me do my job," she said, flashing him what would pass for a smile.

"When we first got here, his SUV, a black Cadillac Escalade, was parked there." Teddy pointed to a vacant spot in the lot. "We found a wallet in the trash barrel."

Prompted, Jens handed her the driver's license salvaged from the fire.

"You can make out a few letters, like 'D' and 'a' in the first name and something 'o' in the last ..." Teddy's voice trailed off at her annoyance.

"We were halfway up the trail when we heard a gunshot coming from the ledge," said Jens. "When we got there the bear had his head between her jaws, likely protecting her cubs on the ledge below."

"Three gunshots were reported by the woman in the cottage at the foot of the trail." She held Jens' eyes.

"The first shot was the victim's, self-inflicted." He held her eyes steadily. "Then I fired twice, at the bear."

"You kill her?"

"Grazed her," answered Teddy.

"That stop her?"

Jens shrugged, nodded.

"So where's the gun?"

———

After climbing back up the trail and beating the brush around the cap rock for the gun, unsuccessfully, they trudged wordlessly back down the trail.

Sgt. Morrison put them in the back seat of her cruiser, insisting on driving them home as a courtesy but, really, Jens knew it was to check out where he would be for future reference. Her suspicions bothered him, making him feel guilty for no reason.

As they drove out of the preserve, past the dried-up riverbed and dense woods, Sgt. Morrison reported back to her station on her two-way radio.

"The unsub is being taken to North Conway Presbyterian," answered a female voice tinged with French Canadian cadences. "Condition unstable; hasn't regained consciousness. You get a positive ID?"

"Negative," answered the trooper, keying in the microphone. "Put out an all points on a black, late model, Escalade Cadillac SUV with Florida tags, though they might've been swapped." She released the transmit button on the two-way and glanced back at Jens and Teddy in the back seat.

"Either of you catch the SUV's plate number?"

Jens met her watchful eyes in the rearview mirror. They were blue-grey, he noticed, not just blue.

"Only that it was a Florida plate."

Jens glanced at Teddy, who mouthed nope without looking away from the fleeting scenery. They had just turned onto Mountain Ledge Rd., with its alternating mix of farms and sprawling, red-roofed country homes carved into the hillsides. The cruiser's engine groaned as it took them up the steep grade.

The radio crackled. "Any sign of foul play?" asked the dispatcher.

"Civilians aboard. Fill you in back at HQ."

"Roger that," said the dispatcher, ending the connection.

"So, Corbin, would I know any of your books?"

Jens named his published titles, beginning with the best known one, *The Killing Kind*, nominated for a "Poe," named after Edgar Alan Poe, he explained.

Sgt. Morrison shrugged.

———

Finally, at a bend high up on the ridge, she pulled into the drive at Jens' cabin, a modest two-story, single family home of notched cedar logs perched on a hillside, with a view of the sloping woods and surrounding mountains. In the driveway, Jens' late model 4-WD Subaru was parked beside a tarp-covered fishing skiff on a trailer.

"Yours?" The trooper pointed her chin at the Subaru.

Jens shook his head in disgust.

"Yes, it is, and no, we're not planning on going anywhere soon and why *the hell* would you need to know that *anyway?*" he said angrily. "If you have any suspicions, spit them out, otherwise, let's go, Teddy."

He jerked the door handle, only to find it locked.

"Shit! Shit!"

He slammed his shoulder against the door. He knew he was acting foolishly, overacting perhaps, but he couldn't stop himself.

Sgt. Morrison took her time writing down the Subaru's plate number. She turned around in her seat.

"There's still the matter of what happened to the gun — I know, small detail." She smiled insincerely.

"Maybe it fell off the ledge in all that chaos," offered Teddy. "It was a rad high ledge."

"Chaos, eh?" After a pause: "Any objection to my searching you?"

Jens shook his head in disgust. "No good deed goes unpunished." He shared a conspiratorial look with Teddy. "Book us or let us go."

He jerked the door handle again.

"Calm down."

She laughed — a lovely trill, thought Jens, that offset all the macho posturing.

"You put a line like that in your next book, you're off the bestseller list." Her smile seemed genuine. "Anyway, be prepared for the likelihood that your friend may not make it."

"His name's Daniel," Teddy barked, having missed the shift in her tone.

Sgt. Morrison released the rear door lock, got out, and leaned against the cruiser, waiting for them to step out.

Jens handed her the doctor's Rolex.

"Found this up on the ledge. We noticed him wearing it back at the convenience store."

"Inscription says 'To Daniel, Always, Leah,'" piped in Teddy.

F. Morrison whistled at the bejeweled watch as she took it from Jens.

"Conscience just kick in?"

"Let's go, Teddy."

"Hey, I'm just doing my job." She laughed unapologetically.

Jens stomped up the gravel path to the cabin, resolved not to look back and give her the satisfaction of seeing how much she'd gotten under his skin.

Yet, he had to admit, he liked her. She reminded him of his former students whose brash confidence belied their insecurity.

Chapter Fourteen

While Trooper Morrison backed out of the drive, Jens sent Teddy ahead to get the key from the realtor lockbox attached to the front door. Walking up the pebbled drive to his cabin always gave Jens a rush of pride, reminding him that this was the house that *The Killing Kind*, his second novel, had financed. The Poe Award had generated book sales, along with a substantial advance on his next two books. Both had fared well, though not as well as expected.

"Whew, it's stuffy in here," Teddy shouted from inside the foyer.

"Open some windows."

Out of habit, Jens surveyed his house and grounds, finding everything in order. He walked around to the back of the house and mounted the deck with a smile. He loved to sight down the grassy slope of his property, which extended deep into the woods without encroachment from other homes. After today's ordeal, he appreciated the solace this view afforded him.

Having to justify his existence as a writer, as he'd been forced to do with Sgt. Morrison, always made him aware of how precarious a livelihood he'd chosen. With the glut of fiction on the market, Jens knew that publishers soon lose interest in older authors, especially ones who fail to regularly make the bestseller list, opting instead to put their money and effort into the next *wunderkind*. It's sexier to promote the young. Youth worship is the malaise of the 21st Century, seen in nearly all media. Jens visualized an infinite influx of twenty-something writers in every genre, all poised over their keyboards, flush with the pride of completion, finger pressing the "Enter" button, their printers spewing manuscripts. It did not matter that their novels were not especially well-written: editors would fix that. What mattered was a youthful point of view and a "fresh" story.

The rest was image, promotion, packaging.

Sitting beside Teddy in the mudroom, Jens removed his dusty trail boots, sighing with relief as he put on house shoes. He inhaled the comforting, familiar odors. He loved the smell of pine pitch coming from the saws and axes clamped to the wood-paneled wall. The familiar smell of wool laced with sweat lingered on ski sweaters and jackets arranged on hooks along the entrance. While Jens unlocked and opened the window, working the hand crank, Teddy brushed past him into the house proper.

Putting his thoughts aside about his value to publishers, Jens gave himself over to the pleasure of deciding what to make for dinner. Cooking was one of his rare indulgences, for it offered timely gratification while engaging his creative impulses. He had a variety of dishes to choose from the shopping he had done earlier. Tonight, he decided, he would keep it simple — chicken breast in spicy mango sauce, basmati brown rice, and steamed broccoli drizzled with olive oil. Under his tutelage, Teddy's palate was becoming sophisticated. Jens looked forward to his son's culinary critique.

"Open all the windows," he called. "Upstairs, too, please."

"I'll get the basement." Teddy headed for the lower level, where there was a recreation room and a bedroom, outfitted with bunk beds where he slept.

Jens felt a twinge of suspicion as he watched Teddy disappear downstairs, wondering why he was volunteering to air the basement. Teddy never did any chores without being asked and coaxed numerous times. Jens knew, from talking with other parents of LDs, Learning Different kids, that volunteering was generally not in their repertoire.

He shrugged it off and stepped inside, gliding on the laminated maple, tongue-in-groove flooring, taking it all in with a rush of pleasure.

Here, more than at the sprawling, two-story farmhouse they owned in Lee, he felt most at home. A library of his favorite books, an eclectic collection that represented twenty years of deep reading in just about every genre and topic imaginable, lined the shelves around the room and continued along the stairway up to the loft and beyond. His wife's vivid watercolors from an earlier period adorned the wall. A sofa flanked by deep leather chairs, positioned before the fireplace, completed the rustic ambiance.

Teddy popped back into the main room, a little out of breath.

"That was fast. Everything all right below?" He could tell when Teddy had something on his mind, like now.

"Daddio, can I play a little Xbox? Just 'til dinner?" He worked the crank on the window in the kitchen alcove, which gave onto the porch.

Jens opened the window beside the sink. He leaned against the butcher block island in front of the stove and took down a copper sautéing pan from among the burnished pots and pans hanging overhead and placed it over a burner on the stove. He loved to cook here. *He loved to be here.* Unconsciously, he ran his hand along the surface of the butcher block, which he kept rubbed with lemon oil. He turned back to Teddy

"We didn't come up here to play Xbox. You can do that in Lee. You got a whole shelf of summer reading to choose from in your room. What about that new Poznanski I saw on your night table — *Erobus.* Have you started it?"

"Can't I just chill?"

Annoyed, Teddy went to the topographical map of the White Mountains mounted beside the fireplace and red-lined the day's trail with a magic marker.

"C'mon, just 'til dinner?"

When Jens didn't answer, Teddy poured himself a tall glass of juice from the refrigerator, gulped it down, and poured himself another. He grew serious.

"What would you have done if the bear hadn't stopped?"

"I'd have shot her."

"Where?"

"In the woods."

"Ha-ha, very funny. *Not.* No really, where?"

Jens chuckled.

"You always want to know the hypothetical 'what if?' You've been doing that since you were old enough to talk."

"And you've told me that at least a thousand times." He sipped his drink. "I'd have shot her in the ear. Blown her brains out." His hand a gun, he pointed it at Jens. "*Bam! Bam! Bam!*"

"Great." Jens pushed his hand away. "What about her cubs?"

Teddy shrugged. "Were you scared?"

"Very. And you?"

"If I say 'yes' will you let me play Xbox?"

Jens really wanted to ask Teddy more about the question he'd raised earlier — about the stability of his marriage. But now was not the right time.

"Just until dinner," he relented.

Teddy threw an arm around him and hugged, making Jens wonder how much longer he could expect to enjoy such tender mercies.

Chapter Fifteen

After putting the chicken in the oven, Jens went to the master bedroom, which he shared with Vivian on the rare occasions she joined him here. She preferred the house in Lee, with its spacious horse barn converted to a studio, where she could disappear to paint when the mood struck her.

Most people would assume that two artists living and working under the same roof would make a perfect match, but he knew that the best marriages between creative types designate one spouse as the artist and the other the nurturer, channeling his or her energy into the home and children. In their marriage, he did both, juggling his time like a miser.

While writing and teaching the occasional fiction-writing class at the university, he nurtured his wife as well as their son. Meanwhile, Vivian neglected them and the house to pursue *her* art, which was little more than a hobby as far as he was concerned, though she took herself quite seriously.

This was a bone of contention between them, especially lately, with the pressure on him from his publisher and agent to produce a bestseller, something that would decisively transcend his dependable, crafted crime stories and catch fire with his readers. Like the Swedish novels of the late Stieg Larsson and those of the husband and wife writing team "Lars Kepler," he needed to let his writing take his readers to unknown territory, with a character or a subject that defied expectations. For this he needed his wife's support — and her faith. Instead, like narcissists who repel one another, they squabbled over household chores and responsibilities and, sadly, over money. Here, at the cabin, he was free at last to indulge his imagination.

He scooped up his pen and composition book, which served as a diary, and went to the kitchen to pour himself a glass of cabernet from a bottle he'd opened to air for dinner.

"Teddy, I'm going out back to work," he called down to the basement, where he pictured Teddy seated in front of the flat screen TV, frenetically thumbing the toggle switches of his Xbox controls, his concentration total. No attention deficit when he was playing, Jens noted cynically.

"Right!" Teddy yelled back.

Glass in one hand, his diary in the other, Jens managed to open the door to the deck and settle into one of the wooden chairs positioned with a view of the mountains in the distance.

He thought about the protagonist of his crime series, a tenacious Portsmouth, New Hampshire police detective of French-Canadian descent and spirited temperament named Honore Poulon.

The distinctive chatter of a mockingbird calling out to its mate gave Jens pause.

A thought occurred to him, no doubt stimulated by the events of the day and the bear's turning on Teddy. What is the worst thing that can happen to a parent? The answer was obvious: to lose a child. And the worst way, bar none? To a predator.

It was a fear that had obsessed him when Teddy was younger and they were living in L.A., an apparent magnet for child molesters. The tabloids were full of sordid stories, and neighborhood watches distributed the names and addresses of registered sex offenders. When Teddy was four, he'd wandered away in a department store, and Jens had panicked before finding him hiding in the clothing racks.

A shadow fell over the curtain of his inner eye. When it lifted, a young woman bodied forth from the recesses of his imagination. Deep sorrow was etched in her face, her cheeks bathed in tears. Like a distant call to arms, Jens heard the mockingbird's mate chatter back. Jens began to write as though possessed.

Cassie Melantree is a thirty-something private investigator, whose seven-year-old daughter was abducted by a pedophile, a local civic leader, and slain only moments before Cassie crashed his secret lair. She's on a mission. Applying the investigative skills of her former profession as a reporter, she devotes herself to helping other families whose children have been abducted. These are the victims whose melancholy faces stare out at us from milk cartons, accusing us of indifference, taunting our naïve complacence.

The land phone was ringing inside, in the kitchen. Jens ignored it, refusing to interrupt the flood spilling through his fingers onto the page.

In some cases, she saves the children in the nick of time, returning them to the safety of their homes; in other cases she's too late, uncovering their mutilated bodies, allowing their families at least the solace of mourning; in still others, she fails to bring closure to the wounded families, either because the culprit is dead, or there just aren't enough clues to rescue the child or pin the heinous act on a particular suspect, even if Cassie knows he's guilty (she has powerful instincts which she trusts implicitly).

The phone continued to ring. Jens ignored it.

These are the hardest cases for Cassie to recover from, as she knows the pain and panic of a parent with a child missing. Her heart goes out to the parents of these children and to the kids themselves, undergoing soul-shattering abuse at the hands of conscienceless monsters, human only in so far as they walk and talk like the rest of us. These are the cases she never puts out of her mind, which haunt her even as she embarks on a new one.

"Teddy, *Teddy!* Get the phone!"

The phone was still ringing, the spell broken.

With a sigh, Jens tucked his pen in his composition notebook and went inside to answer the phone. On the way, he considered how excited and intrigued he was by Cassie's "appearance." He wanted to know all about her. He wanted to stand alongside her in the shadow of evil and vanquish it, sharing her strength and fervor.

His step was lively, almost jaunty, as he went into the house and picked up the receiver.

"Corbin, here."

"Hi, it's me," said the modulated voice on the other end of the line, his wife's.

"Hi. Everything all right?"

He was irritated at being interrupted, and he knew she would pick right up on it.

"I could ask you the same question. You sound disappointed to hear from me." Was she taunting him? *Why?* he wondered.

It seemed to him that their marriage could be summed up by this moment: bad timing and underlying incompatibility. It hadn't always been this way.

"No, no. It's just that I've been working. Something... interesting."

He faltered, not wanting to bring scrutiny to his creation — and not with someone too self-involved to care. He wished it were otherwise.

"Well, I'll let you get back to it. I just wanted to see how my two men were doing. Which mountain did you conquer today?"

He laughed in spite of himself. It allowed him time to consider how much to tell her about the events of the day. She would blast him if he told her that Teddy was nearly mauled by a bear.

"We climbed Black Mountain. You know it, it's not far from the cabin."

"Did something happen?"

Jens knew she could read him like a book.

"Will I have to pry it out of Teddy?" she went on.

"Ah, well, there was a little problem." He cleared his throat.

Using his best editing skills, he launched into a sanitized version of the events of the day, beginning with their brush with the doctor at the convenience store and how Jens had shamed him into saving the cashier. The climax of the tale was the doctor's rescue, when Jens' ran the bear off with a club, making no mention of Daniel's gun. Trooper Morrison handily failed to materialize in this account — no point in raising unnecessary concerns about the Law.

Jens concluded his "tale" with a forced laugh and a gulp of wine. Naturally, she failed to see the humor.

"Where was Teddy when all this was happening?"

He paused long enough to give her food for thought.

"He was with me. Safe."

"You put our son in harm's way?" she accused.

"Viv, it was nothing like that, believe me."

"You're lying." She made no effort to hide her disgust. "Put Teddy on. He'll tell me the truth."

"Ah, I can't do that."

"Why not?"

"He's playing Xbox and can't be disturbed. How was your day, darling? Did you paint?"

"Put Teddy on the phone *NOW!*"

———

After numerous attempts to get Teddy to come upstairs and talk to his mother, Jens decided to bring the phone, an older wireless model with a mobile receiver, to him in the basement game room. Jens ignored Vivian's impatient patter coming over the receiver as she accused Jens of stalling.

Meanwhile, Teddy tried to finish the Xbox episode without getting his assassin killed and losing points. Finally, he took the phone from his father.

"Hi, Mom, sorry but I was in the middle of a game."

Jens was about to return to the dinner he was making when Teddy clapped his hand over the receiver.

"Dad, can I have a little privacy here?"

Jens gave him a quizzical look, Teddy glared back, and Jens left, accustomed to Vivian and Teddy's private conversations.

As he mounted the stairs to the main floor and kitchen, he couldn't help overhearing Teddy answer her defensively.

"Dad didn't do anything — if anything he was a hero. He

saved me, Mom, and that poor man, not to mention the clerk at the convenience store."

Smiling to himself, Jens continued up the stairs, proud of Teddy for standing up to Vivian on his behalf. He stopped when he heard a shift in Teddy's tone. It was sharp, righteous and angry.

"*Excuse me?*" Pause. "So, you found the letters? Good." Pause. "Oh, really?"

He spoke *sotto voce*, forcing Jens to descend a few steps to hear.

"How would you like me to tell Dad?" Pause. "I *will* if you have anything more to do with that bastard Laurent."

Teddy laughed bitterly as he listened to her side of the story.

"*You*, you're the one putting us in jeopardy with that ex-con. *Not* Dad."

He hung up abruptly.

"Dad?" he called, checking to see if Jens had been listening. When Jens didn't answer, he sunk back into the couch, thinking. After a while, he shrugged and went back to his Xbox game.

Jens slipped silently upstairs, closed the basement door, stunned and perplexed by what he'd overheard.

———

Jens and Teddy were just digging into their chicken-mango delight when the phone rang again. Jens expected it was Vivian calling back to deliver a few choice curses and remind him of his failure as a father.

Would she instead address Teddy's reference to an ex-con named Laurent? What had he heard him accuse her of? Some sort of romantic involvement? Ex-con? Convicted of what? How much time served? Where was he now?

Jens, who'd been waiting for the right moment to question Teddy, thought maybe he'd misheard. Would a romantic liaison explain her coldness toward him? He decided to wait and see if she broached it. *Coward*, he chided himself. This was not something he could brush under the rug. Mentally, he prepared himself.

"*Bon soir*, dear. There's something I want to —"

"Corbin?" Jens recognized Sgt. Morrison's North Country nasals.

Jens resisted explaining that he was expecting his wife's call. Had something happened with "the unsub" Daniel?

"Not disturbing anything, am I?"

Jens decided that over the phone she seemed more genuine, sans the defensive armor that came with her job. Did the uniform do that to her?

He pictured her at home, in a small, tidy, modern apartment, in sweats and a jersey either from college or the police academy. He wondered if she had any art on the walls and if so of what? Or photos of her with lovers? What did they look like? Did she live alone?

He mentally chastised himself for making assumptions about her sexual orientation, which was none of his business. But he was curious, an occupational hazard.

He suddenly realized that she was the unconscious model for the character of Cassie in his story — full of intriguing contradictions, still a work in progress. He'd have to get to know Sgt. Morrison better.

"Would it matter if you were?" he sneered, intending to draw her out.

He felt their acquaintance had advanced enough to bear his prickliness, which was not unlike hers. His perception was validated when she stifled a laugh and then grew serious.

"It doesn't look like the unsub is going to make it through the night."

"Oh?"

"Thought you'd like to know."

"Thank you." He exchanged looks with Teddy, who could hear both sides of the conversation.

"Okay, that's it."

"One moment, Sergeant." Jens held his hand over the receiver.

"He has no one," he whispered to Teddy. Teddy nodded back. Jens resumed the conversation.

"Would I be permitted to visit him, even though I'm not next of kin?"

"It could be arranged." The phone line hummed distantly. "Why would you want to do that?"

"It's the right thing to do," answered Jens unequivocally.

"I figured you to say something like that." She paused. "North Conway Presbyterian. Intensive care, west wing, second floor."

"Get his last name yet?" Jens started to say, but the trooper, a woman of few words, he noted, had already hung up.

Chapter Sixteen

Winding the Subaru down Black Mountain Road through a fine mist of fog, Jens arrived at the hospital in North Conway shortly after 9:00 P.M. Teddy had asked to stay home, and Jens hadn't had the heart to drag him out into the night, to watch a stranger die. As for whom Laurent was and what he meant to Vivian — he'd get back to that later.

In the west wing he took the elevator to the second floor. Silhouetted in a cone of light, distributing pills into plastic cups on a tray, the nurse on duty smiled up at him as he approached. Strands of reddish-blonde hair peeking out from her cap identified her to Jens as Irish, corroborated by the name on her badge, which read "N. Leary."

He thought she looked vaguely familiar, deciding it was probably because she was a type. Now that he was standing in front of her, he noticed that she was pretty, *very* pretty, even without make-up.

She looked up at him, arching one of her dark eyebrows, flashing her green and brown-flecked eyes. He was staring and had to force himself to look away.

Like many naturally beautiful women, she was aware of her beauty's power but did not flaunt it. If anything, she was demure.

"Where can I find a patient, ah, who ..." he fumbled.

"The man they brought down from Black Mountain?"

She blew a stray hair from her face. Jens guessed her age at about thirty-something, midrange.

He nodded, relieved that she had come to his rescue. What should he have said?

I'm looking for the man who was mauled by a bear? Who tried to kill himself? Who's dying? In a coma? Whom I barely know?

"And you are?" she asked officiously, belying the twinkle in her eye.

"Jens Corbin."

"Are you really?" she teased, switching gears.

"Excuse me? Want to see my ID?"

"Not necessary." She glanced down at her notepad. "Trooper Morrison told me to expect you."

She looked up at him, enjoying the upper hand.

"Besides, I know you; I took your 'Literature into Film' seminar at UNH, more years ago than I care to admit. Oh, and your Comp. Lit course, too. Really enjoyed your lectures." She searched his eyes for recognition. "Probably don't remember me, do you?"

Jens hesitated, not wanting to be impolite.

"That's okay, it was a big class, and a long time ago."

She smiled as she came out from behind the night desk.

"Follow me." She set off down the corridor.

"Thanks, Miss Leary," he said, recalling her name tag.

"Nola," she tossed over her shoulder.

Was that a mischievous smile he'd glimpsed?

———

She deposited him in front of a private room at the end of a garishly lit corridor.

"Stay as long as you like. I told the staff that you're family."

"Thanks. I'm not, really."

"I heard the story. You were brave."

Embarrassed, he did not know what to say.

"Hey, I'm just around the corner." She started back to her station.

"Shouldn't someone be in here with him?"

She smiled wisely.

"You are. A team of surgeons operated to remove blood clots and relieve brain pressure. There's a shunt draining off cerebrospinal fluids. Really, there's nothing more we can do for him except monitor his vital signs. And pray."

She flashed him an encouraging smile and went back down the corridor.

It was dim in the room, the rheostat turned down. He'd read somewhere that brain trauma patients have low tolerance for light. His eyes adjusting, he found Daniel's hospital bed in the gloom.

There he lay, underneath an oxygen tent, breathing strenuously. His head was bandaged, secured in an apparatus to keep him from moving it. Beneath the rippled plastic of the oxygen tent, he looked fragile, insubstantial. Bundled wires led to monitors on stands behind his bed. An IV dripped fluids into a catheter attached to his arm. A tube leading from his head trailed into a receptacle on a stand — the drain Nola had mentioned.

He placed a metal chair beside the bed and sat down in a crescent of shadow and light. His eyes wandering, he noted the absence of the customary artifacts brought by family and friends — flowers, fruit baskets, get-well cards, framed photos — to bind the ill to the hearts and minds of their loved ones.

It is what it is, he observed sadly, a place to die and pass on to the next place, if there is such a thing. He recalled how his mother used to threaten him and his brother when they were young, that if they didn't show respect, she'd come back to haunt them.

He felt a twinge of bitterness, remembering how she'd half-heartedly forgiven *him* for surviving the hunting incident, instead of her first-born son, Nils, the joy of her life. She'd had to settle for Jens, the black sheep, whose emotional problems in the aftermath of Nils' death and his financial difficulties launching his career as a writer had given her little comfort in her old age. In the end, she'd died alone in a hospital room just like this, feeling abandoned and unappreciated, unloving and unloved.

With an inward shiver he pushed back the memory of his

breakdown so many years ago out on the West Coast when, overwhelmed by shame, he'd purposely cut himself off from everyone, to mourn belatedly for Nils. His inability to be with his mother on her deathbed had compounded his guilt.

He suppressed the sudden urge to cry, which welled up inside like a claw, gripping him by the throat. *Silly*, he told himself, as he talked himself down from a visceral despair he hadn't felt in decades. *Here I am feeling sorry for myself while a man lies dying.* He had a momentary glimpse of the pervasive ironies of life, with its tragedies and joys, cradle to grave.

———

When he felt like himself again, he took out his android phone and called the land line at the cabin. Happily, mobile reception was strong here in Conway. The phone rang and rang until Teddy answered, breathless.

"Corbin residence."

"Teddy, it's me."

"Hey. What's up?"

"I've decided to hang in here, with Daniel." As he said this, he realized how the man's name personalized him, making him more human, deserving of sympathy. "To see him through."

"Okay ..." Teddy answered, tentatively.

"Don't wait up for me."

"You sure?"

"You'll be okay." There was a long pause while static cleared from the line.

"Teddy, is there something you want to tell me?"

The silence became oppressive. Whoever spoke first lost.

"Can I play a little more Xbox?" Teddy giggled nervously.

Jens decided to wait until he was face-to-face with his son before asking about Laurent and his letters to Vivian.

"Haven't you had enough for one day?"

"Just one more game, please?"

"Then lights out?"

"Night, dad."

Jens glanced at Daniel. He seemed unchanged, his breathing ragged though steady.

What am I doing here?

But he knew ... he was doing penance. Still.

Chapter Seventeen

Dawn was breaking when Jens stirred. Sensing purposeful activity around him, he opened his eyes. Nurses just coming on shift hovered around Daniel, observing his monitors, changing the drain receptacle, adjusting electronic sensors. X-rays, CT, and MRI scans were displayed on a backlit case. An upbeat mood circulated.

Jens felt a gentle nudge on his shoulder and looked up to find Nola smiling at him. Feeling in the way, he stood and began to back out of the room.

"You seem to have had a positive effect on our patient," she trilled, barely showing signs of her long shift. "The first twenty-four hours are the most critical after head trauma. He's made it this far. Who knows?"

Jens didn't know what to say. He doubted very much whether he'd had anything to do with Daniel's survival.

"I'll take it from here, nurse," said the IC doctor as he entered to make his morning rounds. He had a slight British accent. A dark-skinned man of thirty-something in a white coat held out his hand for Jens to shake.

"Choudhury, Chief of Neurology." He shook Jens' hand vigorously. Jens noted that despite a freshly perfumed shave, the doctor's blue beard gleamed. "I've read your books. You're a terrific writer," Choudhury added, smiling. "I know a police officer identical to Honore Poulon — in Delhi, of course. Quite the ladies' man, indeed," he chuckled.

Flattered, Jens thanked him. Despite being a bestselling author, it was rare that he ran into anyone who had actually read his books, let alone knew them well enough to comment.

"Goodbye, doctor."

And good luck to you, Daniel. I will not be passing this way again.

———

Jens went back to the nurse's station to say goodbye to Nola, but she was apparently still on her rounds.

Just then the elevator opened, discharging Trooper F. Morrison, sans Smokey-the-Bear hat, revealing a neatly-jelled crew cut rising from her shaven fringe. Jens thought it fit her to a "T." He was beginning to enjoy her abrasive looks and manner, which he found refreshing. *Would he model Cassie after her?* he wondered.

"You look like you've spent the night here, Corbin."

"Is there something, Trooper? I'd like to get home to my son if you don't mind."

She raised an eyebrow. "Home alone, is he? I'm certain child welfare services would be interested in hearing about that."

"Are you serious? After you asked me to come down here and keep your 'unsub' company?"

She broke into a wide grin.

"Naw, I'm just messin' with you. C'mon, let's go down to commissary. I'm treating."

Jens' eyes sought Nola, still on her rounds apparently, before acquiescing. They set off for the cafeteria, located on ground level.

"Doc says the unsub is going to make it." She glanced at Jens, trying to read him. When he didn't respond, she slipped a manila envelope from beneath her arm, and slapped it against her leg as they walked.

"There's something I want to run by you."

Jens smiled to himself: suddenly everyone wanted something from him.

"Why don't you just call me Jens?"

They turned the corner to the stairs to the basement.

"I will if you promise *not* to call me by my first name."

"Why would that be?"

"Because you'll laugh. And then you'll think you *know* me."

76

Her look was unguarded, amused. Jens decided to take the bait.

"Okay, what is it?" They came around the bend leading to the cafeteria.

"Ferdinand."

Jens couldn't suppress a snigger as they entered.

"That's a girl's name?"

She gave him a mock-severe look.

"My parents thought so."

"Oops," he said, retreating. "Anyway, it fits."

She struggled to keep a straight face.

"Thanks, I think. Anyway, *Ferdie*, for short."

"Ferdie, it is, then."

"But only in private." She flicked a hand to her holstered weapon. "Otherwise ..."

He raised a hand in mock protest.

————

The commissary was bright and sunny, with lemon-colored walls that reminded Jens of the 60s, when he assumed this wing of the hospital was built. Wall dividers made of opaque glass squares confirmed his suspicion.

The room was empty aside from a few kitchen workers in white smocks and hairnets bustling about setting the tables. Along one side, windows gave out onto a landscaped park and duck pond. Though it was early, patients in robes sat on benches at the edge of the pond; attendants pushed others in wheelchairs along the arbored paths.

"Ferdie" led Jens to the cafeteria's food line. They slid their trays onto the runners and began helping themselves to breakfast. Jens was starved. He heaped eggs, toast, bacon, and hash browns onto his plate. He glanced at Ferdie taking a Spartan repast of juice, oatmeal, and coffee. Jens caught up with her at the coffee urn and poured himself a cup.

"Long night," said Ferdie sympathetically, as she fished out her wallet to pay.

The cashier, a young Asian, able to dispense with the customary hair net because of his shaved skull, glanced at the larger-than-life female trooper as he rang her up, not even trying to hide his contempt for the uniform and the law it represented. Jens wondered if Ferdie's cross-gender cues, understated as they were, added to his contempt.

Meanwhile, a party of nurses arrived. Leaving their sweaters and jackets at their table, they went to the food line. Jens checked to see if Nola was among them. He tried to downplay his attraction to her — a former student who'd flattered him by remembering him. Though he felt abandoned emotionally by Vivian, he'd never considered cheating on her.

Dismissing his thoughts with an inward shrug, he joined Ferdie at a table overlooking the garden.

"Gangbanger. Thai," said Ferdie without preamble. She nodded at the cashier as they sat down.

Jens followed her eyes, registering her comment. He shoveled scrambled egg onto his fork with his toast, blew on his piping-hot egg.

"Thanks for this."

"Maybe it will help you say yes to what I'm going to ask." Ferdie brought a spoonful of oatmeal to her lips. Jens noted that, as before, she wore no lipstick.

Jens continued eating.

"What changed your mind about me? Yesterday, you seemed ready to accuse me of having something to do with the shooting."

"It's my job to be suspicious. And when we couldn't find the gun, well, you understand."

She reached into her manila envelope and drew out a hardcover of Jens' novel, *The Killing Kind*.

"That was before I read this," she enthused. "Kept me up all night. Your Detective Poulon is one spot-on lawman."

Jens laughed to hide his embarrassment.

"I'm honored."

"No doubt he's modeled after me."

"No doubt. A female version, I'm sure." Jens pursed his lips, waiting.

"I made some inquiries — with law enforcement agencies where you researched your book. They said you know social network tricks even criminologists miss. Help me track down the unsub — Daniel."

Jens shook his head in disbelief. A part of him was held in reserve, studying her as Cassie's prototype.

"You've got local, state, national, and even international law enforcement at your disposal, along with national fingerprinting, DNA, and missing persons dedicated tracking networks, not to mention state DMV, FBI, and Home Security."

"It's not so easy. I warned you that his prints may not be in the system, and they're not. Means he's never served in the armed services, been arrested, or applied for a job with the federal government. Secondly, there's no missing person bulletin out of Florida fitting his description or the car he was driving."

She sipped her coffee.

"Last night his vehicle was spotted crossing a checkpoint on the Canadian border. It's long gone by now, chopped into parts, so that eliminates anything we might have found in his vehicle to track him with, like a VIN number. Further, of the fifteen million motor vehicles registered to drivers in Florida, two thousand are Escalades. And one-hundred and fifty are registered to doctors."

Jens raised an eyebrow.

"And?"

"We're checking those out now, but registrations can be misleading. Savvy doctors use their corporations to register their personal vehicles and drive them as tax write-offs. It could be weeks before we get a hit off the registration, if ever."

"Why is it so important you identify him? His doctor doubts that he'll regain consciousness. I know attempted suicides in New Hampshire undergo mandatory treatment, but that's irrelevant now, with his life hanging in the wind."

Ferdie nodded. She seemed to be debating whether or not to say more. She touched up her crewcut, brushing her hand over the top, careful not to mess her jelled coif. A nervous "tell," noted Jens the writer.

He pushed hash browns onto his fork, glancing up at her.

"I don't get it."

She picked up the manila envelope she'd brought with her.

"I went back to the ledge on Black Mountain and found these."

Three spent cartridges bounced onto the table. Their *clang* attracted looks from the table of nurses.

"NIBID. The National Integrated Ballistics Information Network —"

"I'm familiar with it."

Jens put his fork down. Ferdie had his attention.

"— came back with a match."

Jens scooped up the shells, examined them, and stared at her expectantly.

"According to the markings on the cartridges, the gun that Daniel used to shoot himself matches shell casings left at a crime scene down in Florida last year."

"What kind of crime scene?"

"Double homicide — a young couple in the wrong place at the wrong time — a bank robbery."

"How would someone like Daniel get a gun like that?"

Ferdie shrugged.

Jens squinted at her doubtfully.

"Double homicide?"

Now he felt like a suspect being interrogated. He didn't like it. He crumpled his napkin and tossed it onto the table.

"What exactly do you want from me?"

Her handsome face seemed carved in stone.
"If you don't have the gun then who does?"
Jens stood abruptly. Left without a word.

Chapter Eighteen

Out in the parking lot Jens was pleased, if he was honest, to find Nola waiting for him, leaning against his car.

He'd had time to calm himself after Ferdie's insinuation that he or Teddy had Daniel's gun. He'd wanted to ask her about Laurent, if she knew about him, and whether she would help him make sure he was no threat to him or his family. But her suspicions about the gun had ended any further discussion.

Nola saw him coming and waved. She'd changed into tight jeans and a snug, peach-colored cashmere top that hugged her lithe figure. Her hair was brushed out, falling in rich waves onto her shoulders. She pushed off his car, arching her back, looking younger than the thirty-something years he'd calculated earlier. Jens tried not to stare, but it was hard not to.

"Heard you say you were heading back down to the seacoast." She paused to gauge her effect on him. "Wanted to say goodbye."

"That was nice of you, Nola. Really, you didn't have to." Privately, he was pleased.

"Don't worry," she said, in response to his apparent discomfort, "I don't bite."

"I should hope not." He laughed nervously. "Anyway, I wanted to tell you that I do remember you — class of '05?"

She nodded affirmatively.

"You sat in the second row back, aisle seat, next to one of the" — he started to say 'jocks' but corrected himself — "hockey players, as I recall. Because you two were always whispering, I thought you weren't paying attention, but then when I called on you, your answers were on the mark."

She smiled.

"Wow! You've some memory. I'm flattered you remember me … and Bobby, too. Actually, your class was an inspiration for both of us. Because of you, Bobby took some acting classes before he graduated and went out to the West Coast, where his uncle, a cameraman, helped him land a recurring role on a TV series. He's done really well. Maybe you've heard of him?" She named a TV star always in the news for his romantic links.

"That's Bobby?"

When she looked up, the light splashed across her face, highlighting a sprinkling of freckles. Her green eyes drew him in; her long lashes sun-bleached, iridescent. His eyes darted to her pursed lips. Mesmerized, he forced himself to look away.

"He changed his name." Pause. "We stayed in touch for a while ..." Her voice trailed off.

He knew where this was going. Bobby had dropped her, his college sweetheart, for life in the fast lane. Jens really didn't want to know anymore; it would be too much sharing. She seemed vulnerable. So was he, he realized. Especially now that he suspected his wife of cheating. Where did that leave him?

She brightened.

"I applied to NYU and got accepted to the screenwriting program. But ... other things came up." She smiled wistfully. "I know nursing's not glamorous, but I feel like I'm making a difference."

I can't do this, he told himself. Here he was: forty-seven, married with a sixteen-year-old in an expensive private school, a burdensome mortgage, and an idea for his next book that would take him out on a limb. Not to mention a scary interloper focused on his wife. He pushed it all aside, caught up in the moment, liking her. Wanting, perhaps, to make a fresh start with someone who didn't take him for granted. And *liked* him.

"You *are* making a difference, Nola."

"Oh, I haven't given up on my writing. I write poetry and short stories published on the Internet. I'm waiting to hear back on a script I sent to a contest in L.A."

"Great!"

Interesting and attractive as she was — a writer after all —

he was not going to let himself fall into a romantic mentor relationship. Vivian, the possessive type, oddly, could smell student-worship a mile away. But so what? Hadn't *she* been exchanging love letters with a former lover who just happened to be an ex-con?

"I should let you go," she said, reading his ambivalence. "It was great seeing you again."

"Me, too."

"I think your presence last night saved your friend."

"He's not my friend."

"He is now. I hope you'll be back."

She held out her hand.

Good manners predicated he take it.

"Take care, Nola."

"You, too, *Jens.*"

She smiled and squeezed his hand before letting go.

Dazed, he got into the Subaru. She watched him as he shifted into reverse and backed away. When he looked in the rear-view mirror, she was still standing there, smiling, wistful. Then she shrugged and walked briskly away.

The odor from her hand filled the car. It smelled like peaches and something more feminine and intimate. He recognized it as civet, which seemed to him the tantalizing essence of every Eve since the beginning of time.

Even with the windows down, it was a long time before the scent of her dissipated and his fantasies subsided.

Chapter Nineteen

The phone rang in the Corbins' farmhouse. It interrupted Vivian's painting trance, what she called "being in the zone." The moment when all the words, the mind's negative chatter, consciousness, receded like an ebb tide.

She stepped briskly from the barn to the house, thinking, Jens wouldn't persist, knowing she would be out in the barn painting. Unless it were an emergency.

As she entered the house through the sliding kitchen door, the ringing stopped. Bruzza, their French bulldog, glanced up from his slumber and then dozed off again.

Whoever it was, they were welcome to call back while she fixed herself some lunch. And if it was *him*? Armand Laurent? Well, she'd hang up on him. Too much water under the bridge. Besides, she never went back — only forward. The curtain had been drawn.

———

Halfway through her sandwich, the phone rang again.

"Hello. Jens?"

"Vivi ..." *His* name for her. "Vivi, it's me. Armand..." His first name, intimate, flush with memories.

His voice seemed to fly across the trough of time, jolting her awake, all senses alert. Her heart was pounding.

"Armand? Really? It's really you?"

"I told you I'd come for you." His voice trembled.

Hadn't he promised in his letters to call once he said it was safe? *What had he meant by that?* she wondered. Why wouldn't it be safe? Because of her husband? Her son? What did he want from her that couldn't be dealt with openly, straightforwardly? Surely, he didn't expect her to go around her husband's back.

His letters clearly spelled out his intentions, his desire to reclaim her, a married woman and a mother. Did he really think she would drop her safe, comfortable life to run off with him, a man with no prospects, a convicted murderer, and do what? Play Bonnie to his Clyde? Disappear in Mexico like old hippies? Become starving artists? To beg, con, and steal?

She shook her head unconsciously and gripped the phone to her ear, pulling the wire tight as she paced like an animal in a cage.

"Come for me?"

His silence bespoke disappointment. This was crazy, she told herself. She found herself feeling sorry for him. The least she could do was let him down easy.

"Armand," she said, her voice aquiver. "Is there something you need? Money? I can help you with that."

"Oh, Vivi ... is that why you think I'm calling?"

He sounded like he'd been cut loose from his earthly tether and was careening through darkest space, to his eternal doom.

She did not know what to say.

"Meet me, please," he begged. "Just for a few minutes ... in a public place. Okay? *Please*?"

When she didn't answer, he took a new tack.

"Vivi, you *owe* me," he said, his voice choked with emotion. "*Please,*" he repeated.

Was he crying? she wondered. *Was he*? Or had she heard a tinge of anger?

"Okay ...," she said, her voice subdued. "Where?"

Chapter Twenty

As Jens drove away from the hospital in Conway, the morning sky turned leaden with thunderheads. A light rain began to fall. Within minutes the rain gathered force. It made the Scenic Conway Railroad, a local landmark with its turn of the century train station and locomotives, look like a page out of history.

He breathed a sigh of relief as he pulled into his driveway, watching as the rain poured over his tightly-shingled roof and ran off the eves into the shale beds surrounding the house.

He shut off the engine and listened to the beat of the rain on the Subaru's hood and roof. It was a pleasant sound, reminding him vaguely of his college days: of rented attic rooms with tin roofs that syncopated with the rain; of pots and pans pinging with leaks; of the candlelit nights spent with a girlfriend, hunkered down against the New England weather, a bottle of Liebfraumilch to warm them.

He was unhappy in his marriage, this he knew. And now?

He smiled ruefully to himself, recalling how he'd chased Vivian around Portsmouth until she'd relented. He'd practically stalked her, turning up at her gallery openings, buying her watercolors to flatter her, though he'd not been as taken with her paintings as he had been with her and her dark Arcadian beauty. When she failed to show any interest in him except as a collector, he'd redoubled his efforts, regaling her with roses, taking her to romantic supper clubs, drawing her out. She found herself relying on him for advice about her career and later about her insecurities, which were many.

Had she been in love with someone else the whole time?

He burned with anger and shame at her likely betrayal.

Yet, he did not believe it — did not want to.

He flashed back to the morning a few days ago when he was leaving for Jackson with Teddy. There'd been that shot fired in the woods. Plot-savvy by trade, he began to make connections, unbidden, between the shot and Teddy's reference to that "bastard ex-con Laurent."

Were they in danger? Teddy would have to come clean. And Vivian, too, if he was going to protect his family, the thing that mattered most, his ambition aside.

The rain had stopped. Jens opened the Subaru's door and got out. Tomorrow he and Teddy would drive back down the mountain to the seacoast, where he'd get to the heart of the matter, the truth.

He'd also have to face the consequences of his decision to drop the Honore Poulon book, or postpone it at the very least, to pursue Cassie Melantree. In her he knew he'd found a vehicle to explore his deepest concerns in life: suffering, guilt, redemption.

The phone was ringing in the house. He bounded up the front steps and yanked open the door.

"Teddy, you up yet?" he yelled into the basement. "We've got to get a move on, kiddo." He picked up the phone, prepared to confront Vivian about this Laurent character.

But it was Ferdie, calling to tell him that Daniel, "the unsub," had passed away. A blood clot from the trauma to his brain had dislodged, killing him in his sleep. Jens thought to ask her what would become of Daniel now, but she'd hung up, leaving him with more questions than answers.

And sadness — that could not be entirely accounted for by the death of a stranger whose life he'd saved.

And a pang of jealousy — at the thought of Vivian with another man.

And concern — that a stranger was trying to insinuate himself into their lives — a dangerous stranger.

He reached deeper, looking for the tenacity and resourcefulness he would need to get to the bottom of the Laurent matter.

And the nerve, to protect his family, no matter what.

Chapter Twenty-One

Laurent maneuvered around the newly-cemented sidewalk, cordoned off with yellow tape while it dried; shuffled past exhaust-dusted hedges and chain-link fences that kept the neighborhood pit-bulls and rottweilers from taking off his hide. They lunged and snapped at him, making him scoff, as he considered the irony of upscale homeowners keeping dogs once reserved for parolees and inner-city drug dealers.

Portsmouth had changed in his absence, bought up by the rich.

With real-estate prices skyrocketing in Portsmouth, gentrification had waved its magic wand, transforming this once low-income enclave into an upscale development.

He pushed on through the back alleys and courtyards, a labyrinth of made-over triple-deckers and single-family homes. Ever since Laurent could remember, this end of Portsmouth had always been home to those living, literally, on the wrong side of the tracks. Not anymore. He wondered how his friend, his erstwhile cellmate, could still afford to live here.

At the end of the courtyard, he bounded up the steps of a modest cape, the door glowing with a fresh coat of white paint easy to find in the dusk. His friend, he noted, had been keeping up with the gentrification trend. That meant he must be doing well, even for an ex-con.

Laurent rapped three times in quick succession, paused, rapped again.

From the triple-decker next door, with its widow's walk converted to a dormer, wary eyes peeped from behind closed shades. The widow's walk reminded him of Portsmouth's origins as a whaling town, when wives, keeping faith with sea-faring husbands, scanned the harbor from their iron-gated rooftops.

Laurent pushed back the anger that was always there, simmering beneath the surface. Hadn't he deserved the same treatment from Vivian? Hadn't he risked it all for her?

He was about to rap again when the door swung open. A tall man in his early 40s, his predatory features hard and unforgiving, looked him over.

Warren.

With his long ponytail and black leather vest worn over a work shirt, he looked like an old hippie who'd just climbed down from the roof he'd been working on. This wasn't far from the truth, as earlier he'd been putting up new cedar shingles out back.

But his muscular arms — sleeved with jail-house tattoos — told a different story. This was a man who could kill without blinking.

Warren tossed his braid over his shoulder. His movements were spare, economic like his words, as Laurent knew from sharing a cell with him for more than a decade.

Laurent's voice wavered, caught off guard seeing him in the flesh after so long.

"You're a sight for sore eyes, *brotha*."

He ventured a smile, which went unreturned.

Warren made a deft movement behind his back, tucking a pistol under his belt. Laurent wondered why he would jeopardize his parole and all that he'd worked for by keeping a firearm.

"Supposed to call first, right?"

Laurent fumbled for an answer.

"Don't tell me, no cell phone yet?"

Caught like a schoolboy, Laurent nodded.

"Heard of burner phones?"

Laurent's discomfort was palpable.

"Get in here, chooch!"

Grinning, he yanked Laurent inside and locked the door, but not before scanning the neighborhood for watchful eyes.

———

Laurent followed him into the living room, a cozy space dominated by a matching faux-leather recliner and couch grouped around a wide-screen TV. Lace doilies covered the arms of the furniture. Yarn paintings adorned the walls, depicting homey scenes and sayings: *Home is where they have to take you when you got no place else to go.* Over the fireplace hung a picture of haloed Jesus, morbidly pointing at his bleeding heart. On the coffee table, a spray of white roses scented the room.

Laurent held out his right hand for Warren to shake, forgetting that cons don't shake. Warren gripped his forearm instead, and they tapped each other on the shoulder with the left hand — ensuring that neither was holding a weapon. A standing joke between them while in prison, as they'd trusted each other with their lives.

Warren pushed up the sleeve of Laurent's shirt, exposing his tattoos: a weeping woman, interlocking barbed wire bracelets, a spider web cradled at the elbow, a quincunx of four dots around a center dot on the underside of the wrist, and three dots in a triangle in the web formed by thumb and forefinger on the back of the hand. No color; all faded black and blue.

He held his own arm alongside Laurent's, his tattoos nearly identical, except for the four-petal shamrock reserved for members of the notorious Hell's Kitchen gang, the Westies.

"Some things never change." Grinning, he pushed down Laurent's sleeve.

"You got that right," Laurent answered.

"You want something to drink — or smoke?"

"Both if you don't mind."

Laurent felt Warren's eyes drilling him, stripping him bare of deception and lies, even the ones he told himself. Just like in stir.

"Sit. I'll be right back."

———

He returned carrying a tray with two juice glasses, filled to the brim with colorless alcohol. Laurent knew the lime slices and saltshaker meant tequila, though he'd never tried it before, having missed it while in prison.

Warren set everything down on the coffee table without spilling a drop. He demonstrated the ritual, licking salt from the back of his hand, tossing back the shot, biting the lime — his accompanying grunt of satisfaction optional.

Laurent followed his lead, snuffling back the fiery liquid when it went down the wrong way and seeped from his nose.

"I got this," Laurent said, choking.

Warren gave him a whack on the back

"My pruno never agreed with you neither."

He motioned for Laurent to sit on the couch, angled the recliner to face him, and sat down. He took a glassine bag from his shirt pocket and tossed it to Laurent.

"This gonna do the trick?"

Laurent examined the contents: a verdigris and gold-colored marijuana bud the size of a walnut. He broke the bag's seal and took a whiff.

"Man!" He passed the bag back to Warren. "Your product?"

Warren glared at him.

"Don't even think that. Marie will have my balls if she thinks I'm back in the game."

Laurent knew all about Marie from Warren's endless stories. With a then eleven-year-old daughter from a previous marriage, she'd married him on the condition that he give up his old ways and fly straight.

"Marie's job doesn't cover your nut?"

Warren broke up the bud with a small scissors and rolled a tight joint without losing a crumb.

"RNs don't make shit, even with overtime."

His eyes roamed the room as he licked and sealed the joint.

"House in this neighborhood — not cheap."

He fired up the joint and passed it to Laurent.

"You do the honors."

The pot — which Warren extolled as Merrimack Valley Primo, known for its mellow yet energizing qualities — performed as advertised.

Lubricated by the tequila and smoke, they talked about everything that had transpired in their respective lives since Warren had been paroled seven years earlier, leaving Laurent in Concord to serve out his sentence alone.

By that time, Laurent had no longer needed Warren's protection. He'd proven his resolve not to "swing" by cutting those who wouldn't take no for an answer. Though it had cost him time in solitary away from his job at the library — his only pleasure — it had been worth it.

Grinning, Warren now owned that he'd been a law-abiding citizen since his release — except for the pot farm he'd recently taken a stake in.

"Explains the piece you greeted me with at the door." Laurent toked, held his breath, passed the joint.

"So what are you going to do with your life, genius?"

Laurent's sudden deflation was palpable.

"I screwed up — bad," he said, exhaling between the words.

Warren waited for him to go on.

"How bad?"

"Broke into Vivian's house. Her kid may have spotted me."

Warren waited, sensing there was more.

"I threw a rock at her husband, broke a window on his car. Luckily he didn't see me."

"What were you thinking?"

"I don't know — carjack her old man, get some money out of him. He's loaded."

Laurent gnawed on a knuckle nervously. "Grab Vivian, start a new life."

"You check with her on any of this?"

Laurent stood, agitated, his massive shoulders trembling.

"Easy, bro. Marie will be home soon — we gotta wrap this up."

"That's not all," Laurent blurted. "I went to her art gallery, made a fool of myself." He started to say he'd gone to the Corbin boy's school, but thought better of it.

Warren was the first to break the heavy silence.

"Look, you need a plan. This guy, her husband, what's he do?"

"Believe it or not, he's a writer, damn successful one." He sniggered. "Writes crime novels — had a bestseller a few years back. Fugger's loaded. I know we can take him off," he added. "I'm just not sure how."

Warren stroked his ponytail thoughtfully.

"Okay, say I help you. You gotta stop thinking with your dick and use your head. First thing, get a cell phone, a burner — use it to call me. Lay low. And no more stalking, not unless you're ready to go back."

It was the most he'd ever heard Warren say at one time. He felt better already.

"Vivian ... she's not going to get hurt, right?"

"Nobody's going to get hurt — except in the pocket. We're going to have to be smart and careful. I have no intention of going back to jail, friend."

Warren walked him to the door.

"One more thing. You listening?"

Laurent stiffened.

"Stay away from Vivian."

Out on the doorstep, Laurent congratulated himself on saying nothing about stalking the boy. Or his upcoming meeting with Vivi, for that matter.

———

After Laurent left, Warren tidied up, putting away the drinks and opening windows to air out the pot. Marie didn't like him getting high in the house, setting a bad example for her daughter, as straight an arrow as they come. Marie made him toe the line. Being married to her, he passed for a law-abiding citizen with his front as a contractor, basically a handyman. But that didn't stop him from doing what he did best — drug running and extorting any and all fool enough to fall into his web.

That included his ex-cellie, time spent in stir watching each other's back notwithstanding. Stir was one thing; this was now.

Warren fanned the air in the living room with a towel, chasing away any scent of pot and with it any regrets he might have about taking Laurent for everything he could. Which, naturally, included Laurent's ex-wife and her husband's money, home, possessions, and life, if it came to that.

Laurent, he decided, would be set up as the fall guy.

He smiled to himself as he straightened the doily on the armchair.

Things were looking up. Hopefully, they'd happen quickly enough to appease his business associates from Boston's North End. Time was running out.

Chapter Twenty-Two

Jens and Teddy spent Sunday morning fishing the Saco River, where they each caught three legal-sized brown trout on 5-weight line, using mayfly nymph flies. The flies had been recommended by the bluff, red-faced clerk at the tackle shop, who was sure they would work. Jens cleaned the fish and pan-fried them for lunch with home fries. Eating the fish gratified Teddy, who was incensed by fishermen who turned their catch back into the water, fishing only for sport.

Later, they hiked Red Ridge Trail on the eastern slope of Moat Mountain, north of Conway. Of some difficulty, with a steep incline and a peak elevation of 3,196 feet, the four-hour hike offered spectacular panoramic views of the surrounding ranges. Its chief attraction, because of its difficulty, was the lack of crowds. Jens found it more challenging than the climb up Black Mountain Trail, where they'd had the incident with Daniel.

As they hiked, Jens attempted to get Teddy talking about himself, but he remained reticent, answering in monosyllables. Jens tried to find an opening in which to bring up the letters from Laurent. But a graceful opportunity never arose, and he gave it up, content to enjoy the boy's company without stress. He thought that the ride home back to Lee the next day might be more opportune.

Over a dinner of cheeseburgers, chips, and a rare beer that Jens occasionally permitted, Teddy became more animated, speculating about the identity of Daniel and his motive for wanting to kill himself.

"I think that what got Daniel going probably had to do with a woman, maybe his wife, who is probably dead."

Startled, Jens looked at him, sensing the likelihood in Teddy's observation.

"I think you're right."

Teddy nodded. "Why else would he try to kill himself? If she were gone, he'd have nothing to live for."

Jens smiled at the simplicity of Teddy's logic. He was about to ask him to speculate further when Teddy jumped up from the table.

"Daddio, I challenge you to a game of Xbox. I'll give you twenty bucks if you beat me."

Jens smiled. "Do you even have twenty dollars?"

"C'mon, it will be fun."

"Hey! I got an idea. You don't happen to have a racing car game, like Le Mans, do you?"

Teddy shot him a perplexed look.

"No, Dad … why would I? I'm into … assassins."

"There was a time, back in Los Angeles, when I was writing a script and I needed to take a course in intensive driving offered by a Hollywood stunt car driver. For research. It was awesome," he added, his excitement flagging as he gauged his son's disinterest. "No? Okay. You go ahead then."

———

Jens dutifully called Vivian and listened patiently — despite a raging impulse to interrogate her about Laurent — while she recounted a rambling story about how Bruzza had gotten out. There was an odd excitement in her voice that he hadn't noticed in a long time. Still, what he had to ask her would have to be done face-to-face. It was too easy to lie over the phone.

Besides, he was impatient to end the call and strategize his meeting with his agent, Jean Fillmore-Smart, who was driving up from Boston to Portsmouth, to meet with him to discuss the next Honore Poulon installment.

Vivian, sensing his distraction, curtly ended the conversation with a brusque "Okay, I'll let you go now." Jens was accustomed to her discourtesy, which spoke volumes about their marriage.

Though he enjoyed being with Teddy, he'd planned the trip to give his wife time alone, to work uninterrupted on her painting. And for *him* to get some time off from *her*.

Accompanied by his customary glass of red wine, he settled down before the fireplace with a notebook. He slid a pen out from the spiral coils and wrote in the middle of the green cover, in large bold script: "Forsake Me Not: A Cassie Melantree Novel by Jens Corbin." Now it was official. He turned to the first lined page and began to write.

Background: What does she look like? Where does Cassie live? Why was she a single mom? Who was the father of her abducted daughter? How and when was she taken? How did the local civic leader get away with it? How did she solve her daughter's case?

Jens stopped to consider the questions he'd raised about Cassie. He had a clear picture of her in his mind's eye. She was tall, well-proportioned, and athletic. Pretty, in a wholesome way. Like Ferdie. He saw other physical features, scars, old sports injuries, but he had enough — the rest he would discover as he went along.

Tomorrow, once back in Lee in his attic study, he would flesh out Cassie's personality and finalize her background, then he'd be ready to pick up her story in Mexico. With Tommy Flaherty, a missing persons cop she likes but is reluctant to show feelings for, they track the suspect back to Mexico, taking them deeper into the underworld of Mexico's human trafficking, a world coincidental with that of the drug trade. He had enough to go into a meeting with Jean and infect her with his enthusiasm.

Glancing up from his notes, he saw that Teddy had forgotten to mark off the day's trail on the topographical map over the mantle. As he traced the trail in red magic marker, he thought about how mountain climbing was a metaphor for writing — step by step the incline is surmounted, overcoming all obstacles.

He knew he was no Hemingway, but he cared deeply about his work and his family, and he was resolved to find a way to protect them *and* do his job.

The next morning Jens got up at 7:00, showered, shaved, and awakened Teddy at 7:30. By 8:30 they'd breakfasted and were packing and cleaning.

"Aw," complained Teddy, "what's the point in going to all this bother? Nothing can get in here. It's tight as a drum."

Jens tied off the trash bag and lifted it from the receptacle built into the cabinet beneath the sink.

"You know why, buddy boy."

It was necessary to remove all trash from the house and carry it down to the township's dumpster at the foot of Black Mountain. Food with a shelf life of a month or longer could stay in the refrigerator. Everything else had to be carted back to Lee or dumped. Because of bears and other animals, outdoor trash cans were useless and no one kept them.

"Okay, I'm going to shut off the hot water heater," he added. "Why don't you take the trash out to the car along with your suitcase? I'll lock up."

Teddy stepped in front of him with an upraised hand. "I got this."

He bounded down the stairs, leaving Jens to wonder what had inspired him to be proactive. He shrugged to himself and went for his luggage. When Teddy didn't return immediately, he called down to him.

"Hey, what's taking so long?"

"Coming!"

They were just approaching the town of Ossipee, where they'd had their first run-in with Daniel, the suicidal doctor, and saved the store clerk's life. Jens sensed Teddy glancing his way; they exchanged looks. Their weekend adventure was coming full circle.

"When you get back to school, you've got something to write about on your 'What I did over the summer' essay," said Jens. "I'll bet no one else faced down a bear."

Teddy guffawed. "That bear — think she'll attack someone again? Maybe we should've put her down."

"That's cold."

"Maybe she's got a taste for human blood." Suddenly he reared back and let out a howl halfway between a horse *neighing* and a hysterical laugh.

"*Ahh-ugh-ha*," he whinnied.

Jens chuckled. "Is it that time of day again? I thought you werewolves only came out at night."

"Naw, it's good any old time."

Jens had discovered Teddy's tick when they drove together to Florida one winter, to go fishing in the Gulf. He recognized it as a venting reflex, a way of externalizing tension. Every evening on the road as the sun went down, Teddy howled for approximately a half-minute. Jens bet Teddy that he couldn't stop doing it. Teddy insisted that he could, he just didn't want to. In the end, it became a ritual, though it was never really clear whether Teddy could stop.

Jens' research into ADD informed him that it was likely a mild expression of his OCD, Obsessive Compulsive Disorder, often associated with ADD. Teddy's doctor told Jens not to make his son feel weird about it — he'd outgrow it, like a lot of youthful quirks.

"I think that bear was just protecting her cubs, to answer your question."

Teddy nodded as though he understood the implications. Jens thought this as good a time as any to bring up his unanswered questions.

"Trooper Morrison wanted me to check with you — if you had any idea as to what might have become of Daniel's gun."

Teddy didn't hesitate with his answer.

"I gave that some thought, too. I can only conjecture"— Jens smiled at his word choice — "that the gun fell over the ledge and got trapped in a crevasse or against some roots that Ferdie overlooked. I know you don't like coincidences in fiction, Dad, but they do happen in real life."

Jens smiled to himself, gratified that Teddy had been picking up on the tricks of his trade. Who knew, maybe he would become a writer after all, though he preferred that the boy choose a reliable career, in law, for example, like Jens' college friend Vincent. The insecurity of Jens' early years as a struggling writer was not something he would wish on his son.

"So, when Ferdie calls, I can tell her with confidence that we have no idea what happened to the gun?"

Teddy gave him a serious look. "I assumed you already did, Daddio."

Jens nodded.

Now for the elephant in the room, thought Jens.

"Ted," he began, "I accidentally overheard you say something to your mom about some letters."

Teddy stared straight ahead.

"Look, Dad, you know I love you and Mom, and I want you to stay together, right?"

"Teddy, from what I gathered, this is more serious than a romantic fling. There's a history between Mom and this man that we need to deal with. He's a criminal."

Teddy looked conflicted, on the verge of tears. He nodded slowly to himself.

"This guy, Laurent — they were involved as teenagers. Then he got sent away, for what I haven't been able to figure out. Probably something stupid, like stealing a car, maybe B&E or manslaughter, I don't know, he never mentions it exactly in his letters. Calls it 'the thing that ruined our lives.'"

"What made you hold out the letters from your mom?"

The look Teddy gave him was all the answer Jens needed: he'd done it for him.

"Okay … I get it."

Jens turned back to the road and concentrated on driving. In a few hours they'd be back in the seacoast and home. Perhaps he'd over-reacted and Vivian would reassure him that he had nothing to worry about.

"It's not as bad as you think," said Teddy, mirroring his thoughts. "She had no idea that he'd been writing to her. Maybe he's given up."

"Given what up, exactly?"

Teddy looked away.

"Her. He's out of jail. He wants her back."

Over my dead body, Jens told himself.

Chapter Twenty-Three

Walking briskly from the bus stop, Laurent arrived early for his appointed rendezvous at the park along Dover's scenic Cocheco River.

Ignoring Warren's warning to stay away from Vivian, Laurent rationalized that he could tell Warren, if it came out, that he'd been gathering intel from her.

Getting her to agree to see him was the easy part. Over the phone, she'd sounded as if she hadn't been expecting him. Now, he wondered if she'd even received his letters. No matter; he'd see her soon and he'd know — know exactly how she felt about him.

He'd expected the park to be crowded on such a sunny, breezy, autumn day, but it was a weekday and was practically deserted. He occupied a bench overlooking the river's bend to calm himself and wait.

What would Vivian say when she saw him? he wondered. *And think, once she saw how he'd changed? Would she cringe?* He couldn't bear that.

His thoughts were interrupted by a pair of joggers running past, a middle-aged couple in designer track outfits and sneakers with brand names he'd never heard of, Mizuno, Prono, Balenciaga — expensive no doubt. He envied them their leisure — and their money.

His was dwindling fast, now that he'd bought a phone, paid a month's rent, applied for a state ID, bought a bus pass, and had to eat all of his meals out, as he'd never learned to cook. Money was like sand in an hourglass — slipping through his fingers. What would he do when it was all gone? Get a shit job flipping burgers at McDonald's? Would they even hire him? Did he really believe that he and Warren would get away with blackmailing Vivian's husband?

That part of him that keenly felt everything he'd missed out on and would never have — education, career, family, self-respect — welled up inside him.

He looked to the sky, a cloudless, sparkling, blue canopy. Not for him were the simple blessings of sun, sky, water, and trees. But a curse that he must bear to the end of his days. Murderer!

No, no, not true, he told himself. For he knew in his heart of hearts that the life he'd taken had been justified — just not in the eyes of the law. Familiar leaden thoughts returned — down-spiraling, repeating. He was helpless to stop them.

Across the river, sunlight glanced off the windows of new upscale condos, searing, blinding him.

Was that Vivian ... an apparition?

"Armand," she said.

"You came," he stammered, his voice husky with emotion.

Shielding his eyes from the ring of St. Elmo's fire surrounding her like an aura, he forced himself to look at her.

"You haven't changed," he said, his voice surprisingly firm.

"Nor you," she said, her voice quivering.

He laughed, choking back his tears. He was standing now, without remembering how he'd gotten there.

She took an involuntary step back, caught herself, smiled, and raised her brimming eyes to his.

Locating the youthful image of Armand from memory, she let it merge with the reality of the present. Though he'd changed, nothing had changed. His rugged looks, though scarred and battered, added to his appeal. She felt a shiver down below, tried to ignore it.

"Armand," she whispered.

A cry escaped his lips. "I'm ... ugly."

She shook her head vehemently. "Not to me. Never!"

He thumbed away her tears.

Choking back a cry, she held out her arm for him to take.

"Shall we walk?"

"Like we used to."

He fell in step alongside her.

———

They spent the afternoon leisurely strolling through the park, talking about her life since their sundering years ago. He seemed reluctant to open up about his, like a man guarding a scab over a wound. They found themselves drifting into one of the designer cafes that banked the river.

Here, finding anonymity among the young, boisterous happy hour crowd, they sipped beer and talked passionately about art. It had been the pretext that had brought them together as teenagers. They'd been wildly happy, in the grips of first love. A time of innocence, the world still a safe place, they'd basked in their passion for art as though it were a key to the mysteries of the universe. Coincidentally, their love grew, opening the way to other forbidden worlds.

Recalling their time together was a healing balm. Now, Vivian couldn't take her eyes away from his, which were animated, youthful, and sparkling; no longer the lifeless pools of the prison walking dead. The twinges of desire she'd felt a few days ago, upon discovering his letters, now coursed through her veins like the quicksilver waters of the river swirling below, barely contained by its granite banks.

Their love rekindled, they wasted little time deciding to consummate it at his hotel room, a short drive away in her Volvo.

On the ride over they were silent. Vivian wondered if she were making a big mistake, jeopardizing the comfortable life she was accustomed to. As for him, she knew this was why he had come here.

How could she refuse?

After the sacrifice he'd made for her.

Chapter Twenty-Four

Jens glanced at Teddy as they exited the Spaulding Turnpike onto Route 125. Soon they were passing the country club, then Wheelwright Pond, a silver patch. In a moment, he would turn onto Bennett Rd and then Mast, where they lived.

The afternoon sun lit up the landscape of trees and summer fields in green and gold Technicolor. A cloud of dust followed in their wake. The word "idyllic" popped into Jens' head.

Teddy seemed happy to be home. He grinned to himself and stared out at the countryside. Meanwhile, Jens began to prepare himself for his inevitable confrontation with Vivian.

Her teal blue Volvo was in the drive, parked at a hasty angle. Jens pulled in beside it and turned off the motor. Teddy was already out of the car before he could caution him to keep his account of the shooting on Black Mountain sketchy, and to focus instead on their last day of fishing and hiking.

But this now seemed irrelevant in light of what Jens had learned about Vivian, about Laurent. Had she seen him? Had she been with him?

Bruzza came lumbering out of the barn to investigate their arrival. He lunged on his stubby legs, excited at the sight of Teddy, who scooped him up in his arms and cooed "Bruzza, Bruzza" into his ear. The dog whined and yipped in delight. Jens passed them and entered the barn through the open door.

Her back to him, Vivian was at her easel in a pool of light from the skylight, dabbing at a watercolor of marshlands. She worked off a photo pinned to a corner of the easel. Jens watched as she made feather strokes, supporting her painting hand at the wrist with the other. Her rendition was detailed and realistic, the colors splendid, thought Jens, with vividly contrasting grass, water, sky, and sunlight.

As Jens approached, her body language told him that she knew he was there but wanted him to wait. He waited. Finally, she stepped back, nodded to herself, turned around and smiled faintly, as though indifferent to his return. He whistled in appreciation at her painting.

"Brilliant, darling," he said, gesturing at the painting. "I see our absence did you some good."

She started to say something then shook her head, smiled wanly.

He moved in to kiss her, but she turned and let him buss her on the cheek. He caught her in his arms, staring into her eyes.

Was now the time to confront her about Laurent?

He went on holding her, inhaling her familiar essence, of paint, perfume, and sweat, until she wriggled free, laughing girlishly. She brushed her long brown hair from her face.

"What's gotten into you, anyway? Where's Teddy?" She rinsed her brushes in a jar of water and dried them.

'So you didn't miss me, not even a little?" he asked.

She took his hand and drew him towards the door and the sound of Teddy and Bruzza playing outside, growling and laughter mixed in equal proportions.

He let her draw him out into the bright light, feeling simultaneously a shadow fall across his soul. He looked at his wife, who was oblivious to his discomfort. An old sound-worm rose up inside his head, reverberating with David Bowie singing, "Turn and face the strain ch-ch-changes."

Big as he was, Teddy ran into her arms and she hugged him to her. They walked arm-in-arm toward the house, Bruzza nipping at their heels.

A charming sight, thought Jens, without irony. He watched, abandoned, cooling; wondering if his exclusion was a presentiment of things to come.

Wondering whether his painstakingly arranged life, his marriage, his role as parent, and his satisfying work, was about to come crashing down around his ears.

MY WIFE'S HUSBAND

A killer was on the loose.
And his wife was acting as if nothing was going on.

Chapter Twenty-Five

As usual, Vivian had been too engrossed with her painting to plan for dinner, so Jens ordered pizza from Milo's on Route 9.

With twenty minutes to kill before his order would be ready for pickup, he climbed the stairs to his attic study and pushed open the door, sending dust motes swirling. Sunset poured in through the skylight, washing his office in gold. He stepped behind his desk.

After logging onto his desktop, he Googled "Armand Laurent" and clicked through a series of articles published in the Berlin New Hampshire *Daily News*. He found clips referring to Laurent's arrest and sentencing. Grainy black and white photos captured the face of a callow young man, his boyish features bleak, fearful, shocked.

The images contrasted sharply with the candid shots of him ten years later, on the occasion of his father's death, when he reiterated his claim of innocence. In these, he'd matured, his gaunt face guarded and hostile; gone was the naïveté of youth.

According to the coverage of his trial, there'd been no doubt among the jury that Laurent had killed Leroy D'Arcy, 41, of Berlin. But whether it was premeditated murder, that is murder in the first degree, or murder in the second, making it a crime of passion, had been contested hotly by the jurors. Laurent claimed that D'Arcy, the aggressor, had tried to back his car over him, and when that hadn't worked, he'd come at him with a tire iron. Laurent had only been protecting himself when, in wrestling the tire iron from D'Arcy, he'd accidentally stabbed him in the throat with it and killed him.

Jens wondered if the authorities had been wrong in sending him to prison.

As for the victim, D'Arcy, that was Vivian's maiden name. In what way were they related?

Jens pulled up a final picture, of Laurent another ten years later, as he was released from the Men's Correctional Facility in Concord in August. The Berlin media, it seemed, had been keeping faith with him throughout his time in prison.

But the face that stared back at him — dead eyes under scarred brows — dispelled his lingering sympathy and doubt.

Laurent's was the face of a killer.

Where did Vivian, his wife, come into all of this?

Chapter Twenty-Six

Vivian held the bottle poised over his glass.

"Would you like some more wine, *dear*?"

Her disdain became more apparent the more she drank.

Reluctantly, he nodded yes. She did not like drinking alone. She poured the Chardonnay, spilling it. Then she filled her own glass to the brim. Jens glanced at the nearly empty bottle, noting that she'd had two glasses to his one.

Over pizza, they sat at a padded nook in a corner of the spacious kitchen, with a view onto the lush garden, at summer's peak. Gardening was Vivian's second passion in life, after painting.

Through the sliding glass doors that gave onto the patio, Jens could see her herb garden of neat rows of fennel, anise, laurel, mint, savory and lavender.

It reminded him of the gardens in Aix en Provence they had visited on a belated honeymoon to France with newborn Teddy. It remained in his memory an icon of their first flush of joy and happiness as a married couple, when anything had been possible.

What happened to the promise of those times? wondered Jens, as he was pulled back into the present by Teddy insistently calling his name, and Vivian's unladylike laughter.

Have you been sleeping with that bastard Laurent? he wanted to hurl at her. The wine was loosening his reserve; he'd have to make sure not to drag Teddy into this.

"Dad, Dad, tell me again what happened when you gave Mom pot. What did she say? What did she do?"

"Who, *moi*?" Jens hedged. "I never…"

"C'mon, you know you did. What's the big deal, anyway?" asked Teddy.

Jens read the disapproval in his wife's eyes. She'd stopped

laughing. He knew that she was tired of hearing the story and being made fun of because of her ineptitude years ago, even though it was just pot. Any reference to what she perceived as inadequacy, however far-fetched or unlikely, made her defensive. Moreover, Teddy habitually used the account as an introduction to his favorite topic, marijuana, and the reasons why he, a sixteen-year-old, should be allowed to smoke pot at home.

"The big deal is that you just want to talk about pot — it excites you. And thought precedes action."

Teddy gave him a bored look; Jens ignored it.

"Why don't we talk about your lackluster grades and what you're going to do about passing Algebra I this year? Besides, Mom doesn't like this story."

"This is not about you, Mom, so much as it's about Dad and his wild days." Teddy plucked at his paper napkin, shredding it into a neat mound beside his plate.

Vivian tilted back her wine glass and drank. "Go ahead, you may as well tell him the rest."

"Not if you don't want me to, darling."

"It's not that I object to honesty. I just don't like being made a fool of."

"I know, I know," he said, trying to placate, wanting to talk about the real issue at hand.

"But that's what you *so* like to do: put me down, humiliate me. You're always doing that. You think I'm a fool." Her voice had risen, fueled by alcohol. She turned to Teddy. "Did your father tell you that he took LSD and freaked out?"

Now it was Jens' turn to glare. The steps that had led to his breakdown could not be blamed on LSD alone. It was so much more complicated than that, overlooking the part his brother's death had played and his mother's rejection.

"You took LSD?" Teddy asked, incredulous. "And you flipped out?"

Jens shook his head in stony silence. He had always planned

to tell Teddy about his breakdown at the right moment and use it as a cautionary tale, a "teaching moment," about the dangers of experimenting with psychotropics. Now, Vivian had reduced his breakdown to a weakness in character and judgment. Moreover, he'd wanted to avoid planting another dangerous seed in Teddy — that he might have inherited his father's genes of instability.

"You bitch, Vivian," he said, his voice icy. "I know what you've been up to."

She stared back at him, fury and hate concentrated in her eyes.

"*Screw. You. Asshole,*" she spat.

"You've been —"

"What?" she roared defiantly. "*What?*"

Jens rose from his seat, his balled fists at his sides.

"Don't, Dad," Teddy pleaded.

Jens caught himself. Paused. After a beat the spell was broken. Vivian picked up her wine glass and sipped, a smug look on her face.

Jens slapped the glass from her hand and charged out of the room.

"Bruzza, here boy," Jens called. "Let's go for a walk."

Jens' breathing came in ragged gasps; his blood pressure soared. He told himself to calm down, it would be all right, but he doubted it ever would. He'd married a woman who was not only capable of deceiving him and denying it, but with a convicted murderer no less.

He knew his job now — he had to get his son away from her.

Chapter Twenty-Seven

He found the dog stretched out on his favorite spot, on the leather couch in the den, napping.

"Papa needs some air. C'mon, boy."

From the kitchen he could hear his wife still cursing him — loudly *hissing* under her breath — a thing he hated because it was exactly what his mother used to do.

Outside, faithful Bruzza trundling at his side, he inhaled the cool evening air, sharply scented by Vivian's garden. Intimations of the fall, winter fast on its heels, filled him with gloom, a feeling that he tried to push away. A pang of anxiety, that ancient bugaboo, accompanied the thought that it had been years since he had succumbed to seasonal depression.

Once out the driveway, he turned right, hugging the picket fence surrounding his property until the path forked. With a waxing moon high overhead, the woods were limned with silver, and he easily found his way along the trail. Bruzza darted ahead, drawn by movement in the brush — likely a stray hare tucking into its den for the night, or a swallow settling in its nest.

With a heavy sigh he acknowledged that he and Vivian were headed for a sundering. Most of the couples they had known on the West Coast, during his Hollywood days spec-writing for TV, had separated. He knew what would happen to Teddy if they went that route. He would take him, whether she liked it or not.

He heard Bruzza rooting around in the brush.

"Hey, boy, what you got?"

The dog pawed the earth, letting out a growl that turned into a whine, and suddenly bounded into the bush. Jens shrugged and walked on, deep in thought. The dog would circle back, he had no fear.

With Teddy, Vivian was overprotective and indulgent, thwarting Jens' efforts to instill values and discipline. The result was that Teddy would go to her for permission to do things Jens disapproved of.

"Here, boy," he called, beginning to wonder what had become of the dog.

Lost in thought, Jens found that he had wandered down a heavily wooded path. A carpet of pine needles underfoot added a touch of the surreal, as though he were floating. He looked around in the gloaming, trying to orient himself, searching for a landmark.

———

He tracked Bruzza, aided by the moonlight, arriving at last to a place where the grass was tamped down in a wide circle. Deer had bedded here. A footprint from a boot, the toe dug into the earth, alerted him to evidence of recent human presence.

Puzzled, he examined the scene like a forensic scientist, strafing it with his eyes in quadrants, discovering the outline of a human form imprinted in the grass, made by someone lying prone on his stomach, elbows dug in for support, leaving deep indentations.

How odd. The outline aligned with his house, now visible in the distance through the bracken and thick foliage. Spooked, Jens surveyed the woods, wondering what someone might have been doing here.

Stalking him?

Then he saw the apple tree and thought he understood — it was a hunter's blind, with a clear shot at deer feeding on apple drop. But his relief was short-lived; deer season didn't begin for another two months.

Poacher, maybe?

He recalled the pistol shot he'd heard a few nights ago coming from the woods.

Suddenly, it all seemed to fall into place.

Laurent, that bastard, had been stalking them.

Jens would take it up with her in the privacy of their bedroom, away from Teddy's ears.

Meanwhile, Bruzza had been following his nose deeper into the woods, sniffing out his rabbit quarry. It led him to the base of a venerable oak, its gnarled roots failing to camouflage the track to the rabbit den in the earth beneath. Bruzza began digging frantically, his front paws clawing the dirt like a windmill, spewing earth backward, between his legs. A blur of rabbit tore past his nose and he lit off in pursuit, taking him around the corner to a pine. Here, the rabbit darted into the brush and disappeared, spooked by the presence of someone hiding behind the tree.

Warren cursed the dog under his breath, waving his arms silently at him, hoping that the husband wouldn't come armed with a double-barreled shotgun. Hadn't he killed his own brother in what the papers called "an unfortunate tragic accident?"

Warren had left his own piece at home, not wanting to jeopardize his parole and everything he was now planning. He was not stupid; that's why he'd lasted so long on the "outside." Besides, tonight's sortie was only to gather intel on his mark.

Earlier, he'd watched from Laurent's blind in the woods behind the farmhouse as Jens brought back pizza and sat down with his family to eat in the kitchen.

The sound of footsteps thrashing through the bramble alerted him to someone coming. He snatched up a rock and hurled it at the dog and was rewarded with a pained *yelp*.

He fled into the woods and found his way back to his pickup truck. On the way home, he began to think that perhaps the best way to get at Corbin's loot was through his wife — made vulnerable by her history with Laurent. She could become an accomplice under the right circumstances. He could manipulate her by threatening to harm her son.

The boys from the North End had paid him another visit a few days ago. He had to meet with Laurent right away and put the play in motion. He was running out of time.

———

Jens lay stiffly on his side of the bed, while Vivian curled up, her back to him, on her side. He knew she was not asleep; he could hear her labored breathing. He tried to "read" her but couldn't tell if she was defiant, still.

"We need to talk."

"So talk."

Vivian turned over and looked at him, guarded, waiting for him to continue. He searched her eyes for common ground.

"What is your connection with a convicted murderer? I have a right to know."

She sat up, looked him in the eye.

"Teddy told you?"

He shook his head, not wanting to get Teddy in trouble.

"I overheard your phone conversation about the letters the other night," he said.

"It was something that happened a long time ago. He had... expectations. It's over. I've talked to him. He'll leave me — us— alone now."

Jens' heart was pounding. Did she just admit to sleeping with him?

"There's a hunter's blind at the edge of the woods with a view of the house. Someone's been stalking us. Is it him?"

She shook her head vehemently.

"He would never do that! Just because he's been in prison— convicted of a crime he's innocent of — doesn't mean he's come

124

to harm us."

"According to Teddy, in his letters he promised to come for you. How am I supposed to interpret that?"

"So, you *have* talked to Teddy?"

"Only after I'd done some research of my own. According to the corrections website, he's been out since August. After serving twenty years."

She studied him, searching for a hint of understanding if not sympathy.

"I was the last person he cared about before going away. Jens, you have nothing to worry about."

He tried to read her eyes for the truth. Was Laurent really innocent? What did it matter? In the end, he did not know what to believe, or whether she was deceived herself.

"What is he to you?" He held his breath.

"He's someone I once cared for deeply, before you, who got into trouble because of me. Please don't make me explain that right now — another time maybe. All you need to know is that he's paid his debt to society. And he won't bother me anymore."

Jens' anger flared.

"Vivian, if I even for a moment thought this man meant harm to our family..."

She reached out unexpectedly and stroked his cheek.

"Can't this keep until tomorrow? I've been up since dawn."

"I feel ... shouldn't I call the police?"

She held his eyes.

"In the morning you can show me the blind. Then we'll decide, okay?"

"Last question. Who's the D'Arcy guy he killed?"

She turned away onto her side and pulled the covers over her head.

"My ... uncle," she said stiffly.

Jens collapsed onto his pillow, more perplexed than ever.

———

What do I want from her? he asked himself, as the familiar animal comfort of her body next to his calmed and focused his thoughts.

He found himself winnowing down from the precipice of his fight or flight reflex. Soon his thoughts returned to his habitual preoccupation, his work.

He lay awake thinking through his determination to write the Cassie Melantree novel. He tired himself, applying author John Irving's comment about always knowing the last line of a novel before he began. He thought of a few last lines for his story, but rejected them for these:

In the ambulance Cassie rode alongside Tommy, holding his hand while medics worked on him, trying to staunch the blood pouring from his neck wound, from the bullet that had nicked his carotid. "If you die, you bastard, I'll never forgive you," she whispered over him. At her words, his eyes blinked, and a smile curled his lips.

Jens fell asleep thinking about the implications of the line, knowing now that Emma, the abducted child, had been saved, and her kidnapper, Orozco, was dead, killed in a shoot-out with Tommy Flaherty. Or was he?

He dreamt he was Tommy, dying in Cassie's arms. But then he was Orozco, flush with the pleasure of watching Tommy die.

Strangely, an image of Orozco appeared in his mind's eye.

He looked frighteningly like Laurent.

———

In the morning, coffee mugs in hand, he and Vivian examined the hunter's blind at the edge of the woods. Vivian stood beside the tamped grass where the hunter had lain, staring at the spot for a long time.

The look she gave Jens said it all. He'd let his imagination run wild, fueled by jealousy. She raised an eyebrow.

"Poacher?" he offered.

They walked back to the house, talking about the desiderata — duties, errands, and chores — that hold a marriage, fragile or otherwise, together.

For the time being, things were back on track. Jens would write his new book, Vivian would paint, and Teddy would soon return to school.

Chapter Twenty-Eight

The meeting with his agent Jean Fillmore-Smart did not go well. Not at first, anyway.

Jens had awakened early, showered, and shaved. Dressed smartly in an off-blue broadcloth shirt and light-weight navy trousers, he'd gone up to his study, intending to flesh out his outline for *Forsake Me Not.* And rehearse what he was going to say to her.

The more he thought about his "brilliant" idea for a breakthrough novel, the more it seemed flat and unconvincing. He decided to stick with a pitch, learned from his screenwriting days, and hook her with it. He found his notes written at the cabin the day he and Teddy rescued Daniel, and played with them on his desktop until he was satisfied.

Their melancholy faces stare out at us from milk cartons, accusing us of indifference, taunting our complacence. Cassie Melantree's seven-yea-old daughter was abducted by a pedophile and slain only moments before Cassie crashed his secret lair. Her life's mission is to hunt down these predators and save the children. She'll stop at nothing to save the children. All the children ...

He printed his pitch on an index card. After reading it aloud, he decided to cut it down by eliminating the first and last lines. Less is more, he concluded, drawing a line through the reference to the children on milk cartons and the superfluous line, "All the children." He read it over a few more times and decided it would work.

———

At Portsmouth's "Dock-In," a landmark waterfront restaurant and drinking hole built on a tugboat, he spotted Jean seated on the deck, with a scenic view of the north bank of the Piscataqua River.

She was angled toward the entrance, apparently to keep an eye out for him. She already had a drink in front of her, her usual gin and tonic. She looked up just as Jens waved, and she waved back. Sidestepping the hostess, Jens pointed to his lunch date and went to her table. Jean smiled up at him as he sat down, her serenity total.

A young waitress approached their table with menus. Jens ordered a gin and tonic and offered a refill for Jean. She declined, putting her hand over the top of the glass. The waitress smiled, apparently mistaking them for lovers.

They laughed at the waitress's gaff; it happened all the time. For some reason, thought Jens, people saw them as ideally paired. They were about the same age, athletic, attractive, and youthful. Jens admired Jean's fair Scandinavian looks — her luminous skin, golden hair, arched brows over an aquiline nose that was slightly tilted, broken in a boating accident on the Charles River when she was a teen. There was the matter of the similarity of their names — Jens and Jean — twining them ironically.

A different waitress dropped off his drink and he stirred it compulsively.

"It's good to see you," began Jean. Both took perfunctory sips from their drinks.

Jens nodded. "Likewise. You look great."

He glanced up at the luxury condos that towered over every square foot of prime waterfront property; then he looked east, to the river swirling past the cement stanchions supporting the new Memorial Drawbridge to Maine. The river massed eastward, toward the Atlantic.

"So ..." Jean pushed a blond lock from her face as she studied the menu, "how's Inspector Poulon doing? Well entrenched in a tasty new enigma, I trust? How's his love life?"

Jens, who'd been waiting for this moment of truth, but now

felt preempted, stammered.

"Fine, just fine."

She raised an eyebrow.

"Okay, not so fine."

He paused just as their waitress came to take their food orders.

"Give us a few more minutes, please," he told her, his eyes locked with Jean's.

"I'm afraid it's time to talk about it."

She nodded. "Go on."

Jens took out his pitch card, studied it, and then put it back in his pocket.

"Ah, hell, let me begin at the beginning. Teddy and I were up on Black Mountain for Labor Day Weekend when we saw a bear. No, wait, it starts before that, at a convenience store in Ossipee. We were on the way to Conway, and we saw this black Escalade, you know how much I hate them ..."

Over bowls of chowder and more drinks — Jean had stopped putting her hand over her glass and was keeping up with him — Jens recounted the story of how facing down the bear and saving the doctor's life, and maybe Teddy's too, had opened up something inside him and had led to his "discovery" of the story he *had* to tell, of Cassie Melantree and the missing children.

Perhaps it had been the proximity of death, he went on, that had triggered his own sense of mortality, made him feel the urgency of writing something ... different, before it was too late. Perhaps it had triggered his worst parental horror — that of losing a child, a subject he had never wanted to write about before, for fear, superstitiously, of attracting harm to Teddy. But now he felt compelled to. There was emotion in his voice. He stopped talking, waiting for her reaction.

They had been there so long that they hadn't noticed the sky darkening or the wind picking up, chopping the waters. As the sun ducked behind a cloud, the banks across the river receded against the skyline, looking smudged, painted by an inept artist.

It grew cooler, and Jean shivered, her lips turning blue.

Jens noticed her discomfort. "Let's go inside," he said, pushing away his gin glass. "Get a hot drink."

———

Insulated from the elements by floor-to-ceiling glass windows, they sipped steaming hot coffee and cognac, caught up in their own thoughts. Jens had no doubt that his story had touched her. It had touched chords in him, too — of a vaguely grasped epiphany, hard-won, lurking at the end of a long and treacherous writing journey.

Finally, Jean glanced up and frowned.

"I really don't know what to say, Jens."

She shook her head, looked him square in the eye.

Hers, he noticed, were clouded with anger.

"You're jeopardizing everything we've worked for. Do you have any idea how many publishers I sent your first Honore Poulon to, before we even got anyone to read it?"

He fiddled nervously with the spoon on his coffee saucer. Jens recalled her once telling him, in the heat of landing a major New York publisher on his behalf, that she'd sent his book to over one hundred publishers.

"Are you and Vivian on the same page with this?"

Jens thought about telling her about Laurent and how it might have effectively brought him and Vivian closer together. He hadn't really broached the idea of starting a new series to his wife yet; he wanted things to settle in the aftermath of last night's blowout.

Instead, on an inspiration, he spoke the lines from his pitch card, beginning with the ones he'd cut: *Their melancholy faces stare out at us from milk cartons, accusing us of indifference, taunting our complacence.* Then he repeated his story about when he thought he'd lost Teddy in a department store. He was trembling. Finally, he told her about Daniel's life slipping away the next morning after saving him.

He stopped, grew silent, inward.

———

Jean inhaled deeply and sighed. This was the part of her job she hated — telling artists what to write, knowing that it was their very insecurity that allowed her to influence them. It was harder in Jens' case because she really cared about him.

She knew his foibles as a writer, which included fragile self-confidence common to artists; an overweening need to please, offset by arrogance and a temper to match; and a dark side, the legacy of his childhood trauma, which she'd observed on numerous occasions washing over him unbidden, without warning, in a wave of despair. Like now.

Yet she knew that the darkness was his source of creativity and drive. Therapy had taught him the danger of ignoring it, at the expense of his identity — and sanity. Writing what he believed would free or destroy him. That was his dilemma, cutting both ways.

"I think you should write it. You *have* to write it."

He smiled back. "I was hoping you'd say that." He breathed a troubled sigh.

"How could I not? I heard the conviction in your voice — the call."

He nodded. "But can I afford to? And what if it flops?"

"You can always go back to writing Inspector Poulon novels."

"Will I have to return my advance?"

She grimaced. "I don't know. Do you still have it?"

"Some of it," he answered. "It would be tough if I had to give it back. There'd be a lot of changes at home."

"Look, I'm not going to tell you what you already know — that you're putting aside a well-established literary product and reliable source of income to gamble on an unknowable. At a turning point in your career."

"But?"

"No but. I'll stall Cathcart House as long as I can. You get to work. We'll see how it goes."

He took her hand. "Thank you." He smiled.

She nodded. "Does Vivian know you're doing this?"

He didn't answer.

"Good luck with that."

Chapter Twenty-Nine

Driving home to Lee, Jens took the back roads, using Route 33 through Greenland and Stratham, instead of coming over Route 4 and the Little Bay Bridge at Newington. He found the countryside conducive to thought. He needed to strategize how to approach Vivian about his decision to drop his Poulon series for Cassie.

Despite the tentative encouragement he'd received from Jean, he realized that he was nervous about breaking his decision to his wife.

Even if he didn't have to give back his Poulon book advance, or at least not right away, they would have to economize. Teddy would go to public school instead of his expensive prep school at Exeter. Household expenses would have to be sharply trimmed to make the advance last, which meant little dining out, less entertaining, less alcohol, and no trips.

As for assets, if push came to shove, they owned some valuable art, collected in good times when they lived in L.A., mostly prints and etchings, along with a couple of original model sketches by Aristide Maillol and an exquisite oil from the 17th century French Baroque school of Georges La Tour that together might fetch $250, 000 — 300,000, if placed in the right Sotheby catalogue. He knew that Vivian would object to selling them because they were earmarked for Teddy's college expenses. She'd make Jens sell the cabin in Conway before sacrificing Teddy's "college sketches."

———

As if on cue, his cell phone buzzed, flashing Vivian's thumbnail photo on the mini-screen. He fumbled for it on the seat beside him.

"Where are you?" she asked without preamble.

"I just left a meeting with Jean in Portsmouth. I'm coming home."

"We've got an event this afternoon, or have you forgotten? The Centennial."

"Shit!" As board members of the Lee Library, they were expected to attend the 100th year anniversary celebration.

"Meet me at the library."

"Viv, there's something important I want to talk to you about — it affects us all."

"It's not about —"

"No," he said, cutting her off, "this is about us."

"Okay, let's talk there," she said.

The light had turned green and behind him cars were honking. He stepped on the accelerator and sped off, suppressing the urge to give his impatient fellow citizens a piece of his mind or, at the very least, the finger. So much for the peace and tranquility of the countryside.

———

He spotted Vivian's Volvo at one end of the parking lot and pulled in opposite. They nodded across their dashboards. She turned off her engine and walked over to his car. He felt her looking him over, a snarky look on her face. The discordant din of a brass marching band could be heard seeping from the library. They started for the entrance.

"That must have been some meeting by the looks of you."

"Does it show?"

She nodded, pointing to his shirttail sticking out.

"You may want to do something about that."

"We had a lot to talk about," he said, tucking in his shirt, "and I just kept ordering one drink after another." He turned her to face him. "Jean and I talked it over. I'm putting the Poulon novel on hold; there's another book I have to get out of my system first. A book about stolen children ... the anguish ... how parents can go on …"

He watched her face shift gears, pinch with anxiety.

"Do we have enough money?"

"We do if I don't have to give back the advance."

She walked on, considering.

"And if you do?"

He shrugged. "Let's cross that bridge when we get there."

She turned back and shook her head in dismay. He recognized the flush of anger on her cheeks. "Have you thought about how this will affect us?"

"It'll be tight, but we can do it. I'll be juggling a lot. Jean agreed to look for an advance on the new novel, but it may be a while. We'll just have to tighten our belts. Teddy can go to public school for all the attention he puts into his studies."

"You're *not* going to put us in jeopardy — not again."

He controlled his anger. "What about you bringing in some money for a change?"

He started walking away, aware that her questionable liaison with Laurent put her in a weakened position to argue with him. He regretted lording it over her, but he knew he had to stick to his convictions.

She caught up with him. "I get it — you think you can do anything you want now because of Laurent."

"Vivian, it's not like that, honestly —"

"You'll dump the cabin before I let you take Teddy out of Exeter, away from his friends. And don't even think about selling Teddy's paintings!" She started to walk away, her torso rigid, arms swinging.

"You, you don't get me — I'm not a machine," he said, running after her. "I have to believe in what I write."

"Then believe in the Poulon series, it's our bread and butter."

He said nothing. Thwarted again; nothing had changed.

"You're such a fool, Jens. I've really had it with you."

"And I've had it with you!" he exploded. "Have you ever been there for me? Never! Thank God we don't have to depend on your paintings to support us. Why don't *you* get a job — a real job — instead of dallying at that shit you call art?"

The slap caught him off guard. It stung.

"Fuck you! I want a divorce!" She stormed into the library.

Chapter Thirty

Teddy was waiting for him when he got home, suited up in black Nike gym shorts, a matching body shirt, and sneakers. Jens was glad to see him; it helped diffuse his despair in the aftermath of Vivian's eruption.

"What's up, Daddio? You're late. I already drank my energizer."

"Give me a minute, pal."

He emerged from the bedroom in a blue outfit like Teddy's to find the boy pacing in the foyer. Jens was used to his occasional agitation, a symptom of his ADD.

"Let's do it!" Jens scooped up his car keys. He was hungover from his meeting with Jean, but he knew it would burn off after ten minutes of lifting.

On the road to Durham Teddy was silent, staring out the window. Jens didn't know where to start. He felt it was time to warn Teddy about the changes that were likely coming. They passed a farm on the right, with its rows of cow corn, high and ripe.

"Did they smoke corn silk back in your day, Dad?"

Jens laughed. "They smoked a lot of stuff in my day, but tobacco was the poison of choice."

"I heard the hippies smoked banana peel."

"First off, I was not hippie, I was born way too late. Second, I was too serious about my studies to experiment with every new fad or drug."

"C'mon, Dad, I know you smoked pot and tried LSD. What was your bad trip like?"

"Let me ask you something. If you give me a straight answer, I'll tell you what you want to know. Deal?"

Teddy nodded. They bumped fists.

"How many times have you smoked pot?"

Teddy hesitated. "A couple of times ...okay, maybe three."

"Thank you for your honesty. Anything else you want to tell me?"

"Not until you tell me about the LSD trip. Quid pro quo, right?" Teddy grinned.

"You might benefit from my cautionary tale. Are you listening? It begins with my brother Nils."

Teddy nodded.

"I was fourteen. A few years older than me, Nils could hunt, fish, fight — everything I was never very good at. He had a girlfriend who was in love with him, friends who were loyal, and my parents adored him. One day he asked me to go deer hunting. I was flattered he would want to take me."

Jens shook his head, remembering.

"Because of the damage to his face, the casket was closed."

Teddy looked at him, a quizzical expression on his face.

"How did Nils die? I forget."

"An accident, a horrible stupid accident. We were over in Northwood Meadows, the first day of deer season. Nils had gone on ahead, tracking this buck, and I'd lost sight of him in the woods. He'd taken a grunting tube with him to call deer, so I thought it was him, calling from a position upwind, safe. When the buck — a beautiful eight-pointer — stepped into the clearing, I was so nervous I barely got him in my sights. Just as I fired, Nils stood up, directly in the line of fire. He'd been crouching behind some trees *downwind*. It was horrible ... never a day goes by that I don't think, why did he stand up? Why? If only ... an experienced hunter like him."

"Jesus, Dad."

Jens fumbled, trying to pick up the thread of his narrative.

"I was devastated. In a moment of inattention, I'd shot and killed my own brother. It destroyed our family. Kids are more resilient than adults and I went on with my life. But Dad drank himself into an early grave and my mother ... never forgave me."

The hum of the automobile's tires on asphalt seemed to fill

the car. The road was a blur. He swiped at his eyes.

"Dad, it wasn't your fault."

"Hey, I'm supposed to be the adult here." He smiled at his son. "Thanks, pal."

They were coming into Durham, home of the University of New Hampshire, Jens' alma mater, driving past the horse barns and football stadium on the outskirts of town. Jens glanced at Teddy to see if he still held his attention.

"You want to hear more or you had enough?"

He went on.

"It was my senior year in college; I was very depressed. I was looking for an escape, for a breakthrough. I went from pot to LSD, which was being touted by New Age avatars as the panacea for all psychological and spiritual ills, a silver bullet to mental health and happiness."

"Was it?"

"At first, maybe. There was the illusion of insight, of relief. Then there were vestiges, hangovers ... seeping into waking consciousness. Soon, that's all I saw, pictures in my mind of Nils, and blood and mayhem, disembodiment. And there was a girl ... with whom I was very much in love. It broke us up."

He paused.

"Look, Teddy, I'm not saying the same thing is going to happen to you, but why don't you get on your path before you start destroying your brain cells with pot?"

Teddy shrugged. "Did you?"

They were driving down Main Street, past the ivied brick buildings of the campus. Jens pointed out Thompson Hall with its picturesque clock tower dating back to the 1800s; then Hamilton-Smith Hall, equally venerable, with its white Georgian columns and contrasting brick facade.

"That's where I found myself," he said, pointing at Hamilton-Smith. "Literature, and teachers who wrote novels. It was like manna."

"I don't feel like that about anything."

Jens ruffled his hair, a universal gesture, like his own father had done.

"Don't worry. It will come."

Teddy looked at him sympathetically.

"I'm sorry about your brother," he said paying him back in kind. Suddenly he brightened. "You ready to pound some iron, old man?"

Jens pulled into the mall behind Main Street and parked in front of "Wildcat Fitness," named after the university mascot.

———

Vivian was not home when they got back, so Jens made dinner for the two of them. Over burgers, Jens steered the conversation to the possible changes they'd all have to make, in order for him to write the book he had to.

Teddy nodded, not really sure how it would affect him. Jens thought they'd cross that bridge when the time came.

"Right now, your mother's not onboard with my decision to put the Poulon series on hold. We had a fight this afternoon, and she may be staying away to let things cool down." And punish me, Jens thought.

"Don't worry, she'll show up." There was a pause. It seemed as though Teddy had something he wanted to ask him. He glanced at his father, then looked away.

"What did you fight about? Did it have something to do with me telling you about Laurent?"

He shook his head.

"Because of *him*?"

"No, that's — I think I misunderstood."

"About Laurent?"

Jens nodded. He wondered how much to tell a boy about his parents' relations.

"There's a possibility Mom and I will split up."

Teddy's look was skeptical. "C'mon, she's threatened to kick you out before, but she never does. Buy her some roses like you always do, take her out to a fancy dinner — that'll bring her around."

"Not this time." Jens smiled. "Maybe." He gathered his thoughts. "I'm an aging, mid-sales crime writer, one among dozens, and I need to stand out from the crowd."

"You're a great writer."

"Have you ever read one of my books?" Teddy was silent. "Anyway, up on Black Mountain, facing that bear, I felt ... my mortality."

"You're still young."

"I know this sounds dramatic, but there's a book I have to write before I die, and it means putting the Poulon series on hold."

"I don't see the problem."

"It means the publisher may take back the advance we're living on. It means tightening our belts." He took a deep breath. "It means pulling you out of Exeter."

Teddy stared at him, his brow furrowed. He brightened.

"Do it, Dad."

"What about your friends?"

"I'll make new ones. Do this thing for yourself."

"I don't know, Teddy. It feels selfish ... and scary. What if the book fails?"

Teddy shook his head. "Go for it, old man."

Jens' smile was short-lived. "Your Mom's definitely not on board."

"*Get* her on board. You haven't lost your mojo, have you?"

———

Jens was awakened from a light sleep by sounds coming from the bathroom. The shower was running, which meant that Vivian was home. He wasn't sure how to play this. In the past, if he'd kept quiet, their rifts blew over. He decided to wait and see, taking his cue from her.

He didn't want to split up, though he'd been less certain earlier, after the scene at the library. He knew his reasons were selfish, separating would destroy his ordered writer's world. Family routine was a safe port he gratefully returned to, after riding the high seas of fiction. Besides, it would put his relationship with Teddy into jeopardy. And the boy really needed him.

Though he knew his survival depended on his ability to write, he also knew that he'd choose the path that would be best for Teddy, even if it meant him living apart for a while.

Anyway, she was the one who wanted a divorce. Why? So she could be with Laurent? He flared with jealousy.

Vivian entered from the bathroom, a towel wrapped around her, exposing tawny shoulders beaded with water. Jens lay on his back, watching as she casually removed her towel, dried herself, and wrapped it around her hair. His eyes were adjusted to the dark, and he easily made out his wife's silhouette, admiring her feminine curves: luminous breasts, a flat stomach, shapely hips, and long, slender legs.

He felt her staring in his direction, trying to determine if he was awake. She toweled off her hair and hung the towel over the back of a chair to dry. He expected her to put on the dowdy stringed pajama bottoms and cotton T-shirts she normally slept in, always complaining of the cold, even in summer. He felt a shiver of excitement as she pulled back the covers and slipped between the sheets — naked.

They lay side-by-side, staring at the ceiling, listening to the rhythm of each other's breathing, sensing one another. Gauging, as married couples are wont to do, the emotional and sexual climate.

Jens felt something different about his wife tonight — a subtle shift, an unhinging of habitual reserve, a tempest in the blood. It caught fire with him. The old disaffection he felt for her — borne of tiresome wrangling, repeated snubs, and disappointments affecting most every way a couple interacts — suddenly, miraculously, evaporated.

"Jens," she whispered, her voice hoarse.

"Mmmm." He felt her reaching for him. He rose to meet her embrace. Her hands were hot coals strafing him. He took her in his arms, and they began to make love, flesh cleaving flesh.

"I don't want to leave you. I love us — you, me, Teddy." She was sobbing.

"Shhh. I'm so sorry. I didn't mean what I said about your painting," he answered.

As they made love, he felt new resolve, infusing him with confidence in his ability to deliver the book he dreamed of.

Somewhere deep in his being, buried on the bitter edge of consciousness, lay the worm of doubt. But it wasn't about him — it was about Vivian. As she gave herself to him in a way that she hadn't in a very long time — not since their courting days — he sensed that she had given herself to another.

Someone who'd freed her of the numbing routines couples become accustomed to.

He felt a rougher hand in the works — signaled by Vivian's demanding, grappling, clawing, as they rollercoasted to orgasm.

Laurent's hand. The hand of a murderer.

The knowledge was lost in the passion of the moment, rocketing him away like a meteor flung to the far reaches; lost but for a trail of paranoia that might be traced back one day, to the truth.

———

In the morning he awakened feeling restored and whole. Vivian was already up; he smelled coffee and toast. He lay in bed longer, letting the glow of their intimacy continue to permeate his sensibilities. Forgotten was the worm of doubt.

He suddenly understood that Cassie Melantree, who had cut herself off from feeling because of her daughter's murder, was ready to become whole again, able and willing to risk love. This would be the subtext of his crime story — an exploration of how the human heart mends. He liked the way it fit in with the ending he'd already envisioned — of Cassie confessing her love for Tommy Flaherty.

He congratulated himself on his insight, loving the way an idea acts as a magnet. It was one of the unsung satisfactions of his work, how story comes from incidental strands, semi-conscious threads, woven into a whole.

He jumped into the shower, turning his story over in his mind, priming the pump.

At breakfast, he embraced Vivian, looked into her eyes, and kissed her. She laughed nervously but did not pull away.

He took his coffee and toast on a tray and bounded up the stairs to his office, ready to begin the first chapter of his book, warmed by the thought that with this book, he would take care of his family. And they would stay together.

Chapter Thirty-One

Trying to look casual, Warren glanced around Petronella's Café, nearly deserted in the wake of the lunch crowd. Their booth, just off the bar with a view of the courtyard, gave them as much privacy as was possible in a public place. Meeting Laurent was a violation of Warren's parole, and it made him jumpy. But that was something he'd never allow his disciple to see.

A couple, 30s — tourists, judging from their matching sweatshirts embossed with the familiar Bow St. tugboats — sat at the bar chatting. At their feet were shopping bags full of overpriced "treasures" to haul home. Warren wrote them off as harmless. Still, he lowered his voice.

"Three hundred K, that's what's it's worth?"

Laurent nodded. "Maybe more — housing market's back up — Conway's a popular destination — mountain climbing, hunting, fishing, water sports."

With a toss of his ponytail, Warren looked at him askance. It was a look that Laurent knew well, that said I'm on board, but *you* can't know that, or you'll buy me off cheap.

"Explain to me again — how is it that this log cabin in Conway is not part of their marriage assets?"

"Corbin was smart enough to title it under a shell corporation used for writing off his expenses as a novelist."

"His wife told you that?"

"It slipped out; she said Corbin thought she didn't know about it." Laurent leaned in closer, adding to the drama. "Realistically, if he sells short — and he will once we —"

Warren held up a cautionary hand, shorthand for "don't count your chickens."

"Quarter of a mill," Laurent added, letting it sink in. "Easy money."

"Kidnapping's a federal beef." Warren shook his head. "Too

risky."

Laurent played along — believing himself as good as Warren at the con.

"*Not* kidnapping," he hissed. "Threat. Threat only."

"Still, a *terrorist* threat. And the boy?"

"We leave him alone. I know enough about him to make it sound good."

Warren frowned. "I don't know. I got a lot to lose here."

Laurent shrugged. "Okay, I'll do it alone."

When Warren tossed his ponytail again — *his tell* — Laurent knew he was in, he had him. It was only a matter of the terms.

"You say you've researched this thoroughly. What about..."

Laurent listened patiently while Warren cited his objections. Then he dismissed them one by one, like a car salesman overcoming a buyer's reservations. It only took another fifteen minutes for Warren to say the words.

"I'm in, I'm in," he said, bumping fists with Laurent. "Coupla points, first."

"I'm all ears." Laurent suppressed a grin.

"One: no physical contact whatsoever with this Corbin guy. Phone call only. Scare tactics. Two: I do the cash pickup. Three: I make the call, do all the talking. Four: We split sixty-forty. I get the extra for the use of my truck."

Laurent knew he was expected to do some horse-trading, the first item on the agenda their split.

"Sixty-forty for me. It's my job."

They finally agreed on fifty-fifty.

"We make the cash pickup together." Laurent stared him down, knowing this was critical; though they'd been buddies in prison, he didn't know if he could trust him outside.

Warren nodded. "Okay, but I make the call. You don't want him talking to Vivian and suspecting you."

Laurent rubbed his forehead, made like he was thinking it over.

"No deal, then." He smiled crookedly.

Warren glared. Laurent glared back.

"Okay, okay," Warren said, finally. "You can make the call, but keep it impersonal."

Meaning, do not let Corbin know how much he had it in for him. Laurent slowly nodded yes.

They sealed the pact with shots of tequila. Warren got up to go; they'd agreed not to be seen leaving together.

"You steering clear of the wife?" He threw some bills down on the table.

"Strictly business, now," Laurent lied.

"Keep it that way."

After he left, Laurent glanced at the bill.

Son of a bitch shorted me!

He grudgingly paid the difference, vowing to get Warren back for all his arrogance. As he made his way back to Bow Street, he congratulated himself on how well things were working out. Warren was playing right into his hands and so would Corbin, and eventually Vivian, too, though she could never know he was connected with the blackmail.

After the cash was delivered, well, accidents happen all the time to people like Corbin, don't they?

Chapter Thirty-Two

Deep in thought, Jens drove north along the White Mountain Highway toward Conway, retracing the familiar route he and Teddy had traveled only weeks before, in the aftermath of their experiences on Black Mountain.

For Jens it had been life-changing. He had saved a man's life and in some indefinable way it had quickened his sense of purpose, casting his accomplishments in doubt, and making him avid to bring something new and different into creation while he still possessed talent and will.

The phrase "mid-life crisis" came to mind but instead of having one last fling with a younger woman (Vivian, ten years his junior, was young enough), or buying a James Dean vintage Porsche 550, his dream car, he was committing to a rigorous writing program. He was coming up to the cabin to eliminate all the distractions of home and professional life, so he could concentrate on a book that would come from his heart, not just his head.

Happily, he had the blessings of his wife and son. Vivian, in fact, had encouraged him to go to the cabin so he could concentrate, leaving her to manage the house along with Teddy, who would be starting school in a few weeks. In the meantime, steps had been taken to enroll Teddy at Oyster River High in the event that Jens' writing advance was forfeited. Jean, his agent, was still trying to hold onto it for him. Surprisingly, Vivian said she would begin looking for a job.

Once at the cabin, he planned to take a page from Hemingway's notebook on the disciplined writer, which predicated writing without break for six hours, from six in the morning until noon, and then spending the rest of the day fishing.

He imagined the hypnotic play of sunlight on sparkling water and the rhythmic action of fly-casting as his reward for producing the requisite 1500 - 2000 word goal he set for himself daily.

Already he had completed the first few chapters, which some say is the most difficult because they must hook the reader while revealing enough of the protagonist to be intriguing.

Jens' Subaru climbed the winding road to Black Mountain in the dusk. He was nearly home.

———

After passing through the pleasantly-musty mudroom, with its fragrance of pine and sweat, Jens cranked open the kitchen and living room windows to chase away the stuffy air. He glanced around with satisfaction, happy to be back in his familiar cocoon, where he could indulge his imagination without interruption. Everything seemed to be in order.

He would write well here, he decided.

He went downstairs and turned on the hot water heater, remembering how he had discovered the cover ajar when he returned to lock up the house the day he and Teddy drove back to Lee. The thought released a cloud of doubt and concern surrounding Teddy, tugging at the edge of awareness. About what, specifically, he could not say, so he dismissed it. Under Vivian's care, Teddy would be fine for the month Jens would be away here. He set about making himself dinner, thoughtful and relaxed.

———

While washing up the dinner dishes he was struck by a thought about the hook in Chapter One. It wasn't strong enough. He thought of his Poulon series, in which each novel begins with a scene revealing the "perp" committing his horrendous crime, or showing the results of it, the *corpus delicti. The body of the crime* is what he always introduced Detective Poulon to, according to the formula for police procedurals.

Suddenly, he caught an image of the "perp," Orozco, preparing to mete out punishment to the child on the deck of his yacht. The scene rapidly fleshed itself out, and he was afraid he'd lose it if he didn't capture it immediately on paper, or in Word.

He dried his hands and removed his laptop from the knapsack he used as a carrying case, setting it down on the kitchen table. While the computer booted up, he retrieved his wine glass and took a meditative sip, his thoughts warming in the glow of the screen. He opened a new Word doc and started writing, his fingers gathering speed as he recorded the scene exploding in his mind's eye.

Prologue: The Beast
Emma was sitting on the bunk in one of the staterooms used to indulge the man's wicked fantasies of seduction and punishment ...

After writing non-stop for almost an hour, Jens saved and closed his Word doc, worried that the opening was too salacious, prurient — and borrowed. He did not want to arouse the reader, only horrify, and elicit pathos. He closed his eyes to recapture the moment, but the movie in his mind receded, as Orozco disappeared behind the ship's stateroom door and locked it.

Jens shut down his computer, thinking, *enough threatened mayhem for one night*. Tomorrow he would evaluate the scene and either rewrite it or discard it.

He poured himself another glass of wine and took it along with his cell phone onto the porch and called home. The phone rang and rang but no one picked up.

He sipped his wine, warmed by his developing understanding of Cassie's story, confident that it would unfold

— without much interference from him — now that he was consciously dreaming.

Chapter Thirty-Three

After seeing Teddy off on the bus to Portsmouth to meet his friends at the city pool, Vivian retreated to her studio in the barn to resume work on the painting she'd put aside until Jens returned to his cabin in the mountains. His departure, which she'd gently but persistently encouraged, was necessary as she intended to sort out matters with Laurent before he did something foolish.

She really did not know what he was capable of. Whispering on the phone with him until Jens left, she'd found him to be alternately sensible and demanding, oscillating between Dr. Jekyll and Mr. Hyde. At times she believed him to be considerate of her need to remain with her family. At other times, he sounded like a manic-depressive, high on his demands for *their* life together, sheer fantasy.

And when she reminded him that nothing like that was going to happen, *ever*, he became so morose she feared he would kill himself. She contemplated going to the police, but she knew that would blow back on her, terribly. She had a lot to hide about her former life — things that would hurt her relationship with Teddy, never mind Jens, were it to come out.

Laurent just hadn't moved on. He was obsessed with her.

She knew it had been him out at the hunter's blind, though she'd lied to Jens, a sin of omission to buy time.

And now he still wanted her back?

So angry had the thought of his clingy desire made her, unreasonable and absurd as it was, that she hadn't noticed the paint running from her brush onto the sacred white spaces of her composition, reserved for the light. Cursing Laurent and all the heartache his reappearance brought, she daubed at the paint stain until she'd rubbed through the rag paper, destroying her composition thoroughly, sending her into a paroxysm of teary self-recrimination.

At first, because of her sobbing, she failed to hear another presence in the barn, calling out to her from the hinged door.

"Ma'am?"

She spun around to find a man dressed in a UPS uniform, tendering a clipboard for her to sign. She looked but did not find the company's logo over his shirt pocket.

Odd.

The shorts he wore exposed worm-white legs that likely had never seen daylight. She pictured the UPS delivery men and women depicted in TV ads, always dressed in shorts in summer, outdoorsy types, legs tanned.

His braided silver-streaked ponytail also seemed out of place, as did the tattoos sleeving his muscled arms.

As he talked, he advanced on her in rapid steps.

"Ma'am, pardon me. I'm sorry to interrupt," Warren said, "but I need to get your signature — oh, I see you're an artist. Mind if I have a look?"

Suddenly, he was there — and it was too late to run.

He clapped a calloused hand over her mouth, dragged her to a chair, and roughly plunked her down. He put a finger to his lips, to *shush* her. She knew better than to scream. A look in his eyes told her that he would kill her — and enjoy it.

"What do you want? Money? Jewelry?"

He stared at her, coldly appraising her.

"One word — Teddy."

"What?" she cried.

He smiled, enjoying his easy dominance, her fear.

"Oh, I don't want your son. *You* do — you want him home from that pool he goes to every day. And when school starts, you'll want him back home, too, every evening. And when he goes out on dates, or basketball games, or whatever, you'll want him home then, safe and sound."

She tried to keep the fear from choking her up.

"My husband, he'll be home soon."

He looked at her askance.

"Really? Then who was it I watched load up his trusty Subaru yesterday morning, no doubt headed for the hills?"

She recoiled, shocked: *he'd* been the stalker in the hunter's blind in the orchard. Somehow, he knew about Jens' cabin retreat.

"I'll give you whatever you want —" She caught herself, realizing he could take *that*, too, if he chose to.

"Maybe," he leered. "But for now, I just want the keys to the castle." He gestured about. "To everything of worth." He glared at her fiercely. "*Everything!*"

She nodded through her tears.

"Why?"

He shrugged.

"I need money — you have more than me."

"I don't know where you got that idea, we —"

"*Stop!*" His ferocity blasted her into silence.

"Good. Shall we head on up to the house and begin? We can start with the cash and jewelry and move on to the art, which I've heard so much about ..."

He paused. She looked at him quizzically.

"From my associate Laurent."

She jolted at her ex-lover's name.

He pulled her to her feet. His vise-like grip discouraged her from running.

"That's another thing — you are to have no more contact with Laurent. Understand? You'll let me know if he bothers you anymore. I'll take care of him."

He shoved her in the direction of the farmhouse.

"Consider it part of the service, quid pro quo."

She shook her head, not knowing what to think. Had he been tapping her phone and listening to her conversations? Had Laurent shared privileged information with him about her and Jens' finances? She searched her memory for what she might have let slip to Laurent.

"Obviously, no police, and leave your husband out of this, too."

They stepped into the sunlight and onto the path back to the house.

Where was Bruzza? she wondered. He ought to be barking his head off.

"What have you done to my dog?" she asked, peeking into his kennel as they approached the house. Bruzza lay there, snoring and whimpering.

"He'll be fine in a couple of hours. We need to get going — before your son comes home."

Vivian tried to stifle a sob.

He slid open the glass door to the kitchen and stepped inside, pushing her ahead. Violating the sanctity of her home.

"Now, let's start with the safe. You do have a safe, don't you?"

Chapter Thirty-Four

For Jens, the time at the cabin unfolded in a chrysalis of inner dialogue about *Forsake Me Not* and played out over the course of the day with his usual discipline: at his laptop by 7 AM, done with his word quota by 1 or 2 PM.

He modeled his afternoons after "the Hem," fishing to catch his supper, which afforded him the illusion of killing to survive and the satisfaction of economy. Such notions were inherited from his undergraduate writing teachers, outdoorsmen and novelists, who extolled the virtue of entering the woods and stream with humility, taking only what you needed.

But no amount of rationalization would permit Jens to take up a firearm ever again, with the intention of slaying a large mammal, like a deer. Nils' death had closed that door. Protecting his family from harm was the only exception. The incident with the bear had put his resolve on trial. He hoped it would never be tested again, especially not with a human target.

In the evenings he cooked and ate leisurely, reading police procedurals or surfing the internet, until it was time to call home. Vivian filled him in on the events of the day: Bruzza's antics, her job search, Teddy's activities. She encouraged Jens to talk about the progress he was making on his book, an interest she had never taken before. Jens remarked the change to himself, afraid that calling attention to it would embarrass and discourage her.

"Jens ..." she began casually. "Do you happen to know where Teddy's doctors' assessments validating his ADHD are? I need them for school to get him his accommodations."

Jens mentally shuffled through his memory, organized in folders not unlike the ones on his laptop and computer, remembering that he'd transferred them to an electronic document to reduce paper. They were on his desktop, in his office.

"Ah ... they're on my computer ..."

He kept the password to himself because his backup writing was stored there too. Though it was paranoid, he knew, he didn't trust anyone, not even Vivian, with the password; there were things in his files there — half-baked ideas, autobiographical sketches, story tangents that he felt uncomfortable sharing. The detritus of an active, imaginative intellect, but for his eyes only.

Oh, well, he told himself, *I can change the password when I get home.*

She thanked him for sharing it with her, reassuring him that she wouldn't write it down. Besides, it was easy to remember— "Forsake Me Not".

Jens asked her if Teddy was available. Most nights, if he could be persuaded to pause his Xbox playing, he would come to the phone, reluctant to share at first but then open up. Jens was concerned about his transfer to Oyster River High.

Tonight, his son talked with enthusiasm of the book he'd been assigned for summer reading. Without being heavy-handed, Jens applauded Teddy and encouraged him to read more. Teddy sounded excited about the prospect of making new friends at school and had resolved to turn over a new leaf in his studies.

Jens was in shock. Had his absence from home opened up a space for family members to fill with their own initiative because he wasn't around to micro-manage? Was he *that* overbearing? Or was it because they had risen to his call for support?

"Still there, Dad?"

Jens reacted to the shift in his voice. "Something the matter?"

"Nope, I just wondered ... when are you coming home?"

"I'm not due back for another couple of weeks. Why, do you need something?"

Jens wondered if Teddy had something to report about

Laurent; Vivian had promised she was done with him.

"No, I just ... I miss you, Daddio," he blurted. "Like, when can we go fishing?"

"How about the weekend after next, when I get home? How's that?"

"Great! Can we take the boat out on the bay? The stripers are running."

"What're they biting on?"

"Mackerel, I hear"

"Then plan on it."

Jens started to tell him to put his mother back on, but Teddy had already hung up. Jens considered calling back, but then thought better of it. Everything was going brilliantly; he would call tomorrow, try to get Teddy alone. Seemed like there was something he wanted to tell him.

Sometime in the night Jens awakened with a feeling of dread, which he could not connect to anything in particular. He sat up in the dark and probed for the answer, reviewing the usual culprits — Nils, Teddy, Vivian, his story, money.

Once his eyes adjusted to the dark, Jens found his way into the living room and turned on the light. He made himself a strong gin and tonic, and sipped it as he recomposed his thoughts.

He tossed back the rest of his drink, shrugging off his silliness — a momentary lapse, a night fugue. The story was going well; his family was behind his decision; his finances would work themselves out. Vivian was done with Laurent.

So what was bothering him?

PART TWO

Chapter Thirty-Five

A week later around noon, his answer came at the end of a long and fruitful writing session.

It came in the form of a letter, delivered midday, by a process server in a bad suit, with crooked, yellow teeth — why in God's name did he smile, wondered Jens — knocking loudly on the door to the mudroom.

Jens had stopped typing and gone to the door, thinking there was an emergency and his help was needed with a car accident, a missing dog, or a hunting accident. He stared at the man, unable to account for his presence.

"Sir, are you Jens Corbin, 16 Black Mountain Rd., North Conway, New Hampshire?"

"I am! And just who might you be?"

He took an envelope from the inside breast pocket of his suit and presented it to Jens.

"This is for you, Mr. Corbin." He held out the official looking envelope bearing the seal of the Court of New Hampshire, Division of Divorce Proceedings.

Jens stared at the seal. "Divorce?"

The man pushed the envelope at Jens until he took it, mostly in self-defense.

"I'll need you to sign here, acknowledging receipt." He produced a clipboard with a release form. "Please," he insisted.

"Is this a joke or what?"

The server shook his head. "No, sir, it's not."

It was a stand-off — with the server proffering the clipboard for Jens to sign and Jens balking.

"All right, sir, I'll have to sign it for you, noting your lack of compliance."

Jens glared at him for his answer.

The server turned on his heel and began walking to the rusty Crown Vic, a retired plain-wrapped cruiser, engine idling, blue smoke puffing from the exhaust.

Jens watched, speechless, as the car lurched away, kicking up gravel from the drive. Jens stood there, flummoxed.

"Aw, hell!"

As he walked back inside, he barely took notice of a northern mockingbird foraging in the brush bordering the driveway. Its distinctive wings, with contrasting black and white chevrons, were spread wide in a gesture intended to startle insect prey out of hiding. When Jens let the door slam shut, it startled the bird into flight.

"Chuck-chuck," it called, as though taunting.

Jens lost track of time sitting in the living room, the envelope containing his divorce papers crumpled in his hand. When he came around, he discovered it unfurled beside him. He took it up and slit open the top. The document was printed on linen paper, embossed with the seal of the State of New Hampshire. He unfolded it and smoothed out the pages, began to read.

"Claimant, Vivian Corbin brings complaint against Jens Corbin ... claims for divorce under state law ... respondent is ordered to cease and desist from contacting the plaintiff via phone or letter, except through an attorney ... physical abuse ... reasonable apprehension of physical abuse ... barred from the home ... restraining order ... custody to be determined..."

The cliché of the insensitive male who never sees his divorce coming struck him as glaringly apt. Hadn't he and Vivian patched things up? Why now?

Why was she doing this? He began to review her actions of the last few months, sickened by the unavoidable conclusion that she was still cheating on him with Laurent. She'd been playing him until she was ready to make her move.

A stone crushed his heart. He turned his thoughts to Teddy. Now, he knew the wrenching anguish a parent feels when offspring are torn from them by the law. He would fight her tooth and nail for his son.

He took out his cell, which had better reception lately, aware that he was violating the terms of the divorce claim, and rang Vivian. Her thumbnail image seemed to glare back from the small screen, accusing his folly. She surprised him by picking up.

"What do you want?"

"I want to know one thing — why you're doing this," he said, partially successful in suppressing the emotion in his voice. "Is it because of the book? Or is it because of Laurent?"

After a long pause she answered slowly and deliberately, as though talking to a child.

"No ... yes ... it's everything. It's you, it's me, it's us!" Her voice was rising. "Jens, I want my life back; I don't know who I am anymore." She seemed on the verge of tears.

"You've been seeing Laurent, haven't you?" In his mind, he screamed *bitch*.

"Get yourself an attorney." Her voice was frigid. "I don't have to talk to you."

"And Teddy, *our* boy. What about him?"

"The court will decide what's best for him."

He had a sudden epiphany — remembering that she had asked him for the password to his desktop at home in Lee, on the pretext of getting documents for Teddy's ADHD accommodations. He realized that not only was his writing exposed in the files, but also all his financial business — his passwords for banking, credit cards, annuities, 504's. *Everything!*

"I'm coming down there!"

"Jens, don't you dare!"

"You can't do this — "

"I'm hanging up."

"*Please*, let me talk to Teddy."

The line went dead. He jumped up from the couch, paced; twice he stopped himself from hurling the phone into the fireplace.

"You bitch!" he bellowed. "You rotten bitch!" he cried, collapsing back onto the couch. He squeezed his temples and rubbed his eyes until he was seeing stars. Then he cried like a baby.

————

After a while, cold resolve settled over him. First, he would contact the bank and alert them to his wife's threat to his money.

When he called his bank, he was informed that he no longer had access to his accounts, as they had been transferred out and the name on the account changed.

"Hold on a minute," he screamed into the phone. "I'm co-owner of that account, with my wife."

"Not anymore, sir. I'm sorry. Would you like to file a complaint?"

"I'd like to report criminal activity."

"By your wife, sir? If you didn't want her to have access to your account why did she have the password?"

When he demanded to speak to a manager, he was reminded that it was Saturday, and he might have to wait for his call to be transferred to corporate.

He ended the call, impatient. Stunned. He stared at his hands, noticing that they were clenched tight. He forced himself to breathe deeply, in and out.

Who could he call for help? Ferdie? The last time they'd met, he'd walked out on her. Would she, a woman and a law officer, be willing to advise him?

His cell phone rang on the coffee table repeatedly before he answered, thinking it was Vivian calling back, to tell him what?

Jean Fillmore-Smart's image appeared on the screen.

"Jens?"

All that came out of him was a hoarse whisper.

"Jens? Are you there?"

"Hello," he croaked.

"Am I calling at a bad time?"

"Vivian ... she ..." he was unable to go on.

"Oh, dear. What is it?"

"She's filed for divorce."

"Oh, no!"

"I've just been served. All lies ... she's been cheating...."

He stifled the urge to blurt out that she'd been cheating with a convicted murderer, no less.

"I'm so sorry, Jens. What are you going to do?"

"Fight it! Can't afford not to! For Teddy."

Jean waited for him to cool. "I have some news that might cheer you up ... but I don't know if this is the right time."

Jen sighed. "What?"

"You have a fan at Cathcart — Gabbie."

Jens realized she was talking about Gabbie Halliday, the editor-in-chief of fiction at his publisher.

"When I told her that your new book was from a woman's POV," Jean continued, "she was excited ... said she always wanted to suggest it."

Jens scoffed. "Must be because I'm such a feminist."

"Don't let this throw you." After a beat: "Jens?"

"I'm still here."

"She went to bat for you and got the legal department to apply your advance to the new book on two conditions."

"Which are?"

"One, you send them the first 200 pages in ninety days, with a chapter outline of the rest of the book."

"Okay. Not a problem. What's the second part?"

"They reserve the right to refuse the book if they don't like it. In which case, you return half the advance."

"I can live with that."

"Good."

There was another long pause.

"Jens, are you going to be alright?"

"The book is going well."

"That's not what I meant."

"I gotta go, Jean. Thank you."

"Keep in touch. *Please.*"

Afterward, he wondered why he hadn't asked her for advice about his compromised bank account and his desktop computer back in Lee.

He deliberated about calling Ferdie, but he knew what she would say: stay away from Vivian. Period. Not what he wanted to hear.

———

In the end, he decided not to pack an overnight bag. If Vivian wouldn't let him stay the night, at least she'd let him have some of his things to go to a motel. He drove well over the speed limit, anxious to get home to Lee before dark. He nearly got caught speeding, at the last minute spotting a state trooper's cruiser lurking behind a billboard.

Ironically, the billboard was an advertisement for a divorce attorney. Jens found himself amused by the symbolic juxtaposition of the law, represented by the cruiser, and the ad for an attorney. Tomorrow he'd contact his own attorney in Portsmouth, an old friend from college. It's going to be alright, he told himself.

Yet some part of him knew otherwise. The time bomb in his blood had been set ticking. He'd suspected it days ago, and he knew it now. But, like most, he'd learned to distrust and ignore his instincts. The same inner barometer told him, unequivocally, that going to see Vivian before talking with his lawyer was a mistake.

For the rest of the ride he stayed under the limit, though his mind and heart were racing on a collision course.

Chapter Thirty-Six

Jens pounded on the front door of the home he'd shared with his wife and son for the past fifteen years, calling his wife's name over and over. Ironically, the venerable Schlage cylinder lock that had served them as a first line of defense against intruders was now being used to exclude *him*; it had been re-keyed.

The shades had been drawn on the picture window in the living and dining rooms. Upstairs, the bedroom lamps shone warmly in the gloaming. Jens stood in a parabola of light from a lamp mounted beside the door, triggered by a movement sensor. He felt raw and exposed — unreal. This couldn't be happening to him.

"Teddy!" he shouted at the upstairs window. "Teddy! It's me. Dad! Come down and talk, son!"

There was no answer. He backed away, cupping his hands to make a megaphone.

"Vivian! I don't deserve this! Come on, let's talk!"

On a thought, he pulled out his phone, thinking she might respond to a call on her cell. The script at the bottom of his droid's screen informed him that he had a message, sent minutes earlier. He tapped the text icon from Teddy.

"Get out of here, Dad! Cops on the way. Tried to warn you about Mom earlier."

Jens glanced up at the house, hoping to catch a glimpse of Teddy, to wave "okay." As he backed away, a deep male voice boomed behind him.

"Put your hands on your head and turn around slowly."

A glaring beacon blasted him. Car doors slammed. Another voice rang out, harsh and insistent.

"Hands on your head!"

Jens judged its owner to be smaller, less formidable than the first speaker. He began to turn toward the voices.

"Gun!" the voice screamed.

Jens felt the sudden impact of furious men tackling him from opposite sides, knocking the wind out of him. He collapsed. As he lost consciousness, he felt his cell phone being ripped from his hand.

That's no gun, he wanted to tell them. It's the last thing he remembered.

When he came to, he was prone on his stomach, a bony knee stabbing him in the back. His hands were cuffed with plastic ties, cutting off the circulation.

"Get the fuck off me!" he bellowed.

The smaller of the officers pressed his knee deeper. "Want verbal abuse on a police officer added to the charges?"

The other cop crouched beside Jens and shone a torch in his face, brandishing it with menace. "Jens Corbin?"

"Y-e-s-s-s!" he answered with difficulty.

"I didn't quite catch that."

"I'm. Jens. Corbin!"

"No need to shout," said the lightweight, digging his knees into Jens' kidneys. They laughed at him moaning in pain.

"A beater," one of them sneered. "Tough guy, huh?"

"You are in violation of your restraining order. Do you understand?" said the basso profondo.

"Y-e-e-e-s!" he moaned.

"That means that you are forbidden by law to come within twenty-five yards of this property and its occupants."

"Is that clear?" insisted the monkey on his back.

"Get off!" Teddy hurled himself at the cop.

The weight was suddenly gone from Jens. He glimpsed Teddy wrestling with the smaller cop, getting the better of him. Jens tried to get up, to come to Teddy's assistance, but the other cop held him down.

"Stay where you are!" he commanded, a restraining paw on Jens' shoulder.

From the corner of his eye Jens saw Vivian running toward

them.

"No!" she screamed. "That's my son. Please don't hurt him." She pulled Teddy away from the officer who was scrabbling for the baton at his belt.

"I'll take it from here, officers!" barked a familiar voice. Trooper Morrison, Ferdie, approached. She saluted the officers smartly with the requisite two fingers snapped off the brim of her Smokey.

It was clear to Jens that State Trooper trumped the local Lee Sheriff's Department, though the officers didn't surrender their turf without a fight, especially not to a woman.

The big cop heatedly braced her, face to face, talking in private a few feet away. Jens strained to hear what they were saying.

"This is an RSA 458.16 violation. A local matter," spat the sheriff's deputy, his chauvinism flaring.

"*I know*," barked Ferdie, undaunted. "The restraining order came across my desk. When I saw who it was for, I got here as soon as I could."

The deputy waited for her to go on.

Trooper Morrison lowered her voice. Jens caught only a few words: "Conway ... case in Florida ... famous writer ... *friend*."

"Thanks," said Jens, as Ferdie and the deputy hauled him to his feet. Once his ties were cut, he urged the circulation back into his hands. He sought out Vivian in the darkness. His anger surged.

"This is what you wanted, Vivian? To put Teddy in harm's way?"

Ferdie took him by the arm, led him away.

"To humiliate me in front of my son?" he called over his shoulder.

"You can't be talking to her except through a lawyer." Ferdie faced him. "Shut up or I won't be able to keep you out of jail," she hissed.

"Seventeen years — this is what I get?" He shook Ferdie off, spun on Vivian. "What did I ever do to you, Vivian, except love you and take care of you and our son?"

Tears were flowing down Vivian's cheeks.

"I'm sorry, Jens. You'll never understand. Just let it go," she pleaded.

"This is all about that bastard Laurent, isn't it?"

She pressed her lips together, silent.

"I never put a hand on you."

Ferdie pushed him toward his cruiser.

"You're threatening and abusive," she said, angry again. "You're doing it now, coming here."

Jens started to respond but Ferdie blocked him.

"Don't say another word, Jens. She's baiting you for the record. You'll get your day in court."

"She froze me out of our bank account. Isn't that criminal? You tell me."

Ferdie tipped her hat to the deputies as she steered Jens to the passenger's side of her cruiser.

"Teddy," Jens called over the roof as he got in. "I'm sorry I dragged you into this."

Teddy nodded, his eyes shining.

Ferdie put her hand on Jens' head to keep him from hitting it on the door frame.

As they drove away, Jens asked about going back for his car. Ferdie shook her head.

"Because your wife's call came over 911, the deputies are obliged to charge and book you."

She turned to Jens and winked.

"Unless, of course, you're not available."

Jens stared ahead, in shock.

"I don't know what would have happened if you hadn't come along. Thanks."

She shrugged, smiled mysteriously.

"I'll drive you back later when the deputies are gone."

"Why are you doing this?"

———

They stopped at the diner at the Lee traffic circle, took a booth, and ordered coffee and pie. Ferdie told him about her parents' divorce when she was in high school, and how much it had embarrassed and isolated her.

"You're a good Dad, I know, I see how you are with your son. I don't want him to suffer like I did."

She toyed with her fork while he waited for her to go on. Jens sensed she wanted to talk more about her trials and tribulations as a teen. He wondered if coming out in high school was also part of her painful story.

"Do you have someone now?" he asked sympathetically, before he could stop himself.

She looked at him in mock horror.

"Oh, my goodness," she exclaimed, laughing, surprised. "You mean like a lesbian lover, maybe? Or..."

Jens understood he'd gone too far.

"I'm sorry, Ferdie. I didn't mean to —"

"Bit personal, don't you think?"

Her chest was heaving in spite of herself. She tamped down her flattop, even though it was perfect.

———

Later, when it was safe, Ferdie dropped him at his car at the house in Lee and idled on the side of the road until Jens started up and drove away.

He was headed for Portsmouth, where he had the best chance of finding a Rite Aid or 7-Eleven still open to get some toiletries. To economize, he decided to check into a motel over the state line, in Maine.

He found a trucker's motel on the 1A bypass in Kittery, its shabbiness consistent with his low mood. He spent the night on a lumpy mattress trying to sleep, the tang of the ocean seeping in from the estuary behind the motel, like ghost fingers unhinging latches to his past. Marsh gas recalled the sulfurous stench of paranoia and his bout with madness, decades ago.

In that bewildering half-sleep known only too well to insomniacs and the insane, in the absence of light just before dawn, he reacquainted himself with the morbid attraction of suicide. In his dream, he was flitting through worlds within worlds, calling, crying out. But there was no one there to answer.

Chapter Thirty-Seven

Unbeknownst to Jens, in the very same motel, the River Run, only a floor above and a few doors over, lay his nemesis Laurent.

Also unable to sleep, Laurent was suffering a paroxysm of conscience — whipping him between hope and despair, between heaven and hell, between life and death.

He had been cut off from the object of desire, Vivian, and with it his reason for living. He had no choice. She'd stopped returning his phone calls. Her farmhouse was off-limits now, with Teddy around.

"Armand," she'd hissed at him when he'd surprised her at the State Street gallery where she was working as an art consultant.

He'd dressed up in his "tourist clothes" again — slacks, dress shirt, sports jacket, all looking worse for the wear — and was posing as an art collector, as he had weeks ago when he'd first arrived in Portsmouth. Though now he felt — and looked — even more out of place than he had then.

As she went about her work, she'd been caught off guard by his appearance in one of the exhibition rooms, where he stood staring blankly at a larger than life seascape not hers.

"I'd like to see a *D'Arcy*," he'd garbled, unable to sustain the élan he'd hoped to impress and win her over with. "You must have one here, don't you?"

"I don't want you here!" she'd hissed. "That's all Jens' lawyer needs, to catch me with you! *Now leave!*"

"Vivi," he'd pleaded as she escorted him out. Luckily, for her sake, she'd been alone in the gallery. "I... can't go on like this."

Now, as he relived his humiliation, he recalled how he'd been with Vivian in *this* motel room, on the very same day they'd met at the park, a stolen moment in Paradise. It had felt so right; he'd felt anchored.

Now, he was free-falling.

Back through his hard-won triumphs over the forces of fate. Prison time, slow time, no time, hard time: time spent wrestling strength from defeat, forging the will to survive. Gone all pride and determination. Along with it, tenderness, joy, and hope but briefly tasted. Gone.

Vivian had decreed that they must part — until the divorce was over. Wasn't it enough that she was divorcing her husband of almost twenty years? And there was her son — what about him? She did not want to lose him, accused as an unfit mother because of her liaison with Laurent.

What was left for him?

An idea took shape, one that would either bind him to her permanently or deliver him to hell. He glanced around the shabby room, seeing it for what it was.

How easy it would be to step off this very chair, rope around his neck, noose tied to the light fixture, and surrender to the forces of chaos that nip, always, at the edge of every con's life, once on the outside. Would anyone care? Would she?

No, it was *not* enough that she was divorcing him. Corbin had to be punished, eradicated, expunged. Only then would she turn to him, Laurent, and give herself without reservation.

———

Later that morning, Laurent stepped into the rental office of the motel, to complain that his toilet was backed up and that he'd like it attended to — *today* — while he went about his errands.

The walk to Portsmouth would take him half an hour at best, and he was already running late for an appointment with Warren to put together some equipment and finalize their plans to extort Corbin.

The clerk, a haggard young man, was checking out a guest, a man in his late 40s, tired-looking, dressed in wrinkled clothes that looked slept in. Something about him was familiar.

The tiny rental office, crammed with a counter, computer,

and two rickety wooden chairs for guests, barely accommodated one check-out at a time. Laurent grew impatient, shifting nervously in place, suddenly reminded of the time he'd spent in lockup.

He cleared his throat and gave the clerk a toned-down version of his prison yard stare — why waste it?

"Room 217 backed up toilet. Fix it," he barked. "I gotta get to work," he lied.

The guest glanced at Laurent with bloodshot eyes. Suddenly, they grew wide with recognition.

Laurent jolted with recognition, too.

Corbin! He wanted to take him right there, but knew he couldn't.

He backed out of the office, walked briskly to his room, tossed his meager belongings into the paper bag he'd arrived with.

He was gone. In the wind.

———

Jens waited while Ferdie cautiously peeked into the room Laurent had occupied on the second floor of the motel, where he too had spent the night, never suspecting that the man he hunted, the man he wanted out of his life, was close, oh, so close.

Why hadn't he pounced on Laurent when he had the chance? What would Laurent have said, done? Agreed, Laurent was formidable: prison-bulked, tattooed, dead-eyed. Jens thought about what his alter-ego, Honore Poulon, would have done in a similar situation. If unarmed, like Jens, he'd have called for backup. As had Jens.

Did that make him a coward?

He glanced up at the balcony. Ferdie was no coward.

Her weapon drawn as a precaution, she kneed open the door and advanced, though convinced that Laurent was no longer there.

179

She reappeared on the catwalk outside room 217, shaking her head and confirming the obvious.

Jens watched as she keyed her mini two-way radio attached to the collar of her uniform and called for a BOLO, be on the lookout, for Laurent, a possibly armed and dangerous ex-con.

She gestured for Jens to join her up in the room and he climbed the shabby stairwell to the catwalk leading to room 217.

Taped to the mirror, apparently left behind in Laurent's haste, was an older publicity picture of Jens from a yellowed news clipping, along with a tattered map of Lee with an "X" marking the location of Jens' farmhouse.

If this was the only picture Laurent had of him, it was easy to see why Laurent had been slow to react in the motel office. As for Jens, recognizing Laurent had been instantaneous.

The one thing that Jens hadn't anticipated was how big, how formidable, how intimidating the ex-con was. And this was the man Vivian had been screwing? He burned with anger and shame.

Meanwhile, Ferdie miked her radio, sending a patrol car to Corbin's home in Lee to protect Vivian and Teddy, repeating the BOLO on Laurent.

"We'll get him, don't worry," she reassured Jens as they trudged down the stairs to the parking lot. "Cons like him have few friends and no place to hide."

Chapter Thirty-Eight

While Laurent was breaking into an isolated cabin in nearby Northwood Meadows Park, where he planned to hide out for the next few days, hopscotching from one unoccupied hiker's hut to another, Jens was weaving through Portsmouth's bustling lunch time crowd on Market Street.

He was headed to the professional building around the corner, wedged between two upscale seafood restaurants and a tourist trap selling nautical knickknacks.

His attorney's office.

Exhausted from troubled sleep, his adrenals squeezed dry by worry, he climbed to the loft floor of the restored warehouse on Bow Street. Weeks ago, though it seemed like days, Jens had sat with his agent Jean at the dockside restaurant below on ground level, quaffing gin and tonics, riding the rip curl of his enthusiasm for his book about stolen children.

He remembered glancing up that day, mid-pitch, at the neat chrome and glass condo balconies clinging to the ledges of the high-rent wharf district and thinking how blue-collar Portsmouth had been sold out to stockbrokers and lawyers from Boston and New York. Now, as he dragged himself up the last few steps of one of those very same properties, on a mission to get custody of his son in his impending divorce battle, he too felt beaten and sold out. Sold out, in his case, by a vindictive woman to whom he'd given himself body and soul. Hadn't he? To a cheater with a shady past.

He rang the buzzer alongside the brass plate with his friend's name embossed in raised script: *Vincent Polcarpi, Esquire, Divorce & Family Law Practice.*

The door lock released. He pushed inside and stepped up to the reception desk, commanded by a middle-aged brunette wearing too much makeup, in a silk blouse and half-glasses on a gold lead, the glasses resting on her ample breasts. She flashed him a professional smile, urging him to speak.

"Jens Corbin," he stammered self-consciously. "12 o'clock appointment."

She agreed but only after consulting her computer screen. "Please have a seat, Mr. Corbin." She gestured to the leather couch and recliner comprising the focus of the spot-lit waiting area. "He won't be long."

Lost in thought, Jens stood at the plate glass window partaking of the magnificent view of the harbor — its tugboats, wharf, and three bridges to Maine arching hundreds of feet over the wide Piscataqua River.

He sat down on the couch facing the coffee table, a round glass top balanced on a dramatic trunk of driftwood. Opposite, in a glass case mounted in an alcove of the wall, sat a to-scale whaling ship, replete with linen sails and knotted hemp ropes, its varnished hull reconstructed in authentic detail.

He smiled at his friend's acquired taste in décor, finding it pretentious. It was a far cry from the dusty, plastered dorm rooms and gouged desks that he and Vinny once shared, decades ago at the university, as undergraduates.

Jens had just enough time to wonder what kind of lawyer he himself might have made when the door to his friend's office opened to reveal a balding, middle-aged man, looking as harried as Jens felt. The man cast a hopeful glance backwards as Attorney Polcarpi, Vincent, propelled him out with a reassuring nod.

Vincent turned his sharp gaze on Jens, and his face broke open in a wide grin that looked indecorous for a man in a Hugo Boss suit and gold necktie.

"Jens, c'mon in!" He took him by the arm and drew him into a bear hug.

He ushered Jens into his office, shut the door, and steered him toward a deep leather armchair. He cracked open the door — to tell the nosy receptionist that he wasn't to be disturbed —

then closed it.

"How have you been?" Jens asked as he watched his friend pour generous splashes of designer bourbon into crystal tumblers.

"Excellent. Wish I could say the same for you, Jens."

They sat opposite one another, sipping their drinks, appraising each other.

"You're looking good," said Jens, relaxing — with the help of the whiskey — for the first time since the beginning of his ordeal only a day and a half ago. "You've done well," he added, looking around.

"Thanks. Not bad for a kid from *Dov-ah*," he said, mocking the accent of the locals from the next town over. He put down his drink and opened his hands, inviting Jens to begin.

"So, tell me, what's been going on?"

———

In a rush of angst, Jens recounted the events of the previous day, explaining his motive, once served with divorce papers and a restraining order, for driving down to Lee to see his *wife*, to try to talk reason and to see Teddy. He recounted his mistreatment at the hands of the two Mutt-and-Jeff sheriffs summoned by Vivian, and her outrageous lie accusing him of threatening to slash her face with a broken wine glass. He told of his near run in at the motel with Laurent, the dangerous, jealous ex-con Vivian had been consorting with.

When Jens reported that Officer Morrison, Ferdie, had put out a BOLO on Laurent and round-the-clock protection for Teddy and Vivian, Polcarpi acknowledged that he was in good hands; that Ferdie, a personal friend, would stay on the case until she got "the SOB" and put him back in jail, where he would no longer be a menace to Jens or anyone else.

"How could Vivian do this to me?" Jens lamented. "This is how she thanks me? By bringing danger into our lives and destroying everything we've worked for?"

Vincent studied his manicured hands, folded in his lap. He opened them wide, in a gesture of fake humility.

"I don't claim to understand women — I guess that's why I tend to defend men — and I don't agree with the tactics that the law and society permits them, to compensate for their vulnerability. But, in all fairness, I know that there are always two sides to the story. Since you've come to me, I'm taking your side."

Jens put his drink aside, sensing what was coming.

"With that said, there are two ways we can do this. One is you put your tail between your legs and hope for the best." He glanced at Jens, gauging.

"And the other?" Jens' voice shook.

"We go after your soon-to-be ex-wife tooth and nail to get what's yours. And we have to act fast. Using every trick in the book. Are you with me?"

Jens nodded for him to go on.

"We freeze the marital assets, get an injunction allowing you to enter the home and remove your personal belongings."

Vincent paused, interrupted by Jens' sudden agitation.

"I forgot all about my bank account — it's been frozen. She got my password."

Polcarpi clapped his hands together and raised them, imprecating the gods.

"My friend, you have been gaslighted. I hope it's not too late."

"I've got a right to see my son, don't I? He *needs* me."

"Only after the case has been heard, because of the restraining order."

"Can't you get that lifted?"

"I can try."

"Isn't there something I can do?"

"There is. But you may not like it. You say she's been with Laurent and he's been stalking you. Okay. Let me put my hound dog on it and prove it. She'll be the one with a restraining order, maybe even do some jail time if she's been complicit with her lover in robbing you. It's bound to get ugly, but in my opinion it's your only choice."

Jens shook his head. "I won't put Teddy through that."

"Why not? She's going to drag you down in your son's eyes. I'll put my best detective on it. She'll trip up — they always do."

Jens nodded slowly, his eyes downcast, acquiescing.

"If it will protect my son ... do it."

"Okay." Polcarpi stood, as if to start on his calls. "I'll notify the court and her attorney. Who's representing her, by the way?"

————

At reception, Jens handed Molly his credit card, authorizing her to draw $5000 dollars for Vincent's retainer. She handed it back to him almost immediately.

"I'm sorry, Mr. Corbin, it indicates you've reached your credit limit. Do you have another card you'd like to use?"

"No ... yes. Please try it again," he said, rattled. "I have a $25,000 limit on that card."

He watched her with dread as she swiped another card. She handed it back to him. "What about American Express?"

He let out a moan. When Vincent came out to see what the problem was, he shook his head knowingly.

"Don't worry, Jens, I know you're good for it."

Chapter Thirty-Nine

Jens spent the next few days working with Vincent and waiting for the court order that would allow him to remove his personal articles from the home in Lee that he'd shared with Vivian and Teddy. He was too nervous to write, and besides he'd left his laptop with the chapter files from *Forsake Me Not* at the cabin in Conway.

Instead, he bought a bottle of gin and drank alone in his room, at a different motel, leaving SMS texts for Teddy that went unanswered, and feeling as though he'd stepped off into an alternate universe, one devoid of familiar signposts, emotional or physical.

Vincent hadn't been able to restore his funds, as they'd been removed before the divorce papers were served with exquisite timing by his wife, depleting their joint account legally, if not morally. They'd get it all back in court, he'd promised. Push came to shove, Jens could always put the cabin up for sale — and live where?

Jens couldn't believe that this was the same woman he'd trusted all these years. Why hadn't she made her move earlier, when he was flush with celebrity and cash from movie options and royalties after his Poe Award? Back then, he'd been able to plunk down $275, 000 in cash for his cabin in Conway.

Nothing made sense. Especially not Teddy's silence. Why didn't he reach out to his father? He sank deeper into a funk; the only thing buoying him was the conviction that he needed to be there for his son. Meanwhile, there was no word on Laurent. Ferdie speculated that Jens had spooked him. He was likely in the wind and far away, perhaps over the border into Canada.

In the meantime, Jens hadn't been idle: he'd made a search of the homeless and indigent shelters around the seacoast, looking for Laurent. He'd even checked the bridges and culverts in the

Portsmouth area where the homeless were known to bivouac.

But he had uncovered nothing, no trail. Still, he was not ready to give up. As soon as he could get to a computer, he'd research Laurent on the Internet, sussing out his virtual tracks if there were any.

On the morning of his third day of waiting, Vincent's receptionist-secretary Molly, whom Jens suspected of having an affair with her boss, called on Vincent's behalf to tell him that it was okay for him to pass by the house in Lee and retrieve his belongings.

Vivian would not be there then; arrangements had been made with the Lee Sheriff's Department to handle his visit at 11 A.M., and make sure he didn't remove any property that might be considered a marital asset.

Jens thanked her, then showered and dressed, his heart heavy. If only he could see Teddy, but the court had made that off limits. On a ray of hope, he sent Teddy an SMS telling him that he would be at the house at 11, and that he should meet him there, if possible.

Happily, the sheriff waiting for him was not one of the ones who had put him down on the ground and mistreated him. He was grateful for that. Deputy Chen was polite if distant as he opened the front door with a key to the new lock, making Jens feel estranged, an intruder in his own home. Nevertheless, he thanked him and stepped inside. His shock prompted the deputy to ask him if he was all right. Jens propped himself by the arch to the living room.

"Give me a minute."

"What's wrong?" asked the deputy. "You having difficulty breathing?"

Speechless, Jens gestured at the walls, bare where dark oblong and square shapes unbleached by sunlight marked the places where his paintings had hung for years. He staggered on, into the living room and recreation room, then up the staircase to the second floor, all the while registering his losses. The deputy kept pace with him, understanding his distress.

"My God!" exclaimed Jens. "She's taken it all — every last piece of art! Can she do that?"

The deputy merely shook his head in sympathy. "Nothing restrains her from removing assets before she filed for divorce."

"But all our assets were frozen."

Deputy Chen shrugged. "She beat you to it, I'm afraid."

"Bloody hell!" Jens put his hands to his head to keep it from exploding.

"I suggest you advise your attorney. In the meantime, we need to get on with the business of removing your personals."

———

Under the vigilant eye of Deputy Chen, Jens loaded his diaries into boxes to take down to the car. When Jens started to disassemble his desktop computer and monitor, the sheriff came to life.

"Sorry, Mr. Corbin, that stays."

"What do you mean? It's my property — I need it to conduct my business. I'm a writer."

"I know that, sir." He glanced at the shelves where copies of Jens' novels were stacked, some with foreign titles, in translation. "But the court will need your harddrive in order to assess marital assets. I'm sure you understand."

Jens collapsed into his desk chair. "I give up."

The sheriff nodded sympathetically.

"Can I at least copy some files relating to my book?"

The deputy considered. "Why not. Though I'll have to verify what you download."

Happily, Vivian hadn't bothered changing the password he'd given her.

Jens thanked him and went to work copying his files from *Forsake Me Not* onto a thumb drive. Afterwards, Deputy Chen helped him downstairs with his diaries, clothes, and personal items, and Jens loaded it all into the Subaru.

"Thank you for your help. You've been very decent." Jens considered adding a remark about his colleagues who had assaulted him, but thought better of it, deciding to leave himself at least one ally on the Lee PD.

———

He had just turned out of the driveway and was driving east on Mast Road when a figure rushed from the bushes at the side of the road and flagged him down. It was Teddy. Jens hit the brakes and slowed long enough for Teddy to jump in.

"Go! Go! Drive!" Teddy swiveled around to see if anyone saw him getting in.

"You okay?" Jens floored it and they sped away.

"I'm fine." He looked back. "Let's get out of here. Mom still thinks I'm at school picking up my schedule."

"Good God! Are you being kept prisoner? Why haven't you returned any of my texts?'

"Mom took my phone away. She said the court forbid me from talking with you. Can they do that? Anyway, I convinced her now that school was starting that I would need it for her to pick me up and for emergencies. That's how I knew you'd be here — your text."

"Jesus!" Jens shook his head in dismay. "I wish none of this was happening. Never saw it coming — otherwise I would have taken you with me."

"I know. It's not your fault. This really sucks."

"You're telling me."

Jens was driving too fast for the road, sliding into the curves and crabbing back onto the straightaway.

"Slow down, Dad. This isn't *The Bourne Legacy*."

They laughed. Out on the west coast, when Teddy was small, Jens had owned a red-and-white Mini Cooper, an original, just like the one in the first Bourne movie. He'd shown Teddy pictures of it, even bought him a miniature model. It was a family legend and joke.

Jens slowed to the speed limit. "You hungry?"

———

Jens decided that it would be best if they went someplace far enough from Lee so that he wouldn't be spotted in violation of his restraining order. He drove to a sub shop in Stratham and parked around back.

As soon as they were out of the car, Jens locked his son in a bear hug; Teddy hugged him back. They remained that way for a while, neither wanting to break the spell.

"It's great to see you, son."

He nodded, ducking his head between his shoulders to hide his tears.

Seeing his embarrassment, Jens turned away.

"What do you say we do justice to a couple of footlongs," he said heading for the restaurant.

Teddy pushed ahead to hold open the door. "I've been working out at the gym," he bragged. He flexed for Jens.

"Impressive. What about this?" he said, putting a hand on his son's head and squeezing gently. "This getting any kind of a workout?"

Teddy flicked his hand away with a fake karate chop.

"Not to worry, this year's going to be a breeze after Exeter."

They ate silently, devouring their subs, stopping to take long pulls on the soft drink they shared with two straws, as was their habit since Teddy was old enough to have Coke. Jens couldn't have been happier.

So," he said in between bites, "How're you doing, really?"

"Good, good." Teddy swallowed the last bite of his sub and

washed it down with soda. "School starts next week. Picked up my schedule today. Really looking forward to Algebra II," he added with an ironic grin.

"Hah! I'll believe that when I see it. How're you doing at home?"

Teddy squirmed. "I'm between a rock and a hard place, Dad. I don't want to betray Mom, and I don't want to betray you. And she needs me around, to keep going."

"But you're being treated all right, aren't you?"

"Sure." He smiled. "I get to play Xbox whenever I want. But I've got to help with vacuuming and emptying the dishwasher more, now that it's just me and her."

"There's no one else?"

"Like who? Laurent?"

Teddy stared ahead, as though distracted by an inner vision.

Finally: "Dad, I don't think you should plan on getting back together with us."

"Does that mean you'd rather stay with Mom?"

Teddy swallowed, cleared his throat. "It's not like that. You know I love you — but I've been talking to some of my friends whose parents are divorced, and they say nine out of ten times the mother gets custody."

"What do *you* want to do?" As soon as he said it, he regretted it.

"I want to stay with both of you."

"Teddy, I just want what's best for you. If you decide to stay with Mom, I'll understand. As long as you're safe."

Privately, he felt hurt that Teddy would choose Vivian over him. He'd believed their manly camaraderie was more important to Teddy than his mother's affection. Another illusion evinced.

Teddy nodded, looked away.

"I know she's been unfair to you — taking all the money and the paintings. But she's afraid. She wants to be on her own, but she's petrified she's going to fail — and you'll laugh at her."

"I know. That's one of her biggest fears." Jens didn't know what else to say. *He* was the injured party. How could he forgive her? Why?

"There's something else ... you know how ... ah ... discreet she can be, taking her phone calls in private, leaving the house without explanation, giving none when she gets back?"

"Isn't she working now? At one of the galleries in Portsmouth? Is that where she's selling off our art?"

"Naw, she put it in storage — until after the divorce. For safekeeping."

"Not going to sell your 'college paintings' is she?"

Teddy smiled. "Never." He paused. "She told me a story — about when she was young." He seemed to be weighing his words. "She said she'd made some mistakes, mistakes that hurt people, and now she's paying for it."

He toyed with a potato chip on his plate.

"She shuts herself in her room and cries on the phone. I don't know who she's talking to. It's not Laurent. Sometimes she raises her voice; other times she's sad and compliant. Afterward, when I ask her if there's something I can do for her — God! I'd do anything to see her happy again — she smiles sadly, says that she's paying for the sins of her youth and soon it will all be over. But I don't know, Dad. I'm worried. *Really*."

Chapter Forty

Seated at the kitchen table where he liked to work when he was at the cabin in Jackson, Jens finished the line he'd been working on, gauging its specific gravity, its rhythm and import, before going to answer the phone on the counter nearby.

Seeing his son again had restored his will to continue with *Forsake Me Not.* He would write the best damn book he could — it was the least he could do to thank the gods for a son like Teddy, and the gift of immortality, bestowed by fatherhood.

Some days, he pumped out as many as fifteen pages, a record set with his first novel, when in the grip of his story he'd written an entire book in three and a half months. Now, some twenty years later, he was gratified and thankful for his current productivity. Whether the pages he wrote were good or bad, he did not know, though he suspected they hit the mark. He'd learned a long time ago not to prejudge or censor what he wrote until much later, when he could view it with detachment.

Aside from his lawyer, his agent, and the occasional telemarketer, no one called him on the land line except for local purveyors, whom he contacted for food and liquor deliveries when he didn't want to be distracted from writing.

He picked up the phone. "If this is about life insurance, pain-free urinary catheters, or cremation at sea, I'm hanging up."

There was a girlish laugh on the other end of the line. "I'm nervous enough as it is calling you."

"Nola?" He tried to keep the excitement out of his voice. "How are you?"

"Before I answer that I want to tell you that I got your number from Trooper Morrison —"

"Dear Ferdie."

"Ferdie, yes, she said you were up here on your own."

"Did she tell you I'm on deadline and can't be disturbed?"

Did Nola know about the divorce filing? he wondered. Had she heard about the restraining order and the accusations? There was a pause on the other end of the line.

"Do you *want* to be disturbed?"

"Yes. No ... Yes."

"Oh, okay, I'll leave you alone."

Ironic and serious, thought Jens. He liked that.

"Where are you?"

"Down the mountain from you — at the Wentworth Hotel," she said, tentatively.

Jens looked at his watch, trying to decide whether he should put in another hour, reluctant to abandon his protagonist Cassie just when she was in danger.

He glanced at his watch again. "Give me half an hour."

"I'll be waiting ... on the veranda." She hung up, leaving him to ponder whatever innuendo might be extracted from her factual declaration.

———

There's nothing to feel guilty about. I'm just going to have a drink, one drink, with an ex-student, now a mature woman, who probably wants some advice or help with getting a story published.

Best not to nudge that white lie too vigorously, he told himself, concluding, sadly, that the capacity for self-delusion in matters of the heart is inseparable from the male ego, and only worsens the older one gets.

———

The rain was heavy as Jens parked in the lot behind the Wentworth Hotel, not wanting to be indiscreet by using the valets, notorious for rumoring about locals. He wasn't sure if adultery could be used against him in the divorce, which was scheduled to come before a civil court judge in a few weeks. He'd have to ask Vinny.

For a moment he considered calling off the rendezvous. He wasn't ready for this. He still had feelings for his wife, though she'd betrayed him in the worst possible way.

His reservations multiplied. What would this do to his writing? Would a lover distract him? How would this affect his relationship with his son?

What did Nola see in him anyway? The age gap was discouraging. Though fit, his body was starting to show embarrassing signs of aging, no matter how often or how hard he worked out. When he'd run into Nola at the hospital a little over a month ago, he'd been titillated and flattered, but he hadn't expected things to go any further.

I can't do this.

Her rap on the driver's window shocked him out of his reverie. There she was, holding an umbrella against the wind and rain, her red hair framing her face, her eyes bright under arched brows, lips lush, poised.

She looked great.

"Come with me!" She pulled open the door. "It's too late to back out now!" she added with a knowing laugh, as he scooted under her umbrella.

"Hi."

Surprising himself, he kissed her before she could object.

She looked at him, smiled archly, but didn't kiss him back. The rain pummeled the umbrella. A blast of wind nearly ripped it from her hands.

"Let's get inside."

She took his arm and drew him to the hotel's rear entrance.

Jens couldn't help but wonder if he'd made an awful mistake. There's no fool like an old fool, he told himself. He walked alongside her, sharing the awkward intimacy of the umbrella, obsessed with the idea of extricating himself from this embarrassing situation as soon as possible.

Before he made an even bigger fool of himself.

———

In the restaurant, the glow of candles on the white linen tables seemed a message to Jens, that he was playing with fire, though he was grateful for the psychological cheer they imparted on such a cold, rainy day.

A waitress eyed them as they passed. Jens couldn't help thinking that she disapproved or, worse yet, assumed they were father and daughter.

Vivian was not much older than Nola. Is this what people thought when they'd seen *them* together? That she was his daughter, too?

Nola, seeming to sense his thoughts, drew him to her in an embrace less than filial, her breasts brushing against him. She smiled and drew him to a cocktail area with low couches and a view of the garden. A fire blazed in the fireplace along one wall, and they sat down, side by side but not touching, facing the fireplace to thaw. The waitress took their order of a vodka martini with olives for Nola, and a scotch on the rocks for Jens, his winter drink.

Jens began to recoup his confidence, commenting, like the academic he was, on the romantic wildness of the garden whipped by wind and rain. Pointing out to her the calendulas and larkspur bent over in throngs; the perennials and roses, petals stripped, pooling in red and pink drifts.

"Thomas Praz's *Romantic Agony* comes to mind," Nola said, following his gaze out to the garden. "The sublimity of untamed nature, wherein nature mirrors the moods of man —"

"— and vice versa," Jens cut in excitedly. "Man reflects and amplifies nature."

"Corresponding to the overflow of feeling —"

"Of awe, terror, apprehension and —" Jens glanced at her with anticipation.

"Horror!" she added dramatically.

"Lest we not forget erotic sensibility."

"Stoker's *Dracula*."

She brushed a wing of damp red hair from her face, exposing it to the heat from the fireplace to dry.

"Dikstra's *Idols of Perversity*." She arched her brow.

She seemed to be enjoying their repartee as much as he, noted Jens. He smiled and pointed to her hair. "Red: blood and passion."

"Corrupted by lust." There was a twinkle in her eye.

"Hair as an effluence of feminine sexuality."

"Ibsen's *Hedda Gabler*." She separated another lock of hair to dry.

"Now you've left the romantics for the realists."

Their laughter drew glances from early diners filing in, staid couples and nuclear families with well-behaved, scrubbed children. Just then the waitress arrived with their drinks. If she had an opinion about their relationship, she didn't let it show.

"Will you be dining with us tonight?" She directed the question to Jens.

He exchanged looks with Nola. She nodded.

"Then I'll reserve a table for you."

She smiled, gesturing to an intimate table facing the French windows.

"Overlooking the garden," she added, leaving no doubt in Jens' mind that she had decided theirs was not a father and daughter dalliance at all, but the infinitely more intriguing liaison of winter and spring. *Autumn and spring*, Jens corrected himself.

"Thank you." He turned back to Nola. "Where were we?"

"I believe we'd just abandoned passion corrupted by lust for a full head of hair." She stroked hers unconsciously.

"Nola, I had no idea. You're missing your calling. You should be teaching — and writing."

She shook her head. "Thanks. You think so?"

"My word! You know a lot about the romantics. Where did you get it from?"

"From your Comp. Lit. class."

"Really? And I thought nobody was listening."

"I was." She stared at him pointedly without blinking.

Feeling awkward, he sipped his scotch and she her martini. They stared at each other. Jens recalled his earlier discomfort when he'd kissed her out in the parking lot. He took a deep breath.

"My wife has filed for divorce."

"I know."

"Did you know that she has a restraining order on me — I'm not allowed within twenty-five yards of our home or her person?"

She nodded, adding uncertainly, "Okay."

"She says I assaulted her — hit her and threatened to cut her face with a smashed wine glass."

She stared silently into his eyes.

"I did not lay a finger on her."

Again she nodded. "I know."

"How?"

"Ferdie told me everything. What she did to you behind your back."

Jens shook his head. "I don't know what you want from me. I'm in deep financial shit, I've lost everyone and everything I love, I'm writing a book on a prayer, I'm older than —" He choked on his words.

"Hence the noble overflow of feeling." She winked.

His laugh was charged with sorrow, an apt fusion for a man in his position, he thought.

"Blood and passion," he answered, his voice growing stronger.

"Lust." She smiled suggestively.

The waitress arrived and led them to their table, nodding with approval as she took their order. Later, they rented a room at the hotel, he going first, she following after a discrete time.

———

Jens lay awake in the king-size bed, luxuriating in its opulence, inhaling Nola's intoxicating aroma, floating as though on a cloud of happiness and pheromones.

The place beside him was still warm from her body, and her pillow retained her impression. If he looked beneath the covers, he was sure he would find a snow angel where she'd lain, like the ones he and his brother made in the first snow of winter.

After bestowing a tender parting kiss, Nola had opened the window before she left for work at the hospital. The lace curtains stirred, brushing and caressing him. A diverse assembly of birds, active for some time, quipped back and forth, exchanging pleasantries. They echoed Jens' state of quiet bliss.

He couldn't remember being so happy, not since Teddy's birth, not since his first book deal, and not since the Poe Award launched his career for real.

But this was different. There was no need for fanfare. This, rather, was the joy of stumbling upon one of life's deepest mysteries — how the tuning fork of attraction sends shock waves of renewal down to the very roots of our being. Nola's touch had riven and resurrected. Where it would lead, he did not know. But he would follow — oh, would he follow — of this he was certain.

But for now, he had a book to write, a divorce to resolve, bills to pay, and a son to keep on the straight-and-narrow, regardless of whether the boy was living with him or his mother. For now, there was very little he could do about most of his problems. As for the book, he was confident he was going to meet his deadline: he had one hundred pages to go and the chapter outline.

Jens rose and entered the shower stall. He let the water run hot until steam billowed, before turning it down enough to bear.

He was grateful for the seemingly limitless supply of hot water provided by the better hotels like the Wentworth. His designer log cabin was short on hot water, and the undersized water heater took forever to reheat, especially after one of Teddy's notoriously long showers. Often, Jens' best ideas came to him here, in the shower, or in a steam bath, distracted by sensation.

He found himself picking up the thread of yesterday's writing. Cassie had managed, with Tommy Flaherty's last minute intervention, to extricate herself from the trap Orozco had set for her at a condo in Puerto Vallarta. Today. Jens planned to set the stage for the "honeymoon scene" — the sequence in a thriller when the action slows enough for the protagonist to take stock. The lull before the storm, often taking the form of a romantic interlude.

Cassie had been wounded in the confrontation — a flesh wound luckily — which Tommy insisted on doctoring himself, as he didn't trust the local doctors, or so he said. The bullet had grazed Cassie's thigh, providing the requisite romantic circumstances to unfold in Cassie's timeshare at the shore.

Jens turned off the water and toweled off, satisfied that he could see far enough into his story to have a productive day, bringing the work closer, brick by brick, to meeting his deadline.

As for the quality, he'd have to trust the muse with that. He smiled to himself as he dressed, warmed by the thought of his new muse, Nola. How different and rewarding it would be to have someone who understood him. They had talked long into the night, riding the crest of exhilaration, speaking their hearts.

He knew what she wanted — he was no fool — she wanted to become a writer. Theirs was to be an old-fashioned mentoring relationship, not unlike the kind he'd sought but hadn't found in Los Angeles, during his screenwriting apprenticeship. He knew their romance would flare and fade. He was a father figure, a teacher, and incidentally a lover. How long would it take for that part to play out? Months? Weeks or even days? What did it matter? His troubles would always be there.

But *this*, this was special.

Dressed, his hand on the doorknob, he turned back for a final glance at the love-rumpled bed, the wind-riffled curtains, the tepid moisture from his bath, now settling about the room like a metaphor for the aftermath of love.

Chapter Forty-One

The land phone in the kitchen rang and rang, awakening Jens with a start, his heart pounding. He stumbled in the darkness, down the hall to the breakfast nook and the phone.

"Hello." Silence. "Hello!"

Annoyed, Jens was about to hang up.

"Is this Corbin? *The* Jens Corbin?"

The voice that snaked over the wire reminded him of his deceased brother Nils. For a moment he wondered if he were hallucinating. He pushed aside his panic.

"Who is this?" he said, unable to suppress the tremor in his voice.

"Are you a thief, my friend?"

Jens could hear murmuring in the background, like someone giving instructions.

"What? What did you say?"

Nola, who had been asleep in his bed, came into the room, fully awake. Jens barely registered her hovering beside him.

"Prank call?" she mouthed.

He positioned the phone so she could hear.

"I said," the voice growled, "are you a thief, Corbin?"

Jens recognized the speaker's clipped vowels and sharp nasals typical of the North Country, where his wife — soon to be ex-wife — was from. *Where Laurent was from.*

Jens was wide awake now. "Tell me who you are or I'm hanging up."

"I wouldn't if I were you, pardner."

"I'm not your *pardner*. If you call back, I'll have the police trace you."

"You stole my lady. I'm going to make you pay."

Jens looked at Nola. She shrugged. Nobody she knew.

"Laurent? Is this you? Are you talking about Vivian? Is she

there with you?"

Nola touched his arm. "What should I do?" she mouthed.

He motioned for her to get his cell phone, hoping for at least one connecting bar.

"Call 911," he whispered. "What do you want?" he growled to Laurent.

"The police are tracking you down. You're making a big mistake."

Still, he ignored Jens calling him out by name.

"I want you to be smart, Mr. Crime Writer. *No* police."

"Is this a shakedown, Laurent? If so, you're wasting your time. I get it — you're a wannabe writer. Is this your idea of a pissing match?" *What was keeping Nola?* he wondered.

"How'd you like me to come over there and do that *redhead* you're with?"

Jens anxiously scanned the woods beyond the kitchen window.

Where is he?

"The cops are going to get you, Laurent — your cell phone is traceable. You'd better get the hell out of here. And leave me and my family alone," he shouted.

Nola came back with his cell phone, shaking her head, indicating there was no service. He pulled her down, out of the line of fire.

"I'm talking to you! I know everything about you. I can hurt you *good*," croaked the voice on the line.

"Vivian put you up to this, didn't she? The cops are on their way. You're going back to jail."

"Tell you what — that kid of yours — Teddy? I know where to find him — *oh yeah*. Bus from Oyster River High every day at 3:15, drops him off on Mast Rd. Got your attention now?"

"You lay a hand on him, I swear I'll find you —"

"Listen to me — $300,000 ought to keep him healthy. I know you can raise it."

"You must be joking. Look, I don't know what Vivian told you

—"

"The cabin, your corporate shell — sell it off. Otherwise..."

Jens was in shock. How could he know about that?

"I'll call you with instructions where and when."

"It's going to take time to find a buyer."

"Leave the cops out of this if you want to keep your son healthy. You dig?"

"How do I know this isn't a prank?"

"You left your wine glasses on the porch."

The phone went dead.

Jens exchanged panicked looks with Nola.

"Shit, he's out there. *NOW!*"

"What are we going to do?"

He duck-walked to the porch door to make sure it was locked. Visible on the table where they had been sitting earlier were their wine glasses. He shivered, feeling violated.

It made him realize what a fool he was — isolated in the woods, Laurent at large. New Hampshire's stand-your-ground law legalized his right to shoot an intruder on his property. Where was Daniel's gun now that he needed it?

Armed with an iron poker from the fireplace, he hunkered down with Nola behind the kitchen island, a strategic location, ready to fend off any threat.

Nola wanted them to escape in one of their cars parked in the drive, but Jens didn't want to risk them being sitting ducks if Laurent had a rifle.

They'd tried to call out on the landline for help, but there was no service after the caller had hung up. Laurent must have cut the line.

———

With dawn approaching, the bogeyman faded. They began to downplay the seriousness of the phone call. Still, like trauma victims with OCD, they kept peeking through the blinds.

Finally, when it was fully light out, Jens went onto the porch and scoured the woods behind his cabin. Theirs was the only property this side of the ridge.

"They're gone," he reassured Nola, though he was reluctant to go exploring without a weapon more formidable than a poker.

He went around to the front of the cabin where telephone lines were attached to the house. The line hadn't been cut, only disconnected. He wired it back up.

Inside the house, they breathed a sigh of relief when Jens confirmed that the phone was working. Nola, agitated, began making coffee to calm down.

"Shouldn't you call the Conway police?"

Jens shook his head.

"They're long gone. Besides, it will take the local cops at least a half hour to get up here. I'd rather talk to Ferdie — get her state troopers to hunt them down."

"Why don't you have a gun?"

She poured water into the German coffee maker.

"No, no guns." He hadn't told her about Nils yet.

"Up here in the woods? Don't believe in them?"

"Something like that."

"You said 'they'. Was someone with Laurent?"

"Just a feeling." He sat down at the breakfast nook.

"Obviously he's got a better network provider than you."

"Why?"

"He called you on a cell phone, so he had to have reception."

"Maybe we can get the police to track him."

She put a mug of coffee in front of him and sat down with hers.

"For blackmailers, they're pretty stupid. They should've given you a deadline to have the money. They came a long way just to threaten you."

"You think we're over-reacting?"

Jens was convinced that the caller was Laurent, calling at

Vivian's behest, to scare and intimidate him out of suing for Teddy's custody.

"One thing bothers me." Nola began cleaning up. "Would she use her own son as a pawn?"

Jens pondered this.

"Bottom line, I need to know if Teddy's all right."

"So call him."

"She keeps changing his phone on me so I can't."

"Ferdie will know what to do."

He stroked her cheek while he dialed and waited for Ferdie to pick up.

"Maybe you'd better sleep back in town until this blows over."

"You think the sex is all I'm about?" Her anger flared.

"You wouldn't be here if that's all it was."

She held herself back, reading him until she was certain he was sincere.

———

When Ferdie picked up, Jens told her what had happened. She promised to drive right over to the house in Lee and check on Teddy and Vivian. She wanted to send someone to look in on Jens and Nola, too, but Jens convinced her that the threat was over — for the time being.

Chapter Forty-Two

The blackmailers jumped into Warren's pick-up truck. Warren rolled it a short way down the steep incline before starting the engine, to ensure a silent getaway.

Corbin, he feared, may have been spooked enough to call the cops once he realized they'd been stalking him outside the cabin. This had not been part of the plan. Now they were sitting ducks for the cops patrolling Conway and Jackson's back roads. He gunned the engine and flew over a tar mogul, landing with a thump that rattled the flatbed.

On a bend of the road, he rolled down his window and hurled the chip from the burner phone they'd used to call Corbin.

Warren was cursing under his breath. He pounded the steering wheel.

According to plan, they'd driven up to Conway to view the property and to impress on Corbin how vulnerable he was and that they meant business. Fool that he was, Laurent had given their hand away by talking about Vivian. It wouldn't take the cops long to figure out who was behind this.

Laurent, riding shotgun, guiltily fiddled with the strap to the binoculars hanging at his neck — the ones used to watch Corbin and his girlfriend on the back porch.

"Get rid of those." Warren pointed at the binoculars. "Put 'em in the glove compartment." He gave him a sour look. "If we get stopped, *I'll* do the talking." *This time* hung unspoken in the air.

Meanwhile, Laurent looked like the recently-paroled con that he was. If stopped, they'd both go back to prison, and that was *not* going to happen.

Warren looked away in disgust.

Perched on the edge of the seat like a scolded child, Laurent stared dead ahead, ignoring all the log cabins similar to Jens's bordering the road. Most had for sale signs.

"You can't stay on my boat." Warren had been hiding him on his Boston Whaler moored at the marina in Newington — isolating him from Vivian until Warren was done with her. "I got too much to lose. When we get back to Portsmouth, you clear out."

"What's eating you, anyway?" Laurent glared at him.

"That bit about him being a thief, stealing your woman — that really blew it. He's going to think his wife is in on this, and go right to the police."

Vivian was in the dark about all of this; Warren had made sure of that. She just needed to be terrorized long enough for him to bleed her dry. Using Laurent to scare Corbin off was a perfect play. It would keep the disputed marital assets in Vivian's hands, for Warren to snatch up after the divorce. Laurent, meanwhile, was the ideal patsy: the fall guy. Warren knew he had to do something permanent about him, but for now he served a purpose.

Laurent pounded the dash. "Okay, okay. I was hyped. I wanted to scare him."

"I warned you," he fumed. "But you had to go and make it personal."

Laurent clenched his fists. "He's *not* going to the cops. Not if he wants to keep his son safe."

Warren shook his head. "I was never here."

"What d'you mean? You can't back out now."

Warren touched his Glock, hidden under the seat.

"I can and I will. This better not come back on me if you get pulled in."

"I thought you needed the cash — to cover the rip-off at the pot farm."

Warren snorted. "Who told you that?"

At the bottom of the ridge the development community gave way to farms on either side. Warren turned onto the secondary road and picked up speed.

"What about all your pot, from the harvest? Didn't you tell

me you'd been ripped off?"

"Still mine." Warren smirked.

"*You* ripped it off — conned your partners." *Now it's my turn to get fucked.* "If I collect, you're out?"

"You happen to notice all those for sale signs? Corbin will be lucky if he ever gets an offer." He glared. "Someone didn't do their homework, *pardner.*"

"He doesn't need to sell. He's got book and movie royalties. I don't get it." Then it came to him — *Vivian* was the one with the money. She'd lied to him, told him the marital assets were all tied up in divorce court. Corbin, though a one-time bestselling author, was cash poor.

Was Warren extorting her behind his back? Was that why Vivian had dropped him?

A cloud of hostility settled over them. They drove in silence, taking secondary roads to avoid police checkpoints on the highway.

Laurent considered the events of the last few weeks. Finally, it all came together.

So, that's how it is, he realized. *Warren's going after Vivian's money — he only needed me to get to her. Today was misdirection, to put me off track.*

By the time they got to Portsmouth, Laurent knew what he had to do. He wasn't surprised when Warren dropped him at the traffic circle, not at the marina.

"Give me a call in a couple of days, maybe we can still work something out," Warren told him insincerely before driving away. "Where you going to be if I need to get a hold of you?"

Laurent slammed the door.

"I'll be around, don't worry. I know where to find *you.*"

He set off for the marina, to move to another boat he knew was unoccupied.

Revenge, he consoled himself, was a dish best served cold.

Chapter Forty-Three

Vivian was exhausted from a long day at the State Street gallery "qualifying" prospective buyers who wandered in to look at the art on the walls and socialize, but hardly ever to buy.

The court had tied up what was left of the marital assets and Warren had drained her and Jens' accounts and maxed out their cards. She was left holding the bag, and needed to earn enough to cover the basics. It was tough, but she'd survive. She *had* to, for Teddy's sake.

She made her way to the municipal garage on Hanover Street, resisting the urge to stop for a drink at one of the many watering holes in town.

But she couldn't. She had to pick up Teddy at school, even though Warren had reassured her that as long as she stuck to their "bargain," denying any connection with Laurent that would endanger her share of marital assets or reveal his, Warren's, extortion, he would leave Teddy alone.

Half-dazed, she mounted the steps to the roof level, trying to remember where exactly she'd left her Volvo, confused from one day to the next.

The events since her life-changing first contact with her blackmailer — a man she now knew as a *real* killer from Hell's Kitchen, and not an accidental one like Laurent — had left her numb and drained. She thought back to her ordered, safe existence before Laurent, before Warren, when the hardest thing for her to stomach was a bad night with Jens.

Safety, security, beauty, love. Sanity. Gone, all gone.

She tried not to feel hopeless, but she *was*. Like a trauma victim, her brain churned with toxic acetylcholine, the stress transmitter. Still, she soldiered on, acting as if, hoping for the best.

Teddy was the only thing that mattered, and for his sake she had to keep up pretenses. *And not go to the police.* Warren, no dummy, knew all about her past. And if he didn't make good on his threat to harm Teddy, then he would make sure the divorce court learned about her previous marriage and her crimes. Destroying her in Teddy's eyes and likely eliminating her bid for custody.

In some ways, Warren was the same as her uncle who'd abused her as a teenager, threatening to kill her and Laurent if she hadn't gone along. Thankfully, Warren did not force sex on her as a manipulative tool. Though she knew it was dangling as a possibility, should she balk at following his orders. Repulsed, she imagined his cruelty in "lovemaking" would match his verbal abusiveness.

She clicked the Volvo's key fob and followed the reassuring *chirrup* of her car's locking system to a row of parked cars leading to the roof. Hers was in the shadows.

As she opened the door to get in, she felt a hand block her. Even before she heard the insidious voice of her personal demon, she knew it was Warren; he sent off a vibe, like a predator stalking and toying with its prey.

"Well, fancy running into you, Madam Corbin, or should I say, soon-to-be D'Arcy."

Vivian trembled with fear. She turned her face up to him, exposing her neck like prey hypnotized into surrendering.

"What do you want?" she asked, trying to keep the terror out of her voice.

He smiled.

"Get in, just a few last-minute pointers for your exciting day in court."

There was an odor emanating from him that made her gag. Sulphur, she decided, from his roofing contracts, mixed with cheap underarm deodorant.

"What's the matter?" he sneered. "Got something against the sweat of an honest working man?"

"I have to pick up Teddy," she said, talking through her gag reflex.

"Get in," he growled, "Or would you rather we pick him up together?"

Chapter Forty-Four

The autumn leaves had turned and the colors were high. So much color! Shades of orange, red, mauve, apple green! It was almost painful.

It was a sword slicing him up the middle, tenderizing Jens for the confrontation tomorrow in Dover, at the family circuit court, where he would learn the fate of his relationship with his son and sever ties with Vivian.

As he slowed to pay the toll on Route 16, his cell phone chirped with an incoming call. He glanced at the unfamiliar number.

"Hello," he answered hesitantly, as he tossed three quarters into the collection cage.

"Mr. Corbin, this is Dr. Reese, the assistant principal at Oyster River High. I've been trying to reach you all week."

"One moment, please." Jens pulled off the road and parked. "What's this about? Has something happened to Teddy?"

It was school hours and he thought instantly of Sandy Hook and Parkland. Schools were getting to be as hazardous as state department postings in Middle Eastern countries. His anxiety mushroomed when he remembered the blackmail call, threatening Teddy. Had he discounted it too easily?

"He's all right, isn't he?" asked Jens tensely.

"Don't worry, he's fine. However, there are some issues that I'd like to discuss in person. Are you free tomorrow afternoon?"

"Have you contacted" — Jens almost said 'my wife'— "Mrs. Corbin?"

"Well, that's just it. I've left numerous messages for her for over a week now. You're listed as an emergency contact. Is this the best number to reach you?"

"Yes." The news that Vivian had been unreachable flared his anxiety.

"Will four o'clock be okay?"

"Yes, fine." Jens assumed his court hearing would be finished by then; Oyster River was only one town away.

"Good, we'll hold Teddy over. He can join us after we talk."

"Can you give me some idea what this about? He hasn't been in a fight, has he?"

"I'd rather we talked tomorrow, Mr. Corbin."

Jens disconnected without saying goodbye. Why hadn't Vivian returned the vice principal's calls? That wasn't like her — she'd always been a responsible parent, despite her self-absorption.

Jens pulled back onto the highway, heading for the bridge to Newington. Traffic was moderate as he crossed the Little Bay, which sparkled in the noon sun like a tray of diamonds.

By the time he got to the Newington side, he knew he had to know everything about Vivian before facing her in court. He picked up his phone and speed-dialed Ferdie.

"Hi, Jens. Everything okay?"

He pictured her at her desk at state police headquarters in Epping, the blue from her computer screen casting shadows over her features.

He knew that she was one of only twenty-seven female New Hampshire state troopers and, as she'd told him, she constantly suffered harassment from male colleagues as well as civilians. Jens felt honored by her concern for him and his family. He tried not to take advantage. But this was about Teddy and she would want to know.

"I just had a disturbing phone call from Teddy's vice principal. He says he's been trying to reach Vivian all week about Teddy."

"What's Teddy done?"

"He'll only tell me face to face. I'm seeing him tomorrow, after the hearing."

"Why don't I swing by the house in Lee this afternoon and check up on them?"

"Would you?"

"Call you later."

"Thanks."

"Hang in there, *amigo.*"

"You, too, *amiga,*" he rejoined, to which she scoffed and hung up.

Jens sped up, weaving past slower moving vehicles, anxious to get to his meeting with Vincent. The final report from Spears, the private detective, was in, just in time for Vincent to use in the hearing. Jens would know, once and for all, if Vivian had been in on the blackmail call.

———

"He's waiting for you," Molly said, as she ushered Jens into Vincent's inner office. Jens was not surprised to see another man seated as he entered.

"Jens, I want you to meet Larry Spears. He's the guy I put on the investigation."

Spears, a solid-looking man in his thirties, extended his hand for Jens to shake.

"It's an honor, Mr. Corbin, *sir.*"

Vincent suppressed a laugh.

"Larry's ex-military, as you can see."

Jens sized him up. He was dressed in a tailored suit of gray, light-worsted wool, a rep tie, and Bostonian oxfords. Hair was short but longer than military. Jens nodded to himself as he took the man's hand, prepared to have his own crushed. There was iron in his grip but it was subdued. Jens thought he saw amusement in Spears' eyes, as though he was often misjudged as a brute.

"Larry was with the military police, Navy." Vincent motioned for everyone to sit.

"M.P., like Jack Reacher," Jens commented wryly.

"Reacher is supposedly Army. I'm Navy. We call it 'M.A.,'

Master at Arms, not M.P. You a Lee Child fan, too?"

Spears sat down and straightened the already perfect pleats on his trousers.

Jens smiled affirmatively.

"But then again, Honore Poulon outshines him in the personality department," added Spears affably. "Plus, he's homegrown."

Jens shot Vincent a look.

"I see Vincent's been filling you in on my *who's who*."

Amenities out of the way, Jens was anxious for Vincent to begin.

"Now, about your hearing tomorrow. I've got some good news. You'll be sitting in front of the Dover 7th Circuit Family Court and his Honor, Justice Bartholomew Neadeau." Vincent waited for the name to sink in.

"No, it can't be!" Jens said, surprised.

Vincent nodded back, gratified to see the effect the name from their mutual past was having on Jens.

"I don't believe it!" Jens said, laughing. "Brother Neadeau. Will I need to flash him the fraternity sign for him to remember me?"

"I spoke with him a few days ago. Don't be surprised if he throws the book at Vivian for absconding with your marital assets. She's been ordered to restore everything she took prior to her filing for divorce. Hopefully, your assets haven't been squandered."

"Look, I've thought this over. I want custody of Teddy — especially if she's sunk so low to use him in an attempt to intimidate me in court."

Vincent gave Spears a look that prompted the younger man to pull his pleats, shake hands, and leave.

"How much do you really know about your wife?"

Vincent, his fingers steepled, studied Jens.

Perplexed, Jens motioned him to go on.

"Before you gave me the okay to hire Larry, I did some

research of my own. You may be broke at the moment, Jens, but, aside from your art collection, you have considerable assets in book rights. You may not be on the bestseller list, at least not just now, but why not in the future? And suppose one of your old Hollywood contacts steps in clover and has the funds to make a movie of one of your books?"

"Anything's possible. Where are you going with this?"

"When you and Vivian married you signed a prenuptial excluding your intellectual properties from the marital assets, right?"

He handed Jens a copy of his prenup, which Jens had submitted to the court with all his other marital documents.

Jens perused the document. "Yes, that's it. So?"

Vincent smiled. "Good."

"Why good?"

"Did you know that Vivian was married before you?"

"What're you talking about?" Jens recoiled.

Vincent took a folder from his briefcase.

"Married at sixteen, to a local Berlin boy. The marriage was annulled." He sorted through the documents, extracted a marriage certificate, and gave it to Jens to read.

There it was, Jens thought, in black and white.

He scoured the document for the name of the party she'd been wed to.

When he spoke it aloud the tremor was back in his voice: "Armand Laurent."

He stared at the names on the certificate. He felt a fool. How had she kept it from him? Why? This surely was a woman capable of grand deceits, he conceded. The last seventeen years — all a lie. He shivered. How could he possibly trust her with Teddy? And now that Laurent had served his time, she jumped right back into bed with him.

Jens looked up, his face stony.

"This is news to me."

"I thought as much."

"Why was the marriage annulled?"

Vincent offered another document, a Xerox of a news clipping.

"This was taken from the archives of the Berlin New Hampshire *Daily Sun*, 1997. I had to pull some strings to get it out of archives."

Jens scanned the article about a teenage girl, her name suppressed as a minor, who had been a material witness in a local case of homicide in the second degree, or murder with intent. The convicted man had been sent to the New Hampshire State Prison for Men in Concord, maximum security, receiving a sentence of twenty years. The name of the convicted murderer jumped out at him — again.

"Armand Laurent. My wife's husband," he added, conscious of the irony.

Vincent nodded.

"Released recently, having paid his debt to society by serving his sentence in full."

"In August," affirmed Jens.

Vincent raised an eyebrow.

"She received prison letters from him, which Teddy intercepted. She claims not to have encouraged him."

Jens thought about finding the hunting blind at the farmhouse in Lee.

Now it all made sense: she was divorcing Jens to be with *him*. Still, some part of him refused to believe that the woman he'd been intimate with for so many years, the mother of his son, could have deceived him so thoroughly, for so long, making him believe that she'd loved him. All the while, she'd been biding her time.

"She's divorcing me for a convicted murderer? And she thinks she's going to get Teddy?"

Vincent sighed. "That's why I asked about the prenuptial. We might be able to disqualify her from *all* of the marital assets if she married you under false pretenses."

"Explain to me the part about the annulment."

"I don't know any more than this. I'll keep Spears on it."

Jens rubbed his forehead, frowned. "Vivian's the unnamed minor?"

Vincent shrugged. "The name was expunged from the record by court order. But we know it was her." He reached for the file on Vivian.

"Mind if I hold onto this?"

Vincent nodded. "Sure. We've got copies." He paused, deliberating.

"Don't spare me. What?" Jens tensed like a boxer taking a gut punch.

"According to the internet, Laurent came from money. His father owned the Berlin Paper Company. Vivian was from the wrong side of the tracks. Chances are they paid off Vivian and her family to make the marriage go away. Maybe Vivian went back to the trough one time too many, maybe she offered to sell Laurent's father her testimony to keep Laurent out of jail."

"Lot of conjecture."

"I'll have no problem raising the same doubts with the court about her checkered background."

"Okay, so she's a woman with a past. That doesn't make her a blackmailer."

"If she was involved with a blackmail scheme back then and we can prove that she's involved now, not only will she lose custody, but she'll never get a penny of yours."

Jens considered carefully before answering.

"What if you're wrong and she's the victim in all this? Where would she go if we leave her with nothing?"

Vincent rubbed his hands together. "Don't start waffling on me now, Jens."

"She's still Teddy's mother."

"Are you okay funding her affair with a murderer, who'll be around your son if he isn't already?"

"Would she really use her own son as a pawn?" Jens

wondered aloud.

Vincent smiled, an old pro at this business of divorce, making him a jaded judge of human nature.

"Anything's possible, my friend," he said, ushering Jens out to reception. "See you tomorrow in court."

Chapter Forty-Five

Vivian was perched at the bar at The Brewery, located on the upscale island of shops bordering the Cocheco River in downtown Dover. She'd hoped that the boisterous lunch time crowd would have thinned by 2:30 in the afternoon, but that wasn't the case.

Having consulted with her divorce lawyer earlier, to prep for the hearing the next day, she'd arranged to meet Franny, her confidant. Obviously, she'd said nothing about Warren to her attorney, though she'd been sorely tempted. And she had no intention of saying anything about her true predicament to Franny.

She sipped on her IPA and felt the ale's higher alcohol content go to her head, a welcome distraction, as she stewed in her juices, lamenting her miserable existence.

"Most definitely," she answered curtly, in response to a goateed young man asking if the seat next to her was taken. He was one of a series of idiots trying to hit on her — because she was an attractive woman, she was alone, and she was sitting at the bar. Must mean she wanted to get fucked, right?

I'm old enough to be your mother, for Christ's sake.

A few more beers, she told herself and my answer will not be so polite.

She'd been annoyed to have to find a seat at the bar, put her Coach bag on the stool next to hers to save it for Franny, and fend off the constant inquiries about its availability. Meaning, was *she* available?

Fuck, no! I'm not! I'm taken by killers!

She rebuffed them, second nature after a few beers — she'd lost count — which complimented the shots of vodka she'd downed at home while dressing and putting on her makeup.

I'm fine. Just fine.

But she wasn't and she knew it. Tomorrow she'd be facing Jens in court. How was she going to explain raiding their bank account just before filing for divorce? How was she going to explain all the crimes and misdemeanors since, committed at Warren's behest?

Taking up with Armand again. What was I thinking?

None of that mattered, she told herself, draining her glass in one long, satisfying draught that drew raised eyebrows from the *studderly* men — *is that even a word?* she wondered, realizing that she'd better slow down — who hovered, hoping if she drank enough ... well, you know.

Fug-the-fug off!

Where was Franny, anyway? Standing her up like this?

Armand had wanted to come over last night and comfort her but she'd quashed that idea without even telling Warren. The last thing she needed was his clingy ministrations in the name of love, while she worried about her son's safety.

Maybe it would be better if Jens had custody. Maybe Teddy would be safer.

Here she was, extricating herself from a marriage with a man who, truth be known, she *had* loved but never *really* loved, while trying to get rid of the man she'd *really loved*, but who had now become a burden. How had she let this happen?

Couldn't she have foreseen that Armand would have changed in prison? He was no longer the callow boy she'd easily manipulated in their teens, both of them swept away by hormones, desperation, and blind belief in their love.

Her innocence robbed earlier by a torturer, a blood relation— *my fucking uncle* — the power of sex had been there when she'd needed it, to *voodoo* Armand and make him love and rescue her.

And she really *had* loved him, too, with as much devotion as possible for a damaged young woman.

It wasn't his battered face and scarred body that marked his change — merely outward signs, which she barely registered.

There was, sadly, a deeper corruption, a cancer of the soul.

Ah, what's the use? she asked herself, feeling overwhelmed, just as she had been back then.

She glanced at herself in the mirror behind the bar and quickly brushed away her tears before the losers saw.

And now she had a vampire at her throat, sucking the life out of her.

Warren.

She doubted he'd let her go, even after he got his payoff.

And if he didn't?

"Fug! "Fug! "Fug!

The past was about to show its ugly face again. Her humiliation — the role she'd played in the drama leading up to Armand's arrest twenty years ago — was about to rubbed in her face like shit! All of it coming out in court now, in front of Teddy.

Oh, why? Why?

Tears ran down her face, streaking her mascara.

No Franny.

Everyone in her life had let her down: the father who'd died, leaving her unprotected; the mother who'd abused her, pimped her. Armand, who'd left her for prison and was leaving her now, because he'd changed.

Jens, even that damn Jens, for not loving her enough to make her resist Armand, and for not fighting hard enough to keep her.

She swiped away her tears and waved for her check.

There's Teddy, she thought, brightening. *Dear, dear, beautiful Teddy. The only thing that matters now.*

I've burnt my bridges with you, Jens, I'm so sorry, but I can't let you take the one good thing in my life.

She threw some bills on the bar without waiting for the check and pushed her way through the men — *always the men, with their reachy love and selfish needs* — still hovering, scenting after her like hyenas.

"Get the hell out of my way!" she bellowed, pushing them aside and stumbling drunkenly toward the door.

As she slammed out the door, she bumped into Franny, coming in. Taking in Vivian's condition at a glance, she put her arms around her.

"You poor darling."

Vivian sobbed as Franny led her away.

Chapter Forty-Six

Laurent, having broken into Vivian's house in Lee because he couldn't reach her via phone, went from one desolate room to the next, the bands of shadow and sunlight attuning him to the home's emotional desertion.

He passed kitchen counters cluttered with unwashed dishes. In the living room someone had slept on the couch, leaving a rumpled blanket and pillow. The walls flanking the stairs to the bedrooms were punched and gouged. Upstairs in the bathroom, the door ajar, a pile of soiled towels and clothing lay scattered. Finally, he arrived at the master bedroom, where the bed was stripped down to the mattress.

He sat down on the bed, choosing the side he remembered Vivian had slept on, though he suppressed the image of her making love to Corbin. The few times she and Laurent had been here together, she'd insisted on using the spare bedroom.

The slanted autumn sun shone warmly through the window, which looked out onto the woods beyond the backyard. Without thinking, his eyes sought out the shrub-encircled hunting blind where he'd hidden and spied on Corbin, when he'd first come to town. Though only months ago, it now seemed like a lifetime had passed.

He'd only wanted what others took for granted: love, belonging, hope.

Everything he'd once known as a child and assumed he would always have.

In sharp contrast to the shadow realm he now inhabited — a world devoid of meaning or purpose — without *her.*

Last night she'd begged him to let her go.

Now, he'd half-expected to find her in the bathtub lying in a pool of blood, wrists slashed. Or lying on the bed, an empty bottle of pills beside her, a peaceful look on her face — an angel released from the torments of life.

But she was gone. He swept his hand over her dresser top, caressing it as though his touch might bring her back. He would find her. And together they would go to a safe place, another country; or cross over, into the darkness.

Downstairs in the kitchen, he noticed the answering machine blinking. He clicked on the button for "messages," hoping for a clue to Vivian's whereabouts. The several messages from her realtor — begging her to call ASAP or lose *a very good* offer on the house — confused him, as he didn't understand why she needed the money.

There were several messages from a lawyer named O'Connell. And more than a few from a woman named Franny. And someone named Ferdie — a state trooper, apparently, to judge from her officious references to the hunt for him — left terse messages for her to call her, *ASAP*.

He was about to turn off the machine when he heard a familiar voice that went through him like a blast of adrenalin.

"You know who this is, my sweet," Warren crowed. "In the spirit of camaraderie — hah! — I want to wish us luck tomorrow. Call me on my burner as soon as you have the results of the divorce hearing. Oh, and regards to Teddy. Tata!"

She was sleeping with Warren!

Was she running away with him after the divorce?

Chapter Forty-Seven

After his meeting with Vincent and a failed phone call to Teddy, Jens checked into a bed and breakfast in Kittery, deciding to pay a little more for hospitality, as an antidote to loneliness. Luckily, he'd found a Discover card, apparently overlooked by Vivian, among his personals collected at the house in Lee. He could eat, buy gas, and sleep in comfort.

In his luxurious room, Jens stepped through sliding doors onto a patio, his senses tuned to the fresh smell of the Piscataqua River and harbor. The air was bracing. He let the ultramarine blue sky, peculiar to Portsmouth this time of year, wash over him.

Unwinding, he sipped his drink and told himself everything was going to be alright. Teddy was all that mattered, divorce notwithstanding.

He found himself contemplating the revelations about Vivian's past, learned from Vincent. Her life was no longer the open book he'd arrogantly presumed to know. And Laurent was a threat that could not be ignored.

Especially since Ferdie reported that Laurent had come back on the radar, a sighting at one of the marinas, perhaps drawn by Vivian's day in court. There was an all points bulletin out for his arrest. Jens almost wished the "shoot on sight order" was real, not just a legend from Bonnie & Clyde's time.

Yet, this was the man, concluded Jens, who'd made the crude threatening call to the cabin and talked about nabbing Teddy if he didn't cooperate. He'd been stalking him, in Lee and Jackson. He was a thorn in Jens' side. Maybe it was time for Jens to turn the tables on him. On an inspiration, he dialed Ferdie, getting her on her cell.

"Ferdie, hi. What can you tell me?"

"Fine, thanks, and you?" she said, half-trill, half-guffaw.

"Sorry, I'm a bit wound up. No Laurent yet, I take it."

"I thought you wanted to know about Vivian and Teddy."

"I do. That means bringing down Laurent."

"And how, pray tell, do you plan to do that?"

"We lay a trap for him, with me as the bait."

"Jens, you're a civilian. It's out of the question."

"Why don't you hear me out before you say no?"

"Jens ... I can't ..."

"Tell you what — let me buy you dinner. If you don't like my idea..."

"I can't — I'm having dinner with ... friends."

Jens read between the lines. She was going on a date.

"Oh ... okay, sorry I mentioned it."

The silence was palpable.

"Did you see Teddy today at the house?" he blurted. "Was Vivian there?"

"You like fish?" she asked with a sigh, ignoring his questions.

He started to answer but she cut him off.

"The Dolphin Club. One hour. I'll reschedule my dinner."

Jens wanted to tell her no, not to, not for him, but she'd hung up.

Chapter Forty-Eight

The Dolphin Club was packed when Jens arrived. He stopped at the reception desk on street level and confirmed that Trooper Morrison had made a reservation, but there was a seating delay and Jens was directed to join her at the bar until their table was ready.

Jens took the stairway down to the bar, with its windows giving onto Ceres Street, dense with tourist foot traffic at this hour. His eyes adjusted to the room's dim lighting, which stood in stark contrast to the Klieg spotlights over the veneered bar; here local seacoast players made their moves, dates displayed their "catches," and local celebrities held court.

Ferdie apparently fell into the latter category, noted Jens. Dressed in civvies — a dark blue pant suit over a white silk blouse open at the neck, showing her décolletage to advantage — she was perched in the pivotal seat at the "L" of the bar. Like a reigning queen.

Jens almost felt underdressed in an Oxford shirt and Docker trousers, all he could muster from his limited clothing supply in Jackson.

He pushed through the boisterous crowd to the place Ferdie had reserved for him with a rocks glass on a cocktail napkin. He slid onto his stool, taking in the discrete row of diamonds set in one of Ferdie's ears. On her wrist she wore an elegant bracelet which he recognized as an expensive Swarovski, with its trademark gold-plating and inlaid onyx. He'd bought something like it for Vivian, though less masculine, for one of their anniversaries.

"You look fantastic," he said, facing her and noticing for the first time two women watching her from a nearby high table, a blonde and a brunette, both in their late twenties.

They, like Ferdie, were costumed to fit in while standing

apart. They seemed tuned into him, warned of his arrival no doubt by Ferdie.

They were beautiful, thought Jens, who was fascinated by Ferdie's generation — as it made him aware of just how out of touch he was with Cassie, the youthful heroine of his novel, and what made her tick.

Ferdie seemed to sense his appraisal, blushed.

"Oh, am I not supposed to say that you look great?"

He noticed she was wearing a touch of lipstick, adding to her allure.

Her smile seemed to say she didn't mind.

"What are you drinking?" She had to raise her voice above the din.

"Black Label and soda." Jens mimed a twist for the attentive bartender, summoned with a nod from Ferdie.

Ferdie pointed a finger to her own near-empty martini glass and ordered a round for the two women, who returned her smile with ingratiating looks. When the drinks arrived, Ferdie stepped to their table and clinked glasses with them, exchanging a few words *sotto voce* that set them tittering, and eyeing Jens. Ferdie then led Jens to a high table against the wall.

"Old friends?" asked Jens, when she returned.

Ferdie sipped her drink. "New. Like you."

"How'd you meet?" he asked, realizing his impertinence.

"Tinder." Her eyes sparkled with amusement.

"Nice," he answered, not knowing what else to say. He raised his drink glass in a salute. "I appreciate what you're doing — "

Ferdie stopped him with an upraised hand.

"We're friends, despite your brusqueness on the phone."

"We are, aren't we?"

———

On the other side of town, Laurent was stealing a car. Not just any car — Warren's black pickup truck, parked curbside outside his house.

Having spotted Corbin as he entered the Dolphin, Laurent knew he had a short window in which to steal Warren's truck and get back to town, so that he could follow Corbin and run him off the road. Thereby killing two birds with one stone: get Corbin and implicate Warren for the murder, his truck the weapon.

Brilliant, he congratulated himself.

He bloodied his fingers tearing at the panel under the dash housing the wires connecting the ignition to the battery and starter motor.

He had to vamoose! Hopefully, before Warren looked out his front window, caught him in the act, and blew his brains out.

Finally, the screw holding the panel by a thread let go, and he pulled the bundled wires free. His hands shaking, he separated out the yellow, red, and green leads.

Please be green for ignition.

With his knife, a sling blade, he scraped ¼" bare spots on all three leads, careful to keep them apart. Then he attached double-ended alligator clips to the exposed wires.

He risked a look at Warren's front window — sensing more than seeing him — as he clipped the red lead to the green.

Is that him at the curtain?

Warren's front door banged open, followed by the *clonking* of his boots down the front steps and onto the sidewalk.

Fuck! He's coming!

Laurent touched the two leads to the yellow one from the starter. Sparks flew! He'd gotten it right!

Almost here! Oh, God!

"Motherfucker!" shouted Warren, his voice coming closer, louder. "I'll kill you!"

Motherfucker is right!

He touched them again! *Tzzt! Tzzt!* More sparks!

"Kill you, bitch!"

Oh, God! I'm dead!

Sparks flew from the contact. The engine cranked over, roared to life. Laurent sat up, jammed the shift into gear, stomped the gas pedal, and burned rubber.

He glanced in the rearview mirror just in time to see Warren taking aim. He ducked.

Blam! Blam! The rear window exploded.

Laurent flew around the corner — engine squealing, gears grinding.

"You're a dead man!" Warren shouted.

The wind roared through the shattered window, drowning out Warren's curses, filling the cab with cool night air and the promise of freedom.

Laurent barely heard him above his own disembodied laughter.

Warren, you're the dead man.

But tonight was Corbin's turn. With the divorce hearing tomorrow, a timely accident was just what was needed to get rid of him. Even if Vivian had told him it was over between her and Laurent. Even if she'd been cheating with Warren.

Didn't she deserve his forgiveness?

Unlike that bastard Warren!

He tore onto Islington, picking up speed, racing hell-bent for his appointment with death.

———

Jens and Ferdie sipped their drinks. Jens pushed his lemon twist around with a finger, waiting for Ferdie to report on her visit to the house in Lee.

"So," said Ferdie, taking her cue. "Teddy's fine. He's been working out a lot. He's a good kid. Funny, too."

"Did he talk about the trouble at school?"

Ferdie seemed to be weighing her words.

"Remember up in Conway, at the hospital, when I told you

about the Asian gangs coming into the seacoast?"

Jens nodded, his anxiety rising.

"They're here, at his school, giving him a hard time. Maybe because he's new and doesn't have a lot of friends."

"Is this what the principal wants to talk to me about?"

"He got into a little scrape —"

"*What?*"

"Calm down, *Dad*. Nothing's happened. He can take care of himself in that department, rest assured."

"I'm gone a month, I come back and find out my kid, my boy, is in a turf war with the Yakuza." Jens took a pull on his scotch. "What kind of scrape?"

"Phuket, you mean."

Jens cocked his head, thinking she'd said the "F-word".

"Excuse me?"

"The Thai Mafia — they're called Phuket. Yakuza is Japanese," added Ferdie pedantically. "And no, they're not in a war — at least not yet."

Ferdie took a thoughtful sip of her martini, puckering her mouth at the drink's astringency.

"They planted some pot in his locker and some pills, which turned out to be cold capsules, to make it look like he was dealing. I believe him when he tells me they aren't his, but he's having a hard time convincing the principal they're not."

Jens shook his head. "I've got a meeting at the school tomorrow — I'll straighten *him* out." He took a breath. "I don't get it. Why him?"

Ferdie shrugged. "He's new, he's from a private school, and his dad's a famous author."

Jens scoffed. "The sun's setting on that dream."

"Not to the locals."

"Ferdie, I've got to get him out of there."

"What are the chances you'll get custody?"

"I'll know tomorrow."

"Look, I'll vouch for him with the principal — say I'm a friend of the family."

"Thanks — you *are*."

Jens' innards churned. Hadn't he always defended his son, fiercely and foolishly, perhaps, sheltering him from all the knocks and scrapes of childhood? But now that he was in real danger, caught up in a complex social situation, Jens' instinct to charge in like a bull wouldn't work.

Ferdie clinked her martini glass against Jens'.

"I'll check up on the Thai kids. He'll be okay."

"He'll be okay when *I* get custody." Jens looked away.

"Trooper," interrupted a willowy blonde hostess, "your table is ready." She shot Ferdie an appraising look over her shoulder. Ferdie, as she passed her Tinder friends' table, signaled that she'd catch up with them after dinner.

———

Ferdie insisted on paying the bill for the excellent dinner, for which Jens was grateful, as his credit card was starting to max out.

He invited Ferdie for an ice cream at Danielle's on Ceres St. As they were leaving the crowded shop with their napkin-wrapped cones, Jens began talking about Vivian's marriage to Laurent.

"Victor thinks she may have tried to sell her testimony about Laurent to his defense team, and extort his parents."

They licked their cones as they walked along Market, gazing absently into window displays of souvenirs, nautical knick knacks, and art glass.

"So if you're not going to help me trap him, at least tell me what I can do to protect my son." Jens, hiding his anxiety, peered into a window display.

"Forewarned is forearmed," Ferdie answered. "You opposed to carrying?"

Jens looked away. "Me and guns — don't mix."

She nodded, waiting for him to go on.

"It's a long story — another time." Apparently, not everyone knew about his childhood trauma. Or maybe Ferdie knew but thought it best if he broached it.

They were approaching the public garage on Hanover St. where Jens had parked his Subaru. They finished their cones.

"You writing?" asked Ferdie.

"Always."

"Seriously, are you?"

"Seriously? Too many distractions. Not until I get back to Conway. My deadline is coming due."

"How's Nola?"

"Another kind of distraction," Jens said, with a touch of irony. "By the way, I got something for you."

He reached into his sport jacket.

"You still interested in Daniel's identity?"

He handed Ferdie the black & white snapshot he'd found in Daniel's wallet on Black Mountain.

"A face to go with the inscription on the back of his Rolex— 'With love, always, Leah.'"

Ferdie scowled. "Now you give it to me?"

Jens shrugged. He felt like he ought to give her a hug. Instead, they shook hands awkwardly, sticky from their ice cream cones, and went their separate ways — Jens to his car on the second level, Ferdie back to the bar and her Tinder friends, of whom Jens was jealous, sort of.

He drove down to the gate and paid his parking ticket.

After tomorrow he'd know where he stood on the matter of his son's custody. Maybe he could take him to live with him in Jackson. They must have good schools where a kid could get a decent education without having to fight off gangs.

He swung left onto Market toward the Sarah Mildred Long Bridge, which would take him to Kittery and the inn where he was staying. His thoughts drifted back to Laurent and the danger he'd brought to his family. This was a man who had nothing left to lose.

In his mind's eye, he pictured Laurent walking Teddy into the woods, a gun stuck in his back, readying to execute him.

In his scenario, Jens had no problem picturing himself with a shotgun aimed at the killer's heart.

Maybe it was time, as Ferdie suggested, to arm himself.

Chapter Forty-Nine

Parked in Warren's black pickup truck on Hanover Street, lights off, Laurent ducked down as Jens pulled out of the municipal garage and drove past. Laurent put the truck in gear and followed at a discreet distance.

Accelerating onto Market, Jens waved to Ferdie, a solitary incongruous figure — at once formidable and romantic. Jens was certain she would go back to the bar and enjoy drinks with her Tinder friends, maybe take one of them home, or both, bless her. Everyone needs someone to love, he conceded. He felt oddly protective of her.

As Jens passed the tugboat dock and then the salt piles, images of his misspent youth here on the seacoast crowded out his present anxieties. One winter, after his father had died and he'd cut off from his mother, he'd taken a cottage on the Little Bay in Newington and was trying to write. To make ends meet, he took odd jobs, like unloading the salt that came into Portsmouth on cargo barges, and laying trans-Atlantic cable in the holds of ships, at the cable factory upriver.

By the time he broke from his reverie, he was on the bypass, half-way across the bridge to the Kittery side in Maine. Flickering cones of light from the street lamps lighting up the bridge bounced off the swirling waters of the Piscataqua, rushing past darkly on either side of the two lane bypass. A line of cars came from the opposite direction, headlights glaring.

Suddenly, there was a car behind him, urgently flashing its high beams, trying to pass, despite oncoming traffic. It came closer and closer, nearly bumping him, forcing him to speed up. He took the Subaru up to 65 MPH, faster than he liked on the narrow bridge. There was no breakdown lane for Jens to pull over and let him pass.

Jens was trapped. Was this guy out of his mind?

As though in answer, the driver flashed his high beams and lurched forward, kissing Jens' bumper with the grille of his vehicle, a black flatbed truck.

Panicking, Jens tapped his brakes to force his assailant to fall back, but instead the driver bore down. In the light of the oncoming traffic, Jens could clearly see the driver's face in his mirror.

Laurent.

Jens jammed his foot down on the gas until he was doing 85 then 90 MPH, putting a few car lengths between them. There was a hairpin right turn coming up, leading to a rotary that brought cars onto the bridge heading south, back to New Hampshire. Jens risked a look in the rearview mirror.

Laurent kept coming, his face a rictus of hate.

I'll duck under the bridge and lose him, Jens told himself.

Just before crossing into Maine, Jens spun the wheel sharply to the right. He began a tailspin, gradually braking harder — until he was nearly standing on the pedal, using every trick he had learned so long ago in Hollywood. Hopscotching into the curve, the Subaru's back end lurched and shuddered clockwise, tires smoking.

Once he felt the brakes lock, he released them and downshifted. He reapplied the brakes, feathering off. Miraculously, he regained control as he flew into the rotary. Meanwhile, Laurent stayed on him, nearly touching his rear end. At the bottom of the rotary, Jens lost control.

He smashed through the guard rail, caromed over the edge of the embankment, and plunged down, into the black water.

Who would protect Teddy now?

———

When Jens' Subaru struck the water it had been traveling at 70 MPH. It catapulted off the embankment airborne, tires spinning, flying out over the dark space like a rocket, before plummeting.

The rear struck first, cleaving the water violently, followed by the front end.

The sudden impact, metal meeting water hard as concrete, had smashed Jens against the steering wheel, jerking him sideways, delivering the brunt of the collision to his left side, snapping his upper arm like a wishbone on Thanksgiving. Then, the driver's airbag exploded onto his shattered arm, compounding insult upon injury, pinning him to the seat.

Luckily, the pain was intolerable, for this is what kept him from passing out and drowning in the rising cabin water, as the Subaru came to rest perched on the edge of the channel bed, submerged in ten feet of water. He shrieked with pain as he pounded his damaged arm against the driver's side door, sending jolts of lightning up his arm and flooding his brain with life-saving adrenalin.

Sucking what might have been his last breath from the diminishing pillow of air trapped in the cabin, he squeezed down under freezing water onto the seat, braced himself against the door, and kicked with all his might at the passenger's window, first cracking then breaking it free.

Hoisting himself up with his good arm, he pulled and frog-kicked to the opening and backed out, into the pitch-black water. Lungs bursting, he kicked off, lunging upward, but once adrift in the inky depths he lost his orientation. He kicked and kicked, clawing the water with his one good arm. Soon he could not tell if he was alive or dead.

The last thing he remembered was the fear at the very root of his being, which, strangely, was not for himself, but for his son, whose face wavered like a pale rider in the watery depths, beckoning, leading him on, deeper into the darkness.

Later, once over his shock, he would learn that a pair of local sports fishermen had been trawling the riverbank in their Whaler and had seen him sail off the embankment.

Racing to the spot above the burst of bubbles from his submerged car, they'd shined a strong flashlight over the side, guiding Jens to the surface, where they hauled him aboard like a spent fish.

Chapter Fifty

Jens lay tossing in a hospital bed, heaving and clawing with one arm — the one *not* in a cast — like a drowning man. The strong sedatives administered by the EMT staff had done nothing to mitigate his delusion, or stop him from mentally rehearsing his own obituary.

Ferdie looked on while attendants fumbled with Jens, finally strapping him down for his own protection, and covering him with warming blankets. After a few drinks with her new friends, she had checked her radio upon returning to her car. Hearing a description of the accident and the Subaru, she knew right away it was Jens.

Jens' condition was an unusual but not uncommon shock response, temporary, the EMT doctor said. Jens had not suffered anoxic brain injury from hypothermia and would be himself in a matter of hours. Not to worry, concussion has been eliminated, too, he added. Aside from the broken arm and a gut full of brackish water they'd pumped out, Jens was in good condition, thanks to his speedy rescue, said the doctor, as he rushed to a new emergency.

Ferdie pulled a chair over to the bed and put a calming hand on Jens. Eyes clenched, Jens was still shivering, but his tremors had subsided with the help of the restraint. Teddy and Vivian were on the way in. Nola would be arriving shortly, driving down from Conway. Ferdie, feeling out of place in her dinner clothes and jewelry, settled in to keep vigil over her friend, like an ordinary citizen.

———

Jens drifted in and out of consciousness, not quite aware of his surroundings, nor cognizant of who he was and what had happened to him. The pull of oblivion was a rip tide taking him down, dashing him head over heels, further and further, out to sea.

The sound of talk, the signature and crown of human life, brought him back. Teddy's voice was the first he recognized, followed by Ferdie's.

Jens blinked awake. He was in a hospital bed. When he tried to sit up, he found he couldn't. He bucked and his blankets fell away, revealing the strap across his chest and arms.

"Hey!" he shouted, but all that came out was a hoarse whisper.

It was enough to get Ferdie and Teddy's attention. Ferdie called for a nurse while Teddy hovered over his father.

"Dad! Are you alright?" Jens heard the quiver in his voice. A wave of relief washed over him — Teddy was safe.

"I was worried about you."

"Me? You're the one," said Teddy.

Jens nodded to Ferdie, trying to manage a smile.

"Ferdie, get this thing off me," he croaked, jerking against his restraint.

The nurse Ferdie had summoned approached.

"I see you're back with the living, Mr. Corbin. Are you going to behave yourself?" She hesitated before unbuckling the strap over his chest.

"What do you mean?" asked Jens.

"You were thrashing around. We didn't want you to hurt your arm."

Jens noticed the cast on his arm.

"My deadline! How the hell am I going to write?"

"I can help you with that."

Nola draped her coat over a chair on the way to his bed. She was still wearing her hospital scrubs. She brushed her fingertips over Jens' cheek.

"How are you?" She smiled down at him.

"Good," answered Jens, hiding his embarrassment. He'd not

had a chance to tell Teddy about her.

"How was the drive?" interjected Ferdie, trying to help.

She extended her hand to Teddy, who appeared to be having a hard time accepting the fact that his father had a girlfriend, let alone one as attractive as Nola. She brushed back a lock of golden-red hair that had escaped her bun.

"Hi. I'm Nola, a friend of your dad's."

Teddy glanced at her, then at Jens.

"A student of mine," stammered Jens. "An ex-student, I mean. She's a writer, too. Down from Conway."

"A good friend," she added with a smile.

Teddy raised an eyebrow as he took her hand, appraising her, liking what he saw.

"Charmed, I'm sure," he said gallantly.

Jens exchanged looks with Ferdie.

"See, I told you he'd changed," said Ferdie.

Chapter Fifty-One

Using Jens' updated description of Laurent and the pickup truck he'd used to push Jens off the embankment into the Piscataqua, Ferdie put the wheels in motion to apprehend the convicted murderer. She called in a new BOLO and issued a warrant for his arrest, advising officers to use extreme caution, as their suspect was likely armed and had already proved dangerous.

Once Laurent was apprehended, she told Jens — who was now able to sit up in bed — he would be charged with attempted murder using a motor vehicle, and be returned to prison to serve out a new, extended sentence. In all likelihood, life, added Ferdie.

She questioned Teddy about Laurent. He said he'd had no contact with him and, aside from the letters Ferdie already knew about, had nothing to add.

Ferdie decided to take a ride out to the house in Lee on the unlikely chance that Vivian was hiding Laurent. Though she did not believe Vivian was complicit in the attempt on Jens' life, she wanted to gauge her reaction when she told her about it. She could drop Teddy off at the same time, if it was safe. Promising to return for Teddy after a quick stop at the Portsmouth PD, she left Jens to explain to Teddy his relationship with Nola.

Nola, apparently sensing their need to talk, left them alone on the pretext of scaring up some breakfast and coffee. As soon as she was gone, Teddy let out a guffaw, followed by a whistle of appreciation.

"A friend, Daddio? I'd say you've been rather busy up there on Black Mountain."

Jens hadn't considered when he was going to introduce Teddy to Nola — and what *as*. His brush with death had taken that decision out of his hands. His primary concern in the months following his court-ordered separation from Teddy had been to steer clear of any behavior that would jeopardize his chances of being reunited with him. And bide his time until his day in court.

With a rush of anxiety, he realized that his day in court was today — this very afternoon! He groaned. Could it be postponed, he wondered, without jeopardizing his position? Better to go through with it if the doctors would release him.

"I can't believe it! I'm due in court today about your custody."

"Dad, I've already talked this over with Mom." He paused, choosing his words carefully. "Ah ... you know I've been having some trouble at school."

"I never should have taken you out of Exeter —"

"Naw, that's not your fault. You had no choice. Mom ... she did this ... when she filed for divorce and took your money. Your hands were tied. Anyway, I'll be okay. I can take care of myself."

"Teddy, I'm sorry this ever happened."

"I know, Dad, you got blindsided. I couldn't really warn you as I didn't know what Mom was up to, except that she was divorcing you and needed money."

"Still, I should have seen it coming."

Jens deliberated about how much to tell Teddy about his mother's past and what that may have to do with last night's attack and the terrorist threat on Teddy's life. He gave him an edited version, leaving out his lawyer's speculation about Vivian's alleged role in the events leading to Laurent's incarceration.

"She would never let anyone hurt you, Teddy. She loves you."

They were silent for a moment, regrouping.

"Look," Jens said, talking over Teddy's simultaneous, "Look."

After the nervous laughter died out, Jens asked, "What kind of trouble are you in at school?"

"These Thai kids who moved up from Boston — the Sworn Brothers — they're trying to make a name for themselves controlling the drugs at school."

Jens shook his head, bewildered.

"What's that got to do with you? Is there any truth in what the principal claims — that you were dealing drugs found in your locker?"

"Dad, *Dad*, you know me," protested Teddy, his voice raised stridently. "Do you think I deal drugs? Why would I? I don't use them. I don't even smoke cigarettes."

"I don't know, Teddy. You talked so much about pot before I went away —"

"Okay, sure, I was curious."

"But not anymore? Have you gotten high since the last time we talked?"

"Dad, I made you a promise."

"Well?"

"Do you want to hear the truth or not?"

"Go on, then." Jens watched his son carefully, tuned to the subtle "tells" that give a liar away, even a good one.

"You don't know me. I'm into working out now." He smiled proudly. "I've put on ten pounds — all muscle — since you went away. I work out every day."

He pulled up his sleeve and flexed his bicep — it was the size of a baseball, larger and more defined than the mango Teddy had displayed the last time he'd flexed. His shoulders were starting to bulk up, too, like a man's.

"Look!" Teddy pulled up his shirt to display the beginnings of cut pectorals and a six pack.

"Jesus, Teddy! I'm impressed."

Teddy dropped his shirt and resumed his self-defense.

"One day early in the semester, when I'd just transferred over, I was in gym class. I was watching some of the Thai kids workout — a martial art called *Muay*. It was like nothing I'd ever seen before. Anyway, I didn't think I was staring — and I certainly didn't mean anything by it — but they took it the wrong way. Thought I was, I don't know, putting them down in the way I was looking. Regardless, from that day on, they've had it in for me."

253

"I know what that can be like. I had something like that in high school. First it was my foreign name, then it was ..." He stopped himself, not wanting to bring his dead brother into this. "What about the stuff in your locker?"

"Part of their campaign to mess with me."

Jens stared into his eyes. "I believe you." He grabbed his shoulder and squeezed.

"So, Dad," began Teddy, in a tone that reminded Jens of when he wanted something, "do you think I could come and live with you?"

Teddy's request was just what Jens had been hoping for but hadn't expected. He was encouraged, knowing that the court most often took the dependent's wishes into consideration. He hoped that Teddy's preference would be enough to convince the judge to award Jens custody, but he was prepared to drag out Vivian's dirty laundry in order to win custody and protect his son.

Taking Teddy up to the lodge on Black Mountain would remove him from the Thai threat as well as Laurent's until he was caught, and give Teddy a fresh start. There was a good school nearby in North Conway, he'd learned on Google, and Jens could keep close tabs on his son, who he knew would be facing some rocky roads ahead — in addition to separation from his mother.

This was the best news he'd had to date. It went a long way toward dispelling the depression triggered by Laurent's attack.

There was still the problem of how Jens would write one-handed, but he was certain he'd find a solution. He warned himself not to take Nola for granted. He knew he'd handled her introduction to Teddy poorly. Meanwhile, the prospect of getting his son back was all that he needed to feel like he was on a roll.

———

Teddy devoured the breakfast Nola brought. Seeing how hungry he was, she offered to bring him another, but Teddy begged off until she saw through his shyness and fetched him a second, for which he was grateful. Jens thought they were getting off to a good start. He'd need them both in the months to come.

Dawn brought an assault of medical personnel to Jens' room, and Jens' improved condition and the demands of triage facilitated his early release. Teddy was sent home with Ferdie to await the results of the custody hearing, but not before thanking Nola and hugging his father goodbye.

Chapter Fifty-Two

While Nola showered, Jens stepped out onto the deck of their room at the inn. Awkwardly gripping his cell phone with his cast hand, he used the other to choose a number from the list of previous callers. His injured arm — wrapped in plastic thanks to Nola — had given him little bother aside from a dull, aching pain.

The call was to Dr. Reese, the assistant principal at Oyster River High, to cancel their meeting, explaining that after today Teddy would likely be living with Jens in Jackson and attending school in North Conway. Jens told Reese he would advise him of the results of the custody hearing, adding that State Trooper Morrison would be coming around to check into the Thai students' involvement with the drugs found in Teddy's locker.

"Why would she be doing that?" asked Reese suspiciously.

"Because," answered Jens, suppressing his anger, "you disregarded the explanation of a boy who's never been in trouble with the law, in favor of reputed gang-bangers."

"Are you referring to the Thai students your son accused of planting the drugs?"

"I am."

"That's a lot of suppositions there, Mr. Corbin."

"Isn't that what you're doing?"

"I don't know what stories Theodore has been feeding you, but I can tell you, as the chief disciplinarian here, that his record has been less than exemplary. In fact, if you'd bothered to keep our appointment, I would have told you about the numerous detentions he accrued this semester, two for fighting, and one for disobeying a teacher. Were you aware of this?"

"No, I wasn't."

Jens fumed for a moment before answering sharply.

"Thank you for being candid with me, Dr. Reese. I'll follow up with you on whether or not he'll be returning to Oyster River."

———

Shortly before two o'clock, Nola pulled her Beetle up to the curb at the district courthouse in Dover, squeezed Jens' hand for good luck, and drove off in search of a Starbucks where she could work on her script, fueled by an endless supply of coffee. Jens was to call her cell when he was finished.

Vincent, dressed smartly in a dark suit and cashmere topcoat, was waiting for him at the door of the brick courthouse, a hybrid of municipal architecture from the 90s grafted onto an edifice of indistinct earlier origins. He held the door for Jens, careful not to jar his cast, which Jens cradled protectively.

"You're a lucky man, Jens, from what I hear. Your guardian angel was working overtime. Larry, our investigator, talked to his contacts on the Portsmouth PD. A few more minutes in that icy water and ...."

He paused dramatically.

"Now, the good news. Larry can tie Vivian to Laurent as recently as last night."

As Vincent talked, he led Jens along a stale-smelling corridor banked by courtrooms, where other hearings were being conducted. Interspersed, uniformed marshals stood guard, bracing those who sought to enter, checking their bags and keeping order.

On wooden benches flanking the courtroom doors, taciturn plaintiffs and defendants sat awaiting their turns, the mothers cradling babies and dandling kids too small to be left home. An air of pinched circumstances floated amid their desperation.

"Any update on Laurent's whereabouts?" asked Jens.

"Not from Larry. He's waiting to hear back from the FBI. What's our friend Ferdie have to say?"

Jens shook his head. "He slipped the BOLO. Ferdie thinks he could be in Canada by now."

Vincent paused his client at the door to the courtroom. He brushed some imaginary lint from Jens' suit lapel.

"Look, Jens, you're going to play it cool in there and let me do all the talking and negotiating — no recriminations shouted at your soon-to-be ex-wife, no soft-hearted forgiveness either. She stole from you, cheated on you, gaslighted you, maybe even put your son in the crosshairs — now she's here to bury you, make you pay for everything mean and unfulfilled in her life."

He overrode Jens' attempt to object.

"It's not your fault. You've been the good guy, always played by the book, loved her, took care of her and your son, all the while sustaining a difficult career with no support from her. We show no mercy!" he concluded dramatically, winking at the marshal at the door.

Jens, stunned by Vincent's vehemence, nodded ambiguously.

"All *right*," Vincent said, straight-arming the door, "let's do this!"

———

Jens wondered if Vincent made that speech to all his male clients, or just to him because of their friendship. It hardly seemed professional. Then he caught sight of Vivian, and everything Vincent had warned him of flew from his head. Her back to him as he approached, she was deep in huddled conversation with a man Jens barely noticed — her lawyer presumably.

Her chestnut hair, grown longer and fuller as though licensed by his absence, fell to her shoulders, vivid against her cream-colored silk blouse. He recognized the blouse as the one she reserved for *their* special occasions: anniversaries, Christmas, birthdays. Flowing sleeves accentuated her graceful arms, the padded shoulders counterbalanced by a plunging neckline. He came alongside her table, oblivious to Vincent tugging at his sleeve, pulling him toward their side of the courtroom.

Jens willed her to look up, but she did not, obstinate as always.

"Mr. Corbin," growled the judge. "Would you mind taking your seat, sir? I've got a busy docket this afternoon. Your case is one of many."

Jens tore his eyes from Vivian and managed to stutter an apology.

"Sorry, your honor, ah — Judge Neadeau," he said, recognizing his former fraternity brother, despite the overlay of time thickening his features, limning his head with silver, and imbuing him with the *gravitas* that comes from years spent deciding the fate of others.

A look of mutual recognition seemed to pass between them — one that said, see what we've become? It's not so bad, you a writer, me a judge.

"Let the record show that the plaintiff Vivian Corbin is present, represented by attorney O'Connell. Defendant Jens Corbin is present, represented by attorney Polcarpi. Let us proceed," prompted Neadeau.

———

The two lawyers, circling like pit bulls, politely hurled accusations and objections at each other.

Vincent tied Vivian's checkered past with Armand Laurent, a convicted murderer, to her recent absconding with the couple's marital assets, citing it as a sign of her flawed character, if not criminal behavior. To Jens' surprise, Vincent had proof of her ongoing relationship with this dangerous felon, presenting phone records of calls Laurent made to her cell phone going back several months.

Only yesterday, he added pointedly, Laurent had made an attempt on his client's life. The phone records showed that he'd made a call to Mrs. Corbin some fifteen minutes before running Vincent's client, Jens Corbin, of the Long Bridge into the

Piscataqua River, hoping to kill him.

Over O'Connell's stentorious objections, the judge allowed Vincent to roll out the speculative evidence he'd unearthed about Vivian's part in shaking down Laurent's family in the alleged pregnancy scam. Vincent produced the marriage certificate establishing her annulled marriage to Laurent, and the news clippings hinting at her identity as the minor who'd testified against him.

Vincent cited her attempt to hide Jen's valuable art collection, purchased with the proceeds of his creative endeavors as an artist, *not* hers, as further evidence of criminal conspiracy with the man she'd helped send to prison.

Perhaps she was acting out of some misguided sense of guilt and love for Laurent, he speculated. No matter. The coup de grace, the product of Larry's investigative digging, was a bill of sale made out to Vivian in her maiden name, proof she'd purchased a throw-away handy used by Laurent to make calls to her as recently as last night, when the phone disappeared from the cellular grid.

O'Connell, with a salt-and-pepper coiffeur swept back like the movie stars of the fifties, struggled to recover his aplomb. It was obvious he'd been blind-sided by the revelations about Vivian as a teen. He huddled with his client in counsel, whispering heatedly.

Jens, having scripted courtroom scenes in his fiction, found the lawyer's comeback predictable and uninspired. O'Connell dismissed Vincent's allegations as malicious slander, declaiming that his client had done nothing wrong that couldn't be explained by her fear for her own safety and security. The defendant Mr. Corbin's violent nature, he argued, was well known to the Lee Sheriff's Department, as they'd responded to a call when he violated his restraining order.

Talking over Vincent's objections, O'Connell went on to describe in exaggerated detail Jens' attack on his client — the incident with the wine glass — which precipitated her decision to file for divorce, fearing for her safety. He further cited Corbin's history of mental illness and his ongoing record of psychological cruelty, constantly verbally abusing his wife and son, and recklessly jeopardizing the family's financial security with risky projects, while deriding his wife's efforts to make a living from her art.

Finally, he concluded, the plaintiff's contact with Laurent should not be used to impugn her fitness as a mother. He put his arm around her protectively. She was a victim then, and she is a victim now. O'Connell rose from his seat to make his final argument. His voice dripped with sympathy.

"Her uncle brutally raped her, and then forced her to accuse Laurent on pain of death. She feared for her life, a pattern that followed her in her present marriage. Her only crime has been her trusting nature. She wanted to help Laurent get back on his feet after what she'd been forced to do to him. She has no knowledge of the regrettable assault on the defendant's life, allegedly made by Laurent. We beg the court not to punish her by taking away her son."

Vincent had the final say and he used it to draw the noose around Vivian's neck, by reporting the terrorist call made to Jens at his cabin in Jackson, which was a matter of police record. The caller had attempted to shake Jens down for money, threatening to hurt his son if he didn't cooperate. The caller knew particular details about the boy's movements that had to have come from his mother.

The judge stared at Vivian as though trying to comprehend her corruption. When he spoke, his voice was dispassionate. He questioned Vivian and then Jens, asking them to clarify the claims made by their attorneys, answer further questions about their mutual assets and income, and describe their respective relationships with their son. Vincent capitalized on the moment by introducing a sworn statement by Teddy stating he wanted to live with his father.

Vincent presented Jens' prenuptial agreement, excluding

Vivian from benefiting from his creative efforts, including book, film, and TV rights. O'Connell protested that this was unfair to his client, as she had been a faithful partner all the years of marriage, and had been discouraged from pursuing her own career while his flourished. As a result, she had no visible means of support and limited expectations.

Neadeau took it all in, deliberated, and told them that he had come to a decision. Marital assets were to be shared accordingly: Vivian was awarded the house in Lee and Jens the cabin in Jackson, with all furnishings attached; personal motor vehicles would remain the property of the current registrants; Jens was to retain sole ownership to all copyright to his works, future, past, and present, and all royalties derived thereof; the art collection was awarded to Jens alone. Half the money that Vivian had taken before the divorce was her settlement. She was to return the other half immediately to Jens or suffer imprisonment.

There would be no additional monetary awards nor alimony, as their son — Neadeau paused to consult the custody papers for a name — Theodore, was entrusted to the custody of his father, with bi-monthly visiting privileges assigned to the plaintiff, with the proviso that she sever all ties to Laurent.

"Divorce is granted under these terms by the authority vested in me by the State of New Hampshire and the Fourth District Court of Dover," he concluded. "Oh, I almost forgot, the restraining order on Mr. Corbin is hereby dismissed."

At first O'Connell was too stunned to protest. When he rose to the task, he was full of bluster, which did little to sway the judge.

"Your honor, I've never, in all my years at law, witnessed a decision so cruel and unfair. The plaintiff is destitute, sir. Moreover, alienation from her son will destroy her. Please, I beg the Court, do not punish her for the sins of others."

"Your reservations have been duly noted, Mr. O'Connell," answered the judge, who turned his attention to Jens and

Vincent. "Do you have anything to add, Mr. Polcarpi?"

Vincent, flush with victory, responded with admirable reserve.

"We find the terms quite satisfactory, your honor."

"Mr. Corbin, have you anything?"

Jens, whose eyes had been on Vivian during the judge's pronouncement of the terms, was slow to refocus and respond.

"Your honor, judge," he began. "I just don't know what to say." He glanced back at his now ex-wife. She had collapsed onto the table and was sobbing.

Vincent glared at Jens and shook his head. "Don't," he hissed.

"I'm not sure this is the right thing." Jens' voice quivered with emotion.

"Are you willing to take custody of your son, sir?" asked the judge.

"Most assuredly, your honor."

"The parties will appear back in this courtroom in three months for evaluation. Dismissed."

While Vincent reached for Jens' hand to shake, Jens glanced over at the plaintiff's table, looking for Vivian, planning to say something that would comfort her — reassure her that she would not be cut off from Teddy, that she would be welcome in Jackson, and Teddy could come and stay with her in Lee, no matter the court ruling.

But she was gone, leaving behind a sour attorney to collect her divorce papers, and an ex-husband whose heart, despite everything she'd done to destroy him, went out to her.

Chapter Fifty-Three

Jens was impervious to Vincent's attempts to cheer him up. While Vincent enthused over the judge's findings, they stood on the steps to the courthouse, collars turned up against the chill autumn wind.

Every beat in his son's character arc, to borrow a term from Jens' story analysis, resonated with foreboding. The assistant principal's concerns for Teddy's psychological balance had taken Jens by surprise. Never in a million years would he have expected it. His impression of his son was that while he may be troubled by the divorce, he was at heart a good boy. And still is, he reminded himself.

Taking the boy from his mother now, though Teddy had requested it, seemed questionable, even though Jens had wanted it, especially after Laurent's attempt on Jens' life.

Who was Jens or the judge to presume they knew what a mother's love means to a youth on the verge of manhood? He had seen them together, cozying side-by-side like a calf with its mother — the two made of the same stuff — brushing flanks as they cleared away after dinner.

Jens' own mother may have been physically present when he was growing up, but she had not been available, not emotionally. The damage, he knew, was irreparable; it had stilted his own perception of women and stunted his development. Jens decided to make every effort to reconcile with Vivian, not for his own sake, but for his son's.

"Did you hear what I said?" Vincent was pulling on his sleeve.

It took Jens a while to focus. "Sorry, what were you saying?"

"You'll want to get your art collection out of Vivian's as soon as possible."

"Why's that?"

"I know you think I'm being mercenary, Jens, but this woman

already tried to rob you. *Now*, she's really desperate. Aside from the house, which she'll likely dump on the market as soon as possible, and the half of your savings, she has nothing. I would get my stuff out in the next couple of days if I were you."

He held out his hand for Jens to shake. "Look, she's a survivor, she'll make it, and so will you."

Jens shook his hand absently. "Thanks for everything, Vincent."

"Oh, you won't get rid of me so easily. We've got a court review coming up in three months — and there's my bill, of course." He smiled without irony. "When are you leaving for Jackson?"

"As soon as I can square things for Teddy and put the art in storage."

"How will I get a hold of you?"

"Landline works fine at the cabin. For now, leave a message on Nola's cell — mine went for a swim and I haven't had time to replace it."

"Let me know when you do."

Nola pulled up to the curb in her Beetle and honked. Jens climbed into the compact, careful not to let his arm in its sling bang into the dash. Vincent tapped on the window and Jens pressed the button to roll it down.

"Almost forgot — your agent, Jean, left a message for you to call her. She's in Portsmouth tonight."

Jens nodded his thanks, rolled up the window, and waved goodbye.

Nola glanced at Jens as she turned onto Central Ave., heading out of town in the direction of Dover Point and Portsmouth.

"Well, are you going to keep me in suspense?"

"She got the house in Lee. I got the house in Jackson, my art, my story rights, and half of our savings back. And Teddy," he answered, staring ahead.

She screamed with delight. "That's wonderful!"

"And I thought you'd be excited."

After they had arrived back at the inn and Jens had spoken to Teddy, they celebrated in bed. Later, Jens tried to explain to Nola why he felt ambivalent about Teddy leaving his mother. Nola sensed his discomfort and told him it was okay, he needn't justify his reasons, he was the father after all, she hadn't meant to pry. She started to get up from the bed, pulling the sheet around her as though embarrassed or angry. He wasn't sure which.

"Hey," he said softly, pulling her back into bed and pinning her with his eyes.

"Nola, my muse, my love, my life, what am I going to do with you?"

He tried to kiss her but she turned away, tears welling. He took her in his arms as best he could with one good arm, and she cried. He cooed and shushed and kissed away the tears — *My God, you are beautiful, he thought* — and after a while she stopped with a laugh.

"I don't know what that was about."

"You're worried I'm still in love with my ex."

"Are you?" she asked, holding her breath.

"Nola, *no*. I love *you*."

"Do you?" she asked, growing surer of herself.

"I don't know what I've done to deserve you ... and I worry about keeping you."

She put a finger to his lips. "Shut up, you silly fool." Her lips followed.

Soon they were making love, Nola on top, rocking, her peerless breasts arousing him, making him forget everything — his age, his failures, his concerns for his son — even their match, which might end in heartache for both, cynical as he was about love.

But for now, the moment was perfect. His gargoyle of self-consciousness, which was constantly gnawing at his joy, surrendered in blissful silence. For the moment.

———

The meeting with Jean was more about her personal concern for him than professional considerations, though she did get around to asking about the book and whether he'd be meeting the deadline, which was only weeks away. How was he going to work with only one typing hand?

He told her not to worry, that he was two thirds of the way there and knew where it was all going, and Nola had volunteered to take dictation, and there was always voice recognition software. But she seemed unsure, despite his reassurances.

Jean and Nola hit it off immediately, settling into a cozy familiarity as Nola described her aspirations as a writer and outlined her script, which Jean thought had possibilities as a work of fiction, though style would determine its commercial value.

Jens noted the ease with which they talked, stepping on each other's lines without embarrassment, laughing, segueing effortlessly from one topic to another in ways that left him spinning. He let them run on, content to take in the lights spilling like a painter's impasto on the darkening canvas of the harbor. They were at the Dock-in, his usual choice for meetings with Jean.

In fact, since his brush with death, he hadn't been able to focus at all on his story, and felt terminally out of touch with his characters and their plight. He gulped down his drink, not realizing his abandon was noticed by both Nola and Jean, who glanced at him in surprise and turned away, hoping he hadn't noticed them noticing.

Nola stopped her conversation, put an arm around him, and asked if he was okay. He smiled reassuringly.

"I'm sorry, I forgot my manners." He looked at Jean. "Please forgive me — it's been a rough couple of days."

"Don't give it another thought. You've been to hell and back."

Jens stood to hide his embarrassment. Other's sympathy was not one of the social gestures he was comfortable with.

"Ladies, if you'll pardon me." He pointed to the restrooms behind the bar. "I'll be right back."

He felt their concern following him out, and he tried not to let it rankle. He took his time in the bathroom, dousing his face with cold water, brushing back his hair with his fingers, tucking his shirt into his pants, smoothing himself over. All done with his good arm. He decided he'd had enough to drink. When he got back Jean was alone at their table.

"She's wonderful, Jens — just what you need."

"My muse, eh?" He permitted himself a sincere smile.

Jean laughed. "I thought *I* was your muse."

"You, my dear," he said, rising to guide Nola to her seat as she returned from the bathroom, "are my Janus." He indicated Nola as he pushed in her chair. "She, on the other hand, is my muse."

Nola smiled and nodded.

Soon after, Jean paid the bill, insisting she had invited them. Jens thanked her and told her he would be sending her the manuscript, their "blockbuster," on time as promised. He and Nola walked Jean to her car in the public parking garage and said goodnight.

On the ride back to the inn, crossing the very same bridge to Maine that had nearly cost Jens his life only days before, he told Nola that he was anxious to get back to his book. She nodded enthusiastically. As soon as the art was in storage, he would put all this behind him and dive back into it, just in time to save Cassie and maybe even Emma.

Chapter Fifty-Four

The next day, Nola drove Jens to a truck rental agency on the south side of Portsmouth, where he rented the smallest U-haul van available for taking away the paintings and artwork from his erstwhile home in Lee, which he now thought of as Vivian's.

Because of his broken arm, he drove Nola's VW bug, an automatic, and she drove the truck. He trailed her to Greenland and on to Lee, oblivious to the late autumn landscape of cornfields tamped and weathered, of fallow, harrowed fields, of grey skies giving way to the sun bursting through clouds heavy with the promise of snow. He was preoccupied with thoughts about what he would say to his "ex" if she were home.

He had no illusions about how she was dealing with the judge's harsh ruling. Whatever her reasons for destroying their marriage, she would have to live with the results now. Yet he felt no pleasure in her punishment by the court or her suffering. Her murky past seemed like her cross to bear, regardless of her complicity or innocence.

The sobering fact remained that an ex-husband of hers, whether or not they were together now, had made an attempt on Jens' life. She had let him into her and Jens' private circle and into their bed, bringing danger and the threat of death.

———

Teddy came out to greet them, as first Nola and then Jens pulled into the drive at the farmhouse in Lee. He seemed anxious to keep them from entering the house, as he explained that he had taken down all the artwork and stacked it in the foyer for easy loading.

"I thought it would speed things up," he said, as he walked them to the front door, which was propped open, giving Jens a view of the foyer crowded with canvases.

"Hey, Nola," Teddy said with a smile.

"Hey!" she answered, hanging back until Jens looked her way. "You two don't mind if I wait in the truck, do you? I'd rather not come in."

Jens nodded his understanding and then clapped Teddy on the back.

"Hey, big boy, where's my hug? You're not too old to give your old man a hug, are you?" he said, reaching his arms around Teddy, who bear-hugged him back with a husky "Naw." Jens felt the power in his son's shoulders — man's strength, no longer a boy's.

Jens pulled back to look into his eyes, wet with emotion like his own, yet darting *hinkily*, like one of Jens' fictional characters grilled by the cops. Jens let it go, happy just to be reunited with his son.

"Your mother around?"

Jens stepped into the foyer, peering inside warily, on the lookout for Vivian. This had to be one of the most awkward moments in a divorce, he thought. The distribution of family assets.

"She's gone to town on an errand." Teddy stepped in front of his father, blocking him from going beyond the foyer into the house.

"Dad, why don't we get this all loaded up and on our way? I know she doesn't want to see you, and you likely don't want to see her, right?"

"Teddy, what's going on?" Jens pushed around him and stumbled into the living room.

"What the hell?" His voice rose angrily. "It looks like a wrecking crew's been here."

He surveyed the punched out walls running from the living room into the open-plan kitchen and dining room, up the winding staircase to the hallway and rooms upstairs. Some holes were fist-sized, the handiwork of concentrated, explosive jabs; others were cave-ins, knee to shoulder height, as though from a body blow or a karate kick.

"I can explain," cried Teddy, trying to cut Jens off again.

"You'd better!"

He walked around the room, once the center of family life, redolent with memories of his son's journey to manhood and all the precious moments along the way.

"Jesus, Teddy!"

"Well, you know I've been training in kick-boxing — it's something I can do well, even with my lousy coordination," he said shyly, "and ... see, me and Mom haven't exactly been getting along since you left —"

"Wait a minute, Teddy, I didn't leave you —"

"I know, that's not what I meant —"

Jens was too stunned to say anything.

"I offered to fix the walls, but Mom said she doesn't care anymore about what happens to the house — or about anything — she's in a bad way ... and she's been taking it out on me, now that you're gone. You know how she can be."

"I just don't understand what could make you mad enough to take out one wall, let alone," he swept his arm at the damage, "this."

Teddy stared at the floor, started to answer, fell silent. Finally, he met Jens' eyes.

"I know who Mom's been crying on the phone with," he blurted. "His name's Warren. He's a real bastard — a lot worse than Laurent, believe me." He tensed up, fists balled, muscles rigid. "I'm going to kill him if I ever catch him bothering Mom again."

Jens recoiled from Teddy's anger.

"Warren who?"

"I don't know, I just know he's been blackmailing Mom, threatening to tell about her past."

"That's all out in the open now. He can't hurt her anymore."

"I know." He gestured at the damage inflicted on their once

safe and secure home. "I was trying to cope with Mom's refusal to go to the police. She finally explained why she couldn't — he'd threatened to hurt me."

Jens nodded slowly, forcing his breathing to return to normal.

"I'm so sorry I wasn't here for you."

"I know — Mom got rid of you and you had to write your book."

"I'm here now, son."

They hugged for a long time.

"Let's get loaded," he said softly, leaving the rest unsaid for the moment.

———

While Teddy loaded the van, Jens stepped into the bathroom for privacy and called Ferdie, telling her what Teddy had told him.

"This might explain her behavior the past few months — she was protecting Teddy," rejoined Ferdie.

"All of it," added Jens. "The appropriated bank account, the maxed-out credit cards, the vanished art."

"Warren. Is that a first or last name?"

"Teddy didn't say. He thought he was a friend of Laurent's."

"Laurent doesn't have any friends. *Oh my God*, I'm so stupid."

"What?"

"I forgot to check his prison record for known associates and cell-mates." She went into overdrive. "Jens, I gotta go. I'm sending troopers to both Lee and Jackson to keep an eye on things.

Chapter Fifty-Five

A few houses down from Warren's, Laurent found himself shivering in the thin poplin Members Only jacket he'd brought with him from prison. Only months since his release, it seemed like several lifetimes ago.

He'd called Warren on his burner, informing him that his truck was back, along with some good faith cash on the seat, for its rental and repair.

Laurent had then begged for Warren's understanding. He'd been thinking with his dick, he confessed, not with his head. Now all he wanted was to put things right with his partner. That bitch, Vivian, had scorned him — but not before he'd commandeered her laptop, which was all he needed to get into her bank account, he lied, pretending he didn't already know Warren had sucked her dry. They'd split it, he went on; it would make up for the money they'd planned to extort from her husband.

Now, he watched from his hiding place in the bushes as Warren cautiously peeked through his living room curtain, probing the dark, no doubt with his Glock at his side.

Laurent patted the laptop in his backpack; he'd found it in the trash behind a computer repair shop. Misdirection, the key to besting Warren, he'd decided. The broken laptop would serve that purpose. Laurent did not for a minute believe that Warren was buying any of his bullshit. But that didn't matter— smoke and mirrors was all it was. *How could Warren know that he knew?* Laurent mused.

———

Naturally, Warren knew that Laurent was conning him, knew that the trip to Jackson had been window dressing, knew he'd been blackmailing Vivian. But he went along with it, believing himself wiser, stronger, superior.

From his perch at his front window, he called Laurent back on his cell phone.

"So, can I trust you to meet me in a public place, with witnesses?"

Waiting for an answer, he scanned the street. Laurent, he knew, was out there — under a parked car, behind a fence, hunkered down somewhere in the bushes — ready to pounce.

Warren had been desperate — his investors, up from Boston's North End, had paid him a visit — *in his home* — leaving him no choice but to put the squeeze on Vivian. Laurent, lovesick, would never have agreed.

"Not a problem," said the voice at the other end. "Great minds think alike, eh?"

"Just so you know, I'll be packing."

"Warren, this is *me*. Your *celly*, remember?"

Warren guffawed.

"You got the laptop with you? With her bank access?" He played along.

"I do. Indeed." Laurent had told Warren that he'd set up a bank account on the dark web, where he could deposit her funds as bitcoins and get the cash.

"The Cafe in ten minutes. They've got Wi-Fi. We can do the whole thing from there."

Neither believed either was going to the Café. Each believed himself the winner.

———

Warren slipped out the front door, hugging the hedges and stealthily making his way, his Glock cocked and ready. No street lamps. The surrounding houses cast shadowy light from behind drawn shades.

Reacting to what sounded like a twig snapping underfoot, he

swung his Glock up. His hearing grew attenuated. Panic mounting with every step, he knew he had to see this through. For his family: indoors, unsuspecting, oblivious.

He made his way to the pickup, elbows locked, blindly sweeping the way before him like SWAT. From the grapevine, he knew that his pickup had been used in an attempted murder. It would have to disappear along with Laurent. This had to end fast: the cops were probably already on to him.

Once at the truck, he risked a look inside. *Clear.* Edging around to the driver's side, he risked another look inside. Incredible — a wad of bills on the seat, just as Laurent promised.

Skeptical, he wondered if it was a dummy pack, with a few bills on top and the rest paper cut to bill-size. He wouldn't put it past Laurent. It's what he would have done.

Ducking down alongside the truck, he looked underneath.

Clear.

A rustling nearby!

He whipped around and strafed the hedges.

He shivered with rage, his defense against the mounting certainty that he'd been duped. By the fish he'd schooled himself.

Inching forward, he stabbed his Glock into the bushes and rolled to the other side. Tamped grass and broken branches, no doubt left by Laurent.

Where the frig is he?

Huffing with adrenalin, Warren returned to the street.

All clear! Had that idiot really kept his word and gone to meet him at the café?

There was a backpack in the flatbed of his truck, the zipper half down, exposing a laptop. Approaching cautiously, he leaned over to retrieve it.

That's when he felt a sharp slicing pain on the side of his neck.

"You move, you're a dead man," Laurent whispered in his ear.

"Carotid bleeds out in ten seconds or less."

"I don't move, I'm a dead man." Muscles tensed, Warren acted resigned, playing for time.

Laurent tore the Glock from his hand. "Get in, asshole!"

He opened the passenger's door, pushed him inside, got in beside him. Jamming the Glock into his ribs, he shoved him behind the wheel.

"Now, do exactly what I tell you, and I'll spare Marie and your daughter."

Warren nodded stoically. "Spare them. Yes. Please."

Warren stared at him long and hard, searching for a chink in his armor.

"I was jammed up — owed money to the wrong guys. They came here ...." His voice trailed off. He knew Laurent would show no mercy.

"You screw her?"

Warren's surprise was all the answer he needed.

"It didn't have to end this way," Laurent said finally, almost sounding sad.

Warren glanced up at his home one last time.

"Goodbye," he whispered. He put the truck in gear and drove slowly away.

Chapter Fifty-Six

Once the rental van was loaded, Jens sent Nola on ahead to the storage facility nearby in Greenland, where Jens and Teddy would join her, unload, drop off the truck, and be on their way to Jackson.

But just as Jens was leaving the drive, Vivian pulled in, nearly crashing into them. Jens swerved to avoid her, watching through the rearview mirror as she came to a jerky stop in front of the barn. She stayed in the car, motionless. Jens exchanged worried looks with Teddy, wondering if she was drunk.

"I think she's waiting for you to leave, Dad."

"I need to tell her we *know* and that help is on the way. I called Ferdie, she's sending officers over for her protection."

Jens started to get out of the car, but Teddy stopped him.

"Dad, *Dad*, let me. I need to say goodbye," he said, choking up.

Jens watched Teddy lean into her open window and coax her out of the car. She glanced in Jens' direction as she and Teddy hugged. Reaching up, she bent Teddy's face to hers and kissed him repeatedly.

Teddy circled his arms around her bear-like, hoisted her off her feet, murmuring words of reassurance — Jens' caught "Call you" and "Don't worry, we'll see each other soon" and "I love you, Mom."

Then something Teddy said made them laugh and left them hiccupping between sobs. She held onto his hand as he pulled away, her arm extended long, long after, forlorn. It was the saddest thing Jens had ever seen. He fought back his own tears.

Teddy got in the car and said huskily, "She said she'd wait for Ferdie's troopers. Let's go."

"Shouldn't we keep her company until the police to arrive?"

"She's ashamed, she betrayed you, can't face you now."

Jens pulled out onto the road and drove, afraid to look back,

279

afraid she had turned into a pillar of salt.

———

On the ride back to Black Mountain, while Teddy and Nola kept a running patter going — about music, fashion, slang, school, and whatever else came to mind— Jens was silent. He was having a hard time correlating the garrulous, blithe young man in the back seat, reminiscent of the Teddy Jens knew and loved, with the violent hulk who'd decimated the family home in Lee. Teddy must have felt his sidelong scrutiny because he paused in his conversation with Nola to glance at Jens.

"You okay, Dad?"

Jens nodded noncommittally. Their eyes met. Teddy's were frank with concern. He seemed to nod back, imperceptibly, as if to say, I know what's bothering you, and I will explain everything, later, if you let me. Jens shook off his worried air and smiled.

"I'm fine — just playing around with some ideas for the book," he lied.

"Writer at work," interjected Nola ironically. "What, is our conversation not highbrow enough for you?"

"I doubt you would know the music I was into when I was Teddy's age."

"Give me a try, Daddio."

"All right — 'Heart of Glass.'"

"Easy! Blondie, 1978."

"I'm impressed," said Nola. "Your son's a veritable compendium of music trivia."

Teddy smiled self-consciously. "Is that your best shot, Dad?"

"Okay." Jens considered a moment. "If I fell in love with you."

"Excuse me?"

"The song, Nola," Jens said with a smile.

"I got this," said Teddy smugly. "The Rolling Stones."

"Dringgg!" Jens made a sound half-way between a ringing

bell and a clang. "Wrong. Listen."

He cleared his throat and began singing the lyrics to The Beatles' "If I Fell". His voice rose to a crescendo, drawing out the last note.

"Not bad," said Nola.

"Here's a clue. It came out in '64."

"If it wasn't the Stones," Teddy said, "it had to be The Beatles."

"'If I Fell' from the album *A Hard Day's Night*," added Nola.

"Now *I'm* impressed," said Jens.

"So, Dad, know any Lil Wayne songs?" He winked at Nola.

"Lil *Wang*? Gee, I don't know. You mean like 'She Will' and 'How to Love'? Or what about this?" He rapped the first few military-sounding lines of "6 Foot 7 Foot."

Nola and Teddy joined in, Nola beating a rhythm on the steering wheel, with an occasional honk on the horn, to the annoyance of the drivers of the cars they passed, and Teddy pounding the back of his father's seat, syncopating with mouth beats. *Oh, yeah.*

In this mood the ride to Jackson passed quickly. Soon they were wending up Black Mountain Rd. in the dusk, and Jens was feeling the old excitement of coming home, the home his writing had bought, only now its appeal was imperfect.

Something had changed for him in that frantic moment of disorientation at the bottom of the Piscataqua River, when he didn't know whether he was thrashing toward the surface and life, or downward, to his watery grave. What had changed exactly, he couldn't say. But he hoped it hadn't killed his connection to his story — with Cassie, Tommy, and Emma, and that monster Orozco, who epitomized all the evil in the world, which, Jens could now attest, was real and present.

With his attempt on Jens' life, Laurent had expelled him forever from his cushy world of the imagination, into a harsher reality, one of cold-blooded murder and the mayhem of life in prison, where a brazen glance is provocation for gouging out a man's eyes with a spoon. His actions had declared him Jens' nemesis. No longer could Jens construct his symbolic worlds of fiction without encountering the reality of Laurent. Jens had to stay on guard until Laurent was captured and brought to justice.

And now there was another monster, Warren, whom Ferdie was pursuing, hound dog that she was.

———

The next day Nola drove Jens down to Conway to the Subaru dealer to pick up a loaner covered by his insurance. He soon got used to driving the automatic with one hand, using his sling-arm only to flip the turn signal switch and raise and lower the electric windows. He managed to shop all by himself, though for the first time ever he didn't turn down the bag boy's offer to help him load the bundles into the car. Jens made one more stop before returning home, to the liquor store where he purchased a selection of red and white wines and a 12-pack of Belgian beer.

On the way back to the car, his path took him past the local gun shop. He paused to look at the firearms in the window, noting the prices on the double and single barrel shotguns, like the ones the trooper had recommended.

"I can give you a great deal on a shotgun, if that's what you're interested in," said the clerk, who had come out of the store onto the sidewalk to see what Jens was transfixed by.

He was middle aged, like Jens, with a bald, bullet-shaped head and sallow complexion. He wore an oilcloth apron that accentuated rather than hid his belly.

"You prefer a side-by-side or an over-and-under?"

Jens, holding up a hand to ward him off, started backing away.

"Not in the market, thanks."

"Well, you seem pretty interested, if you don't mind my saying. Why don't you c'mon in and make a deal?"

"Just doing research," Jens mumbled, turning on his heel, and walking away.

"Suit yourself," delivered the clerk as a final salvo.

Chapter Fifty-Seven

It took a few days of phone calls and red tape to get Teddy situated in his new school, Kennett High, in North Conway. That morning, Teddy's first day at school, Jens drove him down Black Mountain to Route 16, branching off the highway at Eastman Rd, to find a new building surrounded by thickets of hemlock and birch.

As Jens pulled up in front to park, they joked about how the school looked like a railroad station, with its central edifice an elongated tower, flanked by the administration offices, classrooms, and gym. Teddy wondered if it was supposed to "allude" to the antique railroad station in North Conway. Jens observed that he had a point, and complimented his use of the literary term. They lapsed into silence, neither apparently wanting to be the first to say goodbye.

"Good luck, son," said Jens at last.

"I know you're worried ... that I might do something stupid, like beat the shit out of the first wanker that looks at me funny ... I promise, I won't."

"Naw, I know you'll wait for the second wanker who steps out of line and clobber *him*."

Teddy turned to him with a smile. "See, I knew you'd understand."

"Get out, already," said Jens, laughing.

"Thanks for the ride, Daddio." He pushed open the door and took his backpack from the rear seat.

"You know what bus to take home, right?"

Teddy waved him off and started toward the school. Jens watched him enter the administration building before pulling away from the curb and driving back onto Eastman Rd. He sent up a prayer for all to go well on Teddy's first day ... and every day thereafter.

———

At the cabin on Black Mountain, Jens sat on the back porch, staring out at the sun-dazzled field behind his cabin, watching the evaporating morning dew tease fledgling ferns open, each one recapitulating, as it unfurled, the miracle of the Fibonacci golden spiral.

He inhaled deeply, relishing the scent of pine mixed with the tang of November. Like the survivor of a shipwreck carried to safety on the waves of chance, he viewed his recent trials and tribulations like a penitent forced to acknowledge the hand of Grace.

Taking stock of himself and his situation, he counted not the shadows but the light. He was still in one piece, albeit slightly worse for the wear, with his arm in a sling. He'd lost a wife but gained a muse. He'd been betrayed, not by his own gullibility, but by his trust in a woman, his wife, an old hand at deceit, apparently. He'd gambled everything on a story that titillated and teased like a Naiad, luring him on, taunting him with the promise of salvation or literary suicide.

He turned his thoughts to his story, of Cassie, the young predator slayer, the savior of the damned, damned herself by guilt for not protecting her own child.

Now, he felt nothing but cold indifference and gray shadows in the absence of his familiar cone of light, his inspiration. They had been back at the cabin a week, and he was still blocked.

———

He spent a good part of the day exploring the speech recognition system on his computer, trying to master it sufficiently so that he could avoid having to type with one hand. But no matter how many times he resorted to the "set-up wizard," he could not get it to respond to his command to "start listening," let alone "correct that."

In the end, he decided to give up on it, instead reviewing his rough notes in his journal and re-reading his earlier chapters, seeking to reconnect with his story and its characters.

When last he'd written of Cassie, she'd surrendered herself to her lover Tommy, afraid that her feelings for him would compromise her discipline and betray her daughter's memory. Having run for years on adrenalin fueled by guilt, she feared her romantic surrender would make her vulnerable. Meanwhile, young Emma, Orozco's victim, a captive on his yacht and a pawn in his dangerous fantasy, was fighting for her life.

Will Cassie find her in time? Will her feelings for Tommy distract her at the critical moment? Jens didn't know. Worse yet, he really didn't know where to begin. The power of his imagination — which had always summoned the heart of each scene and revealed its connecting threads as though by chance — refused to conjure.

Discouraged but not defeated, he decided to call it a day. The years had taught him the wisdom of going "off-line" and letting his unconscious take over. He poured himself a glass of Valpolicella and began planning the tasty dinner he would serve when Teddy came home and Nola joined them.

———

While Teddy cleared the table and Jens and Nola rinsed dishes and put them in the dishwasher, Jens found Nola looking at him pointedly. He waited for Teddy to excuse himself and go downstairs to watch TV.

"Okay, madam, what's on your mind?" he asked, spinning her around with a hand on her backside.

"Mmmm. Some of what could develop if you let your hand move in a slow circular motion."

"Oh, you mean like this?" He dropped his hand lower, feeling beneath the fabric of her skirt, doing as she commanded.

"Mmmmm, precisely," she said in a hoarse whisper.

They kissed. He pulled away and drew her toward the bedroom. As they approached the bed, she let out a shriek and toppled onto him.

"Hey! Watch the arm, please. And shhhh ..." he cautioned. "Teddy ..."

"Shhhh, yourself," she answered, mounting and pinning him. Her long red tresses hung over her face like a veil. It made him think of the Naiads of his earlier metaphor, tantalizing him onto the rocks of literary suicide. The image of Botticelli's *Birth of Venus* popped into his mind once more, with its nubile subject's ropes of hair framing rather than hiding her nudity, accentuating her frank sexuality. He thought of the ever-present proximity of death, and though a cliché, the true subject of all art.

"Shhhh," he repeated, though this time it was more of a challenge than a plea.

"Shhhh?" she asked, smothering him with a kiss. She tossed her head back and laughed archly.

———

Afterward she lay in his arms while she caught her breath. He was in one of those lucid suspended states — detached from his body, aglow, his mind a laser illuminating all the parts of his life.

"Daniel," she whispered.

"What about Daniel?" he asked, emerging from his reverie.

"Do you ever think about him?"

"So this is what's been on your mind all night. What made you think about him?"

She sat up.

"You — your pig-headed refusal to acknowledge the danger that surrounds us."

"Ferdie is convinced that both villains have flown the coop, maybe together. She's on top of this. Why are you so worried?"

"We're unprotected up here. It would take Ferdie and her

troopers a half hour to get here —"

"I need to be here for my book and for Teddy."

"Meaning what — I don't have to be?"

"I didn't say that."

He put an arm around her to reassure her, but she shrugged him off.

Their second fight, noted Jens.

"How's the writing going?" she asked, changing the subject.

"Great!" he lied.

"Are you able to type with one hand?"

"Not a problem," he said without conviction.

"Tell you what — you dictate, I'll type."

"I don't know ... writing's so personal, so ... intuitive."

"Aren't I your muse?"

He nodded, unconvinced.

"Then it's settled."

She rolled over to her side of the bed. Soon she was snoring contentedly, while he lay awake long after, turning over in his mind the scenes he hoped to write tomorrow.

Jens slept fitfully, hovering on the edge of consciousness, sensing but not quite grasping the shadowy contours of images flitting by. He was hurtling through a universe of tonal darkness, surrounded by fathomless space. Curiously, he was not frightened.

They were safe, weren't they?

———

The familiar ringing of the land phone forced him rapidly up through the layers of sleep. He reached groggily for the extension, fumbling it to his ear.

"Hello ... hello?" he said.

There was silence on the other end of the line: baited, pulsing. Someone was there, listening intently, breathing, focused like a pinpoint of light in the darkness.

He knew who it was.

"Laurent," he spat. "My phone is tapped. The cops are here. You come anywhere near us, you're screwed, asshole."

The breathing continued, ragged, erratic. Jens tried to imagine it coming from a brute like Laurent but couldn't.

"Vivian, is this you?" he asked softly. Silence. "I know it's you. Where are you?"

He felt Nola's reassuring hand on his shoulder. He spoke again, even more gently, as though to a child.

"Are you injured? I'll send someone to get you or come for you myself." Pause. "Vivian?"

The ragged breathing built to a crescendo, then burst into muffled cries.

"Vivian," he said soothingly. "Let us help you, please ... Where are you?"

When she didn't answer he lay the phone down on the night table and listened to her crying, bearing witness. After a while, the line went dead.

He hung up and turned to Nola, reading in her eyes the same concern about Vivian — Teddy said he hadn't heard from her in days.

"Do you think she's low enough to hurt herself?" asked Nola.

Jens shook his head. "I don't know. I hope not."

Nola turned away to hide the fear in her eyes.

"What if it's not her? What if it's Laurent?"

Chapter Fifty-Eight

In the morning, Jens phoned Ferdie and asked her to check on Vivian. Again. He described her phone call, and their suspicion, his and Nola's, that she might harm herself.

Ferdie said she would send a sheriff by the house in Lee, as she was up north near the Canadian border, tracking down a lead on Laurent, where some summer cottages had been broken into and pillaged for food.

Meanwhile, Flynn's Ford pickup had been found abandoned on Peirce Island in Portsmouth, at Cliff Overlook, one of the last bits of land before the Piscataqua poured into the Atlantic. She promised to let him know if anything helpful came back from forensics. Its location at the end of Shoreline Trail suggested an escape by sea.

"Could it really be Laurent that far north?" asked Jens, back on the break-ins. He stirred his bowl of hot oatmeal, watching the butter melt in swirls.

"Worth checking out, though it's probably just kids."

"Should I be worried?"

"It's at least a hundred miles from you — way on the other side of the White Mountains."

"Think he might seek refuge in the Berlin area? Ground zero, given his history. Maybe he still has some friends there."

"He'd be a damn fool to try it. There's a new prison there; it's crawling with law enforcement. Anyway, stay sharp."

"Thanks. I will."

"How's Teddy doing?"

"Good, I think. He's pretty excited about an accelerated program at Kennett that would permit him to graduate a year early."

"You approve?"

"We'll see."

———

The cabin was empty with Teddy at school and Nola at work. Jens decided to try word-processing one-handed. If it worked, he wouldn't need Nola, who was certain to distract him, despite her good intentions.

He sat before his computer waiting for it to boot up, conjuring his proverbial cone of light and considering what he wanted to accomplish in the chapter where he'd left off. It seemed like ages ago but in reality no more than a month. He summoned up an image of tall, lithe Cassie, fresh from bedding Tommy, feeling determined to get her game back.

Resting his sling arm on the edge of his writing desk, Jens found that he could type haltingly using his right hand for composing words, and the left only for caps, tabbing and shifting. It was painstakingly slow and frustrating, with his mind racing ahead, his fingers groping the keys unfamiliarly. He assembled the words one by one to form phrases, sentences, and finally paragraphs. It made him think of the typesetters of the 19th century and their frustration of setting a wordy novel by Balzac or Dumas to print. An interminable task, doubtless. But unlike the typesetters, he did not know the text until he saw it processed onto the screen. The story sputtered forth.

The longer Emma was in the monster's clutches, the less likely she would survive. In point of fact, she'd lived a lot longer than predators like Orozco normally allowed, once their victims begin to lose their pubescent allure. Cassie decided the place to begin her rescue was with Cervantes, the PI who had betrayed her to Orozco. He had not counted on her escaping, but he would be ready if she came at him. She knew where his office was, but first she would need to change her identity if she was going to dupe him into setting a trap for Orozco.

Jens paused to review what he had written, finding it devoid of his usual crisp imagery and rhythms, but decided it could be revised later. The important thing was that he was getting it out, however slowly!

As she gave herself a final look-over in the mirror, she asked herself why? Why was she was leaving Tommy out? He would be frantic looking for her. If he knew what she planned, he would stop her. She knew the answer, tried to push it away, but finally had to admit that she cared about him and didn't want him in jeopardy. The admission was an awakening. She would have to do something about her feelings, if she survived the night.

Jens felt the cone of light receding. He had brought Cassie back to life — however blurry the image — and it was a good place to stop, knowing she would be waiting for his vivifying attention.

Chapter Fifty-Nine

As Thanksgiving approached, life at the cabin on Black Mountain settled into a comfortable routine. Jens worked on his book mornings, after seeing Teddy off to school and Nola to work.

The coming holiday provided a goal as well as a welcome respite, with Teddy looking forward to a five-day break from classes, Jens expecting to submit his first draft of *Forsake Me Not* to Jean Fillmore-Smart and his publisher, and Nola planning a gourmet feast for Thanksgiving.

Meantime, Ferdie reported that Vivian was not to be found at the house in Lee, which displayed a for sale sign in the front yard. She'd phoned the realtor with the listing, only to discover that she was desperate to get in touch with Vivian, as she had a motivated client with an attractive offer. But Vivian had not returned her calls. Ferdie checked on her cell phone, too, only to find that it was no longer in service.

Keeping the anxiety out of her voice, Ferdie said she'd called around to the hospitals in and around Portsmouth looking for her, as well as the morgues, asking for a "Jane Doe" answering her description. As a last resort, she contacted the New Hampshire State Hospital Psychiatric Facility, also with no luck.

She had disappeared.

Jens hadn't received any more mysterious phone calls from her.

Ferdie promised to set up a trace on Jens' line in case she did. As for Vivian, hopefully she'd gone off the grid to get herself together. Soon she'd call Teddy and everyone would breathe a sigh of relief. Meanwhile, Ferdie had filed a missing person report on her and was following up on the leads.

Jens thanked her for all that she was doing, and then went on to fill her in on Teddy, honoring her as part of the family.

Teddy seemed to be doing well in the AFEX program, the

alternative learning program that Jens had allowed him to enroll in, relieved as he was of the pressure of homework, also a relief to his dad. Happily, his grades had gone up, and he was working out practically every day, bulking up steadily.

Ferdie agreed that Teddy seemed to be on course, finally, and was to be congratulated on his self-discipline. As was his dad, for seeing him through.

"Who knows," joked Ferdie. "Maybe he'll consider a career in law enforcement when he finishes with school."

"Before or after he wins the Mr. Universe title?"

"He could do worse."

Before hanging up, Jens got Ferdie to commit to joining them for Thanksgiving.

"Oh, I almost forgot," added Ferdie. "If that was Laurent up at the northern lakes, he's long gone over the border."

"So, I've nothing to worry about it?"

"Didn't say that — but chances are he's hiding out in Canada and won't be back for a long time, if he knows what's good for him.

One evening, while Jens and Nola were relaxing after dinner, playing backgammon and listening to Chopin on his Kindle, the phone rang. Jens was expecting Jean, checking on his progress, and was reluctant to answer. But it was "the breather" again, back after a hiatus. Jens put the caller on speaker phone so that Nola could hear.

"Vivian, I know it's you, I know you're there."

Now he was not sure; maybe it was Laurent calling to threaten him again; maybe it had been him the first time, too.

The breathing rose and fell, intimating a well of sadness. Finally, a voice broke through, reedy and arrhythmic, as though from beyond.

"Please, I just want to talk to Teddy," Vivian croaked.

Jens signaled Nola to get Teddy, who was in the basement working out.

"Vivian, where are you? Are you alright? Ferdie's been looking for you everywhere. You're not in danger, are you?"

"Can I please talk to Teddy?" she sobbed. "Please, Jens, don't make me beg. I'm not well."

"No, of course you can, here he comes."

Jens handed the phone to Teddy, whose eyes were wide with anxiety.

"Mom! Are you okay? Where are you?" he said, breaking into tears. He glanced at Jens and Nola, then walked away with the phone to his ear, speaker phone off.

"I've missed you so much," he cried. He let himself into Jens' bedroom for privacy and shut the door.

Jens exchanged worried looks with Nola. "Thank God she's all right."

"It sounds like she's all alone," said Nola. She paused, her face revealing her inner struggle. "Will she come here if you ask her?"

"I don't know if I can do that." Jens hid his surprise. Was she really suggesting his ex-wife share their roof? After everything?

"What about you?"

She nodded yes. "For Teddy's sake I could."

Teddy returned with his hand over the phone. "Mom's at a women's shelter outside Boston. She registered under an assumed name — that's why Ferdie couldn't find her. Can we go see her tomorrow? She wants to tell you how sorry she is about hurting you."

Jens exchanged looks with Nola before answering. Teddy's eyes had softened with pain,

"We can." Jens' voice wobbled.

"I love you, Mom," whispered Teddy, as he hung up.

Teddy put his arm around Jens. "Thanks, Dad." His voice was choked with emotion. He hurried away, not wanting anyone to see him crying.

Later, when Jens and Nola were in bed, the *clank* of Teddy's weightlifting in the basement seemed to keep rhythm with their lovemaking. In the aftermath, he stared at the ceiling, unable to sleep.

Nola propped herself on an elbow.

"You worry too much."

"Do I? Comes with the territory, I guess."

Nola smiled at him, brushed a wave of hair from his eyes.

"I love you."

He turned to her.

"I worry about that too."

She kissed him goodnight and rolled away onto her side.

Chapter Sixty

Jens sat bolt upright in bed.

"Oh, shit!"

"What now?" With a groan, Nola pulled the pillow over her head.

"Shit! Shit!"

"What?"

"All this time I assumed Bruzza was keeping Vivian company. If she's in the shelter, where's the dog?"

He lurched out of bed, fumbled into his robe in the dark, and started for the door.

"Where you going?"

"Maybe Teddy knows."

———

Over breakfast, Jens took some ribbing from Nola and Teddy about his earlier panic attack. Teddy, who could barely be roused from his sleep, had broken into laughter once he understood what Jens was asking.

"The day I left, Mom said she was going to drop him at the Young's farm in Lee," he said, recounting the story for Nola's benefit. "They'd been having a problem with rats at the horse barn — you know what a good ratter Bruzza is. Mom didn't think you'd want him, Dad."

Teddy cut through the stack of pancakes on his plate and shoveled a thick wedge into his mouth.

"Not want him? I love that dog!" Jens exclaimed. "Why didn't you tell me?"

"I guess I forgot, with all the changes."

Jens immediately got the Young's number from information and called.

"Yeah, we still got him," drawled Luke. In his seventies, he sounded disappointed to hear from Jens.

"Fine beast. We thought, what with the divorce and your ... ah ... accident, maybe you didn't want him around anymore."

Jens told him they'd be passing by to collect him, thanked him, and hung up. Bruzza, he explained to Nola, was not only a good ratter but he was also a reliable watchdog.

"Can't hurt to have him looking after us, with Laurent still at-large."

Dressed for work, she kissed Jens goodbye, told him she'd see him that evening and to have a safe trip to the shelter to see Vivian.

"Good luck, Teddy," she said, leaning in to hug him.

Surprised, he hugged her back. "Thanks."

Chapter Sixty-One

They'd agreed to meet Vivian at a Waffle House off Route 95 in Burlington, not far from the Burlington Mall. They'd arrived early, having set out shortly before 8 A.M. to make the three hour drive down from the mountains. Traffic had been light all the way, even on the 95 as they skirted Boston proper. They'd made good time.

Teddy, seated with his dad at the counter with a view of the parking lot, was sipping on a power drink he'd convinced the reluctant counterman to concoct. Vivian had insisted she could drive herself to meet them there, and now that she was a half hour late, Teddy was getting nervous.

"Maybe she's having second thoughts about coming, Dad."

Jens glanced at his son, sipped his coffee, nodded.

"I understand. This can't be easy for her."

"You're so understanding. Why aren't you mad? I'd be, if someone had been double-timing me."

Jens smiled. "I wasn't aware you were messing with the ladies."

"You know what I mean." Teddy spun around on his stool, leaving Jens staring at the fry cook turning burgers on the grill.

"Did you love her, Dad?" he asked quietly.

Jens turned on his stool to face him. "I did, Teddy, with all my heart."

"She hurt you, didn't she? Bad."

Jens nodded. "She did."

"You ready to forgive her?"

"I'm here to try."

"Why?"

"Son, I come from people who didn't know how to forgive — and didn't want to."

Teddy looked at him, thinking. Finally, his eyes brimming, he turned away.

"I love you, Dad," he said.

Jens, choked up, managed to say, "Me too."

———

A few minutes later, they watched Vivian park her Volvo next to Jens's car, get out, and survey the parking lot nervously, before proceeding to the Waffle House entrance.

Jens wondered if she was still worried about Warren or Laurent. He could reassure her that both were likely gone, though he wasn't sure how she'd feel about Laurent's disappearance. She and Jens hadn't spoken since before the divorce. This was the guy she'd divorced him over; this was her first love and maybe her only. This was the guy who had tried to kill him and threatened their son.

She peered in the window and saw them at the counter as she went in. If she'd looked haggard at the divorce hearing, now she looked like a complete stranger. Her hair had been cut unfashionably short, making Jens wonder if she'd had some sort of treatment, like electroshock, that required sheering. She wore no makeup, accentuating the lines of her face. Her dress consisted of a nondescript shift that hung from her gaunt figure.

Only her eyes showed any life, becoming animated once they lighted on Teddy. A cry escaped her lips as she uttered his name. She wept as she went to him.

"Teddy, my dear, dear boy."

"Mom," he cried, burying himself in her arms. "I've missed you so much."

Her eyes brimming, she stood back from Teddy and kissed him. "Me too."

Jens stood apart, waiting for them.

"We can get a booth if you want."

She nodded and they moved to a booth away from the lunch

time crowd.

———

Once seated, Vivian regained her composure and was ready to tell her story.

"Do you mind if Teddy stays to hear what I have to say? I feel he deserves to know who I am. I need your understanding — both of you."

When Jens hesitated, she turned to Teddy.

"This may be rough for you, hearing about your mother's shame."

Teddy exchanged looks with Jens.

"I want to stay." Seated alongside his mom opposite Jens, he reached out and touched his father's hand. "Can I, Dad?"

Jens squeezed his hand. "Okay. Sure. I guess." He turned his attention to Vivian.

Eyes averted, she first thanked him for coming. Then she asked him to try not to judge her but to listen with an open heart. She waited for him to agree before going on, smiling tentatively when he nodded. Her monotone voice was shaky at first but grew stronger.

"I'd just turned fourteen when we first met at the county fair. Armand — for that is how I wish to remember Laurent — was two years older. He was tall and well-mannered, and he treated me with respect, which was rare for someone from my side of town. I later found out that was because he was the only child of one of Berlin's oldest and most respected families, and he'd had all the advantages wealth and status could buy, like attending Philips-Exeter." Here she paused, meeting Jens' gaze. "That's why I insisted Teddy go there."

She seemed to wander in her mind before picking up the thread of her story. Jens wondered how the tale of her first love could possibly serve to elicit his forgiveness for her betraying and destroying their marriage. He had to know if she was still in contact with Laurent, and whether he was a danger to any of them, especially Teddy.

———

The story she recounted over the next hour felt like a punch in the gut. Though Jens tried to detach himself, he couldn't. A strange dislocation took place inside him: the time they'd shared together as husband and wife, with all its attendant joys and miseries, seemed blotted out by the sheer magnitude of her suffering. He was emptied.

And, somehow, he became *her* for the briefest of moments, suffering along with her, as she was seduced, corrupted, and tricked out by D'Arcy, her father's brother, the man she trusted after her father died. He'd forced her to marry Laurent and then betray him, the only man she'd ever loved besides her father. Pregnant by D'Arcy, she'd been left bleeding to death in a motel room, after a botched abortion performed by D'Arcy with a coat hanger. After saving her, Laurent had tried to stop D'Arcy from fleeing, only to kill him in self-defense.

Tears streamed down her face. She wrapped her arms around herself. Teddy tried to put his arm around her to comfort her, but she gently shrugged him off.

"Though our marriage had been annulled, Armand still thought of me as his wife, and I came to visit him as often as I could at the penitentiary, even though his parents tried to get my visiting privileges revoked. A model prisoner for the first few years, he soon changed. He lifted weights and learned how to protect himself. In his third year, he began to get into fights with other prisoners. About this time, he told me to stop coming, as my visits made him sad and weakened his will to survive."

"By then I'd turned eighteen. I came one last time to say goodbye, but he refused to see me. After that, my letters came back unopened. I tried to move on with my life, but I couldn't. After a time, I wrote to him again and finally received an answer.

He begged me to forget him. He said that my success as an artist would be his salvation, but only if I let him go."

Vivian wiped her tears on her sleeve and shook herself, as though trying to rid her mind of unwanted memories. She studied Jens for a reaction; he held his tongue, unsure of what he felt, aside from a well of sadness. She lay her hand on Teddy's.

"I think you know the rest," she went on. "I couldn't abandon him. It turns out that Teddy had been intercepting his letters recently, when he wrote to me again, after all the years, asking to renew our relationship. His parents had died in the interim, after running out of money trying to get his conviction overturned or pardoned. He had no one to turn to except me. He'd given his life for me and I owed him, even if it meant destroying my own in the process. How could I know the depths to which he'd sunk, or the jealousy and hatred he'd developed for you, Jens? You were everything he'd wanted to be in life. And you were married to the only woman he'd ever loved."

The silence was thick with shame and regret. Neither made eye contact. Jens held himself in reserve, thrown back on his thoughts and feelings, touched by Vivian's story. Teddy looked at her with sympathy, shook his head in disbelief.

Meanwhile, Jens was unsure of what *he* felt. Was he supposed to forgive her for ruining their lives? For putting his and Teddy's life in jeopardy? For bringing a killer into their bed?

"What do you want from me?" he said, his voice aquiver, his anger flaring.

"I never meant to hurt you, Jens. I'm so sorry. I'm worthless, I know. But won't you let me make it up to you now? Please?"

"Did you ever love me?"

He studied her, waiting, sad because he already knew the answer. He sighed.

"Your allegiance lies with Teddy, now. Take care not to bring any more harm into our lives. If you can do that, I'll let you stay two weeks until you can get back on your feet, and make sure

Teddy remains a part of your life. But if I suspect that you've gone back on your word and have anything more to do with this killer —"

"No, no, believe me, I won't."

"Do you know where he is?"

She shook her head no. "He disappeared. After I asked him to leave me alone."

"So why are you hiding out in a women's shelter?"

"His friend, his ex-cellmate, Warren Flynn. He's been blackmailing me. He's a *real* killer. He threatened to get at Teddy if I didn't turn over the divorce money. I was afraid to go to the police."

Jens and Teddy exchanged looks.

"Ferdie thinks he's in the wind. They found his pickup abandoned out on Peirce Island," said Jens.

"Laurent, too," added Teddy.

"Flynn's gone?"

"According to Ferdie."

She sighed with relief. "I'm safe. I can't believe it."

She started crying again. Teddy comforted her.

"So, I can stay with you?" She held her breath.

"You'll like Nola," added Teddy, presuming on his father's answer.

Jens bit his lip, hesitating.

"You can stay." He looked at her severely. "But remember what I said about Laurent."

Vivian smiled at him, grateful. Eyes wet with tears, she mouthed thank you.

Chapter Sixty-Two

As Jens drove away from the Waffle House, he felt ambivalent about his decision to take Vivian into his home, even for a few weeks. It seemed ridiculous — now that he wasn't under the spell of her dramatic confession — that he, the injured party, should be responsible for the woman who'd put their lives in turmoil and danger.

What if he'd said no? What if he'd been the one who'd had a breakdown and was being tossed onto the street? Would Vivian have taken him in?

He knew what Vincent, his lawyer, would say: *Are you out of your mind?*

He knew from personal experience how violently people resist change, while holding onto the past for dear life. Only when we are blasted to the roots, like Vivian, do we seek to let it go. And yet, though she'd brought this all on herself, she'd suffered much and deserved his forgiveness. If not for Teddy, though, he would not do it.

She was coming Saturday, driving up by herself. Her counselor at the shelter agreed that it would be a step towards independence. Though she was on medication, Vivian said she's been diagnosed with manic-depression, she could skip it for the drive.

"I almost forgot." Jens slapped the wheel. "We gotta pick up the Bruzza on the way home, right?"

Lost in thought, Teddy started at the sound of his father's voice. He nodded, not really sure of what he was being asked.

Jens plowed on in the stop-and-go traffic on Route 128, headed for Boston and north to New Hampshire.

"You worried about Mom?" Jens braked in the stalled traffic. "Aren't you?"

"She seems to be in good hands with that shrink from the

shelter."

"That's not what I'm worried about. She's tough, she'll bounce back." He hesitated. "I never thought Laurent was a threat, or I would have told you sooner."

"But you did, finally."

He shook his head ruefully.

"I read the letters he'd sent her just before his release, asking for her help. There was nothing in them that seemed like a threat. It wasn't until he tried to kill you ... by then it was too late."

"We all make terrible mistakes in life. What matters is that we grow from them."

"Like you, huh?" he said, deftly tossing back his father's veiled reference to his anger issues.

Jens felt a stab of regret about telling Teddy about his breakdown — he realized that Teddy wasn't above using it against him when he felt threatened.

They did not speak again until Jens turned onto Route 1 north of Boston, weaving through late afternoon traffic, passing old landmarks he'd known since childhood. Like Vivian, Boston had been his cultural Mecca growing up.

He resumed their previous conversation without preamble.

"It's a rite of passage, Teddy. Acknowledging and growing from our mistakes. One day you'll know what I'm talking about."

"Dad, I only care about one thing in all this," he said heatedly, "protecting Mom and protecting you. If that asshole Laurent comes anywhere near us, I'll blow him away."

Jens felt the specter of Daniel's missing pistol, which disappeared at the site of his suicide attempt, raised again.

"You don't have Daniel's gun, do you?"

"No, but trust me, I know where to get one."

"Teddy, Teddy." He shook his head. "What makes you think violence is the only solution?"

"Live by the sword, die by the sword. That's my game avatar's motto."

"What about the Golden Rule, do unto others?" He stared at him.

Teddy fell into a hostile silence, leaving Jens to ponder a better answer.

"Look, Laurent's long gone. He'd be a fool to come back. He's gotten from your mother all he could. Warren, too. I doubt either wants to go back to prison for the rest of their lives."

"It didn't stop Laurent from coming after you, did it?"

———

They sat down to a meal Nola had prepared, of pasta with sauce made from blanched pear tomatoes, topped with aged parmesan. Bruzza, a rare guest at the cabin but not so rare that the pantry wasn't stocked with his kibbles and favorite canned dog food, snuffed up his dinner from a bowl Nola set out for him.

Jens complimented Nola on her *al dente* noodles and her sauce, which she'd learned to make from him. Teddy complimented her by asking for another heaping bowl, with a side of salad. Bruzza came to beg handouts from Nola, but once he realized she was immune to his soulful gaze he plunked down at her feet and went to sleep.

Jens waited until Teddy had eaten his fill and excused himself — he had a game date on Gameboy Advance on Wi-Fi with a friend from Portsmouth — to break the news to Nola about Vivian coming to stay.

"She'll be coming on Saturday and stay through Thanksgiving?"

Jens nodded.

"I'm curious." Nola dried one of Jens' copper pots and hung it over the stove. "What convinced you to say yes? Is she helpless? Did she try to harm herself?"

He took her dish towel, dried another pot, and hung it alongside hers.

"I thought you didn't have a problem with her coming."

"I don't."

"So?"

She leaned against the butcher block island and faced him.

"So what heart strings did she pull?"

Jens told her the story of his ex-wife's horrible childhood abuse and tragic involvement with Laurent, leading to her betrayal of the life she'd built with Jens and her breakdown.

When he mentioned Warren Flynn's role in Vivian's disappearance, Nola nodded with understanding. "She must have been scared to death."

Jens agreed. "She said he was the real killer, not Laurent."

Nola looked at him skeptically. "Does she hate herself for what she did to you."

"It's more about facing what she did to Teddy. Neglecting him for Laurent."

"Teddy's all she has left."

"Do you still want me to stay?"

He struggled to think of a snappy comeback, one that would diffuse Nola's insecurity and reassure her, but none came to mind. He took her in his arms and stared deeply into her eyes.

"My, my, why so serious?" She laughed. "I was only teasing you."

"And?"

"You passed."

———

Later in the privacy of their bedroom, Jens talked about Teddy and his anger, filling her in on the reasons for his concern.

"He's changed so much I barely know him. He talks about blowing people away."

"Have you spent any time with him just doing things he likes, like fathers do? Do you go fishing? Play ball?"

"What, with my book deadline? Not to mention coming to Vivian's rescue," he added heatedly.

"Shhhh," she said, with a calming hand on his arm, only to realize that she'd accidentally stroked his cast.

"When's this damn thing coming off?"

"Shit! Shit! Shit!"

"What did you forget this time?"

"It's supposed to come off tomorrow."

"Perfect."

"Why perfect?"

"So I don't have to make love to a one-armed bandit any longer than I have to."

She kissed him goodnight and rolled over onto her side of the bed.

———

The next morning, Jens sat at the kitchen table, jotting notes in his journal about how Cassie was going to rescue Emma, after sacrificing herself to Orozco. He could think of a number of possible scenarios. One, using her cell phone to put out a rescue signal, another capsizing the boat on a sandbar in the middle of Punta Bay so the Coast Guard would respond. Another, engaging Orozco in one of his sordid movie adaptations, herself the treat, or a combination, even, of all three.

But none of them felt quite right because, he realized with mounting anxiety, he had not planted enough credible scenes to justify Cassie putting herself in harm's way. Now he worried that her dedication to save Emma, while *intellectually* understandable, did not justify her sacrifice *emotionally*. Would he have to go all the way back to the beginning of the book and redraft the backstory of her daughter's murder, making it an abduction instead, her whereabouts unresolved, dead or alive, with Emma her only lead? *Yes*, he told himself, this makes Cassie's actions believable and sympathetic, while upping the ante.

Even as he acknowledged the need to make this fundamental

311

change, which would require considerable rewriting and tweaking throughout the manuscript, he tried to deny it. This is the worst thing that could happen to a writer this late in the game, he moaned, doubting himself, along with his story. It meant weeks of rewriting at the very least, which he no longer had — he'd have to warn Jean Fillmore-Smart immediately. He knew he was right about Cassie's motivation; what he called his *shit-barometer* told him that this plot element, of her own daughter's unresolved fate, was exactly what the story needed to click.

He struggled with the idea of not telling Jean, to keep the advance and get his money due on submission. True, he needed the money desperately: his legal bills were crushing, not to mention household expenses to feed three, and soon four. The court, meanwhile, was taking its time releasing his marital assets — what was left of them.

But he knew he could not deceive his agent or his publisher. This was his work, his life; it's what really mattered. He decided he would go back to the beginning of his manuscript and see what could be done about fixing it. Maybe the changes wouldn't have to be so drastic. Yet he believed they would be; the thought nearly crushed his resolve.

———

It felt great to have the cast off his arm. Jens celebrated by putting his newly liberated hand on the steering wheel, feeling grand, as he drove to the Presbyterian Hospital to have lunch with Nola to celebrate.

"From now on, I'll expect the full use of *all* your appendages," she whispered in his ear, as she met him in the lobby.

"Anyway —" She linked her arm in his — the left, now that it was cast-free — and started him toward the cafe. "What are you going to do about fixing the book?"

"I already talked to Jean. She told me to wait until the editor's read it too."

"You going to wait?"

He nodded. "I have no alternative."

"Thrice good," she said, leading him to a table with a view of the garden and pond, in the newly opened upscale café that had replaced the old cafeteria.

This is where Jens had that fateful meeting with Ferdie, after keeping vigil with Daniel. He marked it as the beginning of his friendship with Ferdie, conflict the precipitating event.

"Thrice good?" He glanced around for a waiter.

"First, because now you have no excuse for not driving down the mountain and having lunch with me more often. Second, because you'll have more time to spend with Teddy, doing fatherly things."

"What's the third reason?"

"Aren't you supposed to be a writer? Use your imagination."

Chapter Sixty-Three

When Jens returned from visiting Nola, he found Teddy in the mud room taking off his running shoes and breathing hard. Jens sat down beside him on the bench.

"Hey, pal, where you been?"

"Went for a run. Why?"

"Without the dog?"

Teddy shrugged. "He holds me back."

Jens pulled off his own shoes and slipped on his house-slippers.

"I'd appreciate it if you'd walk the dog now and then."

"Okay."

"You never walk him. He's your dog, you know."

"*Okay, okay, okay.* I said I would."

"All done with your schoolwork?"

Teddy got up from the bench and pushed into the house, visibly irritated.

"Come back here. I'm talking to you."

Teddy turned back, bristling. Jens noted his arms were away from his body, puffed with adrenalin. There was a dangerous glint in his eyes.

"Hey! What's this all about?"

"This is about you not helping out around here." Jens noted his own breathing was harsh. Teddy's adrenalin was pushing his own. He felt himself rising to a threat. He checked himself.

"What are you going to do? Smash me like you did the walls back home?" His voice was pitched low, to soothe the wild beast in his son, now puffed like a comic book hulk.

Teddy glared at him, his pupils expanded, black. His chest heaved as he labored to bring himself under control. *This is the moment of truth, thought Jens. Either he stands down, or I've lost him.* Gradually the rage seeped from his son's eyes, from his face, from his body. He seemed to shrink a little as he came back to himself.

"I would never, *ever*, lift a finger to hurt you, Dad."

Trembling, he put his mitt-sized hands on Jens' shoulders and looked down into his eyes.

"You know that, don't you?" His voice was almost normal again.

Teddy, the old Teddy, hugged him, and Jens gave him a manly pat on the back.

"Oooh!" said Jens, recoiling. "You need a shower, pal."

"Right after I take out the dog. Here, boy. C'mon, boy," he called.

Reclining like a sybarite, Bruzza grudgingly rose from the couch in front of the fireplace, stretched, and trotted over.

"Does he need the leash?"

Jens nodded. "This is bear country, remember?"

"How could I forget?"

———

After lunch, Jens went over Teddy's online homework with him, finding it surprisingly better than he'd expected. They talked about a new daily routine, going hiking or fishing afternoons, after Teddy had completed his courses for the day.

"Aren't you working on your book, Daddio?"

"It's on hold until Jean reads what I sent her. In the meantime, I thought maybe you and I could spend some time together."

"Sure."

"Would you like that?"

Teddy nodded. "When's Mom coming?"

"Saturday."

"We're going to pick up her up, right?"

"She's driving up by herself. She wants to prove she can be independent — her doctor agreed."

"Wow, that's great." Teddy paused. "I know I have a problem ... with my anger. Sometimes, I feel like I have no control over it. Something wells up inside, a poison like, and once it starts, I see red and there's nothing I can do except ride it out, wherever it takes me."

Jens cuffed his neck and gave him a reassuring squeeze.

"Sometimes ADD will do that. Don't worry, we're going to get you help."

Teddy looked away.

"So, want to go for a hike today? We haven't knocked off any trails lately." Jens gestured to the trail map of the White Mountains, mounted on the wall beside the fireplace. "You'll have a hard time keeping up with me."

"That'll be the day, old man."

"Don't forget to wear red — hunting season."

———

The next day, Jens sat at the kitchen table staring dully out the window onto the patio and the woods beyond. Jean, his agent, still hadn't gotten back to him about his manuscript, and he had little to occupy his mind aside from planning dinner and the afternoon's activity with Teddy. He felt a little bereft without his obsessive preoccupation, his story's characters. He forced himself not to think about them.

Where was Teddy, anyway, he wondered. Wasn't he back from school yet?

Jens went to the mudroom to see if Teddy had left his school bag there, as was his custom — he didn't need his books inside, at his desk, since he had no homework, only online assignments. There it was, dumped on the bench where he'd tossed it. He must be out for a run, Jens concluded.

Just then Bruzza, leash in mouth, trotted up, glaring at Jens impatiently.

"Okay, buddy, I get it. Let's go!"

———

Bruzza, an urban dog despite his life at the farmhouse in Lee, pulled ahead on his leash, intoxicated by the odors of the woods in November, and ready to pounce on any beast, no matter the size, that might cross his path. Jens pulled back on his leash as he startled a covey of woodcock into flight and tried to give chase.

"No, boy, no. There are hunters out there who can't tell the difference between you and a wild turkey. Stay close."

As if in answer, a series of booming shots resounded, coming from deeper in the woods. Bruzza lit off in the opposite direction, stripping all the coils of the leash until it was tight as a bow and he was out of sight, around a bend in the trail.

"Whoa, Bruzza," cried Jens, running after him, pulling on the leash.

Again, there was the distant *boom*. It sounded like a shotgun, decided Jens. Someone hunting pheasant, in season until the end of the year. He had more to worry about from deer hunters and their rifles, this being the height of the season, and the same week Nils had died.

Better head back home, he told himself, even though he was wearing his bright orange cap and vest. Like most New Hampshire natives, he knew better than to tempt the eyesight and aim of out-of-town hunters, especially those up from Jersey and New York, armed with enough firepower to take down a herd of rhino.

"Bruzza! Here, boy!"

He found him sniffing the ground like a hound, racing around a wooded copse that opened onto a field at one end, bordered by a farm wall of fieldstone. Approaching, Jens could see evidence of recent human activity. There was a shallow pit with burnt brush and tree fall, and all around it tamped ground. The glass shards glinting in the sun led him to a place on the wall where bottles had been set for target practice.

He pulled Bruzza back as he examined the broken remains, green and translucent, forming a trail along the wall. Someone's firing range, he concluded.

Warily, he backed away, taking Bruzza with him until he reached the fire pit. Here he found the shell casings scattered about, concluding that this is where he took aim and shot at the bottles on the wall.

"Bruzza, leave those, boy. No good to eat," he said, chasing him off.

He counted the shell casings as he picked them up: nineteen in all. They were small brass jackets, smelling of Cordite, freshly fired. Just like the ones Ferdie had shown him — the ones from Daniel's missing gun.

Jens rolled them in the palm of his hand. He knew where they were from.

If he came to blows with Teddy — then so be it. He intended to take that gun away before it was too late.

What bothered him most — aside from his antipathy for guns — was Teddy's lying to him, denying he had it. Jens rankled with anger at his son's bald-faced deceit — all the times he'd asked him about it.

That's your story and you're sticking with it, eh?

"We'll see about that."

He stomped off in the direction of home, dragging Bruzza by the leash.

———

As he walked back with Bruzza, a funny thought occurred to him. As a Hollywood screenwriter, he'd come across one of the primary principles of dramatic unity: *Chekhov's gun*. It postulated that every element in a narrative must be purposeful, relevant, and necessary.

In the classic case, if you show a rifle in the first chapter of your book, then it must go off in the second, or at the very latest, the third. In Hollywood, the great leveler, it was reduced to this maxim: if you show a gun in the first act, it must be used to kill someone.

Jens did not relish the foreshadowing of Chekhov's gun in his personal life. In his writing, it was okay. Suddenly, he had a glimpse of the ankle biter perched high up on Cassie's sexy thigh, waiting, like Chekhov's gun, to deliver or damn her.

———

Teddy did not want to admit to having the gun all this time, nor did he want to surrender it, along with a box of cartridges he'd brought from Portsmouth. But in the end, he could not stand up to his father's fierce anger and righteous indignation. He handed it over without apology, suggesting that Jens might want to keep it in case *that asshole* Laurent, or his buddy Warren, showed up.

"Does it make you feel like a man?" Jens fumed.

"No, maybe back then when I first found it, but not now," he shot back.

"Then why keep it? You knew Ferdie was looking for it. You knew it might help identify Daniel."

"How?" He shrugged. "Daniel was no hold-up artist or stone-cold killer. He was a romantic, like most suicides. He probably bought it on the street. Anyway, it was cool — knowing I possessed the power of life and death."

Teddy, raised on Xbox games like Assassin's Creed, was a true believer in the elegance of violence, taking CGI for the real thing. Little did he suspect the true ugliness and pain of death. Jens hoped it was not too late to teach him before he found out for himself.

Jens needed to hide the gun in a safe place before he could turn it over to Ferdie. Temporarily, he stuck it under his mattress. When Teddy went out for a walk, he decided to find a place less obvious. He took it down to the basement and slipped it into the compartment behind the water heater, forgetting that he'd once suspected Teddy of utilizing it for the same purpose.

PART THREE

Chapter Sixty-Four

On Saturday morning, Jens puttered around the cabin, cleaning, organizing, and preparing for Vivian's arrival. Teddy, sullen and unrepentant, helped him convert the futon couch in the loft into a queen-sized bed, and make it up with sheets, covers, and pillows.

They hauled a dresser from the basement up the two flights to the loft. Then Jens scrubbed the shower in the bathroom, located behind a curtain in a corner of the loft, while Teddy took care of the toilet, sink, and mirror. Lastly, they drew the screen across the front of the loft overlooking the main room below, making it private.

Jens had received a call on Friday from the psychiatrist at the women's shelter, explaining how Vivian's medication was to be administered, in doses of one 300 mg tablets twice a day with meals, morning and night. Vivian would be responsible for taking her own meds, she added, but it was important that he monitor her discreetly.

"How do I do that?" he asked.

"Suggest she keep her meds in the kitchen so she doesn't forget to take them with meals, and *you* keep count — she has a month's supply."

"You want me to spy on her?"

"Naw," the psychiatrist laughed, "just keep her honest. She must stay hydrated but no alcohol. If she misses a dose she should take it right away. But," she said, her voice rising emphatically, "you definitely don't want her to go off her meds."

"What would happen then?"

"She might become suicidal."

"This is more than I signed on for."

"Don't worry, she's been doing just fine. I tell you the worst, just in case. Remember, routine is important. Anyway, you can expect her around noon."

———

Teddy, camping out in the mudroom, was keeping watch for his mother.

"What time is it, Dad?"

Jens peeked inside, at the clock over the stove.

"Almost noon."

"Shouldn't she be here by now?"

"Have you tried calling her?"

"She doesn't have a cell phone anymore."

"Why don't you come in and we'll play a game of backgammon while we're waiting."

Teddy hesitated.

"C'mon. You're not going to miss her if you're inside. She knows how to knock on the door."

"I just don't want her to have to drag her luggage up all by herself."

"Suit yourself. Want your tablet to listen to music meanwhile?"

"Sure."

Teddy checked the time every half hour — much to Jens' annoyance, as he tried to plow through Hemingway's *A Farewell to Arms*, reading it again after twenty years to find the prose tiresome and repetitive, and the dialogue cute. But it didn't make Vivian arrive any sooner. When it was three o'clock and she still hadn't arrived, Jens got a little worried. Teddy was beside himself.

"Think we should call the shelter, Dad, and make sure Mom left this morning?"

Jens called and was able to get her doctor, even though it was Saturday.

"I'm so sorry," she said, "I forgot to call and tell you that she planned to pick up some clothes and personal items at her house in Lee. She'll be along, I'm sure."

Not long after, Jens heard Teddy let out a cry from the mudroom, where he was still decamped.

"She's here, Mom's here!"

Jens heard the car door open, the excited exchange of voices, the trunk pop, and doors slam.

He looked around one last time to make sure everything was in place. In the next moment, Teddy entered, dragging a massive suitcase that was heavy, even for him.

Vivian, looking wan and road-weary, but better than when he'd seen her last, stepped into the cabin.

"Hi, Jens. How're you?"

"I'm fine. Don't just stand there, c'mon in."

Surrendering his protection, he came out from behind the kitchen butcher block island.

She went toward him, taking in the cabin — its vaulted ceiling, its rose-hued walls of notched logs, its fieldstone fireplace, its glossy oak floors — and stopped. She looked down at her feet.

"I forgot to bring slippers. Can I borrow a pair of house shoes?"

This seemed funny to everyone but Vivian.

"Teddy, get Mom a pair of those padded socks from the mudroom, will you?"

"Soon as I get Mom's bag upstairs," he answered, lifting it up in front of him like a barbell, enjoying the strain as he clumped up the stairs.

Vivian kicked off her shoes and placed them neatly on the strip of carpet inside the door. Jens walked past nervously and returned with a pair of knitted wool socks with leather soles sewn onto the bottoms. He held them out to her. For some reason, she mistook his gesture as a welcome hug. When she stepped forward to meet his embrace, he recoiled behind the socks. She took them, her face red with embarrassment.

"Welcome," he said awkwardly. "Let me show you to your room."

As he mounted the stairs ahead of Vivian, he glanced up to see Teddy standing at the top of the stairs, a smug, judgmental look on his face. Apparently, he disapproved of Jens' failure to welcome his mom with open arms.

Jens glared back as he passed him, led his ex-wife into the makeshift spare bedroom, and pointed out the amenities as though to a distant cousin whose visit would be dutifully tolerated if not exactly enjoyed.

———

As Thanksgiving Day neared, the household settled into an easy routine, with Teddy working on his vacation assignment from school weekday mornings, and Vivian sketching him while he worked. Afternoons, she and Teddy went for long walks in the woods with Bruzza. With Nola off to work in the morning and Vivian temporarily usurping his time with Teddy, Jens was left to entertain himself a good part of the day until dinner.

He was still waiting for Jean to finish reading his manuscript and report back, and he did not want to start another writing project until he knew the fate of his present one; though he felt Detective Honore Poulon chafing to re-enter the cone of light of his imagination.

Jens, talking to himself, placated his venerable fictional detective like an importunate child, with the promise of teaming him up with Cassie Melantree in the next book, should she survive his agent's and editor's respective judgment.

The ringing land phone offered momentary distraction, but

was soon replaced by anxiety when he remembered all the pending concerns in his life, to which he was vulnerable via phone. As he reached for the receiver, he considered, in rapid order, the possibilities.

It could be Jean, calling with news of his literary life or death. Ferdie calling to report that Laurent had just been sighted in the vicinity of Jackson, and that they should clear out immediately and seek refuge at the police station. Or finally, it could be Nola, calling to check up on him, but really because she missed him.

"Corbin here," he said tentatively.

"Ferdie here, your faithful Mountie." She panted like Bruzza.

"Ferdie, you young dog. Good to hear your bark."

"Woof, woof," she answered.

Her trilling laughter reminded him of her feminine side. He pictured her, a modern-day heroine, cruising the state highways and byways, eyes vigilant, protecting the citizenry of New Hampshire. In so many ways, she reminded him of his fictional heroine Cassie.

"Where are you?"

"I'm driving down from Canaan, on the Canadian border."

"Any luck nabbing Laurent?"

Jens could hear the crackle of Ferdie's police radio in the background.

"False alarm. I'm going to check in Berlin, like you suggested. It's on the way."

"I'd love for you to drop by."

"Why's that?"

Jens glanced at Vivian who was working furiously on a sketch at the kitchen table. Teddy, he knew from the sound coming from the water heater, was taking one of his interminable showers after working out.

"Why, then you could say hello to Vivian."

Vivian glanced up; continued working like one possessed.

"She turned up? How? When? Where?"

Speaking *sotto voce*, Jens brought her up to speed on his ex-wife's reappearance, apologizing profusely for forgetting to update her.

"Hey," Ferdie complained, after reaming him for not telling her to cancel the missing person report. "Information's a two-way street, you know. You leave me out, I leave you out."

"I'm sorry, really. Does that mean you won't come for Thanksgiving?"

The crackling on Ferdie's police band rose.

"Sorry, Jens, I gotta take this. Call you right back."

———

Ten minutes passed before she rang back. In the meantime, Vivian kept working on her sketch, glancing up at him occasionally.

"Yes, Ferdie," Jens said without preamble.

"First, I want to know what you think you're doing playing nursemaid to your ex-wife after what she did to you."

Jens found her concern touching.

"There's a story there, but it will have to keep until another time."

There was a pause on the other end of the line.

"I take it you're not alone."

"Correct."

"Okay. Now, don't get your hopes up too soon, we're still running tests, but we think we may have turned up Laurent."

"Where? Around here? In Conway?" blurted Jens, unable to suppress his anxiety.

"Fished out of the Piscataqua — off Peirce Island, near downtown Portsmouth."

"No!"

"Looks like suicide — cut his own throat. We're waiting on the DNA report and his dental records to come down from Concord. But we think we've got our man."

Glancing at Vivian, Jens lowered his voice.

"What makes you think it's him?"

"One, he fits the physical description. Two, the body's tattoos match his on record. Three, the clothes on the corpse are from a local Army Navy store favored by ex-cons. Four, and best of all — you remember I told you that we recovered Warren Flynn's truck, the one Laurent used to run you off the bridge?"

Jens grunted affirmatively, feeling a glimmer of relief but not ready to let go his long-standing angst, like a post-traumatic stress victim unable to let go.

"It's got Laurent's prints all over it," enthused Ferdie, apparently feeling the need to reassure Jens that it was over.

"What about Flynn?"

"Given his resources extorted from Vivian, the money she took from you, he's likely down in the Caribbean, island-hopping in style. I don't think we'll be hearing from him for a long time."

"Okay," said Jens uncertainly.

He dropped his voice to a whisper.

"But what would make a man like Laurent want to kill himself?"

Ferdie said she didn't know, could be a lot of things, starting with Vivian's rejection.

"And there's a high rate of suicide among ex-cons, especially after serving long terms."

Jens let the idea of Laurent's death sink in.

Ferdie, after promising to come for Thanksgiving, ended the call by telling Jens that she didn't want to know how his book was doing, for which Jens thanked her, not wanting to go into it anyway.

Ferdie promised to let him know as soon as they had a positive ID on Laurent. After they hung up, Jens realized that there was something he'd meant to tell her, but he'd lost it in the excitement over her news.

———

He found Vivian staring at him. He wondered how much she'd heard, and how much she'd put together.

"That was Ferdie," he began, deciding not to share the news about Laurent until it was confirmed. He had no idea how she would deal with it. He would tell her once he had a definitive answer.

"She says hi."

She looked at him suspiciously.

"Jens, I'm not a fool, you know."

"I know."

She waited for him to go on. When he didn't, she went back to her sketching. She was furious. It was a rift he'd have to live with for the time being.

———

They spent the rest of the day steering clear of one another. Teddy stayed up in the loft with Vivian, playing backgammon like they used to back in Lee, during the long hours when Jens had labored at his writing up in the attic. When he called up to ask if anyone was hungry, Teddy answered him curtly with a "what's it to you?"

Jens took Bruzza for a walk, all the way to the stream at the foot of the mountain, and stayed there all afternoon, watching him cavort at the water's edge, dipping his paws gingerly into the frigid waters, pawing after winter trout. Jens did not feel like going home and cooking dinner. That night or any other. The tiff with Vivian had brought up all his old, complicated frustration and anger about their marriage. He felt trapped.

Finally, night falling, he put Bruzza on his leash and started back up the road heading home. Soon he heard the familiar whine of Nola's Beetle pitching through its gears. She pulled up alongside him.

"Hop in," she said through her open window.

With Bruzza perched on the back seat, Jens folded himself

stiffly in front.

"You look cold and tired." She observed him through her concerned smile. "Are you okay?"

Her sympathy was enough to open the flood gates. He told her what had happened earlier with Vivian, and how Teddy had reacted.

"Are you surprised? You saw how protective he was at dinner the other night."

"I know, but this is between his mother and me. It doesn't really concern him."

"She'll always be his mother, but you're forgetting she's no longer your wife."

Jens shook his head. "Not the point."

"Jens," she said, shaking her head. "She's very fragile."

"I know. I'm sorry. I'll behave myself, I promise."

"Good! I'll help you fix dinner. We'll patch things up."

"Oh! Almost forgot! Ferdie called — they think they fished Laurent out of the Piscataqua — a suicide."

Nola's mouth dropped.

"You mean I don't have to sleep with one eye open anymore?"

"She's going to confirm it with us once the lab results are in."

"Does Vivian know?"

Jens shook his head.

"Not explicitly — she suspects."

———

Nola made dinner tolerable, providing the social graces that permitted them all to be together. Jens found Teddy distant and cold, but didn't know how to break through. Vivian was reserved but not unfriendly, at least not to Nola. She retired early, taking her pill without being prompted. After kissing his mother good night, Teddy left the table without excusing himself. Moments later, the sound of his Xbox powering up

331

could be heard coming from the basement.

Teddy felt no remorse for lying to his father about Daniel's gun, believing the Glock to be his due, like Daniel's watch. Spoils of conquest. Hadn't they defeated the bear and saved Daniel's life? His father's stubborn anti-gun stance was an aberration, especially up here in the woods. While he loved his father, he did not respect him enough, thinking him weak, damaged. His love for his mother was without reserve. He would do anything to protect her, including kill, were it called for.

Chapter Sixty-Five

In the morning thaw, wrapped in blankets, their breath steaming, Jens sat with Nola on the back porch sipping his cooling coffee. Teddy and Vivian weren't up yet, so they could talk freely.

"I just don't want Teddy to go through life regretting his actions."

"Then you've got nothing to worry about. Accidents don't count as sins."

He'd told her about Nils.

"Don't they? I don't think the heart knows the difference."

"Jens, isn't it time you forgave yourself for your brother's death?"

He brightened with an idea.

"Know what? We could have a little ceremony for Daniel up on Black Mountain, scatter his ashes."

Nola had told him that the hospital had been obliged to preserve Daniel's ashes for at least ninety days in the event a family member turned up to claim them. That time had passed. His remains would soon be interred in a communal pauper's grave, compliments of the township of Jackson, New Hampshire.

"You're a sweet man." She kissed him.

He shook his head. "I'm the lucky one."

"That deserves another kiss." She kissed him again.

They exchanged shy smiles. The sky was overcast, grey and unrelieved. Jens sniffed the air.

"I smell snow."

"No you don't. That's a fishwife's tale."

"Really?" He held out his hand; small, hard flakes began to collect in his palm. "Here it comes."

Snow began to fall steadily.

"You can be a pain in the ass, Mr. Know-it-all."

They went inside, observing the silence signifying mother and son were still in bed. Nola poured out the remains of their coffee, rinsed and set the cups to dry.

"Want to take Bruzza out for a walk with me?" asked Jens, taking the blanket off Nola's shoulders, folding it, and putting it in the chest behind the sofa with his.

Jens scratched behind the dog's ears, evoking grunts of pleasure from him.

"Sure, just give me a minute to brush my teeth."

She slid across the floor in her socks while Jens went to the mudroom, Bruzza trailing.

"Might want to change into foul weather gear," he said a few minutes later, as he pulled on his insulated rubber boots and LL Bean sweater.

He handed her her parka with the faux fur collar. She put it on and tugged on her boots.

"After all, heavy snow is predicted," she teased. "Weatherman says so."

"I never said how heavy it will be."

He buckled Bruzza's collar and attached the leash. The dog pulled him out the door and into the yard.

"Should I lock the door?" called Nola, trailing him out.

He thought about it, acknowledging that he wasn't ready to let his guard down.

"Why not? No point in leaving Teddy and Vivian unprotected."

"Hey, wait for me."

She put on her gloves and ran after him, slipping on the thin layer of crystalline flakes dusting the drive. She managed to scoop up enough for a snowball as she ran.

———

Jens and Nola trudged blithely along the switchbacks through the woods, snow crunching underfoot, the tall pine branches overhead scintillating like Christmas trees in a crèche, though it was Thanksgiving, observed Jens. They walked arm in arm, comfortable with the way their hips and flanks fit, affirming the fact that they were, officially, now a couple. And they were happy together.

So caught up in their talk — about the menu for tomorrow's dinner, about Jens' idea for his next book, about Nola's screenplay revision, about plans to go skiing, both were avid skiers — that they failed to notice that Bruzza had disappeared around a bend in the trail. Jens had decided it was safe to let him off the leash, as long as he stayed within earshot.

"Bruzza," he shouted, his voice drowned out by the wind. He looked up just in time to duck a pocket of snow from a tree branch, flopping on the trail already carpeted in white.

Thick grey stratus clouds blanketing the sky seemed to descend upon them, dimming what little light was left, erasing the skyline.

It was time to get home.

"Bruzza, here boy," they shouted anxiously, almost in unison.

They plunged ahead against the wet wind, following Bruzza's paw prints in the snow.

"I know where he's going. C'mon," Jens shouted, taking Nola by the hand and scrambling up, through the snowy bracken.

———

Jens led them up and up, to the place along the stone wall where he'd discovered Teddy's shooting range on the other side. He helped Nola over the snow-slippery wall, and they separated to walk off the area, but Bruzza was nowhere in sight. Jens, never a great tracker, was confused by the tracks from Bruzza's earlier visit here, days ago.

They were about to give up when Nola called to him, the tremor in her voice alerting him to danger.

"Jens, Jens," she shouted, pointing to a place at the edge of the clearing.

Bright red drops of blood trailed off in the snow, back down the mountain.

"He's hurt," cried Jens. "On the broken glass."

"Pray he's gone home. Vivian will take care of him," she added, hopeful.

———

Ferdie had driven as fast as she could from Berlin, once she got the results back from Epping on the body found off Peirce Island. She'd raced down Rt. 16 through the White Mountains, hampered by the massing snowstorm. Her emergency lights flashing, she swerved around slower moving vehicles, only to get stuck behind snowplows already out scraping and sanding roads turning more slippery by the minute.

She'd tried to reach Jens on his landline repeatedly, to warn him, but no one answered. She'd tried to dispatch a patrol car up the mountain, to put Jens and company under immediate police protection. But the local police wouldn't get there anytime soon, as they were dealing with their own emergencies in Conway and Jackson, brought on by the unexpected snow. A wind advisory had been issued, warning of snow squalls and thirty-mile-an-hour winds.

The body fished out of the Piscataqua had not been Laurent's but Warren Flynn's.

DNA had established that — even if Warren's wife had a hard time identifying him after the fishes had gotten to him. One thing threw her off, she'd said, teary-eyed. Warren's trademark ponytail was missing.

Laurent had chopped it off, apparently to confuse identification, leaving a perfect dead-ringer behind, almost. Ferdie had to concede that his ruse had bought him time.

She knew where Laurent was heading. He had come back to Berlin like a stray returning to its kennel. He'd pistol-whipped a garage attendant and stolen a car. Before leaving the attendant for dead, he'd asked about the condition of the roads to Jackson.

Now it was a race against time — to see who would get there first.

The killer or the cop.

———

Bruzza's blood-trail led Jens and Nola back to the switchback that took them home. They ran after him, the trail soon covered up in snow. Jens prayed he'd made it home.

Meanwhile, Laurent tracked them through the woods, the trees and natural cover camouflaging his movements, the mounting snow muffling his footsteps. He ducked behind a tree, waited, proceeded after his prey.

The dog had almost given him away, barking and nipping at his heels. He'd stabbed at him with his sling blade, but only grazed him.

He was cold in his light jacket and thin dress shoes. He'd had nothing to eat but snack food and was very hungry — and thirsty. He scooped up fresh snow and licked his palm clean. He followed, undetected.

It was not hard to be invisible to people like Corbin and his girlfriend. They were stupid and soft. Lacking in fortitude, perseverance.

He thought of his mission — Vivian. She *had* to be here at Corbin's.

The image of Warren's last moments flared in memory. He'd marched Warren, gun in his back, up to the precipice on Cliff Overlook. He gripped Warren's long rat-tail braid, and chopped it off with his knife. When Warren spun, making a futile last effort to save himself, Laurent slashed his throat, kicked his feet out from under, and shoved him over the edge. He watched him crash onto the half-submerged rocks below.

Though he hadn't realized it at the time, a sob of regret had escaped his lips as he bid goodbye to his old friend. Who'd betrayed him.

———

When Jens and Nola got back to the house, they found the door unlocked.

"That's odd," said Jens, unnerved by Bruzza's blood trail and now this.

"Bruzza," he called.

Warily, he pushed open the door and stepped into the mudroom.

None of the lamps were lit inside the house, except for nightlights with sensors, casting shadows in the hallway. Jens peered inside, wary.

"Teddy? Vivian? Anybody home?"

No answer.

"Where's Bruzza?" Nola peered over his shoulder.

"Shhhh!"

"What is it?" Nola whispered, affected by his tone.

"Wait here!"

He took up the heavy-duty utility flashlight he kept beside the door, turned it on, and stepped into the main room. Nothing was out of place, but to Jens something felt different. Dust motes danced in the beam of the flashlight, swirling in unfamiliar patterns.

Putting on lights as he went, Jens made a tense trip around the house, imitating the cops on TV and in the movies, checking the back door off the kitchen (locked), treading upstairs to the loft, thrusting aside the shower curtain (clear), padding down to the basement (clear), throwing on the lights in Teddy's room, shining his light beneath the bunk beds (no one hiding), checking the back door off the game room (locked), and the utility room where the water heater and washer and dryer were housed (clear).

On a thought, he darted his hand behind the hot water heater, confirming that the gun he'd taken from Teddy was still there. He wavered about taking it now for protection, finally deciding not to — he was probably just overreacting.

———

Ferdie hop-scotched her cruiser around the icy corner leading to Jens' drive and skidded to a stop in the snow. She'd made amazing time, despite the weather. She could only hope she wasn't too late.

Perhaps Laurent had a change of heart and decided to leave Vivian alone, once and for all. But she doubted it. He'd burned all his bridges, and she was certain he was coming here, the only place left where Vivian could be. If not, he'd get it out of Jens, Teddy his pawn.

She tried to reach the trooper station in Jackson, then Conway, but her two-way radio hissed white noise. The windshield wipers groaned, laboring to clear the snow, offering brief glimpses between arcs.

She surveyed Jens' cabin, observing the lights on all over the house, thinking it seemed suspicious. Though she'd never been here, only to the house in Lee, she suspected Jens of being frugal, especially with power on the eve of a gale. He was from New Hampshire after all.

She opened the flap to her service revolver, a non-standard-issue S&W Model 27 .357 Magnum with a six inch barrel, glanced up at the house once more, cracked open her door, and was just drawing her weapon, ready to enter cautiously via the mudroom, when a voice she'd never heard before, though she recognized it immediately, hissed in her ear.

"Take your hands off your gun and step away from the car, bitch!"

Laurent. Back from the dead.

She was not afraid to die.

Indeed, she was her father's daughter, himself a distinguished Vietnam War veteran, a Marine colonel, whom she'd emulated and modeled herself after.

She leaned back, instantly crowding Laurent and chopping backward with all her might, upward with her elbow, catching him squarely on the nose with incredible force.

The cartilage in his nose *cracked* and collapsed; one of his front teeth dangled from her arm.

A shot rang out. Both fell to the ground.

Inside the house, the shot was muffled by the storm. Jens exchanged looks with Nola.

"Could be a car backfiring," ventured Jens, worried about Bruzza, who still hadn't shown up.

The front door creaked open and there was a stir in the mudroom. The sound of someone locking the door behind them seemed odd to Jens.

He whipped around to find Bruzza hightailing it in. He skittered across the floor on his toenails, came to a stop at Jens' feet, and whimpered. There was a slash over one brow, the fur matted with blood. Shocked, Jens reached down to examine him.

"Bruzza, what happened?"

A dark voice opened up a well of terror in Jens.

"Aren't you going to invite me in, Corbin?"

Laurent was holding his bleeding nose with one hand and spitting blood through the tooth gap in his mouth. In the other hand, he waved around the 9mm he'd taken from Warren. Tucked in his belt was Ferdie's revolver.

"I've come a long way to meet you," he lisped. "At no small expense."

He pointed to the damage to his face and then at Nola who was trembling.

"Fix it!" he barked at her.

Nola was frozen in place. Jens started toward her, to protect her, but was stopped by Laurent with a wave of his gun.

"You want to die?"

Jens shook his head almost imperceptibly.

"God damn it!" screamed Laurent, recoiling with sudden pain. "Where's my wife, anyway. Where's Vivian?"

Chapter Sixty-Six

Nola's hand shook as she cleaned up around Laurent's mashed nose. Seated on a kitchen stool, he winced as she applied antiseptic wipes.

"It's broken," she said, her voice quivering. "Do you want me to set it? You'll need pain killer."

Laurent's eyes roamed, looking for something.

"Is that booze over there?"

He pointed his gun at the liquor cabinet off the kitchen.

Laurent followed her with his eyes while she retrieved a bottle of whisky, unscrewed the top, and handed the bottle to him.

"Don't even think about it, asshole," he told Jens. He raised the bottle to his lips and gulped, wincing as the burning liquor washed over his broken lips.

"Uggha!" he spat, his massive head spasming involuntarily.

His two front teeth were missing, making him look like a vampire rabbit, his swollen nose a snout.

"I heard a shot. Is someone hurt?" Jens asked, worried about Vivian and Teddy. He was sitting on the couch, his mind racing, trying to figure out his next move.

One of Laurent's guns, the pistol resting on his knee, was aimed at Nola's midsection as she treated him. Jens could tell she was repulsed — by that tattooed, bleeding, disfigured brute of a man — as she stood as far away as possible, tearing surgical strips from a roll, readying them to support the splint she'd fashioned from wooden salad tongs. Jens was saddened to acknowledge that he'd brought her, too, into his circle of danger.

Vivian and Teddy, where were they? Had they gone for help? He prayed they were in a safe place, far away from here, from Laurent.

Oh my God, that shot we heard. What if Laurent shot Teddy?

Jens *had* to do something. When Nola set his nose — that's when he'd make his move. Jens was poised, ready to hurl himself at the intruder.

"Sit your ass back down or I'll tie you up," growled Laurent, his words muffled.

The gun from his waistband, a revolver with a huge barrel, was pointed at Jens.

"She's going to set my nose, and you're going to sit there like a good boy, aren't you? No heroics," he added, shoving his pistol into Nola's gut. She doubled over in pain.

Jens sat back, cooperating, at least bodily.

"*Now*, sister!" Laurent barked.

"You should be in the hospital, x-rayed, sedated."

"Do it, bitch! Or I'll shoot him — like that trooper I left bleeding like a pig out in the driveway."

Suddenly, Jens recognized the revolver in his lap. Ferdie's.

The bastard shot Ferdie.

Laurent pushed his pistol into Nola again, glared at Jens, eyes twinkling maliciously.

"Do it!"

Nola pushed his gun hand away.

"Get that off me if you want to have a nose when I'm done here."

"Sassy bitch, isn't she?" Laurent spat just before she broke his nose again, resetting it.

Leaving him howling with pain, but still in charge, the revolver cocked, ready to blow Jens into seventh heaven.

———

While Laurent was getting his nose plugged and taped, Jens fished around under the pillows of the sofa, finding the utility flashlight he'd used earlier when he'd cleared the house of a possible intruder.

Jens gripped the flashlight and tensed, ready to lunge.

The *click* of the revolver stopped him cold.

"Put it down, asshole. *Slowly*. On the floor."

Jens rolled the flashlight in his direction.

"I'm getting tired of your antics."

As he pointed the revolver at the phone, Jens noted that the 9mm was back in his waistband. If he was going to make a play, it would be for that one. Ferdie — he had to get to her in time.

"Just in case you're thinking of calling in the cavalry."

He let the hammer fall. There was a deafening *boom* — the phone in its cradle exploded. Jens clapped his hands to his ears. Blue smoke and the smell of cordite filled the room.

Laurent gave his revolver a critical once-over before re-aiming it at Jens.

"Tie her up."

He pushed Nola onto the couch, swung the gun at Jens.

"Where's my fucking *wife*?" he said, enunciating every syllable.

Jens winced at Laurent's reference to Vivian as his wife.

With manic energy, Laurent tore the electrical cord from a nearby lamp and tossed it to him.

"Make it good and tight. Now, where's Vivi? I'm here to collect what belongs to me."

He spoke thickly, lisping, his plugged nose making him sound like a kid on laughing gas. Jens was not amused. This was a deadly game and he didn't know how he was going to get everyone out of harm's way. He hoped it wasn't too late for Ferdie.

"Vivian's gone into town to pick up her meds — she's had a breakdown."

"A breakdown?"

"Why do you think she's here? She's recuperating from what you put her through, *you fucking maniac*," Jens added, unable to stop himself.

Laurent's blue-black gun barrel — all six inches — landed on his head.

———

When Jens came to, he was on the couch next to Nola, trussed up with wire, hands behind his back, feet tied together. Nola was tied as well. Plumber's tape sealed his mouth, making it difficult for him to breathe only through his nose. Blood from his head wound blurred his vision. He glanced at Nola, terror visible in her eyes. Her mouth was taped too.

Laurent back-straddled a kitchen chair, squinting at Vivian's medicine bottle. He looked ridiculous with his nose taped up, like he was wearing a knight's helmet with a long nose plate.

"Lithium carbonate," he read on the label. Again, that laughing gas voice. "Bug juice, that's what it's called in the joint. It's for depression, right?"

He looked up at Jens.

"Just nod your head, asshole. I imagine that's within the range of possibilities, even for a fuckup like you."

Jens nodded.

"Good, we have an understanding. Now, you and her are divorced, right?"

Jens nodded.

"I made sure of that," he said with a laugh. "And she's been in this shelter" — he glanced at the address on the prescription — "in Burlington. That right?"

Jens nodded.

"That her car out front, the Volvo?"

Jens nodded.

"Subaru is yours, the VW hers?" He gestured at Nola with his gun.

Jens nodded again.

"So, wherever she's gone, it has to be on foot."

Jens didn't respond.

"I asked you a question, didn't I?"

Jens nodded, staring at the barbed wire tattoo on Laurent's

neck pulsing menacingly.

"Does that mean yes to my asking you a question or to her going on foot."

Jens nodded ambiguously.

"You want another tap on the head?"

Jens shook his head emphatically *no*. The movement made him dizzy and nauseous.

"The boy, your son," Laurent added distastefully. "He's with her, right?"

Nola darted her eyes away — Laurent noticed.

He leered at her. "You think I didn't see that?"

She was frozen with fear. He could do anything he wanted to her.

He glanced outdoors, onto the patio, where the snow, still falling steadily had formed drifts, swirling like in a snow globe.

"Where could they have gone in this snow?" he said.

Laurent's eyes turned inward, remembering something. He touched his face — tracing his broken nose, pulped brow, bloody lips, scars. His eyes flared.

"I used to be a good looking dude, like your son," he told Jens. He gestured at Nola. "Girls were always hitting on me in high school. I came from money. I could've had the pick of the litter." He smiled to himself. "But I chose only one — Vivi D'Arcy."

His eyes darted about, unfocused, settling on the topographical map mounted over the fireplace.

"Been in jail, Corbin?"

Jens shook his head.

He scoffed.

"Lot of time to think about what might've been. Useless. I read a lot. Lifted weights."

He flexed his massive arms and shoulders.

"Tried to keep my mind off of what a Sancho like you was up to with my wife while I was doing time. Drove me nuts. Want to know why I'm on your case? Vivi wrote to me in the beginning, told me all about you, your big ego, your awards, your movie deals. Why'd you disrespect her painting?" he asked heatedly, glaring at Jens "We started our relationship over art. She tell you that?"

Jens shrugged, deciding that as long as Laurent was talking he wasn't shooting.

There was regret in Laurent's voice.

"Sundays," he reminisced, "at the Gardner and the Museum of Fine Art. Everything ... everything still possible."

He fell into a gloomy silence, his eyes roving, detachedly tracing the cabin's vaulted main room, its cathedral ceiling and exposed beams. Jens wondered if he was falling apart, decompensating.

"Corbin, you got anything more to drink?"

Jens pointed his chin at the liquor cabinet. Laurent got up, poured himself a bourbon, drank it in one draught. His eyes watering, he poured himself another and brought it over to the chair he'd pulled in front of the couch. He straddled it, nodded at Jens, sipped his drink.

More civilized now, talking — a good sign, thought Jens.

"Then her father died, and her mother took up with that lowlife, 'the devil' Vivi called him, for what he'd done to her." His anger erupted. "That 'chomo', molester, pig!" he spat. "He was her uncle."

He flicked at his pants where he'd spilled his drink.

"I'm not sorry I killed him, though it *was* an accident."

There was sadness in his voice — Jens wondered for whom. Himself?

"I'm not a killer." Laurent shook his head. "Never meant to kill anyone."

He looked at Jens steadily, his thousand-yard stare turned inward, struggling with his demons, his guilt. "They'd asked for it. Like Warren."

Jens nodded, hoping to mollify him, delay him from taking action.

"But she'll be here soon. Then we'll be together, *forever*," he blurted.

Does he mean to kill Vivian, too? And commit suicide?

Jens struggled covertly to get his hands free, but the knots held tight.

Impulsively, Laurent darted into the bedroom and peeked out the window. From there — staring out at the falling snow piling up in the drive, covering Ferdie's cruiser and her body — he carried on his one-way conversation with Jens, as he sipped his drink and watched for Vivian to show up.

———

Jens was desperate to do something with Laurent out of the room, though still in earshot. He rolled off the couch, lay on his back with his knees bent to his chest, slipped his hands down over his feet, and stood up. He found the scissors Nola had used to cut Laurent's bandages, snipped through his leg ligatures, and raced over to Nola to free her.

He tore the plumber's tape from his mouth. Nola stifled her cry when he ripped hers.

From the bedroom they could hear Laurent choking on his rage. He laughed, holding back the tears, chugging his bourbon. Suddenly, he hurled his glass against the wall. His crazed laughter told them he was on his way, charging back to the main room.

To do what, exactly?

Jens worked frantically to cut Nola's bonds, but the wires were insulated, too thick for the flimsy surgical scissors.

Nola's eyes filled with terror. She shook her head vehemently, signaling Jens to go — save himself, get help, come back for her.

He started to lift her up, to carry her, but stumbled, woozy from his head wound.

"*GO!*" she hissed.

His eyes tearing, he ran from the room, down the stairs to the basement, to the utility closet, to the water heater, where he'd hidden Daniel's gun.

Laurent's absurd voice sought him from upstairs.

"I'm sick of waiting, where is she?"

He was coming!

As Jens stuck his hand into the compartment where he'd last seen the gun, he heard Laurent roar upon discovering Jens' escape.

"Gonna get you now, *motherfucker*," he sang, squealing, like on laughing gas.

But the compartment was empty.

Teddy had taken the gun.

Jens bolted out into the corridor, cast about for an escape. He crashed through the wood and glass patio doors, running, slipping, sliding in his own blood. His efforts were hampered by his still-bound hands, making him clumsy. There was no time to stop and untie them with his teeth.

A shot rang out just as he made it into the woods.

Blam! Another! *Blam!*

He was hit, grazed in the leg, but kept running — until he collapsed. Then he heaved himself up, kept going. He had to get help. For Nola and Ferdie.

He had to find Vivian and Teddy to warn them away.

Chapter Sixty-Seven

That morning, Vivian had awakened groggy and numbed. It was like this everyday — she had to coax herself into clarity, enough so she could orient herself, collect the illusion of identity scattered by her medication, and meet the world as the functional, creative person she'd once been. It was slow going, but she was almost there.

She glanced out the curtained loft window giving onto the front yard, seeing only grey, overcast skies and the promise of snow. With a groan, she forced herself to get out of bed.

After splashing water on her face and peeing, she dressed hurriedly and climbed down to the main floor. No one was about. Not Jens, not Nola. Not Teddy, probably still sleeping in his room, downstairs in the basement.

She drank juice from a bottle from the refrigerator, knowing she should use a glass but was too lazy. Remembering to take her meds, she went to the cabinet where Jens had stored them, tapped out a pill, and slugged it back with another gulp of OJ.

"Dad hates it when I do that." Teddy emerged from the basement stairs.

"Don't I know it," she answered.

Teddy hugged her. "But I won't tell if you don't."

He took the jug from her and drank deeply. They exchanged smiles.

"It's good to be with you, Mom, I missed you." He put the juice away.

She caressed his cheek.

"Me too, Teddy-bear," she said, calling him by the childhood name that only she still used. He seemed not to mind.

Teddy was dressed in a tracksuit and running shoes.

"Where you going in that gear?" asked Vivian.

"For a run. Want to come?" His voice was charged.

351

Vivian, still groggy from last night's meds, glanced out onto the porch, to the leaden sky beyond.

"You're serious — in this weather? I don't know ..."

"C'mon, Mom, it will do you good. We'll go slow. What do you say?" he pleaded.

She'd always had a hard time resisting him.

"Okay, maybe I'll tag along."

———

Laurent leered over Nola, his nose splint gleaming white, his eyes black unforgiving orbs.

"You'll pay for that, my dear," he fumed, pulling her up by the hair and dragging her to her feet. She screamed.

He whipped out his sling blade. It opened with a flick of the wrist. Nola shrunk back, silenced, expecting to die. He bent over and cut her leg ligatures.

He showed her the full length of the blade, waving it near her eyes before slinging it closed.

She got the message.

"Let's you and I go for a walk — find your asshole boyfriend."

———

Jens had circled back, finding the way slippery in the woods, his grazed leg aching.

He panicked — where were Teddy and Vivian?

All he could think to do was head back to the house and do what? Take one of the cars parked in the drive? All the keys were hung in the kitchen, in case of an emergency. Now under siege by Laurent. As he trudged through the snow, he used his teeth to undo the knots at his wrist.

He could try to talk Laurent out of killing the others, offering to sacrifice himself. With no gun for leverage, that seemed a losing proposition.

Then it struck him. Ferdie. He'd go back to her cruiser and using her two-radio call for help. He'd been too hell-bent on getting Teddy and Vivian to safety to think of it sooner.

Stealthily, he approached the house from the woods.

Jens snaked on his belly across the drive in the snow until he knew he was out of Laurent's line of sight. He stood and quickly ran to Ferdie's cruiser. The door was open. Someone lay prone across the front seat, face down.

Ferdie. She wasn't moving.

Laurent had shot her in the back. She was passed out, apparently from loss of blood.

———

Teddy and Vivian were almost to the driveway when they heard gunshots. The heavy snow had turned their jog into a slow trudge.

Vivan started forward, but Teddy grabbed her arm.

"Mom, I want you to wait here until I tell you it's safe, okay?"

"It's Laurent," she moaned. "I know it." Her face was stricken with fear. "Please don't go near there, please."

"I have to — Dad could be hurt or Nola. Promise me you'll stay here, Mom."

She nodded in agreement. He hugged her and took off into the woods, to circle around to the back of the house. Vivian popped up as soon as he was out of sight, and followed.

No one was going to lay a finger on her boy.

———

Jens pulled Ferdie's State Trooper jacket off her shoulders, tugged on both arms until it came free and he could see the bloody wound in her lower back. He pulled off his sweater, folded it, and applied it to Ferdie's wound to stop the bleeding. He rolled her over onto her back to hold the sweater in place and provide compression. Her breathing was ragged. But she was breathing, thank God.

He started up the cruiser. He tried the two-way radio, but it did not work. No help would be coming.

———

Teddy made his way to the back porch, where he risked a peek inside, into the kitchen and main room.

Though he'd never met Laurent, he was convinced that the brutish giant of a man — his nose in a splint, pacing the floor and waving a knife at Nola — had to be him. The asshole had finally made good on his word — he'd come for his mother.

Teddy crept underneath the porch, making his way to the basement patio doors, surprised to find them smashed, ajar. Stepping carefully over the broken glass, he ducked inside, unseen. He'd hidden Daniel's Glock in plain sight, alongside his Xbox controls, thinking, rightly, that it was the one place his father wouldn't think to look.

His hands trembled.

This was the real world now, and all his posturing would come down to whether or not he was man enough to stand up to a real killer. He could do it; he had to!

Cursing Laurent and the mother that gave him birth, he crept up the basement steps, ready to protect his family. He steeled himself. Remorse was for wimps. This is what he lived for. He was a warrior. Releasing the safety and leading with the Glock, he extended his arm rigidly, as he'd seen the Marines do, on the videos he'd watched online.

Laurent was a dead man.

———

Jens picked up Ferdie's jacket and put it on. He slipped on her

Smokey the Bear hat, pulling it low over his eyes.

In the trunk, he found a megaphone and a roadside flare gun. He shoved its short-barrel into his belt.

He took off in the direction of his house, thinking, *I need a plan*!

———

Laurent perked at the sound of footsteps crunching in the snow outside. He shoved Nola back onto the couch, tapped his revolver against her head, and cautioned her to silence. He went to the bedroom, sidled up to the window, and peeked out.

There was no one. No cavalry charging up the drive.

"Come out with your hands up," barked a voice on a megaphone, the location of the source indeterminate. It sounded to Laurent like it was coming from the woods behind the cabin. Galvanized, he ran to the living room to find Nola wriggling on her back toward the porch door. Cursing, he slung her up and over his shoulder. His human shield.

"Don't you make a sound," he threatened.

She was too frozen with fear to respond. She wanted to scream, her head hanging down his back.

"We've got you surrounded. Put down your weapons NOW and come out with your hands up!"

With both guns drawn, the pistol and the revolver, Laurent crept to the porch door, peeked out, ready to make a dash into the woods where he would not be a sitting duck. If he couldn't make it to his stolen car parked down the road, he could hole up in the woods, Nola his hostage.

He ducked back inside and shouted, "I'm coming out, don't shoot!"

———

His flare gun drawn, Jens ran past the mudroom, rounding the house to the porch, where he ducked down and watched

Laurent peek out the back door. Nola was slung over his shoulder, terror written on her face, her screams muffled by the tape back on her mouth. With Nola in the way, he had no shot with the flare gun.

From the corner of his eye, Jens watched Vivian approach the mudroom and enter.

Another movement caught his eye, inside the game room in the basement — Teddy, Glock in hand, creeping up the backstairs.

Vivian, Teddy, Jens silently screamed. *Get away from here!*

———

Jens hurled himself through the porch window, smashing it, sending ahead a shower of glass. He slid off the breakfast nook counter, rolled and scrambled behind the couch, aiming his flare gun at Laurent, now ducked behind the kitchen island. Nola was propped in front of him, dead weight, apparently passed out.

"You don't have to do this, Laurent. Let her go. She's done nothing to deserve this," pleaded Jens.

Laurent's high-pitched, broken-nosed laughter was his answer.

He held the revolver to Nola's head and pulled back on its hammer.

Jens stood, arms spread, offering to lay down his flare gun.

"Take me instead."

———

"Let off the trigger, asshole. *Now!*"

Teddy was at the top of the basement steps, leaning cautiously into the main room, his elbows locked in a shooter's stance, his Glock pointed at Laurent. His trembling under control.

356

Laurent tossed Nola aside and grabbed Jens by the throat.

"You!" he hissed through his missing teeth.

He jammed the barrel of the revolver against Jens' head.

"Hey, you, asshole! I'm talking to you." Teddy's voice was commanding, though his gun arm shook.

My son, thought Jens.

"Ease off fucker!" Teddy's ferocity was impressive.

Oh, God! He's only a boy. Against a killer.

Laurent sneered but did not ease up on the gun pressed against Jens' head.

"Do it!" Teddy commanded.

Like a trained soldier, he took a step forward. When Laurent did not react, he took two more steps and re-aimed.

"Screw you!" hissed Laurent.

It was a stand-off. Teddy was holding his own.

Jens knew had to do something to save his son.

———

"Don't, Armand, I beg you." Vivian, preternaturally calm, stepped into the room.

Her cheeks were streaked with tears. She reached out to Laurent.

"Stop, both of you. *Please!"*

"Mom, get back."

Teddy, sighting down his gun at Laurent, tried to shield her with his body, but she stepped in front of him.

"Vivian, I'm doing this for you. For *us,"* Laurent cried. "Can't you see, he's stolen our lives?" He pressed his revolver against Jens' head.

Jens prayed that Vivian's appeal would distract Laurent, giving Jens a chance to do something.

"Armand, if you love me, *really love me*, don't do this," she pleaded.

Laurent's gun barrel jerked, but did not ease up.

"Why didn't you come to me instead of *him*?" He glared at Jens. "I would have taken care of you."

She shook her head, came closer.

His face blackened with rage. "You never left him," he accused.

His finger on the trigger was the only thing standing between Jens and death.

Laurent stifled a sob.

"After everything I did for you — for *us*."

"Armand, please, Teddy's all I've got. Don't do this."

"*Lay. Down. Your. Weapon.*" The tension in his Teddy's voice went up a notch. He was going to shoot.

"You took me back and then tossed me away — again!" Laurent cried, his sorrow turning to rage.

Jens tried to catch Teddy's eye — to let him know he was going to make a move, break away. Teddy moved away from Vivian to get a clear shot.

"I'm with you *now*, Armand, aren't I? We'll go to Mexico, my love." She advanced another step. "Just you and me."

"No one else?"

Jens felt Laurent's resolve drift for a split second.

"*Teddy, now!*"

Jens ducked and twisted, grabbing the killer's second gun, the semi-automatic that was tucked in Laurent's belt, and began firing as he fell to the floor. And kept firing.

Laurent, lifted up, slammed backward, fired a shot as he fell.

Vivian threw herself in the line of fire.

Laurent's bullet, intended for Jens, tore a hole in her chest.

As she fell, she screamed Teddy's name.

"Mom, Mom," he bawled, rushing to her. He cradled her in his arms.

She motioned for him to bring his ear close.

"I'll always love you."

She motioned for Jens to come close.

"I'm so sorry, Jens."

"Vivian, don't talk," cried Jens.
She gasped for breath.
Jens put his hand to her heart.

Epilogue

The winter sky was grey, the sun distant, angled low. They were gathered on top of Black Mountain, on the ledge where it all began, on the cap rock where once Daniel's blood had pooled in the late summer sun, gathering like rubies.

Now, the surrounding peaks lay bedded with snow. Pied, a patchwork of white and dark, seen through a vista clear of summer's lush foliage.

Life and death, ashes to ashes, dust to dust.

———

It had all come full circle for Daniel. His flesh and bone cremated, reduced to the spiky ash that each of them took a turn sprinkling into the brisk wind in little puffs, taken from a brass canister, as they thought about the stranger's soul they'd come to honor. Each took a turn, passing the urn along.

Teddy, sad, mourning two passings. Nola, tresses waving in the breeze, Botticelli's Venus, wiping the tears from her cheeks. Ferdie in dress uniform, stiff from her back wound, stoic as always.

Jens — one arm around Teddy, the other around Nola.

When his turn came, he scooped his fingers into the urn and sent his portion of Daniel's ashes into the wind. Each celebrant held balloons — red, blue, yellow, and white — on strings.

"On three, release your balloons — carrying our thoughts of Daniel on high."

"Mom, too," cried Teddy, his voice choked with emotion.

Jens was the last to let his go.

———

They buried Vivian a few days later in Jens' family plot in Lee — where Nils was buried. Now Jens had another grave to stand before, feeling guilty.

The funeral had been well-attended by Vivian's fellow artists and consultants from the Art Association, and by friends and collectors, who, surprisingly, numbered in the high double digits. After the service, they'd spilled out from the Lee Congregational Church, chatting about her art and hinting at how it would likely evaluate, now that she was gone.

Jens, disgusted, had spirited Teddy away from the animated pockets of congregants more interested in Vivian's salacious relationship with a convicted murderer, than her contribution to the art world.

Jens knew that Teddy would have to come to terms with Vivian's death on his own, as would he, but now was not the time or the place. He hoped the healing balm of time would seep into the corners of Teddy's memory of her, suffused with her unconditional love for him. Nola would be a comfort to them both.

Jens was relieved that Teddy had not taken a life to save his father's.

Jens had been the one to take a life, again.

This time in defense of his family.

———

When no one came to claim Laurent's body, he was cremated at the largesse of the Township of Conway, his ashes unceremoniously disposed of in a pauper's grave. Where Daniel would have found his final resting place if Nola hadn't intervened.

Jens was approached by book publishers to recount their sensational story, of life imitating art, but turned them down for Teddy's sake and Vivian's memory.

One day, Teddy, tears in his eyes, told his father that he was done with guns. Soon after, he dropped his Xbox and games off at Goodwill.

As for Jens, his making peace with Vivian and their complicated marriage would come more slowly. Especially since she took the bullet meant for him. Letting go was not something he did well. Maybe his new family would help him with that.

Afterword

Why I Wrote *My Wife's Husband: A Family Thriller*

Years ago when my son was a teenager, we were walking in the woods in New Hampshire's White Mountains when a dark blur off-trail caught the corner of my eye, boggling my senses. What was a man in a *black coat and trousers* doing perched in a tree, and why was he leaping onto the ground, hands first? There was something odd about the way he slinked through the woods, his movements stealthy, animal-like. Hmm. My hackles went up. *Bear,* screamed my primitive brain.

I shushed my son, who was blithely chattering away, and pointed in the direction of the fleeting figure. Without thinking, I had picked up a rock, ready to do battle. But by then, the bear, a black bear, *Ursus americanus* I later learned, was gone. My son chided me for seeing things. But the image stuck, along with my certainty. Having come to fathering late in life, I took my role as my son's protector quite seriously; his Attention Deficit Disorder (ADD or Learning Different) added to my protectiveness. Dangers lurked beyond the muffled patter of our Dunhams on the pine-carpeted trail and in life — especially for a boy so preoccupied.

Months later, the image of that dark blur racing through the woods with primitive grace wouldn't go away. I knew I had to write about it, rife as it was with archetypal potency. What would have happened if the bear attacked? Could I have defended us? All I needed now was a story.

A tale of love, loss, and death evolved from that initial "what if," spilling characters from my imagination that kept upping the ante. My first novel since graduate school, *My Wife's Husband: A Family Thriller* was written over the course of a year-and-half during time stolen, evenings, weekends, and holidays, from my full-time teaching job.

Needless to say, it was a story I *had* to write. Not committing myself to it body and soul would have been bad faith. I taught literature, so why wasn't I contributing? Frankly, I'd reached that age when one begins to worry about a legacy. Aside from the lives gratefully touched in the line of duty teaching, this book and a handful of published poems, articles, and stories would be it.

Long a fan of the literary mystery-thriller genre, I chose the challenges of this sub-genre as the conduit through which I might explore the existential questions that had pre-occupied me for decades: life after death, the transformative power of love, and the tyranny of past traumas to shape our psyche and thwart our best instincts and intentions.

On a personal level, the book was dedicated to and written for my son — a sort of modern day Pilgrim's Progress — for him to gain insight from later in life. Elements of the book are autobiographical in so far as they serve the larger story and its themes. I know he'll recognize himself in the character of Teddy, some of his ticks and tropes, but more importantly I hope he sees how my craft and love have transformed him into a vessel for the story's universal ideas.

———

I hope you found *My Wife's Husband: A Family Thriller* satisfying, and the characters stick with you, as they'll be back in book two of my Jens Corbin trilogy, tentatively called *The Forsaken*, in which female State Trooper Ferdie Morrison shares the stage with Jens Corbin. Together they race the clock to free Jens' lover Nola from a serial killer spotlighted by Jens' research into *his* next book, about a pair of actual, unsolved murders of New Hampshire women from the 1980s.

EH Davis
Boca Raton, Florida

Acknowledgements

This book would not have been possible without the rigor of West Boynton/Wellington Writers Group's weekly meetings and the model set by its leader Caryn Gross-Devincenti, an accomplished writer. Heartfelt thanks to Claudia Marcus, friend and guardian angel, the book's Alpha reader, along with early reader Lindsay Aegerter. Finally, kudos and thanks to Tom Holbrook, publisher, for bringing his sharp editorial eye and keen story instincts to *My Wife's Husband*.

Made in the USA
San Bernardino, CA
28 April 2020